NECRO FILES

NECRO FILES

TWO DECADES OF EXTREME HORROR

EDITED BY CHERYL MULLENAX

WWW.COMETPRESS.US

A Comet Press Book

First Comet Press Trade Paperback Edition
October 2011

Cover Illustration by Guilherme "RazGriz"

ISBN 13: 978-1-936964-52-9

Visit Comet Press on the web at: www.cometpress.us

(The following two pages represents an extension of this copyright page)

Acknowledgements

"Meathouse Man" © Damon Knight, 1976, copyright renewed in 2004. © 2004 by George R.R. Martin. Originally published in *Orbit* 18, 1976. Reprinted by permission of the author.

"Night They Missed the Horror Show" © Joe R. Lansdale, 1988. Originally published in *Silver Scream*, 1988. Reprinted by permission of the author.

"Diary" © Ronald Kelly, 1990. Originally published in *Cemetery Dance* #3, 1990. Reprinted by permission of the author.

"Abed" © Elizabeth Massie, 1992. Originally published in *Still Dead*, 1992. Reprinted by permission of the author.

"I *am* He that Liveth and was Dead . . . & Have the Keys of Hell & Death" (an excerpt from *Duet for the Devil*, 2000) © Randy Chandler and t. Winter-Damon, 1992. Originally published in *Grue* No. 14, Summer 1992. Reprinted by permission of the author.

"Xipe" © Edward Lee, 1993. Originally published in *The Barrelhouse: Excursions into the Unknown*, Winter 1993. Reprinted by permission of the author.

"Bait" © Ray Garton, 1993. Originally published in *Cemetery Dance*, Fall 1993, Volume 5 Number 3/4. Reprinted by permission of the author.

"Painfreak" © Gerard Houarner, 1994. Originally published in *Into the Darkness* #1, April 1994. Reprinted by permission of the author.

"Lover Doll" © Wayne Allen Sallee, 1994. Originally published in *Little Deaths*, 1994. Reprinted by permission of the author.

"The Spirit Wolves" © Charlee Jacob, 1995. Originally published in *Into the Darkness* #4, 1995. Reprinted by permission of the author.

Acknowledgements (cont.)

"Godflesh" © Brian Hodge, 1995. Originally published in *The Hot Blood Series: Stranger By Night*, 1995. Reprinted by permission of the author.

"Every Last Drop" © John Everson, 1998. Originally published in *Bloodsongs*, Spring 1998. Reprinted by permission of the author.

"Blind in the House of the Headsman" © Mehitobel Wilson, 2001. Originally published in *Brainbox 2: Son of Brainbox*, 2001. Reprinted by permission of the author.

"An Experiment in Human Nature" © Monica J. O'Rourke, 2001. Originally published in *The Rare Anthology*, 2001. Reprinted by permission of the author.

"The Burgers of Calais" © Graham Masterton, 2002. Originally published in *Dark Terrors 6, The Gollancz Book of Horror*, 2002. Reprinted by permission of the author.

"Ecstasy" © Nancy Kilpatrick, 2004. Originally published in *Master/Slave*, Venus Books, 2004. Reprinted by permission of the author.

"Pop Star in the Ugly Bar" © Bentley Little, 2005. Originally published in *Outsiders: 22 All-New Stories From the Edge*, 2005. Reprinted by permission of the author.

"The Sooner They Learn" © Wrath James White, 2005. Originally published in *The Book Of A Thousand Sins*, 2005. Reprinted by permission of the author.

"Addict" © J.F. Gonzalez, 2006. Originally published in *Insidious Reflections* #5, January 2006. Reprinted by permission of the author.

CONTENTS

Introduction

Cannibalism, necrophilia, aberrant sex, gore, murder, serial killers, mutilation, torture, child abductions, even werewolves and zombies are all common themes of extreme horror and in this book. But often more than anything it gives us a frightening glimpse into the dark side of humanity, and sometimes even closely reflects true events. We like to be scared, and while the supernatural is very scary, reality is downright disturbing. We are fascinated by mysterious things, and nothing is more mysterious than the unspeakable mayhem and horrors that humans are capable of. Heinous, motiveless crimes fill us with fear and revulsion, yet we are overwhelmingly compelled to read about them. Maybe it is a fear of what may lie dormant within us as well, or perhaps provides an outlet for our own dark thoughts. The media is very aware of this innate human trait and feeds us increasingly over-the-top descriptions of violent crimes and graphic images. And the recent rise in popularity of so-called "torture porn" films like Saw and Hostel underscores this compulsion to experience our violent side from a safe distance.

Necro Files is a collection spanning over twenty years, from the early formative years of extreme horror to the recent past, by twenty great masters and modern authors who have broken down the barriers of traditional horror to explore the most sinister and controversial topics that both challenge and offend our sensibilities. You'll find here an author's first steps into the realm of the extreme, stories that were banned by the publisher, stories based on true events, and many include a quote or comment by the author. Most were first published in the small press, and nowadays, luckily, it's much easier to get a hold of extreme horror, largely thanks to the wider availability of small press books. And what you have now in your hands is an ungodly collection of edgy, unrestrained terrors that delve into the dark recesses of the mind and ultimately satisfy your primal instinct.

Enjoy the ride into hell.

—Cheryl Mullenax

Meathouse Man

George R.R. Martin

"Meathouse Man" was originally published in *Orbit* 18, by Harper & Row in 1976.

George R.R. Martin was born September 20, 1948 in Bayonne, New Jersey. He became a comic book fan and collector in high school, and began to write fiction for comic fanzines. Martin's first professional sale was made in 1970 at age 21: "The Hero," sold to *Galaxy*, published in February, 1971 issue. Since then he has published more than seventy pieces of short fiction, edited thirty anthologies, and written screenplays, teleplays, comic books, and eleven novels. He is best known for his best-selling epic fantasy series, *A Song of Ice and Fire*, the basis for the hit HBO television series, *Game of Thrones*.

Martin's present home is Santa Fe, New Mexico, where he lives happily with his wife Parris and four cats.

♦ ♦ ♦ ♦

I
IN THE MEATHOUSE

THEY CAME STRAIGHT FROM THE ORE-FIELDS that first time, Trager with the others, the older boys, the almost-men who worked their corpses next to his. Cox was the oldest of the group, and he'd been around the most, and he said that Trager had to come even if he didn't want to. Then one of the others laughed and said that Trager wouldn't even know what to do, but Cox the kind-of leader shoved him until he was quiet. And when payday came, Trager trailed the rest to the meathouse, scared but somehow eager, and he paid his money to a man downstairs and got a room key.

He came into the dim room trembling, nervous. The others had gone to other rooms, had left him alone with her (no, *it*, not her but *it*, he reminded himself, and promptly forgot again). In a shabby gray cubicle with a single smoky light.

He stank of sweat and sulfur, like all who walked the streets of Skrakky, but there was no help for that. It would be better if he could bathe first, but the room did not have a bath. Just a sink, double bed with sheets that looked dirty even in the dimness, a corpse.

She lay there naked, staring at nothing, breathing shallow breaths. Her legs were spread, ready. Was she always that way, Trager wondered, or had the man before him arranged her like that? He didn't know. He knew how to do it (he did, he *did*, he'd read the books Cox gave him, and there were films you could see, and all sorts of things), but he didn't know much of anything else. Except maybe how to handle corpses. That he was good at, the youngest handler on Skrakky, but he had to be. They had forced him into the handlers' school when his mother died, and they made him learn, so that was the thing he did. This, this he had never done (but he knew how, yes, yes, he *did*); it was his first time.

He came to the bed slowly and sat to a chorus of creaking springs. He touched her and the flesh was warm. Of course. She was not a corpse, not really, no; the body was alive enough, a heartbeat under the heavy white breasts, she breathed. Only the brain was gone, ripped from her, replaced with a deadman's synthabrain. She was meat now, an extra body for a corpsehandler to control, just like the crew he worked each day under sulfur skies. She was not a woman. So it did not matter that Trager was just a boy, a jowly frog-faced boy who smelled of Skrakky. She (no *it*, remember?) would not care, could not care.

Emboldened, aroused and hard, the boy stripped off his corpse-handler's clothing and climbed in bed with the female meat. He was very excited; his hands shook as he stroked her, studied her. Her skin was very white, her hair dark and long, but even the boy could not call her pretty. Her face was too flat and wide, her mouth hung open, and her limbs were loose and sagging with fat.

On her huge breasts, all around the fat dark nipples, the last customer had left tooth-marks where he'd chewed her. Trager touched the marks tentatively, traced them with a finger. Then, sheepish about his hesitations, he grabbed one breast, squeezed it hard, pinched the nipple until he imagined a real girl would squeal with pain. The corpse did not move. Still squeezing, he rolled over on her and took the other breast into his mouth.

And the corpse responded.

She thrust up at him, hard, and meaty arms wrapped around his pimpled back to pull him to her. Trager groaned and reached down between her legs. She was hot, wet, excited. He trembled. How did they do that? Could she really get excited without a mind, or did they have lubricating tubes stuck into her, or what?

Then he stopped caring. He fumbled, found his penis, put it into her, thrust. The corpse hooked her legs around him and thrust back. It felt good, real good, better than anything he'd ever done to himself, and in some obscure way he felt proud that she was so wet and excited.

It only took a few strokes; he was too new, too young, too eager to last long. A few strokes was all he needed—but it was all she needed too. They came together, a red flush washing over her skin as she arched against him and shook soundlessly.

Afterwards she lay again like a corpse.

Trager was drained and satisfied, but he had more time left, and he was determined to get his money's worth. He explored her thoroughly, sticking his fingers everywhere they would go, touching her everywhere, rolling it over, looking at everything. The corpse moved like dead meat.

He left her as he'd found her, lying face up on the bed with her legs apart. Meathouse courtesy.

The horizon was a wall of factories, all factories, vast belching factories that sent red shadows to flick against the sulfur-dark skies. The boy saw but hardly noticed. He was strapped in place high atop his automill, two stories up on a monster machine of corroding yellow-painted metal with savage teeth of diamond and duralloy, and his eyes were blurred with triple images. Clear and strong and hard he saw the control panel before him, the wheel, the fuel-feed, the bright handle of the ore-scoops, the banks of light that would tell of trouble in the refinery under his feet, the brake and emergency brake. But that was not all he saw. Dimly, faintly, there were echoes; overlaid images of two other control cabs, almost identical to his, where corpse hands moved clumsily over the instruments.

Trager moved those hands, slow and careful, while another part of his mind held his own hands, his real hands, very still. The corpse controller hummed thinly on his belt.

On either side of him, the other two automills moved into flanking positions. The corpse hands squeezed the brakes; the machines rumbled to a halt. On the edge of the great sloping pit, they stood in a row, shabby pitted juggernauts ready to descend into the gloom. The pit was growing steadily larger; each day new layers of rock and ore were stripped away.

Once a mountain range had stood here, but Trager did not remember that.

The rest was easy. The automills were aligned now. To move the crew in unison was a cinch, any decent handler could do *that*. It was only when you had to keep several corpses busy at several different tasks that things got tricky. But a good corpsehandler could do that too. Eight-crews were not unknown to veterans; eight bodies linked to a single corpse controller moved by a single mind and eight synthabrains. The deadmen were each tuned to one controller, and only one; the handler who wore that controller and thought corpse-thoughts in its proximity field could move those deadmen like secondary bodies. Or like his own body. If he was good enough.

Trager checked his filtermask and earplugs quickly, then touched the fuel-feed, engaged, flicked on the laser-knives and the drills. His corpses echoed his moves, and pulses of light spit through the twilight of Skrakky. Even through his plugs he could hear the awful whine as the ore-scoops revved up and lowered. The rock-eating maw of an automill was even wider than the machine was tall.

Rumbling and screeching, in perfect formation, Trager and his corpse crew descended into the pit. Before they reached the factories on the far side of the plain, tons of metal would have been torn from the earth, melted and refined and processed, while the worthless rock was reduced to powder and blown out into the already unbreathable air. He would deliver finished steel at dusk, on the horizon.

He was a good handler, Trager thought as the automills started down. But the handler in the meathouse—now, she must be an artist. He imagined her down in the cellar somewhere, watching each of her corpses through holos and psi circuits, humping them all to please her patrons. Was it just a fluke, then, that his fuck had been so perfect? Or was she always that good? But how, *how*, to move a dozen corpses without even being near them, to have them doing different things, to keep them all excited, to match the needs and rhythm of each customer so exactly?

The air behind him was black and choked by rock-dust, his ears were full of screams, and the far horizon was a glowering red wall beneath which yellow ants crawled and ate rock. But Trager kept his hard-on all across the plain as the automill shook beneath him.

* * *

The corpses were company owned; they stayed in the company deadman depot. But Trager had a room, a slice of the space that was his own in a steel-and-concrete warehouse with a thousand other slices. He only knew a handful of his neighbors, but he knew all of them too; they were corpsehandlers. It was a world of silent shadowed corridors and endless closed doors. The lobby-lounge, all air and plastic, was a dusty deserted place where none of the tenants ever gathered.

The evenings were long there, the nights eternal. Trager had bought extra light-panels for his particular cube, and when all of them were on they burned so bright that his infrequent visitors blinked and complained about the glare. But always there came a time when he could read no more, and then he had to turn them out, and the darkness returned once more.

His father, long gone and barely remembered, had left a wealth of books and tapes, and Trager kept them still. The room was lined with them, and others stood in great piles against the foot of the bed and on either side of the bathroom door. Infrequently he went out with Cox and the others, to drink and joke and prowl for real women. He imitated them as best he could, but he always felt out of place. So most of his nights were spent at home, reading and listening to the music, remembering and thinking.

That week he thought long after he'd faded his light panels into black, and his thoughts were a frightened jumble. Payday was coming again, and Cox would be after him to return to the meathouse, and yes, yes, he wanted to. It had been good, exciting; for once he had felt confident and virile. But it was so easy, cheap, *dirty*. There had to be more, didn't there? Love, whatever that was? It had to be better with a real woman, had to, and he wouldn't find one of those in a meathouse. He'd never found one outside, either, but then he'd never really had the courage to try. But he had to try, *had* to, or what sort of live would he ever have?

Beneath the covers he masturbated, hardly thinking of it, while he resolved not to return to the meathouse.

But a few days later, Cox laughed at him and he had to go along. Somehow he felt it would prove something.

A different room this time, a different corpse. Fat and black, with bright orange hair, less attractive than his first, if that was possible. But Trager came to her ready and eager, and this time he lasted longer. Again, the performance was superb. Her rhythm matched his stroke for stroke, she came with him, she seemed to know exactly what he wanted.

Other visits; two of them, four, six. He was a regular now at the meathouse, along with the others, and he had stopped worrying about it. Cox and the others accepted him in a strange half-hearted way, but his dislike of them had grown, if anything. He was better than they were, he thought. He could hold his own in a meathouse, he could run his corpses and his automills as good as any of them, and he still thought and dreamed. In time he'd leave them all behind, leave Skrakky, be something. They would be meathouse men as long as they would live, but Trager knew he could do better. He believed. He would find love.

He found none in the meathouse, but the sex got better and better, though it was perfect to begin with. In bed with the corpses, Trager was never dissatisfied; he did everything he'd ever read about, heard about, dreamt about. The corpses knew his needs before he did. When he needed it slow, they were slow. When he wanted to have it hard and quick and brutal, then they gave it to him that way, perfectly. He used every orifice they had; they always knew which one to present to him.

His admiration of the meathouse handler grew steadily for months, until it was almost worship. Perhaps somehow he could meet her, he thought at last. Still a boy, still hopelessly naive, he was sure he would love her. Then he would take her away from the meathouse to a clean, corpseless world where they would be happy together.

One day, in a moment of weakness, he told Cox and the others. Cox looked at him, shook his head, grinned. Somebody else snickered. Then they all began to laugh. "What an ass you are, Trager," Cox said at last. "There is no fucking *handler*! Don't tell me you never heard of a feedback circuit?"

He explained it all, to laughter; explained how each corpse was tuned to a controller built into its bed, explained how each customer handled its own meat, explained why non-handlers found meathouse women dead and still. And the boy realized suddenly why the sex was always perfect. He was a better handler than even he had thought.

That night, alone in his room with all the lights burning white and hot, Trager faced himself. And turned away, sickened. He was good at his job, he was proud of that, but the rest . . .

It was the meathouse, he decided. There was a trap there in the meathouse, a trap that could ruin him, destroy life and dream and hope. He would not go back; it was too easy. He would show Cox, show all of them. He could take the hard way, take the risks, feel the pain if he had to. And maybe the joy, maybe the love. He'd gone the other way too long.

Trager did not go back to the meathouse. Feeling strong and decisive and superior, he went back to his room. There, as years passed, he read and dreamed and waited for life to begin.

1
WHEN I WAS ONE-AND-TWENTY

Josie was the first.

She was beautiful, had always been beautiful, knew she was beautiful; all that had shaped her, made her what she was. She was a free spirit. She was aggressive, confident, conquering. Like Trager, she was only twenty when they met, but she had lived more than he had, and she seemed to have the answers. He loved her from the first.

And Trager? Trager before Josie, but years beyond the meathouse? He was taller now, broad and heavy with both muscle and fat, often moody, silent and self-contained. He ran a full five-crew in the ore fields, more than Cox, more than any of them. At night, he read books; sometimes in his room, sometimes in the lobby. He had long since forgotten that he went there to meet someone. Stable, solid, unemotional; that was Trager. He touched no one, and no one touched him. Even the tortures had stopped, though the scars remained *inside*. Trager hardly knew they were there; he never looked at them.

He fit in well now. With his corpses.

Yet—not completely. Inside, the dream. Something believed, something hungered, something yearned. It was strong enough to keep him away from the meathouse, from the vegetable life the others had all chosen. And sometimes, on bleak lonely nights, it would grow stronger still. Then Trager would rise from his empty bed, dress, and walk the corridors for hours with his hands shoved deep into his pockets while something twisted, clawed, and whimpered in his gut. Always, before his walks were over, he would resolve to do something, to change his life tomorrow.

But when tomorrow came, the silent gray corridors were half-forgotten, the demons had faded, and he had six roaring, shaking automills to drive across the pit. He would lose himself in routine, and it would be long months before the feelings came again.

Then Josie: They met like this:

It was a new field, rich and unmined, a vast expanse of broken rock and rubble that filled the plain. Low hills a few weeks ago, but the company skimmers had leveled the area with systematic nuclear blast mining, and now the automills were moving in. Trager's five-crew had been one of the first, and the change had been exhilarating at first. The old pit had been just about worked out; here there was a new terrain to contend with, boulders and jagged rock fragments, baseball-sized fists of stone that came shrieking at you on the dusty wind. It all seemed exciting, dangerous. Trager, wearing a leather jacket and filter-mask and goggles and earplugs, drove his six machines and six bodies with a fierce pride, reducing boulders to powder, clearing a path for the later machines, fighting his way yard by yard to get whatever ore he could.

And one day, suddenly, one of the eye echoes suddenly caught his attention. A light flashed red on a corpse-driven automill. Trager reached, with his hands, with his mind, with five sets of corpse-hands. Six machines stopped, but still another light went red. Then another, and another. Then the whole board, all twelve. One of his automills was out. Cursing, he looked across the rock field towards the machine in question, used his corpse to give it a kick. The lights stayed red. He beamed out for a tech.

By the time she got there—in a one-man skimmer that looked like a teardrop of pitted black metal—Trager had unstrapped, climbed down the metal rings on the side of the automill, walked across the rocks to where the dead machine stopped. He was just starting to climb up when Josie arrived; they met at the foot of the yellow-metal mountain, in the shadow of its treads.

She was field-wise, he knew at once. She wore a handler's coverall, earplugs, heavy goggles, and her face was smeared with grease to prevent dust abrasions. But still she was beautiful. Her hair was short, light brown, cut in a shag that was jumbled by the wind; her eyes, when she lifted the goggles, were bright green. She took charge immediately.

All business, she introduced herself, asked him a few questions, then opened a repair bay and crawled inside, into the guts of the drive and the ore-smelt and the refinery. It didn't take her long; ten minutes, maybe, and she was back outside.

"Don't go in there," she said, tossing her hair from in front of her goggles with a flick of her head. "You've got a damper failure. The nukes are running away."

"Oh," said Trager. His mind was hardly on the automill, but he had to make an impression, had to say something intelligent. "Is it going to blow up?" he asked, and as soon as he said it he knew that *that* hadn't been intelligent at all. Of course it wasn't going to blow up; runaway nuclear reactors didn't work that way, he knew that.

But Josie seemed amused. She smiled—the first time he saw her distinctive flashing grin—and seemed to see him, *him*, Trager, not just a corpsehandler. "No," she said. "It will just melt itself down. Won't even get hot out here, since you've got shields built into the walls. Just don't go in there."

"All right." Pause. What could he say now? "What do I do?"

"Work the rest of your crew, I guess. This machine'll have to be scrapped. It should have been overhauled a long time ago. From the looks of it, there's been a lot of patching done in the past. Stupid. It breaks down, it breaks down, it breaks down, and they keep sending it out. Should realize that something is wrong. After that many failures, it's sheer self-delusion to think the thing's going to work right next time out."

"I guess," Trager said. Josie smiled at him again, sealed up the panel, and started to turn.

"Wait," he said. It came out before he could stop it, almost in spite of him. Josie turned, cocked her head, looked at him questioningly. And Trager drew a sudden strength from the steel and the stone and the wind; under sulfur skies, his dreams seemed less impossible. Maybe, he thought. Maybe.

"Uh. I'm Greg Trager. Will I see you again?"

Josie grinned. "Sure. Come tonight." She gave him the address.

He climbed back into his automill after she had left, exulting in his six strong bodies, all fire and life, and he chewed up rock with something near to joy. The dark red glow in the distance looked almost like a sunrise.

When he got to Josie's, he found four other people there, friends of hers. It was a party of sorts. Josie threw a lot of parties and Trager—from that night on—went to all of them. Josie talked to him, laughed with him, *liked* him, and suddenly his life was no longer the same.

With Josie, he saw parts of Skrakky he had never seen before, did things he had never done.

—he stood with her in the crowds that gathered on the streets at night, stood in the dusty wind and sickly yellow light between the windowless concrete buildings, stood and bet and cheered himself hoarse while grease-stained mechs raced yellow rumbly tractor-trucks up and down and down and up.

—he walked with her through the strangely silent and white and clean underground Offices, and sealed air-conditioned corridors where off-worlders and paper-shufflers and company executives lived and worked.

—he prowled the rec-malls with her, those huge low buildings so like a warehouse from the outside, but full of colored lights and game rooms and cafeterias and tape shops and endless bars where handlers made their rounds.

—he went with her to dormitory gyms, where they watched handlers less skillful than himself send their corpses against each other with clumsy fists.

—he sat with her and her friends, and they woke dark quiet taverns with their talk and with their laughter, and once Trager saw someone looking much like Cox staring at him from across the room, and he smiled and leaned a bit closer to Josie.

He hardly noticed the other people, the crowds that Josie surrounded herself with; when they went out on one of her wild jaunts, six of them or eight or ten, Trager would tell himself that he and Josie were going out, and that some others had come along with them.

Once in a great while, things would work out so they were alone together, at her place, or his. Then they would talk. Of distant worlds, of politics, of corpses and life on Skrakky, of the books they both consumed, of sports or games or friends they had in common. They shared a good deal. Trager talked a lot with Josie. And never said a word.

He loved her, of course. He suspected it the first month, and soon he was convinced of it. He loved her. This was the real thing, the thing he had been waiting for, and it had happened just as he knew it would.

But with his love: agony. He could not tell her. A dozen times he tried; the words would never come. What if she did not love him back?

His nights were still alone, in the small room with the white lights and the books and the pain. He was more alone than ever now; the peace of his routine, of his half-life with his corpses, was gone, stripped from him. By day he rode the great automills, moved his corpses, smashed rock and melted ore, and in his head rehearsed the words he'd say to Josie. And dreamed of those that she'd speak back. She was trapped too, he thought. She'd had men, of course, but she didn't love them, she loved him. But she couldn't tell him, any more than he could tell her. When he broke through, when he found the words and the courage, then everything would be all right. Each day he said that to himself, and dug swift and deep into the earth.

But back home, the sureness faded. Then, with awful despair, he knew that he was kidding himself. He was a friend to her, nothing more, never would be more. Why did he lie to himself? He'd had hints enough. They had never been lovers, never would be; on the few times he'd worked up the courage to touch her, she would smile, move away on some pretext, so he was never quite sure that he was being rejected. But he got the idea, and in the dark it tore at him. He walked the corridors weekly now, sullen, desperate, wanting to talk to someone without knowing how. And all the old scars woke up to bleed again.

Until the next day. When he would return to his machines, and believe again. He must believe in himself, he knew that, he shouted it out loud. He must stop feeling sorry for himself. He must do something. He must tell Josie. He would.

And she would love him, cried the day.

And she would laugh, the nights replied.

Trager chased her for a year, a year of pain and promise, the first year that he had ever *lived*. On that the night-fears and the day-voice agreed; he was alive now. He would never return to the emptiness of his time before Josie; he would never go back to the meathouse. That far, at least, he had come. He could change, and someday he would be strong enough to tell her.

Josie and two friends dropped by his room that night, but the friends had to leave early. For an hour or so they were alone, talking about nothing. Finally she had to go. Trager said he'd walk her home.

He kept his arm around her down the long corridors, and he watched her face, watched the play of light and shadow on her cheeks as they walked from light to darkness. "Josie," he started. He felt so fine, so good, so warm, and it came out. "I love you."

And she stopped, pulled away from him, stepped back. Her mouth opened, just a little, and something flickered in her eyes. "Oh, Greg," she said. Softly. Sadly. "No, Greg, no, don't, don't." And she shook her head.

Trembling slightly, mouthing silent words, Trager held out his hand. Josie did not take it. He touched her cheek, gently, and wordless she spun away from him.

Then, for the first time ever, Trager shook. And the tears came.

Josie took him to her room. There, sitting across from each other on the floor, never touching, they talked.

J: . . . *known it for a long time . . . tried to discourage you, Greg, but I didn't just want to come right out and . . . I never wanted to hurt you . . . a good person . . . don't worry. . . .*

T: . . . *knew it all along . . . that it would never . . . lied to myself . . . wanted to believe, even if it wasn't true . . . I'm sorry, Josie, I'm sorry, I'm sorry, I'm sorryimsorryimsorry.* . . .

J: . . . *afraid you would go back to what you were . . . don't Greg, promise me . . . can't give up . . . have to believe.* . . .

T: *why?*

J: . . . *stop believing, then you have nothing . . . dead . . . you can do better . . . a good handler . . . get off Skrakky find something . . . no life here . . . someone . . . you will, you will, just believe, keep on believing.* . . .

T: . . . *you . . . love you forever, Josie . . . forever . . . how can I find someone . . . never anyone like you, never . . . special . . .*

J: . . . *oh, Greg . . . lots of people . . . just look . . . open . . .*

T: (laughter) . . . *open?* . . . *first time I ever talked to anyone . . .*

J: . . . *talk to me again, if you have to . . . I can talk to you . . . had enough lovers, everyone wants to get in bed with me, better just to be friends.* . . .

T: . . . *friends* . . . (laughter) . . . (tears) . . .

II
PROMISES OF SOMEDAY

The fire had burned out long ago, and Stevens and the forester had retired, but Trager and Donelly still sat around the ashes on the edges of the clear zone. They talked softly, so as not to wake the others, yet their words hung long in the restless night air. The uncut forest, standing dark behind them, was dead still; the wildlife of Vendalia had all fled the noise that the fleet of buzztrucks made during the day.

". . . a full six-crew, running buzztrucks, I know enough to know that's not easy," Donelly was saying. He was a pale, timid youth, likeable but self-conscious about everything he did. Trager heard echoes of himself in Donelly's stiff words. "You'd do well in the arena."

Trager nodded, thoughtful, his eyes on the ashes as he moved them with a stick. "I came to Vendalia with that in mind. Went to the gladiatorial once, only once. That was enough to change my mind. I could take them, I guess, but the whole idea made me sick. Out here, well, the money doesn't even match what I was getting on Skrakky, but the work is, well, clean. You know?"

"Sort of," said Donelly. "Still, you know, it isn't like they were real people out there in the arena. Only meat. All you can do is make the bodies as dead as the minds. That's the logical way to look at it."

Trager chuckled. "You're too logical, Don. You ought to *feel* more. Listen, next time you're in Gidyon, go to the gladiatorials and take a look. It's ugly, *ugly*. Corpses stumbling around with axes and swords and morningstars, hacking and hewing at each other. Butchery, that's all it is. And the audience, the way they cheer at each blow. And *laugh*. They *laugh*, Don! No." He shook his head sharply. "No."

Donelly never abandoned an argument. "But why not? I don't understand, Greg. You'd be good at it, the best. I've seen the way you work your crew."

Trager looked up, studied Donelly briefly while the youth sat quietly, waiting. Josie's words came back; open, be open. The old Trager, the Trager who lived friendless and alone and closed inside a Skrakky handlers' dorm, was gone. He had grown, changed.

"There was a girl," he said, slowly, with measured words. Opening. "Back on Skrakky, Don, there was a girl I loved. It, well, it didn't work out. That's why I'm here, I guess. I'm looking for someone else, for something better. That's all part of it, you see." He stopped, paused, tried to think his words out. "This girl, Josie, I wanted her to love me. You know." The words came hard. "Admire me, all that stuff. Now, yeah, sure, I could do good running corpses in the arena. But Josie could never love someone who had a job like *that*. She's gone now, of course, but still . . . the kind of person I'm looking for, I couldn't find them as an arena corpse-master." He stood up, abruptly. "I don't know. That's what's important, though, to me. Josie, somebody like her, someday. Soon, I hope."

Donelly sat quiet in the moonlight, chewing his lip, not looking at Trager, his logic suddenly useless. While Trager, his corridors long gone, walked off alone into the woods.

They had a tight knit group; three handlers, a forester, thirteen corpses. Each day they drove the forest back, with Trager in the forefront. Against the Vendalian wilderness, against the blackbriars and the hard gray ironspike trees and the bulbous rubbery snaplimbs, against the tangled hostile forest, he would throw his six-crew and their buzztrucks. Smaller than the automills he'd run on Skrakky, fast and airborne, complex and demanding, those were buzztrucks. Trager ran six of them with corpse hands, a seventh with his own. Before his screaming blades and laser knives, the wall of wilderness fell each day. Donelly came behind him, pushing three of the mountain-sized rolling mills, to turn the fallen trees into lumber for Gidyon and other cities of Vendalia. Then Stevens, the third handler, with a flame-cannon to burn down stumps and melt rocks, and the soilpumps that would ready the fresh clear land for farming. The forester was their foreman. The procedure was a science.

Clean, hard, demanding work; Trager thrived on it by day. He grew lean, almost athletic; the lines of his face tightened and tanned, he grew steadily browner under Vendalia's hot bright sun. His corpses were almost part of him, so easily did he move them, fly their buzztrucks. As an ordinary man might move a hand, a foot. Sometimes his control grew so firm, the echoes so clear and strong, that Trager felt he was not a handler working a crew at all, but rather a man with seven bodies. Seven strong bodies that rode the sultry forest winds. He exulted in their sweat.

And the evenings, after work ceased, they were good too. Trager found a sort of peace there, a sense of belonging he had never known on Skrakky. The Vendalian foresters, rotated back and forth from Gidyon, were decent enough, and friendly. Stevens was a hearty slab of a man who seldom stopped joking long enough to talk about anything serious. Trager always found him amusing. And Donelly, the self-conscious youth, the quiet logical voice, he became a friend. He was a good listener, empathetic, compassionate, and the new open Trager was a good talker. Something close to envy shone in Donelly's eyes when he spoke of Josie and exorcised his soul. And Trager knew, or thought he knew, that Donelly was himself, the old Trager, the one before Josie who could not find the words.

In time, though, after days and weeks of talking, Donelly found his words. Then Trager listened, and shared another's pain. And he felt good about it. He was helping; he was lending strength; he was needed.

Each night around the ashes, the two men traded dreams. And wove a hopeful tapestry of promise and lies.

Yet still the nights would come.

Those were the worst times, as always; those were the hours of Trager's long lonely walks. If Josie had given Trager much, she had taken something too; she had taken the curious deadness he had once had, the trick of not-thinking, the pain-blotter of his mind. On Skrakky, he had walked the corridors infrequently; the forest knew him far more often.

After the talking all had stopped, after Donelly had gone to bed, that was when it would happen, when Josie would come to him in the loneliness of his tent. A thousand nights he lay there with his hands hooked behind his head, staring at the plastic tent film while he relived the night he'd told her. A thousand times he touched her cheek, and saw her spin away.

He would think of it, and fight it, and lose. Then, restless, he would rise and go outside. He would walk across the clear area, into the silent looming forest, brushing aside low branches and tripping on the underbrush; he would walk until he found water. Then he would sit down, by a scum-choked lake or a gurgling stream that ran swift and oily in the moonlight. He would fling rocks into the water, hurl them hard and flat into the night to hear them when they splashed.

He would sit for hours, throwing rocks and thinking, till finally he could convince himself the sun would rise.

Gidyon; the city; the heart of Vendalia, and through it of Slagg and Skrakky and New Pittsburg and all the other corpseworlds, the harsh ugly places where men would not work and corpses had to. Great towers of black and silver metal, floating aerial sculpture that flashed in the sunlight and shone softly at night, the vast bustling spaceport where freighters rose and fell on invisible firewands, malls where the pavement was polished, ironspike wood that gleamed a gentle gray; Gidyon.

The city with the rot. The corpse city. The meatmart.

For the freighters carried cargoes of men, criminals and derelicts and troublemakers from a dozen worlds bought with hard Vendalian cash (and there were darker rumors, of liners that had vanished mysteriously on routine tourist hops). And the soaring towers were hospitals and corpseyards, where men and women died and deadmen were born to walk anew. And all along the ironspike boardwalks were corpse-seller's shops and meathouses.

The meathouses of Vendalia were far-famed. The corpses were guaranteed beautiful.

Trager sat across from one, on the other side of the wide gray avenue, under the umbrella of an outdoor cafe. He sipped a bittersweet wine, thought about how his leave had evaporated too quickly, and tried to keep his eyes from wandering across the street. The wine was warm on his tongue, and his eyes were very restless.

Up and down the avenue, between him and the meathouse, strangers moved. Dark-faced corpsehandlers from Vendalia, Skrakky, Slagg; pudgy merchants, gawking tourists from the Clean Worlds like Old Earth and Zephyr, and dozens of question marks whose names and occupations and errands Trager would never know. Sitting there, drinking his wine and watching, Trager felt utterly cut off. He could not touch these people, could not reach them; he didn't know how, it wasn't possible, it wouldn't work. He could rise and walk out into the street and grab one, and still they would not touch. The stranger would only pull free and run. All his leave like that, all of it; he'd run through all the bars of Gidyon, forced a thousand contacts, and nothing had clicked.

His wine was gone. Trager looked at the glass dully, turning it in his hands, blinking. Then, abruptly, he stood up and paid his bill. His hands trembled.

It had been so many years, he thought as he started across the street. Josie, he thought, forgive me.

Trager returned to the wilderness camp, and his corpses flew their buzztrucks like men gone wild. But he was strangely silent around the campfire, and he did not talk to Donelly at night. Until finally, hurt and puzzled, Donelly followed him into the forest. And found him by a languid death-dark stream, sitting on the bank with a pile of throwing stones at his feet.

T: . . . *went in . . . after all I said, all I promised . . . still I went in.* . . .

D: . . . *nothing to worry . . . remember what you told me . . . keep on believing.* . . .

T: . . . *did believe, DID . . . no difficulties . . . Josie* . . .

D: . . . *you say I shouldn't give up, you better not . . . repeat everything you told me, everything Josie told you . . . everybody finds someone . . . if they keep looking . . . give up, dead . . . all you need . . . openness . . . courage to look . . . stop feeling sorry for yourself . . . told me that a hundred times.* . . .

T: . . . *fucking lot easier to tell you than do it myself* . . .

D: . . . *Greg . . . not a meathouse man . . . a dreamer . . . better than they are* . . .

T: (sighing) . . . *yeah . . . hard, though . . . why do I do this to myself?* . . .

D: . . . *rather be like you were? . . . not hurting, not living? . . . like me?* . . .

T: . . . *no . . . no . . . you're right.* . . .

2
THE PILGRIM, UP AND DOWN

Her name was Laurel. She was nothing like Josie, save in one thing alone. Trager loved her.

Pretty? Trager didn't think so, not at first. She was too tall, a half-foot taller than he was, and she was a bit on the heavy side, and more than a bit on the awkward side. Her hair was her best feature, her hair that was red-brown in winter and glowing blonde in summer, that fell long and straight down past her shoulders and did wild beautiful things in the wind. But she was not beautiful, not the way Josie had been beautiful. Although, oddly, she grew more beautiful with time, and maybe that was because she was losing weight, and maybe that was because Trager was falling in love with her and seeing her through kinder eyes, and maybe that was because he told her she was pretty and the very telling made it so. Just as Laurel told him he was wise, and her belief gave him wisdom. Whatever the reason, Laurel was very beautiful indeed after he had known her for a time.

She was five years younger than he, clean-scrubbed and innocent, shy where Josie had been assertive. She was intelligent, romantic, a dreamer; she was wondrously fresh and eager; she was painfully insecure, and full of hungry need.

She was new to Gidyon, fresh from the Vendalian outback, a student forester. Trager, on leave again, was visiting the forestry college to say hello to a teacher who'd once worked with his crew. They met in the teacher's office. Trager had two weeks free in a city of strangers and meathouses; Laurel was alone. He showed her the glittering decadence of Gidyon, feeling smooth and sophisticated, and she was suitably impressed.

Two weeks went quickly. They came to the last night. Trager, suddenly afraid, took her to the park by the river that ran through Gidyon and they sat together on the low stone wall by the water's edge. Close, not touching.

"Time runs too fast," he said. He had a stone in his hand. He flicked it out over the water, flat and hard. Thoughtfully, he watched it splash and sink. Then he looked at her. "I'm nervous," he said, laughing. "I— Laurel. I don't want to leave."

Her face was unreadable (wary?). "The city is nice," she agreed.

Trager shook his head violently. "No. *No!* Not the city, you. Laurel, I think I . . . well . . ."

Laurel smiled for him. Her eyes were bright, very happy. "I know," she said.

Trager could hardly believe it. He reached out, touched her cheek. She turned her head and kissed his hand. They smiled at each other.

He flew back to the forest camp to quit. "Don, Don, you've got to meet her," he shouted. "See, you can do it, *I did* it, just keep believing, keep trying. I feel so goddamn good it's obscene."

Donelly, stiff and logical, smiled for him, at a loss as how to handle such a flood of happiness. "What will you do?" he asked, a little awkwardly. "The arena?"

Trager laughed. "Hardly, you know I feel. But something like that. There's a theatre near the spaceport, puts on a pantomime with corpse actors. I've got a job there. The pay is rotten, but it'll be near Laurel. That's all that matters."

They hardly slept at night. Instead they talked and cuddled and made love. The lovemaking was a joy, a game, a glorious discovery; never as good technically as the meathouse, but Trager hardly cared. He taught her to be open. He told her every secret he had, and wished he had more secrets.

"Poor Josie," Lauren would often say at night, her body warm against his. "She doesn't know what she missed. I'm lucky. There couldn't be anyone else like you."

"No," said Trager, "*I'm* lucky."

They would argue about it, laughing.

Donelly came to Gidyon and joined the theatre. Without Trager, the forest work had been no fun, he said. The three of them spent a lot of time together, and Trager glowed. He wanted to share his friends with Laurel, and he'd already mentioned Donelly a lot. And he wanted Donelly to see how happy he'd become, to see what belief could accomplish.

"I like her," Donelly said, smiling, the first night after Laurel had left.

"Good," Trager replied, nodding.

"No," said Donelly. "Greg, I *really* like her."

They spent a lot of time together.

"Greg," Laurel said one night in bed, "I think that Don is . . . well, after me. You know."

Trager rolled over and propped his head up on his elbow. "God," he said. He sounded concerned.

"I don't know how to handle it."

"Carefully," Trager said. "He's very vulnerable. You're probably the first woman he's ever been interested in. Don't be too hard on him. He shouldn't have to go through the stuff I went through, you know?"

The sex was never as good as a meathouse. And, after a while, Laurel began to close. More and more nights now she went to sleep after they made love; the days when they talked till dawn were gone. Perhaps they had nothing left to say. Trager had noticed that she had a tendency to finish his stories for him. It was nearly impossible to come up with one he hadn't already told her.

"He said that?" Trager got out of bed, turned on a light, and sat down frowning. Laurel pulled the covers up to her chin.

"Well, what did *you* say?"

She hesitated. "I can't tell you. It's between Don and me. He said it wasn't fair, the way I turn around and tell you everything that goes on between us, and he's right."

"*Right!* But I tell you everything. Don't you remember what we . . ."

"I know, but . . ."

Trager shook his head. His voice lost some of its anger. "What's going on, Laurel, huh? I'm scared, all of a sudden. I love you, remember? How can everything change so fast?"

Her face softened. She sat up, and held out her arms, and the covers fell back from full soft breasts. "Oh, Greg," she said. "Don't worry. I love you, I always will, but it's just that I love him too, I guess. You know?"

Trager, mollified, came into her arms, and kissed her with fervor. Then, suddenly, he broke off. "Hey," he said, with mock sternness to hide the trembling in his voice, "who do you love *more*?"

"You, of course, always you."

Smiling, he returned the kiss.

"I know you know," Donelly said. "I guess we have to talk about it."

Trager nodded. They were backstage in the theatre. Three of his corpses walked up behind him, and stood arms crossed, like a guard. "All right." He looked straight at Donelly, and his face—smiling until the other's words—was suddenly stern. "Laurel asked me to pretend I didn't know anything. She said you felt guilty. But pretending was quite a strain, Don. I guess it's time we got everything out in the open."

Donelly's pale blue eyes shifted to the floor, and he stuck his hands into his pockets. "I don't want to hurt you," he said.

"Then don't."

"But I'm not going to pretend I'm dead, either. I'm not. I love her too."

"You're supposed to be my friend, Don. Love someone else. You're just going to get yourself hurt this way."

"I have more in common with her than you do."

Trager just stared.

Donelly looked up at him. Then, abashed, back down again. "I don't know. Oh, Greg. She loves you more anyway, she said so. I never should have expected anything else. I feel like I've stabbed you in the back. I . . ."

Trager watched him. Finally, he laughed softly. "Oh, shit, I can't take this. Look, Don, you haven't stabbed me, c'mon, don't talk like that. I guess, if you love her, this is the way it's got to be, you know. I just hope everything comes out all right."

Later that night, in bed with Laurel; "I'm worried about him," he told her.

His face, once tanned, now ashen. "Laurel?" he said. Not believing.

"I don't love you anymore. I'm sorry. I don't. It seemed real at the time, but now it's almost like a dream. I don't even know if I ever loved you, really."

"Don," he said woodenly.

Laurel flushed. "Don't say anything bad about Don. I'm tired of hearing you run him down. He never says anything except good about you."

"Oh, Laurel. Don't you *remember*? The things we said, the way we felt? I'm the same person you said those words to."

"But I've grown," Laurel said, hard and tearless, tossing her red-gold hair. "I remember perfectly well, but I just don't feel that way anymore."

"Don't," he said. He reached for her.

She stepped back. "Keep your hands off me. I told you, Greg, it's *over*. You have to leave now. Don is coming by."

It was worse than Josie. A thousand times worse.

III
WANDERINGS

He tried to keep on at the theatre; he enjoyed the work, he had friends there. But it was impossible. Donelly was there every day, smiling and being friendly, and sometimes Laurel came to meet him after the day's show and they went off together, arm in arm. Trager would stand and watch, try not to notice. While the twisted thing inside him shrieked and clawed.

He quit. He would not see them again. He would keep his pride.

* * *

The sky was bright with the lights of Gidyon and full of laughter, but it was dark and quiet in the park.

Trager stood stiff against a tree, his eyes on the river, his hands folded tightly against his chest. He was a statue. He hardly seemed to breathe. Not even his eyes moved.

Kneeling near the low wall, the corpse pounded until the stone was slick with blood and its hands were mangled clots of torn meat. The sounds of the blows were dull and wet, but for the infrequent scraping of bone against rock.

They made him pay first, before he could even enter the booth. Then he sat there for an hour while they found her and punched through. Finally, though, finally; "Josie."

"Greg," she said, grinning her distinctive grin. "I should have known. Who else would call all the way from Vendalia? How are you?"

He told her.

Her grin vanished. "Oh, Greg," she said. "I'm sorry. But don't let it get to you. Keep going. The next one will work out better. They always do."

Her words didn't satisfy him. "Josie," he said, "How are things back there? You miss me?"

"Oh, sure. Things are pretty good. It's still Skrakky, though. Stay where you are, you're better off." She looked offscreen, then back. "I should go, before your bill gets enormous. Glad you called, love."

"*Josie*," Trager started. But the screen was already dark.

Sometimes, at night, he couldn't help himself. He would move to his home screen and ring Laurel. Invariably her eyes would narrow when she saw who it was. Then she would hang up.

And Trager would sit in a dark room and recall how once the sound of his voice made her so very, very happy.

The streets of Gidyon are not the best of places for lonely midnight walks. They are brightly lit, even in the darkest hours, and jammed with men and deadmen. And there are meathouses, all up and down the boulevards and the ironspike boardwalks.

Josie's words had lost their power. In the meathouses, Trager abandoned dreams and found cheap solace. The sensuous evenings with Laurel and the fumbling sex of his boyhood were things of yesterday; Trager took his meatmates hard and quick, almost brutally, fucked them with a wordless savage power to the inevitable perfect orgasm. Sometimes, remembering the theatre, he would have them act out short erotic playlets to get him in the mood.

In the night. Agony.

He was in the corridors again, the low dim corridors of the corpsehandlers' dorm on Skrakky, but now the corridors were twisted and torturous and Trager had long since lost his way. The air was thick with a rotting gray haze, and growing thicker. Soon, he feared, he would be all but blind.

Around and around he walked, up and down, but always there was more corridor, and all of them led nowhere. The doors were grim black rectangles, knobless, locked to him forever; he passed them by without thinking, most of them. Once or twice, though, he paused, before doors where light leaked around the frame. He would listen, and inside there were no sounds, and then he would begin to knock wildly. But no one ever answered.

So he would move on, through the haze that got darker and thicker and seemed to burn his skin, past door after door after door, until he was weeping and his feet were tired and bloody. And then, off a ways, down a long, long corridor that loomed straight before him, he would see an open door. From it came light so hot and white it hurt the eyes, and music bright and joyful, and the sounds of people laughing. Then Trager would run, though his feet were raw bundles of pain and his lungs burned with the haze he was breathing. He would run and run until he reached the room with the open door.

Only when he got there, it was his room, and it was empty.

Once, in the middle of their brief time together, they'd gone out into the wilderness and made love under the stars. Afterwards she had snuggled hard against him, and he stroked her gently. "What are you thinking?" he asked.

"About us," Laurel said. She shivered. The wind was brisk and cold. "Sometimes I get scared, Greg. I'm so afraid something will happen to us, something that will ruin it. I don't ever want you to leave me."

"Don't worry," he told her. "I won't."

Now, each night before sleep came, he tortured himself with her words. The good memories left him with ashes and tears; the bad ones with a wordless rage.

He slept with a ghost beside him, a supernaturally beautiful ghost, the husk of a dead dream. He woke to her each morning.

He hated them. He hated himself for hating.

3
DUVALIER'S DREAM

Her name does not matter. Her looks are not important. All that counts is that she *was*, that Trager tried again, that he forced himself on and made himself believe and didn't give up. He *tried*.

But something was missing. Magic?

The words were the same.

How many times can you speak them, Trager wondered, *speak them and believe them, like you believe them the first time you said them? Once? Twice? Three times, maybe? Or a hundred? And the people who say it a hundred times, are they really so much better at loving? Or only at fooling themselves? Aren't they really people who long ago abandoned the dream, who use its name for something else?*

He said the words, holding her, cradling her, and kissing her. He said the words, with a knowledge that was surer and heavier and more dead than any belief. He said the words and *tried*, but no longer could he mean them.

And she said the words back, and Trager realized that they meant nothing to him. Over and over again they said the things each wanted to hear, and both of them knew they were pretending.

They tried *hard*. But when he reached out, like an actor caught in his role, doomed to play out the same part over and over again, when he reached out his hand and touched her cheek—the skin was smooth and soft and lovely. And wet with tears.

IV
ECHOES

"I don't want to hurt you," said Donelly, shuffling and looking guilty, until Trager felt ashamed for having hurt a friend.

He touched her cheek, and she spun away from him.

"I never wanted to hurt you," Josie said, and Trager was sad. She had given him so much; he'd only made her guilty. Yes, he was hurt, but a stronger man would never have let her know.

"I'm sorry, I don't," Laurel said. And Trager was lost. What had he done, where was his fault, how had he ruined it? She had been so sure. They had had so much.

He touched her cheek, and she wept.

How many times can you speak them, his voice echoed, *speak them and believe them, like you believed them the first time you said them?*

The wind was dark and dust heavy, the sky throbbed painfully with flickering scarlet flame. In the pit, in the darkness, stood a young woman with goggles and a filtermask and short brown hair and answers. "It breaks down, it breaks down, it breaks down, and they keep sending it out," she said. "Should realize that something is wrong. After that many failures, it's sheer self-delusion to think the thing's going to work right next time out."

The enemy corpse is huge and black, its torso rippling with muscle, a product of months of exercise, the biggest thing that Trager has ever faced. It advances across the sawdust in a slow, clumsy crouch, holding the gleaming broadsword in one hand. Trager watches it come from his chair atop one end of the fighting arena. The other corpsemaster is careful, cautious.

His own deadman, a wiry blond, stands and waits, a morningstar trailing down in the blood-soaked arena dust. Trager will move him fast enough and well enough when the time is right. The enemy knows it, and the crowd.

The black corpse suddenly lifts its broadsword and scrambles forward in a run, hoping to use reach and speed to get its kill. But Trager's corpse is no longer there when the enemy's measured blow cuts the air where he had been.

Sitting comfortably above the fighting pit/down in the arena, his feet grimy with blood and sawdust—Trager/the corpse—snaps the command/ swings the morningstar—and the great studded ball drifts up and around, almost lazily, almost gracefully. Into the back of the enemy's head, as he tries to recover and turn. A flower of blood and brain blooms swift and sudden, and the crowd cheers.

Trager walks his corpse from the arena, then stands up to receive applause. It is his tenth kill. Soon the championship will be his. He is building such a record that they can no longer deny him a match.

* * *

She is beautiful, his lady, his love. Her hair is short and blond, her body very slim, graceful, almost athletic, with trim legs and small hard breasts. Her eyes are bright green, and they always welcome him. And there is a strange erotic innocence in her smile.

She waits for him in bed, waits for his return from the arena, waits for him eager and playful and loving. When he enters, she is sitting up, smiling for him, the covers bunched around her waist. From the door he admires her nipples.

Aware of his eyes, shy, she covers her breasts and blushes. Trager knows it is all false modesty, all playing. He moves to the bedside, sits, reaches out to stroke her cheek. Her skin is very soft; she nuzzles against his hand as it brushes her. Then Trager draws her hands aside, plants one gentle kiss on each breast, and a not-so-gentle kiss on her mouth. She kisses back, with ardor; their tongues dance.

They make love, he and she, slow and sensuous, locked together in a loving embrace that goes on and on. Two bodies move flawlessly in perfect rhythm, each knowing the other's needs. Trager thrusts, and his other body meets the thrusts. He reaches, and her hand is there. They come together (always, *always*, both orgasms triggered by the handler's brain), and a bright red flush burns on her breasts and earlobes. They kiss.

Afterwards, he talks to her, his love, his lady. You should always talk afterwards; he learned that long ago.

"You're lucky," he tells her sometimes, and she snuggles up to him and plants tiny kisses all across his chest. "Very lucky. They lie to you out there, love. They teach you a silly shining dream and they tell you to believe and chase it and they tell you that for you, for everyone, there is someone. But it's all wrong. The universe isn't fair, it never has been, so why do they tell you so? You run after the phantom, and lose, and they tell you next time, but it's all rot, all empty rot. Nobody ever finds the dream at all, they just kid themselves, trick themselves so they can go on believing. It's just a clutching lie that desperate people tell each other, hoping to convince themselves."

But then he can't talk anymore, for her kisses have gone lower and lower, and now she takes him in her mouth. And Trager smiles at his love and gently strokes her hair.

Of all the bright cruel lies they tell you, the cruelest is the one called love.

Night They Missed the Horror Show

Joe R. Lansdale

"Night They Missed the Horror Show" was originally published in the 1988 anthology *Silver Scream*, edited by David Schow, from Dark Harvest Press. It later appeared in *By Bizarre Hands*, a collection of Lansdale's short stories published by Avon Books, and in *High Cotton: Selected Short Stories of Joe R. Lansdale*, published in 2000 by Golden Gryphon Press.

"Night They Missed the Horror Show" won a Bram Stoker award for Best Short Story, 1988.

Joe R. Lansdale is the author of over 30 novels and numerous short story collections. His work has been filmed and adapted to comics. He is the editor or co-editor of a dozen anthologies. He has received the Edgar Award, The British Fantasy Award, Seven Bram Stokers, The Grinzani Cavour Prize for literature, and numerous other awards. He lives in Nacogdoches with his wife and near his son and daughter.

♦ ♦ ♦

For Lew Shiner, a story that doesn't flinch

IF THEY'D GONE TO THE DRIVE-IN like they'd planned, none of this would have happened. But Leonard didn't like drive-ins when he didn't have a date, and he'd heard about *Night of the Living Dead,* and he knew a nigger starred in it. He didn't want to see no movie with a nigger star. Niggers chopped cotton, fixed flats, and pimped nigger girls, but he'd never heard of one that killed zombies. And he'd heard too that there was a white girl in the movie that let the nigger touch her, and that peeved him. Any white gal that would let a nigger touch her must be the lowest trash in the world. Probably from Hollywood, New York, or Waco, some god-forsaken place like that.

Now Steve McQueen would have been all right for zombie killing and girl handling. He would have been the ticket. But a nigger? No sir.

Boy, that Steve McQueen was one cool head. Way he said stuff in them pictures was so good you couldn't help but think someone had written it down for him. He could sure think fast on his feet to come up with the things he said, and he had that real cool, mean look.

Leonard wished he could be Steve McQueen, or Paul Newman even. Someone like that always knew what to say, and he figured they got plenty of bush too. Certainly they didn't get as bored as he did. He was so bored he felt as if he were going to die from it before the night was out. Bored, bored, bored. Just wasn't nothing exciting about being in the Dairy Queen parking lot leaning on the front of his '64 Impala looking out at the highway. He figured maybe old crazy Harry who janitored at the high school might be right about them flying saucers. Harry was always seeing something. Bigfoot, six-legged weasels, all manner of things. But maybe he was right about the saucers. He'd said he'd seen one a couple nights back hovering over Mud Creek and it was shooting down these rays that looked like wet peppermint sticks. Leonard figured if Harry really had seen the saucers and the rays, then those rays were boredom rays. It would be a way for space critters to get at earth folks, boring them to death. Getting melted down by heat rays would have been better. That was at least quick, but being bored to death was sort of like being nibbled to death by ducks.

Leonard continued looking at the highway, trying to imagine flying saucers and boredom rays, but he couldn't keep his mind on it. He finally focused on something in the highway. A dead dog.

Not just a dead dog. But a DEAD DOG. The mutt had been hit by a semi at least, maybe several. It looked as if it had rained dog. There were pieces of that pooch all over the concrete and one leg was lying on the curbing on the opposite side, stuck up in such a way that it seemed to be waving hello. Doctor Frankenstein with a grant from Johns Hopkins and assistance from NASA couldn't have put that sucker together again.

Leonard leaned over to his faithful, drunk companion, Billy—known among the gang as Farto, because he was fart-lighting champion of Mud Creek—and said, "See that dog there?"

Farto looked where Leonard was pointing. He hadn't noticed the dog before, and he wasn't nearly as casual about it as Leonard. The puzzle-piece hound brought back memories. It reminded him of a dog he'd had when he was thirteen. A big, fine German Shepherd that loved him better than his Mama.

Sonofabitch dog tangled its chain through and over a barbed wire fence somehow and hung itself. When Farto found the dog its tongue looked like a stuffed, black sock and he could see where its claws had just been able to scrape the ground, but not quite enough to get a toe hold.

It looked as if the dog had been scratching out some sort of a coded message in the dirt. When Farto told his old man about it later, crying as he did, his old man laughed and said, "Probably a goddamn suicide note."

Now, as he looked out at the highway, and his whiskey-laced Coke collected warmly in his gut, he felt a tear form in his eyes. Last time he'd felt that sappy was when he'd won the fart-lighting championship with a four-inch burner that singed the hairs of his ass and the gang awarded him with a pair of colored boxing shorts. Brown and yellow ones so he could wear them without having to change them too often.

So there they were, Leonard and Farto, parked outside the DQ, leaning on the hood of Leonard's Impala, sipping Coke and whiskey, feeling bored and blue and horny, looking at a dead dog and having nothing to do but go to a show with a nigger starring in it. Which, to be up front, wouldn't have been so bad if they'd had dates. Dates could make up for a lot of sins, or help make a few good ones, depending on one's outlook.

But the night was criminal. Dates they didn't have. Worse yet, wasn't a girl in the entire high school would date them. Not even Marylou Flowers, and she had some kind of disease.

All this nagged Leonard something awful. He could see what the problem was with Farto. He was ugly. Had the kind of face that attracted flies. And though being fart-lighting champion of Mud Creek had a certain prestige among the gang, it lacked a certain something when it came to charming the gals.

But for the life of him, Leonard couldn't figure his own problem. He was handsome, had some good clothes, and his car ran good when he didn't buy that old cheap gas. He even had a few bucks in his jeans from breaking into washaterias. Yet his right arm had damn near grown to the size of his thigh from all the whacking off he did. Last time he'd been out with a girl had been a month ago, and as he'd been out with her along with nine other guys, he wasn't rightly sure he could call that a date. He wondered about it so much, he'd asked Farto if he thought it qualified as a date. Farto, who had been fifth in line, said he didn't think so, but if Leonard wanted to call it one, wasn't no skin off his back.

But Leonard didn't want to call it a date. It just didn't have the feel of one, lacked that something special. There was no romance to it.

True, Big Red had called him Honey when he put the mule in the barn, but she called everyone Honey—except Stoney. Stoney was Possum Sweets, and he was the one who talked her into wearing the grocery bag with the mouth and eyeholes. Stoney was like that. He could sweet talk the camel out from under a sand nigger. When he got through chatting Big Red down, she was plumb proud to wear that bag.

When finally it came his turn to do Big Red, Leonard had let her take the bag off as a gesture of goodwill. That was a mistake. He just hadn't known a good thing when he had it. Stoney had had the right idea. The bag coming off spoiled everything. With it on, it was sort of like balling the Lone Hippo or some such thing, but with the bag off, you were absolutely certain what you were getting, and it wasn't pretty.

Even closing his eyes hadn't helped. He found that the ugliness of that face had branded itself on the back of his eyeballs. He couldn't even imagine the sack back over her head. All he could think about was that puffy, too-painted face with the sort of bad complexion that began at the bone.

He'd gotten so disappointed, he'd had to fake an orgasm and get off before his hooter shriveled up and his Trojan fell off and was lost in the vacuum.

Thinking back on it, Leonard sighed. It would certainly be nice for a change to go with a girl that didn't pull the train or have a hole between her legs that looked like a manhole cover ought to be on it. Sometimes he wished he could be like Farto, who was as happy as if he had good sense. Anything thrilled him. Give him a can of Wolf Brand Chili, a big moon pie, Coke and whiskey and he could spend the rest of his life fucking Big Red and lighting the gas out of his asshole.

God, but this was no way to live. No women and no fun. Bored, bored, bored. Leonard found himself looking overhead for spaceships and peppermint-colored boredom rays, but he saw only a few moths fluttering drunkenly through the beams of the DQ's lights.

Lowering his eyes back to the highway and the dog, Leonard had a sudden flash. "Why don't we get the chain out of the back and hook it up to Rex there? Take him for a ride?"

"You mean drag his dead ass around?" Farto asked.

Leonard nodded.

"Beats stepping on a tack," Farto said.

They drove the Impala into the middle of the highway at a safe moment and got out for a look. Up close the mutt was a lot worse. Its innards had been mashed out of its mouth and asshole and it stunk something awful. The dog was wearing a thick, metal-studded collar and they fastened one end of their fifteen-foot chain to that and the other to the rear bumper.

Bob, the Dairy Queen manager, noticed them through the window, came outside and yelled, "What are you fucking morons doing?"

"Taking this doggie to the vet," Leonard said. "We think this sumbitch looks a might peeked. He may have been hit by a car."

"That's so fucking funny I'm about to piss myself," Bob said.

"Old folks have that problem," Leonard said.

Leonard got behind the wheel and Farto climbed in on the passenger side. They maneuvered the car and dog around and out of the path of a tractor-trailer truck just in time. As they drove off, Bob screamed after them, "I hope you two no-dicks wrap that Chevy piece of shit around a goddamn pole."

As they roared along, parts of the dog, like crumbs from a flaky loaf of bread, came off. A tooth here. Some hair there. A string of guts. A dew claw. And some unidentifiable pink stuff. The metal-studded collar and chain threw up sparks now and then like fiery crickets. Finally they hit seventy-five and the dog was swinging wider and wider on the chain, like it was looking for an opportunity to pass.

Farto poured him and Leonard up Cokes and whiskey as they drove along. He handed Leonard his paper cup and Leonard knocked it back, a lot happier now than he had been a moment ago. Maybe this night wasn't going to turn out so bad after all.

They drove by a crowd at the side of the road, a tan station wagon and a wreck of a Ford up on a jack. At a glance they could see that there was a nigger in the middle of the crowd and he wasn't witnessing to the white boys. He was hopping around like a pig with a hotshot up his ass, trying to find a break in the white boys so he could make a run for it. But there wasn't any break to be found and there were too many to fight. Nine white boys were knocking him around like he was a pinball and they were a malicious machine.

"Ain't that one of our niggers?" Farto asked. "And ain't that some of the White Tree football players that's trying to kill him?"

"Scott," Leonard said, and the name was dogshit in his mouth. It had been Scott who had outdone him for the position of quarterback on the team. That damn jig could put together a play more tangled than a can of fishing worms, but it damn near always worked. And he could run like a spotted-ass ape.

As they passed, Farto said, "We'll read about him tomorrow in the papers."

But Leonard drove only a short way before slamming on the brakes and whipping the Impala around. Rex swung way out and clipped off some tall, dried sunflowers at the edge of the road like a scythe.

"We gonna go back and watch?" Farto asked. "I don't think them White Tree boys would bother us none if that's all we was gonna do, watch."

"He may be a nigger," Leonard said, not liking himself, "but he's our nigger and we can't let them do that. They kill him, they'll beat us in football."

Farto saw the truth of this immediately. "Damn right. They can't do that to our nigger."

Leonard crossed the road again and went straight for the White Tree boys, hit down hard on the horn. The White Tree boys abandoned beating their prey and jumped in all directions. Bullfrogs couldn't have done any better.

Scott stood startled and weak where he was, his knees bent in and touching one another, his eyes as big as pizza pans. He had never noticed how big grillwork was. It looked like teeth there in the night and the headlights looked like eyes. He felt like a stupid fish about to be eaten by a shark.

Leonard braked hard, but off the highway in the dirt it wasn't enough to keep from bumping Scott, sending him flying over the hood and against the glass where his face mashed to it then rolled away, his shirt snagging one of the windshield wipers and pulling it off.

Leonard opened the car door and called to Scott who lay on the ground, "It's now or never."

A White Tree boy made for the car, and Leonard pulled the taped hammer handle out from beneath the seat and stepped out of the car and hit him with it. The White Tree boy went down to his knees and said something that sounded like French but wasn't. Leonard grabbed Scott by the back of the shirt and pulled him up and guided him around and threw him into the open door. Scott scrambled over the front seat and into the back. Leonard threw the hammer handle at one of the White Tree boys and stepped back, whirled into the car behind the wheel. He put the car in gear again and stepped on the gas. The Impala lurched forward, and with one hand on the door Leonard flipped it wider and clipped a White Tree boy with it as if he were flexing a wing. The car bumped back on the highway and the chain swung out and Rex cut the feet out from under two White Tree boys as neatly as he had taken down the dried sunflowers.

Leonard looked in his rear-view mirror and saw two White Tree boys carrying the one he had clubbed with the hammer handle to the station wagon. The others he and the dog had knocked down were getting up. One had kicked the jack out from under Scott's car and was using it to smash the headlights and windshield.

"Hope you got insurance on that thing," Leonard said.

"I borrowed it," Scott said, peeling the windshield wiper out of his T-shirt. "Here, you might want this." He dropped the wiper over the seat and between Leonard and Farto.

"That's a borrowed car?" Farto said. "That's worse."

"Nah," Scott said. "Owner don't know I borrowed it. I'd have had that flat changed if that sucker had had him a spare tire, but I got back there and wasn't nothing but the rim, man. Say, thanks for not letting me get killed, else we couldn't have run that ole pig together no more. Course, you almost run over me. My chest hurts."

Leonard checked the rear-view again. The White Tree boys were coming fast. "You complaining?" Leonard said.

"Nah," Scott said, and turned to look through the back glass. He could see the dog swinging in short arcs and pieces of it going wide and far. "Hope you didn't go off and forget your dog tied to the bumper."

"Goddamn," said Farto, "and him registered too."

"This ain't so funny," Leonard said. "Them White Tree boys are gaining."

"Well speed it up," Scott said.

Leonard gnashed his teeth. "I could always get rid of some excess baggage, you know."

"Throwing that windshield wiper out ain't gonna help," Scott said.

Leonard looked in his mirror and saw the grinning nigger in the back seat. Nothing worse than a comic coon. He didn't even look grateful. Leonard had a sudden horrid vision of being overtaken by the White Tree boys. What if he were killed with the nigger? Getting killed was bad enough, but what if tomorrow they found him in a ditch with Farto and the nigger? Or maybe them White Tree boys would make him do something awful with the nigger before they killed them. Like making him suck the nigger's dick or some such thing. Leonard held his foot all the way to the floor; as they passed the Dairy Queen he took a hard left and the car just made it and Rex swung out and slammed a light pole then popped back in line behind them.

The White Tree boys couldn't make the corner in the station wagon and they didn't even try. They screeched into a car lot down a piece, turned around and came back. By that time the tail lights of the Impala were moving away from them rapidly, looking like two inflamed hemorrhoids in a dark asshole.

"Take the next right coming up," Scott said, "then you'll see a little road off to the left. Kill your lights and take that."

Leonard hated taking orders from Scott on the field, but this was worse. Insulting. Still, Scott called good plays on the field, and the habit of following instructions from the quarterback died hard. Leonard made the right and Rex made it with them after taking a dip in a water-filled bar ditch.

Leonard saw the little road and killed his lights and took it. It carried them down between several rows of large tin storage buildings, and Leonard pulled between two of them and drove down a little alley lined with more. He stopped the car and they waited and listened. After about five minutes, Farto said, "I think we skunked those father rapers."

"Ain't we a team?" Scott said.

In spite of himself, Leonard felt good. It was like when the nigger called a play that worked and they were all patting each other on the ass and not minding what color the other was because they were just creatures in football suits.

"Let's have a drink," Leonard said.

Farto got a paper cup off the floorboard for Scott and poured him up some warm Coke and whiskey. Last time they had gone to Longview, he had peed in that paper cup so they wouldn't have to stop, but that had long since been poured out, and besides, it was for a nigger. He poured Leonard and himself drinks in their same cups.

Scott took a sip and said, "Shit, man, that tastes kind of rank."

"Like piss," Farto said.

Leonard held up his cup. "To the Mud Creek Wildcats and fuck them White Tree boys."

"You fuck 'em," Scott said. They touched their cups, and at that moment the car filled with light.

Cups upraised, the Three Musketeers turned blinking toward it. The light was coming from an open storage-building door and there was a fat man standing in the center of the glow like a bloated fly on a lemon wedge. Behind him was a big screen made of a sheet and there was some kind of movie playing on it. And though the light was bright and fading out the movie, Leonard, who was in the best position to see, got a look at it. What he could make out looked like a gal down on her knees sucking this fat guy's dick (the man was visible only from the belly down) and the guy had a short, black revolver pressed to her forehead. She pulled her mouth off of him for an instant and the man came in her face then fired the revolver. The woman's head snapped out of frame and the sheet seemed to drip blood, like dark condensation on a windowpane. Then Leonard couldn't see anymore because another man had appeared in the doorway, and like the first he was fat. Both looked like huge bowling balls that had been set on top of shoes. More men appeared behind these two, but one of the fat men turned and held up his hand and the others moved out of sight. The two fat guys stepped outside and one pulled the door almost shut, except for a thin band of light that fell across the front seat of the Impala.

Fat Man Number One went over to the car and opened Farto's door and said, "You fucks and the nigger get out." It was the voice of doom. They had only thought the White Tree boys were dangerous. They realized now they had been kidding themselves. This was the real article. This guy would have eaten the hammer handle and shit a two-by-four.

They got out of the car and the fat man waved them around and lined them up on Farto's side and looked at them. The boys still had their drinks in their hands, and sparing that, they looked like cons in a lineup.

Fat Man Number Two came over and looked at the trio and smiled. It was obvious the fatties were twins. They had the same bad features in the same fat faces. They wore Hawaiian shirts that varied only in profiles and color of parrots and had on white socks and too-short black slacks and black, shiny, Italian shoes with toes sharp enough to thread needles.

Fat Man Number One took the cup away from Scott and sniffed it. "A nigger with liquor," he said. "That's like a cunt with brains. It don't go together. Guess you was getting tanked up so you could put the old black snake to some chocolate pudding after a while. Or maybe you was wantin' some vanilla and these boys were gonna set it up."

"I'm not wanting anything but to go home," Scott said. Fat Man Number Two looked at Fat Man Number One and said, "So he can fuck his mother."

The fatties looked at Scott to see what he'd say but he didn't say anything. They could say he screwed dogs and that was all right with him. Hell, bring one on and he'd fuck it now if they'd let him go afterwards.

Fat Man Number One said, "You boys running around with a jungle bunny makes me sick."

"He's just a nigger from school," Farto said. "We don't like him none. We just picked him up because some White Tree boys were beating on him and we didn't want him to get wrecked on account of he's our quarterback."

"Ah," Fat Man Number One said, "I see. Personally, me and Vinnie don't cotton to niggers in sports. They start taking showers with white boys the next thing they want is to take white girls to bed. It's just one step from one to the other."

"We don't have nothing to do with him playing," Leonard said. "We didn't integrate the schools."

"No," Fat Man Number One said, "that was ole Big Ears Johnson, but you're running around with him and drinking with him."

"His cup's been peed in," Farto said. "That was kind of a joke on him, you see. He ain't our friend, I swear it. He's just a nigger that plays football."

"Peed in his cup, huh?" said the one called Vinnie. "I like that, Pork, don't you? Peed in his fucking cup."

Pork dropped Scott's cup on the ground and smiled at him. "Come here, nigger. I got something to tell you."

Scott looked at Farto and Leonard. No help there. They had suddenly become interested in the toes of their shoes; they examined them as if they were true marvels of the world.

Scott moved toward Pork, and Pork, still smiling, put his arm around Scott's shoulders and walked him toward the big storage building. Scott said, "What are we doing?"

Pork turned Scott around so they were facing Leonard and Farto who still stood holding their drinks and contemplating their shoes. "I didn't want to get it on the new gravel drive," Pork said and pulled Scott's head in close to his own and with his free hand reached back and under his Hawaiian shirt and brought out a short, black revolver and put it to Scott's temple and pulled the trigger. There was a snap like a bad knee going out and Scott's feet lifted in unison and went to the side and something dark squirted from his head and his feet swung back toward Pork and his shoes shuffled, snapped, and twisted on the concrete in front of the building.

"Ain't that somethin'," Pork said as Scott went limp and dangled from the thick crook of his arm. "The rhythm is the last thing to go."

Leonard couldn't make a sound. His guts were in his throat. He wanted to melt and run under the car. Scott was dead and the brains that had made plays twisted as fishing worms and commanded his feet on down the football field were scrambled like breakfast eggs.

Farto said, "Holy shit."

Pork let go of Scott and Scott's legs split and he sat down and his head went forward and clapped on the cement between his knees. A dark pool formed under his face.

"He's better off, boys," Vinnie said. "Nigger was begat by Cain and the ape and he ain't quite monkey and he ain't quite man. He's got no place in this world 'cept as a beast of burden. You start trying to train them to do things like drive cars and run with footballs it ain't nothing but grief to them and the whites too. Get any on your shirt, Pork?"

"Nary a drop."

Vinnie went inside the building and said something to the men there that could be heard but not understood, then he came back with some crumpled newspapers. He went over to Scott and wrapped them around the bloody head and let it drop back on the cement. "You try hosing down that shit when it's dried, Pork, and you wouldn't worry none about that gravel. The gravel ain't nothing."

Then Vinnie said to Farto, "Open the back door of that car." Farto nearly twisted an ankle doing it. Vinnie picked Scott up by the back of the neck and the seat of his pants and threw him onto the floorboard of the Impala.

Pork used the short barrel of his revolver to scratch his nuts, then put the gun behind him, under his Hawaiian shirt. "You boys are gonna go to the river bottoms with us and help us get shed of this nigger."

"Yes, sir," Farto said. "We'll toss his ass in the Sabine for you."

"How about you?" Pork asked Leonard. "You trying to go weak sister?"

"No," Leonard croaked, "I'm with you."

"That's good," Pork said. "Vinnie, you take the truck and lead the way."

Vinnie took a key from his pocket and unlocked the building door next to the one with the light, went inside, and backed out a sharp-looking gold Dodge pickup. He backed it in front of the Impala and sat there with the motor running.

"You boys keep your place," Pork said. He went inside the lighted building for a moment. They heard him say to the men inside, "Go on and watch the movies. And save some of them beers for us. We'll be back." Then the light went out and Pork came out, shutting the door. He looked at Leonard and Farto and said, "Drink up, boys."

Leonard and Farto tossed off their warm Coke and whiskey and dropped the cups on the ground.

"Now," Pork said, "you get in the back with the nigger, I'll ride with the driver."

Farto got in the back and put his feet on Scott's knees. He tried not to look at the head wrapped in newspaper, but he couldn't help it. When Pork opened the front door and the overhead light came on Farto saw there was a split in the paper and Scott's eye was visible behind it. Across the forehead the wrapping had turned dark. Down by the mouth and chin was an ad for a fish sale.

Leonard got behind the wheel and started the car. Pork reached over and honked the horn. Vinnie rolled the pickup forward and Leonard followed him to the river bottoms. No one spoke. Leonard found himself wishing with all his heart that he had gone to the outdoor picture show to see the movie with the nigger starring in it.

The river bottoms were steamy and hot from the closeness of the trees and the under and overgrowth. As Leonard wound the Impala down the narrow, red clay roads amidst the dense foliage, he felt as if his car were a crab crawling about in a pubic thatch. He could feel from the way the steering wheel handled that the dog and the chain were catching brush and limbs here and there. He had forgotten all about the dog and now being reminded of it worried him. What if the dog got tangled and he had to stop? He didn't think Pork would take kindly to stopping, not with the dead burrhead on the floorboards and him wanting to get rid of the body.

Finally they came to where the woods cleared out a spell and they drove along the edge of the Sabine River. Leonard hated water and always had. In the moonlight the river looked like poisoned coffee flowing there. Leonard knew there were alligators and gars big as little alligators and water moccasins by the thousands swimming underneath the water, and just the thought of all those slick, darting bodies made him queasy.

They came to what was known as Broken Bridge. It was an old wornout bridge that had fallen apart in the middle and it was connected to the land on this side only. People sometimes fished off of it. There was no one fishing tonight.

Vinnie stopped the pickup and Leonard pulled up beside it, the nose of the Chevy pointing at the mouth of the bridge. They all got out and Pork made Farto pull Scott out by the feet. Some of the newspapers came loose from Scott's head exposing an ear and part of the face. Farto patted the newspaper back into place.

"Fuck that," Vinnie said. "It don't hurt if he stains the fucking ground. You two idgits find some stuff to weight this coon down so we can sink him."

Farto and Leonard started scurrying about like squirrels, looking for rocks or big, heavy logs. Suddenly they heard Vinnie cry out. "Godamighty, fucking A. Pork. Come look at this."

Leonard looked over and saw that Vinnie had discovered Rex. He was standing looking down with his hands on his hips. Pork went over to stand by him, then Pork turned around and looked at them. "Hey, you fucks, come here."

Leonard and Farto joined them in looking at the dog. There was mostly just a head now, with a little bit of meat and fur hanging off a spine and some broken ribs.

"That's the sickest fucking thing I've ever fucking seen," Pork said.

"Godamighty," Vinnie said.

"Doing a dog like that. Shit, don't you got no heart? A dog. Man's best fucking goddamn friend and you two killed him like this."

"We didn't kill him," Farto said.

"You trying to fucking tell me he done this to himself? Had a bad fucking day and done this."

"Godamighty," Vinnie said.

"No, sir," Leonard said. "We chained him on there after he was dead."

"I believe that," Vinnie said. "That's some rich shit. You guys murdered this dog. Godamighty."

"Just thinking about him trying to keep up and you fucks driving faster and faster makes me mad as a wasp," Pork said.

"No," Farto said. "It wasn't like that. He was dead and we were drunk and we didn't have anything to do, so we—"

"Shut the fuck up," Pork said, sticking a finger hard against Farto's forehead. "You just shut the fuck up. We can see what the fuck you fucks did. You drug this here dog around until all his goddamn hide came off . . . What kind of mothers you boys got anyhow that they didn't tell you better about animals?"

"Godamighty," Vinnie said.

Everyone grew silent, stood looking at the dog. Finally Farto said,

"You want us to go back to getting some stuff to hold the nigger down?"

Pork looked at Farto as if he had just grown up whole from the ground. "You fucks are worse than niggers, doing a dog like that. Get on back over to the car."

Leonard and Farto went over to the Impala and stood looking down at Scott's body in much the same way they had stared at the dog. There, in the dim moonlight shadowed by trees, the paper wrapped around Scott's head made him look like a giant papier-mâché doll. Pork came up and kicked Scott in the face with a swift motion that sent newspapers flying and sent a thonking sound across the water that made frogs jump.

"Forget the nigger," Pork said. "Give me your car keys, ball sweat." Leonard took out his keys and gave them to Pork and Pork went around to the trunk and opened it. "Drag the nigger over here."

Leonard took one of Scott's arms and Farto took the other and they pulled him over to the back of the car.

"Put him in the trunk," Pork said.

"What for?" Leonard asked.

"'Cause I fucking said so," Pork said.

Leonard and Farto heaved Scott into the trunk. He looked pathetic lying there next to the spare tire, his face partially covered with newspaper. Leonard thought, if only the nigger had stolen a car with a spare he might not be here tonight. He could have gotten that flat changed and driven on before the White Tree boys even came along.

"All right, you get in there with him," Pork said, gesturing to Farto.

"Me?" Farto said.

"Nah, not fucking you, the fucking elephant on your fucking shoulder. Yeah, you, get in the trunk. I ain't got all night."

"Jesus, we didn't do anything to that dog, mister. We told you that. I swear. Me and Leonard hooked him up after he was dead . . . It was Leonard's idea."

Pork didn't say a word. He just stood there with one hand on the trunk lid looking at Farto. Farto looked at Pork, then the trunk, then back to Pork. Lastly he looked at Leonard, then climbed into the trunk, his back to Scott.

"Like spoons," Pork said, and closed the lid. "Now you, whatsit, Leonard? You come over here." But Pork didn't wait for Leonard to move. He scooped the back of Leonard's neck with a chubby hand and pushed him over to where Rex lay at the end of the chain with Vinnie still looking down at him.

"What you think, Vinnie?" Pork asked. "You got what I got in mind?"

Vinnie nodded. He bent down and took the collar off the dog. He fastened it on Leonard. Leonard could smell the odor of the dead dog in his nostrils. He bent his head and puked.

"There goes my shoeshine," Vinnie said, and he hit Leonard a short one in the stomach. Leonard went to his knees and puked some more of the hot Coke and whiskey.

"You fucks are the lowest pieces of shit on this earth, doing a dog like that," Vinnie said. "A nigger ain't no lower."

Vinnie got some strong fishing line out of the back of the truck and they tied Leonard's hands behind his back. Leonard began to cry.

"Oh shut up," Pork said. "It ain't that bad. Ain't nothing that bad."

But Leonard couldn't shut up. He was caterwauling now and it was echoing through the trees. He closed his eyes and tried to pretend he had gone to the show with the nigger starring in it and had fallen asleep in his car and was having a bad dream, but he couldn't imagine that. He thought about Harry the janitor's flying saucers with the peppermint rays, and he knew if there were any saucers shooting rays down, they weren't boredom rays after all. He wasn't a bit bored.

Pork pulled off Leonard's shoes and pushed him back flat on the ground and pulled off the socks and stuck them in Leonard's mouth so tight he couldn't spit them out. It wasn't that Pork thought anyone was going to hear Leonard, he just didn't like the noise. It hurt his ears.

Leonard lay on the ground in the vomit next to the dog and cried silently. Pork and Vinnie went over to the Impala and opened the doors and stood so they could get a grip on the car to push. Vinnie reached in and moved the gear from park to neutral and he and Pork began to shove the car forward. It moved slowly at first, but as it made the slight incline that led down to the old bridge, it picked up speed. From inside the trunk, Farto hammered lightly at the lid as if he didn't really mean it. The chain took up slack and Leonard felt it jerk and pop his neck. He began to slide along the ground like a snake.

Vinnie and Pork jumped out of the way and watched the car make the bridge and go over the edge and disappear into the water with amazing quietness. Leonard, pulled by the weight of the car, rustled past them. When he hit the bridge, splinters tugged at his clothes so hard they ripped his pants and underwear down almost to his knees.

The chain swung out once toward the edge of the bridge and the rotten railing, and Leonard tried to hook a leg around an upright board there, but that proved wasted. The weight of the car just pulled his knee out of joint and jerked the board out of place with a screech of nails and lumber.

Leonard picked up speed and the chain rattled over the edge of the bridge, into the water and out of sight, pulling its connection after it like a pull toy. The last sight of Leonard was the soles of his bare feet, white as the bellies of fish.

"It's deep there," Vinnie said. "I caught an old channel cat there once, remember? Big sucker. I bet it's over fifty-feet deep down there."

They got in the truck and Vinnie cranked it.

"I think we did them boys a favor," Pork said. "Them running around with niggers and what they did to that dog and all. They weren't worth a thing."

"I know it," Vinnie said. "We should have filmed this, Pork, it would have been good. Where the car and that nigger lover went off in the water was choice."

"Nah, there wasn't any women."

"Point," Vinnie said, and he backed around and drove onto the trail that wound its way out of the bottoms.

Diary

Ronald Kelly

"Diary" was first published in *Cemetery Dance* magazine #3 in 1990.

Ronald Kelly is the author of such Southern horror novels as *Hindsight, Pitfall, Something Out There, Father's Little Helper, The Possession, Fear,* and *Blood Kin.* His audio collection, *Dark Dixie: Tales of Southern Horror* was nominated for a Grammy Award in 1992 for Best Spoken or Non-Musical Recording. His first short story collection, *Midnight Grinding & Other Twilight Terrors,* was published by Cemetery Dance Publications in 2009, and his latest novel, *Hell Hollow,* was released in 2010. His upcoming publications include *Undertaker's Moon, After the Burn, Cumberland Furnace & Other Fear-Forged Fables,* and the *Essential Ronald Kelly Collection.*

He lives in Brush Creek, Tennessee with his wife and three young'uns.

This was my first truly extreme horror story. Upon publication, Richard Chizmar of Cemetery Dance Magazine said "This tale is much darker and nastier than your typical Ronald Kelly story", and he was right. I broke past some personal barriers, fiction-wise, with Diary and I haven't let up since.

♦ ♦ ♦

AUGUST 21

They want to know why I killed those people in Tennessee. They want to know why a no-account bum like Jerry Weller crossed paths with the All-American family and systematically tortured, raped, and slaughtered them, one by one.

They seem very insistent for answers. But I give them none. I only counter their questions with questions of my own.

Why did Satan drive me to commit such atrocities?

Why did God allow such atrocities to take place?

They think they have me pegged. They brand me a violent psychopath and spout their psychiatric crap, but they're still missing the point. If they weren't so damned stupid, they would be able to look into my eyes and see the squirming, maggot-infested soul that lies decaying within.

You see, perversity is my forte.

It is normality that drives me insane.

August 29

My parents didn't tell me for a very long time that I once had a twin brother. When they did, they only said that he had died shortly after birth. I knew they were concealing all the gory details. Eventually, they told me the whole story . . . and, boy, was it a doozy!

It seems that there were once twin brothers named Jerry and Jamie. Shortly after their arrival home from the hospital, Mom and Dad went out for a night on the town, leaving the little ones in the care of teenaged babysitter Caroline. An hour later, Caroline's beatnik boyfriend, Rodney, showed up with a big bag of goodies. There was much drinking and pot smoking and airplane glue sniffing. Soon, Caroline and Rodney had gotten wildly high and thought it would be incredibly funny to put little Jamie in the kitchen oven. They chug-a-lugged vodka and reds as they turned the flame to the max and cooked the squawling infant like a meatloaf.

Supposedly, I witnessed the whole thing, but I don't remember. Hell, I was only three months old at the time.

Those freaking junkheads had the right idea, but they made one mistake.

They baked the wrong gingerbread boy.

September 5

How about a nice bedtime story?

Once upon a time there was a clean-cut, All-American family. They never fought with one another, they attended church regularly, and lived by the Golden Rule. They lived in a cozy, suburban home, drove a Volvo, and sent their children to public school . . . just like those perfect television families of the fifties and sixties—the Nelsons, the Cleavers, the Brady Bunch.

One summer, this family decided to take a trip to Smoky Mountain National Park. They took snapshots of the sights, watched the Cherokee Indians do their rain dance, and found a secluded campsite so they could commune with nature and enjoy the great outdoors. They sang songs, roasted marshmallows over the campfire, and swapped ghost stories. They had a wonderful time.

Then the man showed up out of nowhere, wearing a friendly smile and a stolen park ranger's uniform.

September 12

When I was six years old, I would visit my grandmother. She had this sweet, little canary named Penny. Penny would fly right out of its cage in the corner of Grandmother's sewing room and land in the palm of your hand. It would sit perfectly still and sing you the most beautiful song.

One day, while Grandmother was out working in her flower garden, I slipped into the sewing room and opened Penny's door. It flew out of its cage and lit lightly in my hand.

"Sing me a song, Penny," I said, but it remained silent.

I took a straight pin from Grandmother's sewing basket and shoved it into Penny's little, black eye. It pierced the bird's tiny brain and emerged out the other side.

Penny sang me a song then, a very loud and frantic song . . . but not for very long.

September 23

Bedtime story. Part Two.

The park ranger said hello, sat down beside the fire, and drank a cup of coffee offered to him. As pleasant conversation was exchanged, he studied the All-American family. Father, mother, gray-haired grandmother, and two children, a boy and a girl. He enjoyed their company for a while, as long as he could possibly stand it. And then that damned urge crept into his demented mind . . .

October 7

They sent me to reform school when I was seventeen for cutting off my girlfriend's breasts with a pocket knife. After all these years, I still haven't figured out what my true motive had been. Maybe someday I'll call her up at the state asylum and ask her if she remembers why I did such a horrible thing.

October 14

Bedtime story. Part Three.

Father went first.

The friendly park ranger took a hunting knife from his belt and, with an upward thrust, drove the point up under Father's jaw. The razor-honed blade sliced effortlessly up through his tongue, the roof of his mouth, and into his tender brain. He fell forward into the campfire and burnt his face off while the ranger rounded up the rest of the All-American family . . .

October 19

My attorney wanted me to go for an insanity plea. I fired him and got myself another lawyer with a less attractive track record.

I keep telling them what I want, but they don't seem to take me seriously.

I want to fry.

I want the juice to surge through my body until my veins pop and I begin to sizzle like a slab of raw meat on a hot griddle.

October 31

Bedtime story. Part Four.

My, Grandma, what big eyes you have . . . lying in the palm of my hand.

November 4

Boy, do I miss Nam. Sometimes I cry myself to sleep, I miss it so.

I volunteered to go, you know. Not because I was patriotic, but because I heard there was a lot of weird shit going on over there. Some of the other grunts thought I was nuts for signing up, but they didn't understand. They all hated the Nam, while, for me, it was pure paradise.

The first day there, the platoon sergeant took us cherries out behind a quonset hut. There were four dead gooks lying in a ditch, riddled with bullet holes and flies. The sarge made us get down into that ditch and kick them in the head. He said it was to drive the squeamishness out of our systems before he turned us loose in the jungle. He made us kick and kick and kick until their skulls split open and their brains covered our combat boots.

Some of the guys puked their pussy guts up. I would have been down in that ditch all day if they hadn't pulled me out.

Be all that you can be . . .

November 8

Yesterday, some big guy named Alfonso tried to pull a caboose on me in the jailhouse showers. I was all lathered up and too fast for him, though. I backed him into a corner and, finding him to be an attentive audience, did one of my favorite impressions to entertain the sonuvabitch.

By the time the guards got there, poor Alfonso was lying on the wet tiles of the shower stall, clutching at himself as he bled to death. Me, I just stood there and watched with a bloodstained smile as they searched for the missing part of Alfonso's anatomy . . . one that they will never find.

You know, I do a lot of neat impressions—Bogart, Cagney . . . the Donner Party.

November 11

Bedtime story. Part Five.

Hey, kids, let's pretend that it's Christmas time!

That pine tree over there can be the Christmas tree and we can decorate it, too . . . with pieces of dear, old Mom.

We can use her fingers for tinsel and her organs for ornaments. It'll be lots of fun, just you wait and see.

Deck the halls with bowels of Mommy . . .

November 28

After coming back to the World, I spent some time in Mexico, smuggling drugs and wetbacks across the border. The money was good and kept me in tequila and cheap whores. Then I met up with this guy and we started making movies.

We would lure some chick off the street and take her back to our motel room. We would get her half drunk and give her a snort of coke laced with Spanish Fly. By the time my partner had his camera set up, she would be hot and ready.

Then I would come out of the bathroom, naked except for one of those weird, leather bondage masks. I would then proceed to make love to her. When she opened her mouth to scream in ecstasy, I would take the linoleum knife and, reaching between our heaving bodies . . .

I had that snuff film stashed somewhere in my van with all my other scrapbooks and trophies, but I didn't have an 8mm projector to watch it with. I once considered taking it to a Fotomat to have it transferred to DVD . . . but I chickened out at the last moment.

December 1

Bedtime story. Part Six.

How about a nursery rhyme for the children?

This little piggie went to the market.
SNAP!
This little piggie stayed home.
CRACK!
This little piggie ate roast beef.
SNAP! CRACKLE! POP!

December 13

I robbed a gas station in Tucson once and made the attendant eat a turd out of the men's room toilet, promising to spare his miserable life if he would only perform that one, simple act.

He did.

I didn't.

December 22

Bedtime story. Part Seven.

Oh, did I forget to tell you? The All-American family had a baby with them.

I was going to let it live, honest I was. But then I figured, hey, what kind of life is the kid going to have if I do? He will probably be shuffled off to some sleazy orphanage and be adopted by sadistic parents who will beat and abuse him and he will grow up to be a sick bastard . . . just like me.

So I took him down to the campground trash cans and left him there.

You know, where all the hungry bears hang out for breakfast.

January 7

Well, it's official now. The jury handed down their verdict and the trial is over. The death penalty. I get off just thinking about it.

In some states it is lethal injection, in others the gas chamber. Here in Tennessee it is Old Sparky . . . the tried and true electric chair.

As for my journal, this will be the last entry. The wire that I pried from the springs of my bunk is getting dull and the words are barely legible now. For, you see, the exploits I have penned have not been committed to paper . . . but to human flesh. I am a living tome; all my sins and atrocities have been carved into every inch of skin, or at least the places that I could reach.

Perhaps, following my execution, the grisly accounts of my life's work will be made public. Perhaps some unscrupulous individual will bribe a morgue attendant into letting them take photos of my body and they will end up in a sleazy tabloid or on some off-beat website. Then all the world will be privy to my pursuit of barbarity and perversion.

So, if you are browsing the internet during the late hours of the night, and come upon me . . . please, indulge your morbid curiosity.

Come . . . read my diary.

Abed

Elizabeth Massie

"Abed" first appeared in *Still Dead*, edited by John Skipp and Craig Spector and published by Bantam Books in 1992.

Elizabeth Massie is a Scribe Award-winning and two time Bram Stoker Award-winning author of horror novels, short fiction, media tie ins, historical novels, contemporary mainstream fiction, and units and features in American history textbooks, among other things. Her first love is horror, and since 1984 she has had over 100 horror shorts in numerous magazines and anthologies as well as 5 horror collections and 7 horror novels published by Berkley, Simon & Schuster, Carroll & Graf, Leisure, and others. Recently, some of her works have begun appearing in e-book form through Crossroad Press and Necon E-Books. These include her Stoker-winning *Sineater*, her collections *The Fear Report* and new collection *Afraid*, and a new mainstream novel, *Homegrown*. Currently she is hard at work on a new zombie novel (as of yet untitled) set in the wild mountains of western Virginia. Beth lives in the Shenandoah Valley with the talented illustrator Cortney Skinner. She loves hiking, camping, chai, and World's Softest Socks. She thinks cheese is the food of nightmares. I mean, come on. It's old, rotted, coagulated milk. What's not to fear? Her website is: www.elizabethmassie.com.

"Abed" has had a rather controversial life. Following the initial publication in Still Dead, it was rejected for a later zombie anthology (as a reprint) because the publisher (not the editor) thought it was too graphic. Twice, independent movie makers had to shelve it because others who were to be involved with the production got cold feet and said they just couldn't go that far. Now, however, it looks like it may be made into a short film . . . fingers crossed. (My preference is that most of what goes on in the story will happen "off stage"; you'll know what I mean once you've read it.) Personally,

I see it as a sad story of isolation, despair, and resignation . . .
but it's all wrapped up in a pretty graphic package. :) In a recent
interview, John Skipp said, "Elizabeth Massie's 'Abed' is prob-
ably still the hardest-punching zombie short story I've ever read."

◆ ◆ ◆ ◆

MEGGIE'S A-LINE DRESS IS YELLOW, bright like a new dandelion in the
side yard and as soft as the throats of the tiny toads Meggie used to find
in the woods that surround the farm. There aren't many stains on the
dress, just some spots on the hem. Mama Randolph, Quint's mother and
Meggie's mother-in-law, ironed the dress this morning, and then gave it
to Meggie with a patient and expectant smile before locking the bedroom
door once more. Meggie knows that Mama likes the dress because it isn't
quite as much a reminder of the bad situation as are the other blotted
and bloodied outfits in Meggie's footed wardrobe.

From the open window, a benign breeze passes through the screen,
stirring the curtains. But the breeze dies in the middle of the floor because there are no other windows in the room to allow it to leave. The
summer heat, however, is quite at home in the room, and has settled
for a long stay.

There has been no rain for the past fourteen days. Meggie has been
marking the days off on the Shenandoah Dairy calendar she keeps under
her bed. Mama has not talked about a grandchild in almost a month now;
Meggie keeps the calendar marked for that, as well. Mama Randolph's
smile and the freshly ironed dress lets Meggie know that the cycle has
come 'round again.

Meggie moves from the bed to the window to the bed. There is a
chair in the comer by the door, but the cushion smells bad and so she
doesn't like to sit on it. The mattress on the bed smells worse than the
chair, but there is a clean comer that she uses when she is tired. She paces
about, feeling the soft swing of her hair about her shoulders as she rocks
her head back and forth, remembering the feel of Quint's own warm
hair in the sunlight of past Julys and the softness of the dark curls that
made a sweet pillow of his chest.

At the window, Meggie glances out through the screen, down to
the chain-linked yard below. The weeds there are wild and a tall and
tangled like briars in the forest. The fence is covered with honeysuckle.
There is the remainder of the sandbox Quint used as a child. It is nearly
returned to the soil now, and black-eyed Susans have found themselves

a home. Mama says it will be a fine thing when there is a child to enjoy the yard once again. She says when the child comes she and Meggie will clean up the yard and make it into a playground that any other child in Norton County will envy.

Mama had slapped Meggie when Meggie said she didn't know if there would ever be any more children in the county.

On the nightstand beside Meggie's bed is a chipped vase with a bouquet of Queen Anne's lace, sweet peas, red clover, and chicory. Mama said it was a gift from Quint, but Meggie knows Quint is long past picking gifts of wildflowers. Beside the vase is a picture of Meggie and Quint on their wedding day three years ago. Meggie wears a white floor length dress and clutches a single white carnation. Quint grins shyly at the camera, the new beard Meggie had loved just a dark shadow across his lower face. It would be four months before the beard was full enough to satisfy him, although it never satisfied his mother.

"You live in my house, you do as I say, you hear me?" she had told Quint. And although Meggie believed in the premise of that command, and managed to follow the rules, Quint always had a way of getting by with what he wanted by joking and cajoling his mother. And in the dark privacy of night, while cuddling with Meggie in bed, he would promise that it wouldn't be long before he had saved enough money to build them their own small house on the back acre Mama had given him by the river.

But that was back when Quint worked the farm for his mother and held an evening job at the Joy Food Mart and Gas Station out on Route 146. Back when they had a savings account in the Farmers' Bank in Henford and Meggie happily collected her mother-in-law's cast off dishes to use as her own when the house by the river was built.

And then came the change. Things in Norton County flipped ass over teakettle. Old dead Mrs. Lowry had sat up in her coffin at the funeral home, grunting and snarling, her eyes washed white with the preserving chemicals but her mouth chattering for something hot and living to eat. Then Mr. Conrad, Quint's boss down at the Joy Food Mart and Gas Station, had keeled over while changing a tire and died on the spot of a heart attack. Before Quint could finish dialing the number of the Norton volunteer rescue squad, Conrad was up again and licking his newly dead lips, his hands racked with spasms but his teeth keen for a taste of Quint-neck. Quint hosed him down with unleaded and tossed in his Bic lighter and then cried when it was over because he couldn't believe what had happened.

They all believe now, alrighty.

The dead wander the gravel roads and eat what they may, and everyone in Norton County knows it is no joke because they've all seen one or two of the dead, at least. The newspapers say it's a problem all over now; the big cities like Richmond and D.C. and Chicago got dead coming out of their ears. There is a constant battle in the cities because there are so many. In Norton County it is a problem, and a couple people have been eaten, but mostly the walking dead get burned with gasoline or get avoided by the careful.

A thud in the downstairs hallway causes Meggie to jump and clasp her hands to the bodice of her yellow dress. The permanent chicken bone of fear that resides in her chest makes a painful turn. She presses her fists deep into the pain. She waits. Sweat beads on her arms and between her breasts. Mama Randolph does not come yet.

Meggie turns away from the wedding portrait on the nightstand and tries to remember the songs she sang in church before the church closed down. But all she can remember are some psalms. She walks to the clean spot on the bed and sits. She looks at the window, at the footed wardrobe, at the stained chair near the locked door. Above the chair is a Jesus picture. If there was some way to know what Jesus thought of the change, Meggie thinks she could bear it. If Meggie truly believed that Jesus had a handle on the walking dead, and that it was just a matter of time before He put a stop to it all, then Meggie would live out her confinement with more faith. But the picture shows a happy, smiling Jesus, holding a little white lamb with other white lambs gathered at His feet. He does not look like He has any comprehension of the horror that walks the world today. If He did, shouldn't He be crashing from the sky in a wailing river of fire to throw the dead back into their graves until the rapture?

Meggie slips from the bed and kneels before the picture, Jesus' smiling face moves her and His detachment haunts her. Her hands fold into a sweaty attitude of prayer, and in a gritty voice, she repeats, "The Lord is my shepherd, I shall not want . . ."

The crash in the hall just outside the door hurls Meggie to her feet. Her hands are still folded but she raises them like a club. The sound was that of a food tray being carelessly plopped onto the bare hall floor, and of dishes rattling with the impact. Mama Randolph brings Meggie her breakfast, lunch, and dinner every day, but today Mama is early.

Meggie looks at the screened window and wishes she could throw herself to the ground below without risking everlasting damnation from suicide. There is no clock in the room, but Meggie knows Mama is early. The sun on the floor is not yet straddling the stain on the carpet, and so it is still a ways from noon. But Meggie knows that Mama has something on her mind today besides food. Mama's excitement has interrupted the schedule. Mama has been marking a calendar as well. Today, Mama is thinking about grandchildren.

Meggie holds the club of fingers before her. It will do no good, she knows. She could not strike Mama Randolph. Maybe Jesus will think it is a prayer and come to help her.

The door opens, and Mama Randolph comes in with a swish of old apron and a flourish of cloth napkin. The tray and its contents are visible behind her in the hall, but the meal is the last of Mama's concerns. When business is tended, the meal will be remembered.

"Meggie," says Mama. "What a pretty sight you are there in your dress. Makes me think of a little yellow kitten." The cloth napkin is dropped onto the back of the stinking chair, and Mama straightens to take appraisal of her daughter-in-law. There is something in Mama's apron pocket that clinks faintly.

"Well, you gonna stand there or do you have a 'good morning'?"

Meggie looks toward the window. Two stories is not enough to die. And if she died, she would only become one of the walking dead. She looks back at Mama.

"Good morning," she whispers.

"And to you," Mama says cheerily. "Can you believe the heat? I pity the farmers this year. Corn is just cooking on the stalks. You look to the right out that window and just over the trees and you can see a bit of John Johnson's crop. Pitiful thing, all burned and brown." Mama tips her head and smiles. The apron clinks.

Neither says anything for a minute. Mama's eyes sparkle in the heavy, hot air. The dead folks' eyes sparkle when they walk about, but Meggie knows Mama is not dead. The older woman is very much alive, with all manner of plans for her family.

Then Mama says, "Sit down."

Meggie sits on the clean spot on the mattress.

Mama touches her dry lips. She says, "You know a home ain't a home without the singing of little children."

Oh, dear Jesus, thinks Meggie.

"When Quint was born, I was complete. I was a woman then. I was whole; I'd done what I was made to do. A woman with no children can't understand that till she's been through it herself."

Meggie feels a large drop of sweat fall and lodge above her navel. She looks at the floor and remembers what Quint's shoes looked like there, beside hers in the night after they'd climbed beneath the covers. Precious shoes, farmer's shoes, with the sides worn down and the dark coating of earth on the toes. Shoes that bore the weight of hard work and love. Shoes Quint swore he would throw away when he'd earned enough money to build the new house. Shoes that Meggie was going to keep in her cedar chest as a memory of the early days.

Quint doesn't wear shoes anymore.

"You know in my concern for you and Quint, I would do anything to make you happy." Mama nods slowly. "And if I've got it figured right, you're in your time again. I know it ain't worked the last couple months, but it took me near'n to a year and a half before I was with Quint."

Mama steps over to Meggie. She leans in close. Her breath smells of ginger and soured milk. "A baby is what'll help make some of the bad things right again, Meggie. It's a different world now. And we's got to cope. But a baby will bring Joy back."

"A baby," echoes Meggie. "Mama, please, I can't . . ."

"Hush, now," barks Mama. The smile disappears as quickly as the picture from a turned-off television set. She is all business now. Family making is a serious matter. "Get abed."

The word stings Meggie's gut.

"Abed!" commands Mama Randolph, and slowly, obediently, Meggie slides along the mattress until her head is even with the pillow.

Mama purses her mouth in approval. "Now let's check and see if our timing is right." Meggie closes her eyes and one hand moves to the spotted hem of the yellow dress. In her chest, the bone of pain swells, hard and suffocating. She cannot swallow around it. Her breath hitches. She pulls the hem up. She is naked beneath. Mama Randolph has not allowed undergarments.

"Roll over." Meggie rolls over. She hears the clinking as Mama reaches into her pocket. Meggie gropes for the edge of the pillow and holds to it like a drowning child to a life preserver. Her face presses into the stinking pillowcase.

The thermometer goes in deeply. Mama makes a tsking sound and moves it about until it is wedged to her satisfaction. Meggie's bowels contract; her gut lurches with disgust. She does not move.

"Just a minute here and we'll know what we need to know," crows Mama. "Do you know that I thought Quint was going to be a girl and I bought all sorts of little pink things before he was born? Was cute, but I couldn't rightly put such a little man into them pale, frilly clothes. I always thought a little girl would be a nice addition. Wouldn't a little girl just be the icing on the cake?"

Jesus help me, prays Meggie.

"Here, now," says Mama. The thermometer comes out and Meggie draws her legs up beneath the hem of the dress. She does not want to hear the reading.

"Bless me, looks like we done hit it on the head!" Mama is almost laughing. "Up nearly a whole degree. Time is right. My little calendar book keeps me thinking straight, now don't it? I'll go get Quint."

Mama goes out into the hall. Meggie watches her go. Then she falls from the bed and crawls on her knees to the Jesus picture. "Oh dear blessed Lord you are my shepherd, I shall not want I shall not want." Jesus watches the lambs and does not see Meggie.

Meggie runs to the window and looks out at the flowers and the dead sandbox and the burned cornfield over the top of the joy woods. It was those woods that killed Quint. One second of carelessness that crushed Quint's skull beneath John Johnson's felled tree. Quint had gone to help the neighbor clear a little more land for crops. John and Quint had been best buddies since school, and they were always trading favors. But when Quint went down under the tree trunk, brains and blood spraying, and he died, and when he rose up again, he was through trading favors. He wanted a lot more of John than he'd ever wanted before. And he got it. There wasn't enough of John left to rise with the other dead folks, just some chunks of spine and some chewed up feet.

Mama Randolph found Quint after this meal. He showed no immediate urge to eat her as well, so she brought him home and found he was just as happy eating raw goats and the squealing pigs he had tended as a live man.

Mama is in the doorway again. Behind her is Quint. He is dressed in only a pair of trousers that are gathered to his bony waist with a brown, tooth-marked leather belt.

"Abed!" says Mama. "Let's have this done."

Meggie goes back to the bed. She lies down. She knows what Mama will do next. It is the worst to come.

Quint is directed to stand in front of the old chair. Meggie cannot see Jesus anymore but that is a good thing. What is to happen is not for anyone's eyes, especially the Savior's. Meggie looks at her husband. His hair is gone as is the flesh of his mouth and the bulk of his nose. There is a tongue, but it is slimy and gray like an old rotted trout. The left side of his head is flattened, with the exposed brain now blackened and shimmering, reminding Meggie of a mushroom she tried to save once in a sandwich bag. The eye on the left is missing, but the right eye is wide and wet. The skin of Quint's abdomen is swollen and it ripples like maggots have gotten inside. One hand has no fingers, but the other has three, and they grope awkwardly for the zipper of his trousers. Quint somehow knows why he has been brought upstairs.

Mama Randolph moves beside Meggie and motions for her to hoist up her dress. Meggie flinches, hesitating, and Mama slaps her. Meggie does not hesitate again.

Mama then rolls up her sleeves. She says, "Quint needs the extra stimulation to do what he has to do. Watching helps him. You know that. So be still and let me do my job."

With the perfunctory movements of someone changing a fouled diaper, Mama coaxes the younger woman's legs open, and parts the private folds so Quint can have a better view. Then she begins to rub Meggie's clitoris slowly, while stroking the sensitive skin of Meggie's inner thighs with the other hand. Meggie will not watch. She digs her fingernails into her sides until the pain sings with the rush of blood to her genitals.

"Quint, do you remember? Do you see Meggie? Her pretty dress?" says Mama. "Look Quint, now isn't this lovely?" She leans her face into Meggie's crotch and licks the whole length of slit. The breath from her nose is warm; the wetness of her saliva is cool. Meggie groans. Shame boils her mind and soul. Pleasure teases her body.

Mama, Quint, Jesus, no! I shall not want I shall not want!

Quint grunts. Meggie bucks her head and shoulders and glances at him. He has opened his fly and has found his penis. It is yellowed and decaying, like a bloated fish on a riverbank. As he pulls, it rises slightly. The pre-cum is purpled.

Mama sucks gently and then with a fury, Meggie's body arcs reflexively. Bile rushes a burning path up her throat and dribbles from the corners of her mouth. When Mama's lips move away for a second, Meggie crashes back to the mattress. The acid rockets upward once more and Meggie gags. Mama brings her tongue to Meggie's spot again, and then thrusts her thumb into the opening. Meggie feels the walls of her vagina gush, betraying her in her ultimate moment of revulsion and horror.

I shall not oh dear God Jesus I shall not!

"Good girl," Mama says matter-of-factly.

Meggie writhes on the bed, enraged tears spilling from her eyes and soaking the mattress. Mama stands up.

Quint has a line of moisture on what is left of his upper lip. One side of his mouth twitches as if it would try to grin.

Mama gestures to her son. "Come now, Quint, Meggie can't wait for you." Quint stares, grunts, then stumbles forward. As he passes his mother, she says, "I'd really love a granddaughter."

Meggie turns her face away. She closes her eyes and tries to remember last summer. Days of light and shadows and swimming and play, days of work and trials and promises of forever. But all she can do is smell the creature climbing onto her. All she can do is feel the slopping of the trout-tongue on her cheek and taste the running, blackened brain matter as it drips to the edge of her lips. He burrows clumsily; his body wriggles as his knees work between her knees, and his sore-covered penis reaches like a dazed, half-dead snake for her center.

Meggie bites her tongue until it bleeds to keep from feeling the cold explosion of semen. And as if in some insane answer to it all, her vaginal walls contract suddenly in a horrific, humiliating orgasm.

It is all over quickly. Mama pulls Quint off, then gives Meggie a kiss on the forehead and tells her to stay abed for at least an hour to give the seed time to find the soil.

Alone, with the door locked and the lunch tray balanced on the smelly chair seat, Meggie lies still, her dress still hunched up. She holds her left hand in her right, pretending the right one is that of a living, breathing Quint. She puts the hand to her face and feels the tender stroking. And then she lowers the hand to her abdomen, and presses firmly. There will be a new human in there soon, if Mama has her way. There could be one already. This could be Mama's magic moment. Meggie wishes she could know. It is not knowing if or when that brings her mind to the edge of twisting inside out.

She looks at the window. There is no breeze now, only the persistent heat. The edge of sunlight stands on the carpet stain.

"S'different," Mama Randolph had said. "Different world now. Just adjustin' to cold water is all. Might not wanta do it, but sometimes just can't be helped. Gotta survive, after all."

Meggie holds herself and closes her eyes. She wonders about the different world. She wonders if there will be a baby to grow and use the playground outside her room. And she wonders if the baby, when it comes, will be cuddly and bouncy and take after his mother.

Or if it will be stillborn, and take after its father.

I *am* He that Liveth and was Dead . . . & Have the Keys of Hell & Death

Randy Chandler and t. Winter-Damon

"I *am* He that Liveth and was Dead . . . & Have the Keys of Hell & Death" was first published in *Grue* magazine No. 14, summer 1992. The story is an excerpt from their novel *Duet for the Devil*, published by Necro Publications in 2000.

Randy Chandler is the author of *Bad Juju, Hellz Bellz, Dead Juju*, and various short stories. He is also the author of *Daemon of the Dark Wood* and *Dime Detective*, both coming soon from Comet Press. He lives in Georgia.

t. Winter-Damon was a writer and illustrator from Tucson, Arizona whose works of fiction, non-fiction, and poetry appeared in hundreds of magazines and anthologies. Tim passed away in 2009.

Tim Winter-Damon would be pleased that this piece of Duet for the Devil is included in this book. I have the feeling that he is looking on from the Vast Beyond with a wicked grin on his mug.

♦ ♦ ♦ ♦

BEFORE HE BECAME SOMETHING MORE THAN HUMAN, he liked to hang out in punk joints & coffee houses like Nouveau Expresso & 90 Night—funky little clubs where young radicals & Post Beat post-hip poets & punk musicians gather for mutual ego massage or to have their philosophies styled in the latest fashion. In that previous life, Slice was an angry young poet known as "The Bard of Bones," because he always wore his hand-tooled leather-&-bones outfit when he read his mad poetry in public. T-bones, chicken bones, porkchop bones, dog bones, cat bones (painted black), squirrel skulls, a human femur, all rattling musically as he moved about like a demented witch doctor, mouthing his bone-chilling poems & death hymns. His outfit was topped off with a spooky hoodoo headdress made of a cow's skull & hung with chicken feet & bird feathers. He strutted his killer stuff & the tight little pussies in the audience (those with the kinkier libidos that flamed darkly to the spark of his hellcoals-&-gris-gris laden rap) would get wet & squirmy, aching for that big bone bulging beneath his loincloth. The Bard of Bones got a lot of pussy in those days.

Then came his Bloodbone Poems & his subsequent arrest on obscenity charges. The arresting stormtroopers were pretty riled about his stack of photo albums filled with their lurid headline clippings screaming an obsession with sordid sex, urban bloodbath & megaviolence. Neither did they appreciate his state-of-the-art collection of S&M, fetishist & bondage zines. Their bootheels & balled-fists-in-the-gut made that rather clear . . .

He was convicted, placed on probation & ordered to undergo psychiatric counseling. He enjoyed the cat-&-mouse mindgames he played with the shrink, entertaining private fantasies of extremely creative carnage. The drawback was that he lost interest in writing poetry. But he convinced Dr. Howard (who looked too much like Moe of the Three Stooges) that he had no desire to perform in public again. The baggy-eyed quack never scratched the surface of his mind's core—that dark chamber of id-horrors inhabited by a psyche blown wild by storms of evil. The stupid shrink never even caught a glimpse of the bloodlust boiling behind those hooded eyes. His Freudian flimflam was a total flop. The Bard of Bones became "Slice" right under Herr Doktor's big nose, & now he is someone else—*something* else. Something more than human. A nocturnal predator attuned to the poetry of the blooded flesh. He sees the universe in bones laid bare by his blade. Slice became the hunter of the blue nocturne.

He blows into 90 Night like a storm-building thunderhead.

"Bones! Is that you, man?" squeaks a rat-faced faggot.

Slice shakes his head.

Negative, asshole.

He picks up the sultry scent of choice prey.

His bootknife shifts against his ankle.

A pretty drag queen is sitting on a stool, reading into the mike a long poem about the gay plague.

Slice slinks across the room & sits at a vacant table. A butch lesbian wearing a dildo on a rope around her neck looks into his face, then quickly looks away. He can imagine what she saw there: saw him stuffing that dildo dick down her fucking throat, fucking her with it till blood filled up the torn crater of her mouth. *You ain't butch enough to handle me, cunt. Choke on it, you half-human bitch.*

The queen on the stool ends his epic by ripping off his blonde wig & spinning around on the stool to reveal a death's-head mask on the back of his head. The audience applauds & cheers. Slice hawks up thick phlegm from the back of his throat & spits the blue glob on the floor, causing three punks at the next table to look in disgust at him & move to another table. *Don't you know artistic criticism when you see it?*

The scent comes in stronger.

Something dark & powerful stirs in his belly & groin.

A prettyboy MC steps to the mike & says: "Ladies & gentlemen— Miss Phaedra Flame!"

The prey mounts the stage. The black sheen of her long hair, the black body stocking & black lip gloss accent her milk-white face.

A demonic grin sharpens the predator's face.

Phaedra Flame holds up a slim red-bound book, & says, "These are my Torch Poems." She holds up a blowtorch in her other hand & a tongue of fire licks at the book. Then flames engulf the book, & she tosses it into a bucket of water. "I hereby proclaim the death of the printed word!"

The audience whistles & cheers. *Mindless sheep.*

"Now I do real poetry," Phaedra says with a sly smile.

From the Olympus of his heightened blue awareness, the new god Slice looks down upon the roomful of ragged mortals & savors the coming creation. *Destruction in creation. Reductionist to the Nth.* His artistic medium will be flesh/bone/blood. Each slaughtered lamb a work of art, impermanent like ice sculpture. Art that literally sends spirits soaring into the great unknown.

Phaedra is putting her body & soul into her impromptu scat poetry, moving with feline grace, slinky and seductive, speaking directly to the new god, though she is not consciously aware that she is doing so. ". . . hungry in the hamburger air, tossed aside like a used condom, wearing the emblem of a washed-out revolution, alone with my own bloody abortion . . ."

Slice studies her every move, the jiggle of her full breasts, the quiver of her firm thighs, the pucker of her lips as she wraps them around every word. He is mentally outlining his artistic approach, planning the impetus of his strokes, finding cosmic inspiration in the poetry of her moving body.

The revelation hits him with such force that he is thrown back in his chair, his long hands dangling below the seat. He sees it all with crystal blue clarity: his handiwork must be exhibited for the masses, not merely for the homicide police & the coroner. He will display his blood art, like human graffiti, to the public. Phaedra Flame will be his first message to the world. The more sensitive souls will see the meaning beyond the carved & flayed flesh. Perhaps a few will even glimpse the coming *blue doom.*

The demonic grin returns & remains on his face like a mask.

As he follows her out the rear door of 90 Night & into the poorly-lit parking lot, he suddenly feels fear. Not his own fear, but the wimpy emotion of that intruding mind from Mermaid's Inn. The mind of the four-eyed professor, the one who inadvertently turned him into the new god.

Welcome aboard, Professor. Welcome to mindfuck. Come along & I'll show you what I'm going to do to you. You're in my orbit now.

He can feel the wimp squirm, taste his terror, sense his futile resistance.

You can't hide from me, cuntface. You know that now. You're just beginning to see my power.

Across town, the helpless one cringes.

You thought you could control me? Fat chance. We'll do her, you & me, then we'll turn her into raw art. I know you get off on death. Imagine the rush you'll get when I do you . . .

She bends to unlock the door of her battered bronze Toyota, & Slice puts the tip of the blade against the small of her back.

"Don't make a sound—" he hisses.

Phaedra's body tenses & her breath catches in her throat.

He steps beside her, putting an arm around her like a lover, shifting the knifepoint to the underside of her right breast.

"I loved your poems," he whispered. "They put me in an abstract mood."

He walks her to a garbage-filled green dumpster behind the coffee house.

"I'm going to do something very abstract," he tells her. "You'll be the talk of the art world."

He leads her behind the dumpster & pushes her back against its cool surface.

"If you scream, I'll slit your pretty throat."

He slits the thin material of her body stocking from the neck to the crotch, then peels it off her supple body.

"I smell your essence. I hear your blood rushing through your veins, wanting to come out."

He deftly works his fingers through her pubic bush & into the warm lips of her quim.

She tries to draw back from his touch, but her buttocks are already pressed flush against the dumpster.

His zipper opens with a loud rasp & his ponderous penis nudges against her dry slit.

"Please . . . don't . . ." she whispers.

"You're dry as a bone," he giggles, "but I can fix that."

He clamps his left hand over her mouth & runs the blade downward, over her belly.

"I'm going to *fuck you*," he says & jabs the blade deep into her vagina.

Professor feels a twinge of envy as the huge cock slides deep into the bloodslick tunnel of ruined flesh. Had he been so well-endowed, he may never have gone through his various bookwormish stages of transformation, womanless through high school & college, through a series of bungled sexual encounters with prostitutes & sluts who made light of his inchworm cock, & on into the solitary pursuit of science. Had fate given this magnificent dong to him instead of this crazed sadist, then maybe he would not have summoned the succubus, in his LSD ritual of sex & self-destruction, she who tipped him to the formula & possibilities of Li Di 1 . . .

Envy, regret, &, now, revulsion—as he is trapped in the monster's mind, bearing sick witness to the slaughter of the dying woman. Her mind screams in terror and disbelief as the blade slices off her breast.

A short-handled axe flashes in the dim light from a distant street lamp & strikes the woman's shoulder, completely separating her arm from her body. A fountain of blood gushes from the severed socket, drenching you/her psychotic slayer & the litter-strewn pavement alike in the hot spill of her life-essence. She enters into numbing & merciful shock/you feel the center of her mind melting, dispersing randomly/each dripping direction going to death/butchershop *chic/a little off the top* . . .?

Her head comes off with ease, though the axe keeps slipping in your blood-greased hands. Like the cries of a kitten down a well, the beheaded woman's mewling echoes somewhere in your backroombrain, psychic screams from a locked corridor. Then dead silence. You start to hum a tuneless stream of bluenotes as you sculpt meat & bone. With your eyes ablaze with blue fire, it's easy to work in the dark.

He/you/she/IT . . . spiritflesh bliss blowing back eons . . . back to the bigfucking bang!

From your angle-less corner of the blinding blue galaxy you feel her ghost fly away.

You work blind, by feel, by the sound of rending flesh & grinding bone, by the light of an inner blue radiance, out where interstellar radio messages bleed into curved mirrors & broken space & time, keying a haunted memory of idiotic phone conversations breaking into your old reality like that CB breaker-breaker shit coming out of your TV & making you want to find those rednecked motherfuckers & make them bleed like stuck pigs. Ah, sweet memories. Whose memories . . .?

Bad to the last bone. Blistering blue heat bending mirrors, mirrors catching the bluenotes you hum as you do your best work. Monster art. Opening soon at *your* guerilla theater.

The satellite's orbit begins to decay as it passes over Manila. Its inevitable entrance by fire into Earth's dense atmosphere has not yet been calculated by those paid to monitor such things; when the Com-Sat's demise is plotted, it will be deemed one more hunk of expensive space junk likely to shed a minimum of dangerous debris upon the planet. Scant minutes later, the doomed satellite passes high above & to the south of Hong Kong, &, eventually, over Miami, where Lucy Nation & Pynchon are coupling aboard her yacht *Hellraiser*, & several miles inland, where the squad car lurches to a stop in front of the coffee house 90 Night. If the satellite's onboard equipment were still operational, its camera could snap pictures of the bloody, contorted corpse hanging by a rope from the roof of the coffee house, could zoom in on the horrified & sickened faces of some of the individuals in the crowd, gathered to bear witness to the bizarre abominations. But the Com-Sat is shut down, making its silent way to inevitable destruction somewhere over an ocean of the southern hemisphere, sometime after it flashes by the beaches of Galveston, its bulk visible only as a brilliant pinpoint above the extreme horizon where the sea meets sky . . .

It was the biggest goddamn fly he had ever seen. Not a horsefly, not a green fly, but a goddamn housefly so big that Officer Robbins thought it must be a goddamn mutant, what with all the pollution & shit in the air. & why was it, in unflylike behavior, still out making its rounds in the dead of night . . .?

Now he's staring into the bloody cavern that the fly disappeared into a moment ago. That's what the gaping wound in the girl's chest reminds him of—a raw cavern. Christ! It could be two girls, Robbins thinks, the way all the body parts are hanging there, oozing all that gore & shit, the hand jammed up her ass so it looks like she's shitting a fucking severed arm, & the head, *oh Jesus*, the head clamped between the thighs like she's giving birth to her own fucking head. Some sicko had a field day with this poor babe. From what's visible of her face she was probably a looker. Before the butcher worked her over.

A guy in a business suit steps up for a better look at the mutilated thing twisting a little on the rope as the salt-edged breeze from the shore seems to invest it with a momentary, mocking breath of pseudo-life.

"Get back," Robbins orders the wide-eyed suit. "Something drops off her, you get it smack in the face." He turns to the small crowd of onlookers & closet ghouls & says, "Everybody stay back. This ain't a sideshow. Jesus!"

He lights a cigar & waits for the homicide boys to arrive. While he waits, he watches for that goddamned mutant fly to come out of that bloodyfucking cave.

Xipe

Edward Lee

"Xipe" first appeared in *The Barrelhouse: Excursions into the Unknown*, Winter 1993, and later published in his collection *The Ushers and Other Stories* by Obsidian Books, May 1999.

Edward Lee is the author of almost fifty books and numerous short stories. Several of his properties have been optioned for film, while *Header* was released on DVD in 2009; also, he has been published in Germany, England, Romania, Greece, and Austria. Recent releases include *Bullet Through Your Face* and *Brain Cheese Buffet* (story collections), *Header 2*, and the hardcore Lovecraftian books *The Innswich Horror, Trolley No. 1852, Pages Torn From A Travel Journal, Going Monstering*, and *Haunter of the Threshold*. Upcoming works include the novel *Header 3*, the Lovecraftian novella *The Dunwich Romance*, and the story collection *Carnal Surgery*. Lee lives in Largo, Florida.

♦ ♦ ♦ ♦

THE SMILE—VAST, EMPTY—oozed across the back of his mind. Pudgy hands reached out for him through a rain of blood.

Smith's eyes snapped open. The ceiling was rushing past; he was flat on his back. Dark faces, like blobs, hovered over him. He heard casters squeal and bottles clink.

A voice, a man's, exclaimed: "Desé prisa!"

Smith had a pretty good idea he was going to die.

The smile again, huge, empty—what was it? He closed his eyes and saw a muzzle flash, smelled cordite. He saw twin figures falling through dark. Then he heard a scream—his own.

A sign loomed: STAFF ONLY/PERSONAL UNICAMENTE. Doors parted clumsily. The gurney wheeled into a padded elevator, and at once the breathless, jagged motion ceased.

Images dripped back into his head: memories. Smith's heart shimmied.

I was set up, he thought, astonished. *That swine Ramirez, he must've turned.* The guy must've gotten himself fingered and was trying to deal his way out. There'd been a fed in the room, hadn't there?

More pieces fell into place: a clawing weight on his back, a window bursting, the unmistakable kick of a .38 full of hot loads. But Smith carried a Glock. *Did I shoot a Justice agent tonight?* With his own piece? And good luck to that scum Ramirez if he thought he could spin on Vinchetti's network. Smith couldn't remember a whole lot, but he was sure of one thing: Ramirez was dead.

The elevator hummed. Smith felt dreamy. "What hospital is this?"

"San Cristobal de la Gras, Meester Smeeth," said the blurred doctor. "We are taking you to where you will be safe."

Great, Smith mused. *More Mexicans.* But what could he expect down here? At first he thought they must be taking him to the jail wing, but then a nurse said in a warm whisper, "The government men do not know you're here." She squeezed his hand. "We will protect you."

Smith felt exorcized. Vinchetti must've arranged this, must've paid off the right people to have Ramirez protected. Otherwise, Justice would be all over the place.

Thank God, he thought.

Then, in a jolt, he remembered the rest. The face behind the empty smile, and the name.

Xipe.

"It's Xipe," said the barkeep.

Smith was staring at the tiny stone figure which sat atop the register. It was black. It looked like a Buddha with a feathered headdress. Squatting, it held its arms out and smiled.

"What?" Smith said.

The keep, rail-thin, enthused in a thick Mexican accent. "Xipe protects the faithful. He is the Giver of the Harvest, the Seer of Beauty and Growth. He is the Great God of Good Will. Like your severed rabbit foot, Xipe brings luck."

You look like you've had plenty, buddy, Smith concluded. La Fiesta Del Sol, like all the bars down here, was an erect dump. Sticky floors and walls, seamy light, jabbering Mexican music. A young G.I. fussed with two whores at a corner booth, but that was it. Ramirez always picked shithouses like this. Perhaps they reminded him of home.

Smith was Vinchetti's coverman; he handled the southern region of what the feds called "The Circuit," the mob-operated underground porn network. Vinchetti said the southern region grossed a couple of million per year, a far cry from what they'd been taking before the advent of VCRs and x-rated videos; but then they weren't losing anything anymore, either. Nobody worked in loops and stills now; it was all video. A single 3/4-inch master could be duplicated a thousand times and sold to point-men for a thousand dollars apiece. From there they stepped on them any way they wanted, depending on the orders. In other words, the days of running truckloads of the stuff out of South Texas were long gone. Just a handful of masters kept The Circuit going for months. It was almost too easy, and risk free. Vinchetti's plants in Justice, working with set-ups from Smith, gave the feds plenty of old stuff and overstock to seize, and a couple of wetbacks to bust. Justice thought they were effectively fighting underground pornography, while Vinchetti lost nothing and made millions per year. The net was even safer from the distribution end; everything was mail drops these days, coded mailing lists and untraceable names. Even Vinchetti didn't know who most of his point clients were, and on rare occasions when Postal agents busted a point at a drop, Vinchetti skated because the points didn't know who he was, either.

The stuff, of course, was all made on the Mex side; the states were too hot, unless you were pure-ass stupid like those Dixie Mafia lightweights or the Lavender Hill people. The Circuit dealt only in what the feds called "Underground"; real S&M, torture, snuff, and lots of kiddie. The fucking perverts stateside paid big money for "kp," as much as three bills for a 20 minute double dupe, as long as the kids were white. Smith made the buys and had the masters muled to San Angelo; Vinchetti's dupe labs took it from there. Smith saw no shame in what he did. Supply and demand—hey, it was a free country, wasn't it? The only real worry was getting the masters across the border, and that was Ramirez' problem. Smith didn't know how the guy did it—he was either a very good mule, or a very lucky one.

Where the hell is he? Smith thought. Lapeto was a ghost-town, like any of the notorious Texas border stops, a grim meld of rapid babble, dark faces, and sneers. The pop was 99% Mex, half or more wet. All that kept these little pisshole towns alive were the EMs from Lackland and Fort Sam. The kids would come here, rent rooms, then cross over to catch the donkey shows in Acuña and Fuenté. For all Smith cared, the entire border could burn.

"I've never been robbed," the keep said. He was drying glasses, grinning.

"Huh?"

"Never been robbed like other bars, never been shaken. Never problems."

"Big deal," Smith sputtered.

"Is Xipe. He is good luck."

Idiot. Smith stared at the figure again. It smiled much like the keep, emptily. Smith didn't believe in gods, stone or otherwise. Gods were bad for business. "Another," he said, and hopped off his stool.

In the john, he scanned incomprehensible graffiti. Most of it seemed to lack Spanish extraction altogether. Xoclan, ti coatl. Ut zetl! Huctar, Coatlicue, ay! Me socorro! Someone had drawn a hummingbird eating the heads off stick figures. Smith grimaced and zipped his fly. A shadow swung behind him. He spun, shucked his Glock, and drew down . . .

But it was only a trinket swinging from the light. A black plastic figure with pudgy hands and a big, empty smile.

Xipe.

This place gives me the creeps. He couldn't wait to get back to San Angelo and the real world. A little coke, a little pussy—enough of this wasteland. A slim figure in a smudged azure-blue suit sat stooped beside Smith's bar stool. The head turned as if psychic, big white smile with a gold tooth, greasy hair, greasy face.

"Amigo," Ramirez greeted. "How is my favoreet yankee?" He offered a pale hand, which Smith declined to shake.

"I've been waiting a fucking hour."

"Hey, we Mexicans, we're always late, isn't that right?"

"Come on, we've got business."

Ramirez nodded, grinning, and paid the tab. The gold-flecked grin seemed permanently fixed. He led Smith out, slinking like a junkie after a mainline.

The street stood empty. It stank of dust. A lone whore yammered at a couple of G.I.s getting out of a cab. She gazed at Smith once, then quickly looked away. The main drag wasn't even paved; it was dirt, strewn with litter. Smith checked the alleys for tails, but only emptiness returned his glances.

"I have much good stuff for you tonight, Meester Smeeth." Ramirez held the door for him at the motel. PARADISA, the neon sign glowed. *Jesus,* Smith thought. Dark lamps lit the lobby. Ridiculous felt prints of matadors and Spanish women adorned the stained walls. A greasily rouged fat woman tended the counter, hair in a black bun. From a shelf of curios, the tiny figure of Xipe smiled.

Smith frowned.

They mounted stairs which smelled of beer-piss and smoke. Ramirez' room smelled worse. *La Biblia* rested on a nightstand, beside a stained bed. Used condoms stuck to the side of the wastebasket. Ramirez was zipping open a battered suitcase, but Smith's gaze turned to the room's only wall painting. The quetzl-feathered head on a plump, squatting body. Its arms outstretched as if to invite embrace. The smile huge yet empty.

"Xipe," Smith muttered at it.

Ramirez looked up, grinning gold. "The Giver of the Harvest, who protects the faithful. The Great God of—"

"Good Will, I know," Smith interrupted. Xipe's eyes were empty as its smile, its fat hands empty. Perhaps it was the *mode* of the trinket's emptiness that distressed Smith so. It seemed to him a kind of vitality— a *knowledge*—hidden deep beneath the black facade. An emptiness that somehow yearned to be filled.

"He brings luck, Meester Smeeth. He guards us from our enemies."

Smith blinked. A shiver of vertigo, like standing up too quickly after a neat shot of Uzzo, seemed to transpose Xipe's smile to a momentary hollow grimace.

Smith turned away. He didn't feel good—bad beer or something. In dismay, he glanced down. "Jesus Christ, you bring the stuff in a suitcase?"

"My people, like yours, we pay."

"You can't buy every Customs officer on the line."

"Of course not." Ramirez grinned at Xipe. "The rest is *buena snerte*."

"What?"

"Luck."

Smith felt a chill. The painting distracted him. "How many masters?"

"Ten. New faces, all new stuff. And chiquitas—the best."

Smith carried forty large. He was authorized to pay three grand per master, but only if the production was good. The way it worked, if the larger-formatted master wasn't excellent, the second dupes would look piss-poor. Ramirez plugged the first tape into the VCR he'd set up on the dresser. Now came the grueling part, having to watch a sample of each. Smith steeled himself, crossed his arms, and addressed the screen.

His eyes bulged when the image formed.

He expected the usual phantom scenes: stark-lighted rooms, hollow-eyed children and sneering spic studs, women gagged and tied and jerking as fingers sunk needles into banded breasts. Instead he saw a grainy black and white of a man getting out of a car in front of a San Angelo warehouse.

The man was Smith.

Next: himself walking down the concourse at the Dallas/Ft. Worth air terminal. And next: himself giving Vinchetti's Justice plant some pad and a list of phony bust points in a vacant Del Rio parking lot.

Ramirez' gold grin glowed. "Good stuff, eh, Meester Smeeth?"

"You greaseball pepper-belly motherfucker!" But before Smith could even think about yanking his heat, a hammer cocked behind his head. Smith's face felt huge as he turned. He was now looking down the barrel of a 3-inch S&W Model 13.

"Good evening. Mr. Smith. My name is Peterson. I work for the Department of Justice. I'm arresting you for multiple violations of Section 18 of the United States Code." It was just a young punk, the "G.I." in the bar. He gave Smith an empty smile. "Mr. Ramirez has given us enough documentation to send you up for thirty years. I want you to know that you have the right to remain . . .

The words melted. Behind him, Ramirez was giggling. All Smith could think was *I'm not going down,* over and over. Federal time on a kiddie porn rap was as good as a death sentence. He'd be "boy-cherry." They'd turn him into a cellblock bitch in five minutes.

From the wall, Xipe smiled, seemed to lean over Peterson's shoulder. Smith made his move. The half-second disarm he'd learned in the Army worked well enough; his hands snapped up, grabbed the revolver and Peterson's wrist, and pushed. A round went off and burned a line across Smith's scalp. Peterson's wrist broke, and suddenly Smith had the piece. He squeezed off two Q-loads into Peterson's chest. The kid crumpled beneath Xipe like a tossed offering.

Ramirez jumped on his back. Smith tried an elbow jab but missed. The Mexican was clawing at him, biting into his ear. The revolver hit the floor. Smith staggered back, screaming as his right ear was separated from his head between Ramirez' teeth. The front wall diminished, yet the framed, grinning Xipe seemed not to; the empty smile followed him. Smith meant to slam Ramirez into the back wall.

Instead, he collided with the window, and the window gave.

It was nothing so trite as slow motion. Smith and his piggyback rider fell very quickly, but the hot night seemed to rise more than they seemed to fall. The street greeted them like a brick slammed down onto copulating frogs.

Something crunched, then collapsed. Smith rolled off Ramirez, who'd broken his fall. Was something looking down at them? Stupefied, Smith managed to stand, shuddering as he removed a long glass shard from his armpit and another from his belly. He was cut bad, but perhaps Xipe had brought him luck after all—Smith had risen from the two-story drop intact, while Ramirez lay crushed, organs punctured by cracked bones.

Smith caught an overhead movement, or he thought he did. He stared up. Was someone leaning out of the window, looking down at him? Maybe Peterson had had a backup man. Smith shucked his Glock, but when he lined up the three-dot sights, the window was empty.

Giggling bubbled at his feet. Ramirez spat out Smith's chewed ear. Despite ruptured organs and a broken spine, the Mexican grinned, somehow, in glory.

"Looks like today is not your lucky day, Meester Smeeth."

"Luckier than yours, bean-eater." Smith pumped eight rounds of 9mm hardball into Ramirez' head. The skull divided, as if trying to expel its contents. The gold-toothed smile froze emptily up at the night.

Smith limped away. Heads popped out of La Fiesta de la Sol. Curtains fluttered in lit windows; faces queried down. Several seemed to wear smiles like empty gouges, like cut-out masks.

Numbness throbbed where his ear had been. His breath rattled, and blood ran freely down his leg. He'd probably cut arteries, punctured a lung. Like a dimmer, his vision began to fade.

I'm losing it, he thought. *I'm . . .*

But, more good luck. The cab idled in the alley, as if expecting him. He fell into the back seat, slammed the door, consciousness draining in pulses.

"I'm bleeding like a fucking tap. Get me to a hospital."

The cabbie turned, a blurred, vacant grin. "No hablo Ingles, señor."

Smith peeled off a grand in ball notes from his roll. "Hospitala!" he attempted, throwing cash. "Pronto!"

"Anytheen you say, Meester."

The cab pulled off into dust. Before Smith passed out, he sensed plump outstretched hands, a smile vast as a mountain rift. A plastic toy, like a kewpie doll, swung fitfully from the rearview.

Xipe.

Smith blinked from the gurney. They'd rushed him to an ICU. Around him stood a coven of hospital staff. Starched white uniforms and intent faces. A beautiful dark-eyed nurse patted his brow with a damp cloth, while another timed his pulse.

Am I dying? Smith thought.

"You are safe now," said the doctor. "We have stopped the bleeding."

But like a mirage, a man had risen from the corner. He wore a black suit, a white collar.

Smith gulped. A priest.

Indeed he was. He took Smith's hand and asked, "Are you sorry for your sins?"

Smith felt plunged into darkness. "No, no," he muttered. "Don't let me die. Please . . ."

The holy man's crucifix glittered in the light. He looked solemn and kind. He was holding a book.

"Are you sorry for your sins?" the heavy accent repeated.

But Smith didn't hear the words. His eyes were busy, having at last noticed the incongruity of the priest's silver crucifix. No Jesus could be found at the end of the chain—it was another figure, who wore a crown of quetzl feathers instead of thorns. Pudgy, dark hands bore no nails. The bottomless smile beseeched him.

"Xipe," Smith whispered.

In Nahuati, the native language of the Toltecs, the priest began to speak. The knife he raised was not of steel but of flint. And from the book he commenced the recital, not the Catholic Sacrament For The Dying, but the Aztec Psalter of the Sacrifice, and the Great Rites of the Giver of the Harvest.

Smith's heart beat like thunder in his chest.

Bait

Ray Garton

"Bait" was originally published in *Cemetery Dance* magazine Volume 5
Number 3/4, Fall 1993 and reprinted in his 2006 short story collection
Pieces of Hate.

Ray Garton is the author of more than 60 books, including the horror
novels *Scissors* and *Ravenous* and the thrillers *Sex and Violence in
Hollywood* and *Meds*. His short stories have appeared in magazines,
anthologies and in eight collections. His 1987 vampire novel *Live Girls*
was nominated for the Bram Stoker Award and in 2006, he received
the Grand Master of Horror Award. He lives in northern California with
his wife Dawn and their seven cats, where he is currently at work
on something or other.

◆ ◆ ◆ ◆

"GO OVER TO THE DAIRY STUFF and get a gallon of milk," Mom told them
as she stood in the produce section of the Seaside Supermarket, squeezing
one avocado after another, looking for ripe ones. "Low-fat, remember."

They knew, both of them: nine-year-old Cole and his seven-year-
old sister, Janelle. Their mother always ate and drank low-fat or non-fat
everything. And besides, they knew the brand of milk on sight. The two
children headed down the aisle between two long produce display cases.

"And hurry up!" Mom called behind them. "I wanna get out of here
so I can have a smoke. Meet me up in the front."

"She's always in a hurry," Janelle said matter-of-factly.

"Yeah. Usually to have a smoke."

They found the dairy section and went to the refrigerated cases,
scanning the shelves of milk cartons—different sizes, different brands.
When he spotted the right one, Cole pulled the glass door open, stood on
tip-toes, reached up and tilted the carton off the fourth shelf up, nearly
dropping it. He let the door swing closed behind him as they started to
head for the front of the store to find their mother. But Cole stopped.

"Here's another one," he said quietly.

Janelle turned back. "Another what?"

He turned the carton so she could see the splotchy black-and-white depiction of a little boy's smiling face. It was such a bad picture—as if someone had run the boy's face through a dysfunctioning copy machine—that he looked more nightmarish than pitiful. But pity was exactly what the black writing on the carton seemed to be aiming for. Cole read it aloud to Janelle:

HAVE YOU SEEN THIS BOY?
9-YEAR-OLD PETER MULRAKES
Last seen in Eureka, CA parking lot of Safeway supermarket.
Missing—1 year, 7 months.

There were a few more details that Cole skipped over, along with a phone number to call if anyone should see the boy or have information regarding his whereabouts. At the very bottom, he read silently to himself:

A NON-PROFIT COMMUNITY SERVICE
OF VALENCIA DAIRIES, INC.

"Where's Eureka?" Janelle asked.

"Couple hours down the coast from here, I think," Cole replied, staring at the haunting face with its smeared features and splotchy eyes. "I wonder where they go," he muttered to himself. "I wonder what happens to them when they disappear . . . who takes them . . . and why."

He turned and went back to the dairy case, opened the door and began turning other milk cartons around.

"Mom said to hurry," Janelle said. "She wants to smoke."

"In a second."

Each carton had a face on it, some different than others: little boys, little girls, some black, some white and some asian . . . but all with the same splotchy features and blurred lines that would make the children almost impossible to identify, even if they were standing right there in front of Cole.

"They have 'em on the grocery bags, too, y'know," Janelle said in her usual casual, detached way.

"Yeah . . . I know."

"What the hell are you two doing?"

Cole spun around, letting the door close again. Their mother stood with her cart, frowning at them.

"C'mon, now, I forgot the fish," she said, waving at them. "Hurry up, I wanna get out of here."

So you can have a smoke, Cole thought.

They went to the seafood counter where, beyond the glass of the display case, Cole and Janelle looked at all the shrimp and scallops, squid and octopus, fish, clams, oysters, crabs, lobster, eel . . .

Like a dead National Geographic *special,* Cole thought.

Some of the fish were still whole and their dead, staring eyes looked like glass.

"How did they kill 'em, Cole?" Janelle asked.

He blinked; at first, he thought she was still talking about the faces on the milk cartons because they were still on his mind. "The fish? Oh, they caught 'em on hooks."

"How?"

"With bait."

"What kinda bait?"

He hated it when she did this. "Sometimes other fish. Y'know, smaller fish. And sometimes other things . . . whatever the fish like to eat."

The man behind the counter offered to help Mom, and she said, "I'd like a couple of swordfish steaks, please."

"Sorry, but we're all out. Till tomorrow."

She sighed. "You mean, we live right here on the coast and you're out of *swordfish?*"

"It happens."

"Okay, then . . . how about shark?"

"Oh, yeah, got some fresh shark steaks here. How many?"

"Two. And, uh—" She looked down at Cole and Janelle. "What do you guys want for dinner?"

"Not fish," Cole said. "I hate fish."

Janelle added, "So does Daddy. He said so."

"Well, that's just too bad for him. He could stand to lose weight and red meat is really fattening. Besides, it causes cancer. Fish is good for you, so what kind do you want?"

When they wouldn't respond, she ordered some whitefish.

Janelle leaned over and whispered to Cole, "Poor fish. I don't wanna eat 'em if they've been tricked into bein' killed."

Cole looked over the top of the counter at the enormous swordfish on the wall behind it. It was shiny and regal, with its long, needle-like nose jutting into the air. And, of course, it was very dead.

Once they had the fish, they had to walk fast to keep up with Mom on her way to the register. They stood in line for a while, then when they got up to the counter, they started looking over the racks of candy bars and gum to their right, asking Mom if they could have some.

"No, absolutely not, you know what that stuff *does* to you?" she hissed, bending toward them. "Just go on outside and wait by the car. I'll be right out."

So, they did. But not before Cole noticed the brown paper bags that were being packed with groceries at each counter.

Smeared faces looked back at him from the sides of the bags as if they were watching him lead his sister out of the store. The faces were haunted . . . and haunting.

On the way to the car, they passed the newspaper vending boxes and Cole stopped when he saw a picture of a little baby on the front page of the local paper with the word MISSING! beneath it. The word made him stop. He read the headline, frowning:

2 MONTH OLD BABY STOLEN FROM CRIB
IN MIDDLE OF NIGHT—
POLICE HAVE NO SUSPECTS

Cole stared at the baby for a while, frowning, wondering what had happened to it. Who would want to take a little baby? Why?

With a slight burning in his gut, he turned and hurried after his little sister toward the car.

They stood by the car, kicking a smashed soda can back and forth between them over the dirty pavement. The nearby ocean gave the chilly, damp breeze a salty smell and seagulls circled overhead, calling out sharply.

The musical voice of a little girl called to them from a few yards away.

"Hey! Wanna see my puppies?"

She stood beside a gray van. The sliding door on the side was half open.

"What kind of puppies?" Cole asked as he and Janelle took a few steps toward her.

"Little bitty ones." She held her palms a few inches apart to demonstrate.

"Let's go see the puppies!" Janelle said, grinning.

"Okay. But keep an eye out for Mom."

* * *

Mom pushed her cart of grocery bags through the automatic door and stopped just outside the store. The door closed behind her with a hum as she fished a Marlboro out of her purse and turned against the wind, leaning her head forward to light up.

It was while she was lighting her cigarette that the gray van drove by.

By the time she lifted her head, taking a deep drag on the cigarette, the van was already gone.

So were the children.

Cole awoke in complete, solid, almost *tangible* darkness.

His ears rang loudly and his head throbbed. The ringing eventually subsided—slowly, gradually—and was replaced by the cry of a baby.

No, no, the cry of two . . . no, three, maybe four . . . no, *several* babies.

Somewhere nearby, there were voices that barely rose above the crying of the babies.

But there was something else . . . something weird . . . something *wrong* . . .

The ground beneath him and the damp, cold darkness all around him was moving . . . tilting back and forth . . . this way, that way, back and forth.

He reached down to feel the surface beneath him, but suddenly realized that he could not move his arms. His wrists were tied together behind him and his ankles were tied together before him.

Then he noticed something else: A low rumble that made its way through the surface beneath him and up into his body, gathering in his chest like quivering indigestion. It sounded like an engine.

Are we on a bus, or something? he thought, then: *We? We?*

"Janelle?" he said, his voice hoarse and weak. "Janelle, you here? C'mon, Janelle, say something!"

"Who you talkin' to?" another voice asked. It was the voice of a child, a boy, somewhere around Cole's age.

"What? I'm . . . talking to my sister," Cole said quietly, uncertainly.

"Who?" a little girl asked from somewhere in the darkness, her voice trembling. It wasn't Janelle. "Who are you talking to?"

"My sister, Janelle. Janelle? You there? C'mon, Janelle, you *gotta* be there!"

The voices paused for a long moment. Cole could hear the babies crying, some of them gurgling and making spitting sounds, and when he listened very closely, he could hear the breathing of other children. Some were making purring little snoring sounds. There was a lot of rustling in the dark, squirming movement.

He called for Janelle a few more times, raising his voice in spite of how much it hurt his head, in spite of the way his stomach was beginning to feel sick because of the lurching back-and-forth movements.

Finally, there was a little voice . . . so small and weak and frightened: "Cole? You . . . are you there?"

"Yeah, Munchkin. I'm here. I'm right here."

"Where?"

"I'm here, real close. You *hear* me?"

"I can't see you."

"Yeah, I know, but you can hear me, right?"

"Uh-huh."

"Good, then that's all that counts right now. We'll see each other soon, okay? You just stay still and don't be afraid, 'cause I'm here."

"Okay. Good. Okay."

Her voice was so small, like a thread being pulled through the darkness by a dull needle.

They were all quiet.

A few of the babies had stopped crying.

Cole thought of the faces on the milk cartons and grocery bags.

We've been taken, he thought. *Just like them.*

He wondered what he and Janelle would look like on those cartons and bags. Would their faces be as splotchy and smeared? Would Mom even recognize them if she saw them?

The voices outside were more audible now, easier to make out. But Cole was able to catch only snatches of what they were saying.

"—'cause these here sharks are damned easy to catch, and 'cause most of the shoppers goin' to their local fish counter in the grocery store are so fuckin' stupid that they—"

"—don't know what you're figurin', that they're goin' in to buy shark steaks and they don't even know that we're—"

One of the babies wailed for a moment and the voices melted together into a single meaningless sound, and then:

"—go into the grocery stores and restaurants as cheap scallops and swordfish steaks and, a course, shark steaks, so we pick up the money and they can—"

"—why that stuff's so cheap in some places, 'cause we're out here—"

"—people eating more fish these days to stay healthy and lose weight, so we're able to—"

There was another noise behind the voices, a noise that was hard to identify at first although it was so familiar, as if it were a sound Cole had heard just yesterday, a sound he heard frequently.

Then, quite suddenly, he realized it was a sound he heard almost every day—the *ocean*! He was on the ocean! That was why everything was tilting back and forth—they were in a boat!

A door burst open loudly and sudden blinding light cut through the darkness. Cole turned his head away and clenched his eyes tightly shut.

Heavy footsteps sounded on wood and there was a sharp *click!* and the room filled with light that was bright enough to stab through Cole's eyelids and into his head like a hot knife.

There was deep, booming laughter from one man while another barked, "See? Here they are! All we need! Lessee, whatta we want here, now, huh? Lessee . . ."

Cole tried to open his eyes. It was hard at first, painful because of the sudden bright light . . . then he tried opening them gradually, just a little bit at a time, until he was squinting. First, he saw only bright light . . . then shapes moving back and forth . . . then the light began to diminish and the shapes became more distinct and took on faces and features.

"Well, we'll need a few a-them," one man said, pointing to some shelves with rows of cardboard boxes on them.

The other man—taller, bigger, with broad shoulders and big arms—said, "Yeah, okay, you get them. I'll get these. A couple of 'em. Lessee, lessee . . . which ones?"

By that time, Cole's vision had cleared enough to see the enormous, bearded man looking down at him.

"You awake, boy?" the man growled through a grin.

"Huh? *What?*"

The man kicked him, digging the toe of his boot beneath Cole's right knee. Hard.

"*Owww!*" Cole shouted, trying not to cry.

"Yeah, yeah, you're awake, all right. You'll do."

The man reached down and slung an arm around Cole's chest, carrying him over his shoulder like a sack of potatoes, until Cole could see only the wet wooden floor below.

"And *you*!" the man growled, his voice passing through Cole's entire body. Cole could feel the man picking up another child. Then the man turned and said to his partner, "Go ahead and take four of 'em outta those boxes, just go ahead. We'll need at least that many. Fact, we'll prob'ly hafta come back in here and get more."

Cole raised his head and saw all the children tied up with their backs against the wall or lying on the wooden floor. Then he saw Janelle. She looked up and their eyes met.

"Cole!" she shouted, her voice thick and trembling.

"Don't worry, Munchkin, just stay right there, don't you move, and don't worry about a thing. I'll see you in a little while, okay? Okay?"

With her little mouth hanging open, all she could do was nod.

The man carrying Cole laughed long and hard. Cole wondered if he was laughing at the exchange between him and Janelle.

The children disappeared the moment the man slammed the door behind him.

Then there was sunlight, brilliant and blinding, and Cole groaned as he clenched both his teeth and his eyes.

Cole was dropped and hit the floor hard. The wind was knocked from his lungs. He gasped for breath, thrashed around straining against the ties on his hands and feet until he was on his back, staring up at the sky: patches of blue surrounded by dark, pregnant clouds.

He saw the other man with things under his arms . . . things wrapped in white cloths . . . things that wailed . . . cried . . . sobbed . . .

Babies. They were babies.

"Okay, here they are," said the man who had carried them out. "Let's get to it, guys."

Lying on his back and watching, Cole tried to count the babies. There were three . . . no, four men. Or was that guy over there the fifth? He couldn't tell, and quickly didn't care.

One of the men lifted a baby high by the ankles. He unwrapped the white cloth until the baby was naked, then he handed it to another man, saying, "Remember, the shoulder, that's where it's gotta go."

"I know, I know, whatta you think I am, some kinda amateur?" He took the baby roughly in his left hand.

Cole gasped when he saw the large, barbed hook in the man's right hand.

The hook went through the baby's shoulder.

Blood spurted, then flowed from the wound.

The baby screamed so hard and so long that its face turned dark red as its arms and legs flailed and kicked.

The hook was attached to a cable and was thrown over the side of the boat. A couple of the men laughed loudly.

Cole's eyes were so wide they hurt as he gawked at the men. He felt as if he might throw up.

A man at the other end of the boat holding an enormous fishing pole—like no fishing pole Cole had ever seen before—shouted, "Oh-ho, well, I guess we'll see what I get here, huh?"

One of the men bent over Cole then, clutched him with both hands and lifted him up.

"I'll hold him," he said to another. "You cut the ropes."

Another of the men some distance away bellowed, "You know, I never thought about it before, but hey, this way we'll make the liberals happy 'cause we ain't killin' any dolphins, right?"

The others, including the one holding Cole, roared with laughter.

Someone cut the ropes and his limbs were free.

Big hands with fat, rough fingers ripped his shirt off and peeled his pants from his legs like the thin seal from a sausage. They pulled his shoes and socks off and tore his underwear away until he was completely naked and shivering.

"Okay, you take him," the man said. "Give 'im to Corny—he's good at hooking the bigger ones."

Moments later, Cole was looking at a big man with huge moles on his face. He smiled at Cole. "Tell ya what, kid, I ain't gonna hit any a your organs or arteries or nothin'. It'll hurt, but you'll be okay, I promise."

The man stabbed a large barbed hook through Cole's right shoulder. The excruciating pain made him scream for an instant, then he passed out.

He woke to big hands slapping his face.

"Kid! Hey, *kid*!" the man slapping him shouted. "You gotta be awake for this, okay? You gotta be awake and kickin'!"

Once Cole was alert and crying out for help, one of the big men wrapped his thick arms around Cole, sending explosions of pain from his pierced shoulder through his entire body, lifted him and threw him over the side of the boat and into the cold water.

Under the water, Cole held his breath, cheeks puffed out like little balloons on each side of his face. The pain was unbearable, but at the moment, he was more interested in breathing.

He began to thrash and kick.

He found the surface, got his head above it and cried, "Help me! Please help me help me help me help—"

Through bleary, watery eyes, he saw the men looking over the edge of the boat, grinning at him.

"Go get 'em, boy!" one of them shouted with a laugh.

He went under again, quite unexpectedly, still kicking and flailing, mouth closed and eyes open. He saw it.

The shark.

It came out of the darkness aimed directly at him, its predatory, dead-black eyes staring, teeth showing in his half-open mouth, rows and rows of crooked razors.

Cole felt the impact and was jerked through the water.

His own blood clouded the water around him until the silent predator looked like a nightmarish ghost moving through the night.

Cole let out his breath and screamed under the water as the shark's face came out of the darkness again, mouth open.

Closer and closer . . .

Painfreak

Gerard Houarner

"Painfreak" was first published in *Into the Darkness* #1, April 1994.

Gerard Houarner works in a psychiatric institution by day and writes at night, mostly about the dark. Recent publications include "Tree of Shadows," in the Crossroads Press electronic edition of the novel *The Beast That Was Max*, "Mourning With the Bones of the Dead," *Horror Library 4*, "The Flea Market ," Eibonvale Press anthology *Blind Swimmer*, "Lightning Can't Catch Me," *Darkness On The Edge: Dark Tales Inspired by the Songs of Bruce Springsteen*, and "Dead Medicine Snake Woman," *Indian Country Noir*. He also serves as fiction editor for *Space and Time* magazine.

Painfreak started as a (slightly) warped view of an elite club scene and the not-so-elite desires such scenes serve to satisfy. The club has since appeared here and there in my work, sometimes as a kind of gateway to hell, other times a crossroads between worlds and desires. It's not a place where good things happen.

◆ ◆ ◆

FEAR KNOTTED TONY LAMBERT'S STOMACH as Lisa hopped out of the cab that had stopped in front of the closed Brooklyn warehouse half way down the block from his hiding place under the Belt Parkway. Once again, she was going to Painfreak.

Lisa, anonymous in her black rain coat and hat, trotted through the night's light drizzle to the loading docks. Her slim, petite figure danced in and out of the light from the occasional functioning street lamp. He had followed her from her girlfriend's apartment to the floating club's latest secret location a week ago, and had watched her enter every night since then. He had not yet gone in after her. The fear in his stomach warned him not to pursue her any further. Guy had said people didn't always come out from Painfreak.

So far, Lisa had. Of course, Guy had called the both of them tourists, not players, the night seven years ago when he had introduced Tony to the club and they had met Lisa. Players took the real risks. Like Guy, who Painfreak had claimed with AIDS. Tourists just watched, and wished they had the guts to join in the fun. To give themselves up, surrender to their fantasies. Tourists were afraid to go all the way. Guy had been right; Tony and Lisa had given up the club circuit, and Painfreak in particular, after they met. But they were still alive.

Except now Lisa had left him and gone back to Painfreak. Tony didn't know why. They had started living together the night they met, and had married soon afterwards. In the seven years since, Tony had never been tempted to chase after another woman. Lisa had paid her share of the expenses, never complained or mentioned kids. They had lived quietly, with few friends or family to distract them from their private games. And it was the private games, like the milder ones at Painfreak and the scene to which it belonged, that had kept him faithful to Lisa. They always had sex the way Tony liked it. The way he always thought she liked it. Fantasy not quite over the edge. Love with costumes and devices out of video porn and catalogs; games without points; play with roles and body parts. It had been enough for him and, he thought, for her. He had no idea what other desires had gone unfulfilled in Lisa, any more than he knew the source of the fear that kept him from following her in.

He knew only that he was afraid of finding out.

Tony pressed himself against one of the Parkway's steel support beams, as if trying to draw strength from the vibration of cars passing overhead. Cold metal stole the warmth from his hands and face. The sussuration of tires on the wet highway pavement overhead whispered urgently to him as Lisa knocked on the steel rolling gate at one of the bays. She waited, perfectly still, looking down. A side door cracked opened. She held out her hand towards the darkness in the entrance for a moment. She nodded and slipped into the darkness beyond the doorway.

Tony shuffled his feet. Thunder rolled in from Manhattan; lightning flashed. Soon, the drizzle would turn to hard rain. Soon, perhaps tonight, Painfreak would move. Vanish from the city altogether, re-settle for a while in Paris, Bangkok, Berlin, Los Angeles, or some other travellers' city. Guy had said clubs like Painfreak were only an idea that stayed on the mind of a big city for a little while. The various social scenes from which such elite clubs erupted did not have the energy to sustain the kind of activities that went on inside. There were only so many players at any given time, in any given place. Once depleted of energy, the idea simply moved to another mind. Another city.

Lisa might be swept away with the scene and find herself lost in a strange land. Or, driven by whatever pain and desperation that had brought her to the club in the first place, knowing the club might be out of her reach for a long time, she might make the move from tourist to player. And even if she emerged once more, unscathed, and returned tomorrow night to find Painfreak gone, Tony doubted she would come back to him. He would still not know the source of the pain and desperation that had made her suddenly abandon him, refuse any contact with him, and flee to Painfreak. And if he did not find out, then she would be lost to him forever.

The warehouse stood silent in the abandoned business district. No lights escaped its windows. No music, or any other sound, drifted along the street to him. Tony glanced back at his Lexus parked by the service road curb. Water dripped from the highway into shallow pools, splashed on to concrete. The city waited around him, vast and enigmatic, offering neither encouragement nor menace. He had to make his move on his own. Tonight. Or give Lisa up.

He took a step, then another. He left the comforting darkness under the Belt Parkway, crossed the service road, hit the sidewalk at a steady pace. He tried not to think about where he was going, what he was doing. He tried to keep his mind on Lisa: on her strong legs, gentle hands, her wide mouth and full lips, the way she laughed, and sighed, and turned her head away from him after they were both satiated with sex.

Tony hunched his shoulders against the rain and the breeze, which had chilled and grown brisk. Cold rain trickled down his neck. The warehouse loomed over him, but he was still not at the loading docks.

Thinking about her reminded him of the barren apartment that was now his home, the loneliness he felt sleeping alone. He missed her sitting on the sofa, reading, while he watched television. He missed her cleaning up in the kitchen after he cooked their meals, and coming back from the laundry with their clothes bundled in sacks, and pulling out coupons as they shopped in the supermarket. He missed the click of her high heels on ceramic floor tile, the play of muscle under skin when she tightened straps and flicked a crop or whip, the way leather and latex hugged her body. Without Lisa, he was empty. He could not give her up.

He realized suddenly, as he put his foot on the concrete step leading to the loading dock, that it was emptiness driving him into Painfreak.

The hollow feeling within him had been growing since she left him days ago without a word. Each failure to re-establish contact with her had sucked another piece of his inner self away. She had not gone to work in a week; Tony had called her line and waited outside her office building. She had run away from him outside her girlfriend's apartment building, from which he had followed her to Painfreak. She had the doorman warn him the police would be called it he persisted in trying to talk to her.

He wondered how he had coped with the terrible, raw and aching hole at the center of his being before he met her. It was the pain of that emptiness that was overcoming his fear, making him return to Painfreak to find what he had lost.

On the loading docks, Tony took a deep breath and let it out slowly. Though he was afraid, the desperation of pain was stronger. And now he had something to tell Lisa. He understood there was more than fear inside of him. Surely, she could relate to his emptiness. Perhaps, he thought as thunder rumbled nearby and the rain suddenly began to pour, she felt the same way. Empty. Missing something essential. Perhaps he had failed her in some unknown way. Perhaps he had driven her to Painfreak with his failure.

He had words, now, other than the pathetic: please come back, don't leave me. He had questions: are you as empty as I? what are you looking for in this place? how can I fill your emptiness, as you've filled mine?

Fist trembling, Tony knocked on the gate. The steel rattled. A gust swept rain across the open dock. The side door opened, and Tony approached the darkness.

Shadows stirred, then a tall, wide form separated itself from the deeper blackness and blocked the entrance. A thick-necked, bald-headed man crossed his arms over his chest and looked down on Tony.

Tony reached into his pocket for money, then stopped and stared at the doorman. He had a few more scars on his face and hands, and he was dressed in grey and black instead of the more colorful styles fashionable on his first visit, but there was no doubt the doorman was the same as when Guy had brought him in. It did not seem as if he had aged.

Someone reached out and grabbed Tony's right wrist while he was pulling out his money. Strong fingers wrenched his hand back and twisted, paralyzing him in a painful joint lock. Tony knelt to escape the agony of tearing muscles and ligaments, then looked up. A slightly built Asian man dressed in a dark suit and turtleneck regarded him impassively while the doorman, his arms still crossed, stood behind him. Tony's money fluttered away on the breeze.

"Referrals only," the Asian man said softly. "Please leave."

"My wife just went in—" Tony began, but then gasped as the Asian man twisted his hand a fraction more.

Wrong answer, but what was the right one? Guy had led him in the first time, talked to the doorman. No money, but what? The hand. Like Lisa, he had shown the doorman his hand. There had been a hand stamp, with invisible ink, to allow patrons to leave and return the same night. Both Guy and Tony had been stamped, but that was so many years ago. Stupid to even think—

"Been here, Guy brought me, long time . . ."

The Asian man released him, and the doorman gently helped him to his feet. They gazed at the back of his left hand. The faint outline of a bone mark glowed on his skin. Tony searched for the UV lamp, but found only blackness beyond the two men.

The Asian man stepped back while the doorman pressed a stamp down on the back of Tony's left hand. His flesh tingled, and he remembered the sensation from his first visit. The doorman stepped aside and motioned him to enter.

"Always show the mark," the Asian man said reproachfully before melting into the darkness.

Tony nodded and hurried into the warehouse, his heart beating fast and his wrist still throbbing. All those years he had worn Painfreak's mark without knowing it had been burned into his flesh. Lisa had worn it as well. He had no doubt she had known about the invisible bone on her hand, just as she had always known how to find the club. A pair of secrets she had kept from him, like the unfulfilled dreams that haunted her, like the pain that was driving her back to Painfreak. He wondered how many marks she wore on her hand.

The narrow corridor he followed was dimly lit at the opposite end by a single bulb over a tight, winding set of metal stairs that led down. Seeing no other way to go, Tony descended the stairs. Bass pulsed up the stair well from the club's speakers, sending tremors through the steel hand rails. A repetitive, mechanical tune echoed through the wider hallway he found at the bottom of the stairs. He headed towards another distant bulb, and the music became louder, bass beating inside of him like a second heart; cold, synthesized notes drawing his thoughts into an endless, pointless loop. At the steel double doors under the bulb, Tony shook his head, wiped his palms against his thighs, and pushed a heavy door.

The music washed over him like a cold wave of water. Something in the music, like the combination of electricity crackling and a faint feedback whine, made the short hairs on the back of his neck stand on end. Things had changed since his last visit. The music was different, for one thing. And he didn't remember seeing so many cages.

Seven years was too long away from Painfreak to return.

Tony walked to the long bar—battered tables of different heights and widths set end to end, behind which two naked barkeepers patrolled—and found an empty storage drum to sit on. Something whimpered inside the drum as his weight made the walls pop. He shifted uneasily on the warm metal. Nails or claws scratched feebly at the barrel walls. A new variation in Painfreak's perversions, he decided.

The male barkeeper came to him and set down a tall styrofoam cup of what looked like frothy fruit punch. Tony reached into his pocket and remembered he had lost his money. He turned to hold his empty hands up in a gesture of apology. The barkeeper shook his head, wiped his palms together in a gesture of dismissal and moved away. Tony didn't remember paying for any drinks the last time, either.

He took a careful sip of the concoction, aware from news reports that drugs might have been mixed in with the punch. The sweet scent of tropical fruit masked for a moment the warehouse basement's stale odors. Tangy flavors danced on his tongue, before a slightly bitter aftertaste and a spot of cold numbness told him there was a potent spell hiding behind the drink's seductive enticement. Shaking his head, he put the cup down. Cocaine had been the drug of choice in his day, when things had seemed simpler.

Tony scanned the bodies jumping, gyrating, hurling, convulsing spasmodically on the dance floor. In single cages suspended at varying heights from the ceiling, naked women and men, some locked two and three to a cage, writhed and sweated and rattled the bars to their prisons. Colored lights flashed stroboscopically over the crowd, illuminating for an instant individual faces contorted by ecstasy. He was not surprised Lisa was not among them. They were both too old for this nonsense. How could Lisa stand it? Over thirty, now, and slowing down, neither one of them had the energy or the stamina anymore to throw themselves into such a bacchanal. In fact, meeting each other had been a graceful means of exiting the world of clubs and scenes and parties for both of them. Was it the adventurousness of youth that she missed? The daring? Was she trying to recapture the feeling that came from being young and living life on the edge? His appetites were no longer as keen or as sharp.

Watching the frantic motions of the dancers and the twisting cages, he understood that now more than ever he had limits. He did not want to abandon himself to music screaming around him or drugs humming from within, or join in tired, panting games that tried to capture dreams of sex and power and life and death. He did not want to dance on the edge. He wanted only Lisa.

The emptiness twisted inside of him as he imagined her as weary of the scene as he was, but wanting something else, something more. His grip on the cup tightened as he imagined her feeling that she had made the wrong choice in leaving with him that night, that she should have stayed, and gone deeper into Painfreak. He shut his eyes against the moment's vertigo when he imagined her needing to go over the edge, to fall into the emptiness. To enter Painfreak and never come out.

Without thinking, he took a long swallow from the cup, then quickly put it down when he realized what he was doing. He wiped froth from his lips and pushed the cup away. When he looked around, he noticed an older couple standing against the wall, watching him. They were both stout, dressed in formal evening wear, and glittering with jewelry. The woman smiled and nodded to him, a hungry glint in her eye.

Tony remembered seeing their kind the last time. They were not tourists or players, Guy had said when Tony asked about the ones who looked so completely out of place in the club. They were the ones who paid the bills, made the arrangements, worked the bureaucratic magic that enabled Painfreak to appear and disappear without a trace. They were the part of the urban mind that sensed the need for Painfreak in the fabric of the city's life. They did more than just make arrangements and watch; they filled their own emptiness when others danced on and over the edge. They fed, and when there was nothing more to feed on, they arranged for Painfreak to move on.

More and more, Tony remembered why he had abandoned the scene. He shuddered and looked away.

And found Lisa.

He saw brown hair cut short, a head bobbing up and down in a familiar rhythm, a quick profile that showed the long line of the forehead and nose. Lisa, slicing through the crowd, heading towards a door on the other side of the club floor.

Tony was up and on his feet, shouting her name. The music drowned his voice. Lisa vanished for a moment and he pushed his way through the dancers, frantically searching for her. He caught a glimpse of the older couple standing against the wall; they were laughing and talking to another elderly pair while pointing in his direction.

Someone who might have been Lisa went through the door. Tony staggered as a teenaged girl slammed her body into his back. Her raw-edged howl bored through his mind before hands dragged her back into the dancing pack, lifted her into the air, and carried her to the center of the floor. Tony cast a final quick glance for Lisa, then went through the door.

He passed through a series of sound baffles made of strips of plastic and material hanging from ceiling pipes. He emerged into a darkened cavern lit by hazy fires. Tony froze, looked up, expecting to see stars through the thin smoke. Street grating set into the vaulted ceiling reassured him he had not been transported to some alien world. The place must have been a municipal storage depot at one time, like the ones inside bridge supports and off subway tunnels. Abandoned, the cavern had been transformed into an incubator for Painfreak's more serious games.

Tony coughed from the smoke tainted air, and he massaged a tearing eye. The music was absent; in its place, human voices cried out, wailed, shouted, screamed, singly and in small groups. Their rhythms were random, the volume nowhere near as high as in the club's dancing area. Other noises mingled with the voices; metal grinding on metal, chains rattling, water splashing, the hiss of escaping gases, the soft thump of crashing bodies, wood splintering. Or bone. The sounds chilled him, though the cavern was hot and stuffy.

A few people ran past him, their naked feet slapping on the concrete floor. They faded quickly into the gloom, but he had seen enough to know none of them had been Lisa. Tony began trotting to the nearest fire.

He had almost reached the flames when he became aware of someone running alongside of him. Startled, he turned, anticipating seeing Lisa.

The tall, thin man was naked, and his long, white hair trailed behind him as he kept pace with Tony. His face was bony, beardless, and his eyes were black in the dim, flickering light. He smiled, acknowledging his discovery. "I never had the chance to show you the back rooms," the man said, and his smile broadened. "You and Lisa hit it off so fast the first time you came here."

It wasn't Guy. Guy was dead. The toothy smile was his, as was the jutting jaw and the body that had been flesh draped over bones even before AIDS claimed it. The man's voice sounded like Guy's, sarcastic and dry, on the edge of a caustic observation. But it couldn't be Guy. The cavern spun once around Tony, and he nearly fell.

Tony stopped beyond the fire's inner circle of light, and the man coasted to a stop a few steps later. They faced each other, the man putting his hands on his hips. Through his body, Tony could see the flames jump as if through a translucent curtain.

"See anything you like, sailor boy?" The man wiggled his hips.

"Who the fuck are you?" Not believing, never, it wasn't possible.

The man pouted. "I could understand you forgetting me if we'd fucked, Tony. But damn, after two years of rooming together, I figured the sexual tension between us would've made me memorable." The man exploded into hysterical laughter, holding his arms across his stomach and stamping a foot repeatedly. "Nothing like unrequited lust to bring back the dead," he said after catching his breath, and laughed again.

Tony circled around the man and approached the fire. It was Guy. Alive, or dead, but still Guy. Not possible, but real. Suddenly, the world did not feel so solid or tangible.

"College was a long time ago," Tony said, measuring his words carefully. He glanced at the figures at the periphery of the fire's light, trying to deny the fact that he was talking to Guy as he searched for Lisa.

"Oh, please, stop acting like a tourist bitch," Guy said, his good humor gaining an angry edge. "I'm the fucker that's dead, asshole."

Tony wandered to the other side of the fire, trying to put distance between himself and the apparition. Guy strolled languidly around the fire after him. Tony glanced at the cavern entrance, a distant grey splotch in the darkness. He thought of emptiness, and Lisa.

"I'm sorry about what happened to you, Guy." Was he really talking to a ghost? "But I'm here looking for Lisa." Tony started turning away, desperately pushing the idea of Guy, of talking to a ghost, out of his mind. Lisa. He was after Lisa. That was his anchor to what was real.

"You always were looking for a bitch, Tony," Guy said in a mocking tone. "That's why you liked rooming with me. Didn't give a shit about what the guys said. I was a good bitch to you, even if you never touched me, even if you never let me touch you. And I made your other bitches feel good when they came over. Mister sensitive and self-confident, so masculine you could relate to a homosexual," he said, rolling his eyes, shoulders, hips, and snaking his arms up and down, "and not feel threatened. Ooooo, they really ate it up, didn't they?"

Tony's face flushed, and he turned back quickly as a flash of anger washed over his fear. "Why don't you spare me the helpless faggot routine, Guy."

"And if they freaked when they met me, you knew they weren't going to be any fun, right? Too uptight and serious. They'd start in on your image and reputation, like I was going to drag the both of you into a social gutter. And I would've, too." Guy laughed, but kept his gaze fixed on Tony. "No, you liked the ones who asked if you ever watched me have sex with my lovers, who were curious about how gays did it, who'd listen to you talk about leather and cock rings and fist fucking."

Tony jabbed a finger at Guy. "I used you, and you used me. You liked it when your little studs played seduction games with me, or when the two of you sat back and made fun of me while I was in the house. And you knew things were wrong when your prick got jealous and macho around me. You didn't mind it when I got some of those wackos off your tail, either."

"You know how I love it when you get angry, Tony. Sure you don't want to find out what the real thing's all about?"

"Go fuck yourself."

"Only as a last resort." Guy waited a moment, then smiled. "Just like old times, right?"

Tony's anger evaporated. Guy was right; he had fallen right into a petty argument they had re-hashed hundreds times, a standard eruption of the pent-up frustrations that built whenever two people chose to live together. Only now he was arguing with a ghost. His fear returned, stronger than before. To fight it he had to close his eyes and picture Lisa, on his bed, waiting for him with a seductive smile. He had gone too far to run away. He was too close to her to give up, just because a ghost from his past chose to haunt him in Painfreak.

His fear would not go away.

Drugs. Hallucinogens in the drink, in the smoke from the fires, giving life to memories brought up by his return to Painfreak. A bad trip.

Reason calmed his fear to a manageable level. He took a deep breath, let it out slowly. He could handle what was going on. It wasn't real. Just play along, he told himself. Remember Lisa.

"What a pair of predators we were, Tony," Guy said, stepping to the fire light's edge and sitting cross-legged on the floor. "To tell you the truth, I can't even give myself a good fuck anymore. Why don't you sit for a while and help bring back the good times? It's the only way I can get off nowadays."

"I can't," said Tony. "Lisa left me, came here. She's looking for something, I guess, but I need her. I have to find her, make her come back."

Guy shook his head from side to side. "I know where she went. I can lead you to her, if you sit with me for a few minutes. That's not too much of a price to pay, is it?"

Tony hesitated. He listened to the sounds, stared into the darkness between the fires. There were exits at the far end of the cavern, and Tony imagined a network of tunnels spreading out under Brooklyn and the rest of the city. Lisa could be anywhere. Real, or unreal, there was a chance this vision of Guy might help.

He sat down next to his old roommate.

"You look worse than a tourist, Tony," said Guy, with a touch of sadness. "You look like prey. What happened to you?"

Tony sighed and passed a hand over his face. His palm and fingertips came away slick with grimy sweat.

"Please, don't tell me," Guy continued, breaking into a chuckle. "Please don't tell me you fell in love."

"Not quite. Not in love. But I fell into something." He searched for words to capture what he had with Lisa. "Safety, companionship. Maybe I just fell into sex. But there's nothing now, there's just emptiness."

"That's all there ever is, especially for people like us. You just don't realize it. You don't know the emptiness, how deep it runs. That's why you never made the move to being a real player. But don't feel bad. Even I didn't understand the emptiness completely when I was alive, and I was a player there, towards the end. We thought that empty feeling we had was a hunger for something other people could give us. It didn't bother us most of the time 'cause we thought we were filling ourselves up every time we came. What a pair of sharks we were, cruising our own little scenes. You know what it was that let us live so well together? We were the same kind of people underneath all the bullshit. Predators. We went after the same kind of people. Hollow little nobodies who didn't know their asses from their pricks, or cunts. But the beauty of us being together was that we had our own little territories. You went after the cunts, and I went after the pricks. Tell me about those times, Tony. I want to remember, I want the details. There's nothing inside of me anymore. No feelings, no memories. It's all shadows and emptiness."

Guy stared at him without blinking, as if ghosts forgot to blink. His mouth hung open, his hands lay in his lap, palms up. He looked like a child waiting to be fed.

Tony closed his eyes and trawled for memories, eager to put Guy to rest. The specter's talk of emptiness and predators had only made his own need for Lisa stronger. And if this ghost could not help him find her, at least its guilty presence would not distract him while he caught up to Lisa and tried to win her back.

Names from his own adventures as well as Guy's returned to him, and their faces. Anne, Shanelle, Kiko. Thurman, George, Larry. Episodes he hadn't thought about in years came back: sex on the dorm roof, in the closet while others listened and commented outside, using the early model video recorders the college owned. There were the games of humiliation, the games of pain, and the entertainments in costume. Simple and complex, he had repeated them all with Lisa. But he had discovered them first with the disposable partners he and Guy had enjoyed. He began to talk, and as the memories rushed out Tony opened his eyes and looked up, letting the words flow, the past catching up to him.

And as the past flooded him, the darkness beyond the fire seemed to lighten. He began to see what was happening between the fires. He looked away, at first. He spoke quickly, felt as if he were babbling, but Guy did not interrupt or ask him to be clearer, only sat and watched him with his blank expression, his dull, lifeless eyes. The more he talked, the clearer the air became, until he could not help but see the expression on the face of the squirming woman being hauled by giggling men up to the ceiling on a hook and length of chain; until he could see the sweat running down the body of the man suspended at an angle by his outstretched arms and legs, desperately thrusting his erect penis into a fat, laughing woman dancing wildly to the electronic howl of a band that had just started playing; until he could see the broken bones pushing against muscle and skin, warping the smooth lines of the bodies of the two wrestlers fighting and screaming in a pool of water to the cheers and jeers of a few people standing near.

Blood spurted from a nearby atrocity and sprayed across his face, tickling his lips. Shocked, he raised his arm to wipe the blood away, to spit and rub his skin and shield his face from any more splattering. A sudden impulse made him stop. The blood was hot on his flesh, like Lisa's sweat mingling with his own when they made love. His tongue darted out like a snake's, licked his lips as he would Lisa's body. He tasted coppery saltiness, then swallowed. Surprised by his act, he shuddered. The emptiness within him yawned, threatened to take him. Expecting a surge of fear, he was even more surprised when he became excited by what he had done. His erection pressed against his pants' zipper, as if he had just heard the click of Lisa's heels on ceramic tile.

Blood. He worried for a moment that it was contaminated, tainted by Death. Death's blood. He thought of Guy, dead, a ghost, and of the times he had given in to Guy's nagging and participated in his sex games by disinterestedly watching him with his lover. Kissing, stroking, mouthing, they had ended by swallowing each other's cum.

An electric shock of pleasure passed through him as he described the scene he had just remembered to Guy. He put himself in Guy's place, and in the scene his lover was not another man, but Death. Death's bloody cum was on his lips, in his mouth, in him.

The stream of his words faltered, his memories stumbled over one another. The emptiness that had driven him to follow Lisa into Painfreak blossomed with the promise of secret fulfillment. He saw clearly into the void around which he had lived his entire life. The games, the costumes, the mix of pain and pleasure he had pursued with such desperation were suddenly nothing more than shimmering veils hiding his true desire. He did not want to fill the emptiness with sex. He did not want to master, or be mastered by, pleasure and pain. He did not want to feed the hollow hunger with experience, sensation, life. He wanted to surrender to the emptiness. He wanted to be consumed by Death.

Tony stopped talking. Moments later, the electronic howl of music changed, became louder, erupted with sudden energy as if the band had found its groove. A roar like a raging beast echoed through the cavern, deep and raw and edged with the ragged wail of electric guitars. Buried in the roar like a dim heartbeat was the frantic pulsing of drums and bass. Feedback screeched, pierced ear and mind and thought. Tony doubled over in pain, pressing his palms to his ears. Through tears, he saw the elderly couple nearby, pointing to him and laughing. They looked away. He followed their gaze to a crude cage construction surrounded by a frenetic mob trying to tear down the walls to reach the band playing within.

Tony got up, but the music kept him hunched over. Had Lisa wanted to play in a band? Had that been her fantasy? The band members were shadow forms prancing and miming and sawing the air with their instruments, lost in the passion of the moment. He had no idea if she was among them, or their audience. He took a step towards the cage.

A cage wall fell, bringing down one musician. The mob spilled into the stage space as the other walls collapsed. One by one, the instruments died. Last to go was the pulsing bass, quivering with a life of its own before drowning in the squeals and cries of the mob fighting for any morsel of meat.

He heard bones crack, flesh tear.

"Beautiful, isn't it?" Guy said, standing beside him and looking at the orgy. "It's all so . . . romantic, don't you think? Art and death and, hell, even audience participation." He giggled.

Tony took another step towards the mob, then stopped when he felt Guy's touch on his arm. It was not a solid touch; Guy's fingers felt like a cold breeze blowing against his skin.

"She's not there," he said, suddenly serious. "That's not her game."

"What is?" Tony asked.

"Is that what you want to know? Or do you want to find out what yours is? I can show you that, too." He stroked Tony's arm, and the cold tightened his skin, seemed to burn in the bone of his arm. "Want to be a player, Tony?"

Tony groaned as the emptiness reached for him. He wanted it, he wanted Lisa. "Lisa," he croaked, trying to hang on to the crumbling edifice of his past desires and pleasures while his future called to him.

Guy tsked. "Well, you never really were the truly adventurous type, Tony. You would never have found Painfreak on your own. Not like Lisa. She's been on the scene since she was fifteen. She never told you? I used to see her around, when I was still around. Surprised the hell out of me when she latched on to you. Last chance romance, I think. One final try at a normal life with a guy who could give her at least a little action. Oh, what would my old therapist say? An abused child, obviously. Running away from something terrible, running back into it from the long way around. Dear, dear, the story of all our lives, I'm sure."

Tony pulled his arm away. "Fuck you."

Guy came up next to Tony, careful not to touch him. "Say something like that again," he whispered into Tony's ear, "and it might come true."

Tony stepped back and glanced to his left and right, looking for a direction to walk in. He shivered from the cold Guy had brought with him, and the cold in his words.

"No? Turned down again? Right. I really tried to seduce you once, didn't I? After we graduated?"

"You tried to move in with me when I got my own place," Tony replied. He remembered the panic in Guy's voice as he had offered himself, promised to do whatever Tony wanted, just so they could continue being together, continue playing their games. Fear had leaked from every pore in his body, as raw and powerful as Tony's own when Lisa left him. Graduation, expectations of the adult world, Tony moving out had all sharpened the edges to Guy's panic. "I kicked you back into the elevator," Tony continued. He had had his own panic, his own burgeoning emptiness, to deal with. "To make up, you took me out to Painfreak."

"My shrink'd say that was a very hostile move. Couldn't get to you, so I brought you here for Painfreak to seduce you. Damn, but I wish I could remember that elevator scene. I wonder what I used on you. No, no, don't tell me. Imagining it will entertain me to no end, at least until your next visit. Maybe then I'll ask you to tell me about it."

"I'm never coming back here after I get Lisa out."

"Of course you'll be back. What else are you going do when Lisa's gone?"

Tony recoiled, looked away from Guy. He moved off in a random direction, searched out the next fire, headed for its flames. Guy caught his arm, and the cold staggered Tony. Painfreak's bone mark glowed on Tony's hand.

"Don't go off half-cocked, lover. You'll miss her moment as a player. Here, let me show you."

Guy pulled on Tony's arm, dragged him past women pounding on the bodies of men stretched out and tied down to the floor with wild, dancing steps; past a woman bound, blind, gagged, being raped by another woman with a dildo strapped across her sex; past men wrestling one another in shallow pits, breaking each other's limbs, biting off pieces of flesh, licking the blood spilling from their mouths; past a man with a bloody machete across his stomach, reclining among the severed heads of women and busying himself with pulling out the tongue from one head's mouth and running her blue lips across his skin.

Lisa was not among any of the women.

Guy stopped before another pit, but held fast to Tony's arm. Below, two naked women approached a nude fat man whose spread-eagled limbs were held fast by manacles to stakes. One woman sat behind his head and secured it between her thighs. Her leg muscles bulged as she applied pressure, and he twitched and choked as his eyes widened. The other woman settled herself on his face, covered it completely, and began to move her hips.

"Lisa," Tony whispered. He leaned forward, but Guy's cold grip kept him frozen in place.

Lisa looked up as her hands massaged her breasts and she thrust her hips harder into the face trapped under her. Her eyes saw through Tony, as if he were as much a ghost as Guy. Sweat filmed her body. A smile, sweet and self-involved, danced across her lips. The fat man's body jerked, spasmed. His hands grasped at something elusive in the air. His back arched and a desperate, muffled moan escaped from the pit. Lisa threw her head back, gasped. The fat man collapsed, and his body slackened. Lisa jerked forward and cried out. She slid off the man's face and fell to the ground, eyes closed, smiling to herself. The other woman raised her hips, twisted her legs over until the man's neck cracked, then released him. She moved over Lisa, straddled her, closed her thighs over Lisa's face.

"Lisa," Tony called out. His voice was still a whisper, Guy's hand still served as a cold anchor.

Lisa's hands fluttered in the air. Her legs twitched like caught fish thrown on a dock. The woman bore down, hunched forward, used her hands to keep her thighs pressed closed over Lisa's face. Lisa's struggles weakened until her last feeble movements finally subsided. The woman remained over her, locked in a tight embrace.

"Lisa," Tony cried out as he fell to his knees.

The woman rose, took Lisa by the feet and dragged her up a ramp. She was heading in the direction of the machete man when Tony lost sight of them. He realized then that Guy had released him and had vanished. There was only the cold ache in his bone and muscle to remind him of the ghost's hand.

"Come along, dear," an old woman's voice said behind him. Someone tapped him gently on the shoulder.

"I think you've had enough for one night, young fella," an old man said, slipping his arm under Tony's and helping him to his feet. "Time for you to go home. There's always tomorrow night, you know."

The old, well-dressed couple who had been watching him throughout the evening bracketed him as he stood up. They each hooked an arm around him and helped him walk away from the pit. The woman's diamond bracelet bit into his flesh. Tony felt like a child being taken home from a hard day at the playground by his grandparents. Would there be milk and cookies in the kitchen? Bedtime stories tonight?

Tony tried to remember his grandparents, and found that he could not.

The elderly couple guided him back to the cavern entrance, took him through the sound baffles, helped him maneuver through the dancing crowds in the outer club. At the steel double door entrance to the club, the couple released him.

"You come right back when you're feeling better," the woman said. She smiled, and cracks widened in the caked make-up covering her face.

"We'll be here another couple of nights," said the old man. He patted Tony's shoulder in an amiable, fatherly way. His breath was stale, like the air in a den abandoned by a predator. "Of course, you can always come along when the place moves. There's always a need for help. Lots of turnover, you know."

The couple looked to each other and laughed as they gently pushed him to the doors. Tony leaned against metal, felt it give, and found himself in a hallway under a single bright light bulb.

There was the taste of ash in his mouth as he made his way back to the loading docks. Exhaustion made him rest for a few moments on the stairs, but the faint echo of Painfreak's dance music finally drove him on. He passed no one on his way out to the loading dock, where the rain had stopped and dawn had lightened the sky. The ground was still wet, the air humid. Tony glanced over his shoulder at the warehouse entrance. The two doormen returned his gaze. Behind them, Guy hung upside down, suspended by his feet on a length of chain, swinging back and forth like a clock pendulum.

"Do you feel it?" Guy asked, his voice pitched high, almost hysterical.

And in that moment, the emptiness within him opened up like a bottomless well. Tony felt himself standing by the well, leaning out over the edge, wind whistling by his ears. He licked his lips, searching for the taste of blood. His erection strained as if it wanted to break out of its confines and search for satisfaction.

"You want it?" Guy teased. "Tell me what that's like, to want it. To want the nothingness. The extinction. Tell me first, what that emptiness is like. It's so hard when you're in it to understand. Tell me what the void is like, from the outside. Then tell me what it feels like to want it."

"Tomorrow night," Tony answered, his voice quavering. After you show me the games I'll really like. After I become a player.

"Tomorrow night, sir," the Asian doorman replied, with a slight bow. Guy was gone.

Tony went back to his car and drove home. He did not bother picking up his mail or answering his telephone messages. Though his fear was gone and he was tired, he still had trouble falling asleep. Excitement kept him up, until he began to relax as he gently stroked the back of his left hand with his thumb. Slowly, he fell asleep while caressing Painfreak's invisible marks on his flesh.

Lover Doll

Wayne Allen Sallee

"Lover Doll" was first published in *Little Deaths*, edited by Ellen Datlow and published by TOR in 1994.

Wayne's most recent collection is *Fiends By Torchlight*, which was published by Annihilation Press in 2007, and one of the original stories, "High Moon," will be reprinted in *Best Horror of The 21st Century: The First Decade* (Wicker Park Press). "Rail Rider" appeared in J. N. Williamson's *The Illustrated Masques* (Gauntlet Press), and his novel, *The Holy Terror*, and a collection from 1995, *With Wounds Still Wet*, are available on Kindle (CrossRoads Press). His meta memoir, *Proactive Contrition*, and *Can I End Now?* are both exclusive works published in Germany by Blitz Verlag. He is currently writing a crime novel, *City With No Second Chances*, and a series of dystopian stories with their beginnings set in the recent future fraught of our current political climate. His website is www.wayneallensallee.com and his blog is www.frankenstein1959.blogspot.com.

This is my favorite story in that the first part is almost entirely true, drawn from my childhood in the Humboldt Park neighborhood of Chicago.

◆ ◆ ◆ ◆

SHE IS ASLEEP.

It is Memorial Day 1994, and perhaps it is fitting that I dwell on my past. Our past.

I stare out the window, the one facing east. Where dawn will eventually take away the night with cancerous washes of summer sun and lake breezes. The plasma-coloured digital clock blinks in three-second intervals. It is 4:57 a.m.

Celandine snuggles a little closer to me, caught up in her REM dreams. She tells me that she dreams in black and white. We rent an apartment on Wolcott Street, a common area for gangster films shot here in the forties and fifties. I dream *in colour, and in my dreams, it always seems to be the hours before dawn. Like now. Streets deserted. My mind alert. I can hear my heartbeat in my nostrils, in my ears.*

Celly has the sheets pulled down to her waist. She sleeps in the nude. I wear shorts and an old t-shirt. I hear soft snoring, a peaceful sound. Soft waves hitting the shores of Fullerton Beach.

I look over, recognizing the sound. More nasal than Celly's.

The vestigial twin growing out of my lover's ribcage is the one who is snoring. The gentle sounds bring back memories.

I. 1959 BABIES

The world breaks everyone and afterward many are strong at the broken places—Hemingway

Crystal Street in those days was a world removed from the gang territory it is now. There were no burned-out tenements, no need for orange signs in each window of the three-flats telling passers-by that they were treading through a Neighbourhood Crime Watch Zone. There were social clubs. But we all saw *The Blackboard Jungle* and knew things were on the verge of change.

My parents were living off Crystal and Washtenaw when I was born. It was a Polish neighbourhood, the kind where nobody ever moved. They just died, and after that, their sons and daughters stayed until they married and moved to a bigger house in Bucktown or Logan Square. Or maybe they died as well.

The summer of 1959 was sweltering. I recall hearing this much later in my life from relatives who had gone to the World Series game to see the White Sox. It was ninety-eight degrees on my birthdate, September ninth.

My mother and two of her friends from the radium watch plant she worked at—painting the dials with the luminous ink, in ten-hour shifts—had gone up and down Division and Milwaukee to the shows to get out of the heat that summer. The Banner, The Royal, the Biltmore; they were all air-conditioned.

My mother had to work into her second trimester; back then, my father was pulling in barely enough to feed a family of two working as a security guard at RB's, a now-defunct department store on Milwaukee. I fondly remember getting a Whamm-O Monster Magnet and a Rock-'em Sock-'em Robot from the store in honour of kindergarten graduation.

My father let me pick out whatever I wanted, and by the time I was six, the word monster was embedded in my brain.

My umbilical cord was wrapped around my neck when I was born, and I'm certain my mother's exposure to the radium didn't help. (The factory was eventually closed, after many years of court battles; if you stand on Ogden Avenue overpass, you can still look down and see the ghoulish lime-green glow in those windows that haven't been painted black.)

In September of 1959, my mother and her friends went to the Biltmore on Division to see the premiere of *Ben Hur.* I've been told that she went into labour with me then and there.

The ambulance made it to Lutheran Deaconess in time. When I made my entrance into the world, my face was blue and there were traces of blood coming from my nose and ears. To give you an idea of how limited we were medically just thirty-five years ago, all the doctors could really tell my parents was that I had a degenerative muscle disease caused by trauma to the womb.

My mother blamed herself for many years.

When I was in grade school, one of the class trips was to Ripley's Believe It Or Not Museum in Oldtown, where there was an exhibit of freaks from the Barnum & Bailey circus. Freaks was actually Phineas Barnum's get-rich-quick term. His partner later referred to people like me and Celandine as "human curiosities." Me with my bulging head and wrap-around eyes, Celly with the second head sticking out of her ribcage.

One of the displays was for Tom Thumb. His mother truly believed her son's diminutiveness was caused by grief she held over her puppy drowning while she carried Charlie, the boy's real name. I went home and told my mother this story, how Tom Thumb became rich and married a woman who told him he was just as beautiful as she, so that my mother needn't worry about me.

My mother smiled sadly when I told her this, and now I realize it was because she knew how my adult years would hurt me, and that my coming school years would only foreshadow this hurt. She smiled the way one does when they are recalling that the person they are talking to used to be so young and tiny. The sadness of the first recognition of mortality. My mother expected the worst. And so I would still hear her cry at night.

But the school I went to was Childermas Research, one of the Cook County clinics.

During my first year of classes, I met Celandine Tomei. Some of the other children and their parents whispered about her.

The ages of the children in class varied; some learned slower, others had inhibited body functions and needed to be taught with much patience.

Celly was a 1959 baby, just like me.

She was the first girl I ever saw naked.

Childermas Research was one weird fucking place. You entered this maze of buildings at Eighteenth and Honore, passing a little sliver of what looked like a Philadelphia rowhouse; this building that was the burn ward for the entire county, and the Lighthouse For The Blind. On the northeast horizon, a huge pair of red neon lips, advertising Magikist carpets, beckoned.

The classes of reading and spelling lessons weren't too difficult; our rehab sessions reflected our needs. The therapists were great. Vonnie Llewellyn and Ron Szawlus had the patience of saints, I swear. Rehab mostly consisted of coordination exercises, games to make each person use their right and left sides independently, or in tandem.

What was weird about Childermas was my classmates. Not all of us were allowed out on class trips, like the one to Ripley's. Sometimes I felt as if it was a prison. I was never treated badly, but I felt as if all of us were being manipulated in some way that I could never hope to comprehend.

Juvenile Rehab—where we were—was Room 18, big black numerals on an orange door. Room 20 should have housed the burn ward, but there were people of all ages in there, hooked up to various machines. I heard several orderlies grousing about having to work the Pain Detail, which was kat-corner to Room 20. A blank blue door.

I never saw any of what went on in that long corridor of sub-rooms. But I heard the screams. Several times over the years, I have vomited into my palm or my garbage can, whichever is more convenient, when I recall those damnable, high-pitched, keening screams.

Once it had nothing to do with memories. In a medical magazine, I came across photos of stillborn thalidomide babies like Celandine.

One of these "stillborn" children was nothing more than a nerve column wrapped around bone in the placenta.

I come back into the bedroom, my hands washed fresh. I can still smell the vomit in the faint spring air. May 31st, Chicago's first real breakaway-from-the-throes-of-winter days. It is not a bad smell. It will go away within a few minutes, like when me and Celly were kids and sneaking smokes on the back porch of the Plichtas' two-flat.

Celandine is sleeping soundly. The sun will rise soon, the sky already aqua. Her breasts rise and fall, rise again. The head beneath her left breasts lolls to the side.

As Celandine breathes, the head looks like a buoy bobbing off Fullerton Beach. Its eyes are open, and it is staring at me.

Silently staring.

So many deformities in one classroom. A boy who looked like his skull had been caved in with a lead rod, another with one bug-eye, as if his head was a bubble being blown from a plastic pipe. Many could barely stand. I was able to, but the weight of the excess blood in my brain made my head slump down. My chin often touching my chest, I'd stare up, my eyebrows framing my view, at the lovely Celandine.

There was nothing visibly wrong with her. Compared to the others, at least. Her spine was curved to the right; I heard Ron Szawlus mention that it might eventually realign itself. She always wore billowy, flowered dresses. Of course, this was 1966, and all girls dressed in clothes that covered every possible aspect of their young sexuality, the flowers exuding innocence. These days I see the same patterns on women wearing maternity outfits.

By the middle of 1967 the schedules of many of my classmates changed. Both Celandine and I, as well as several others, had improved enough with our mobility and coordination that we only had to come for therapy three times a month. This would continue until I was thirteen. The therapy offices—a two-flat on Aberdeen—were closer to our respective houses.

Gone were the memories of the boy in the burn ward, the one the nurses in the pain detail talked about. His mother had left him asleep on the top of a coil heater. Instead of doing skin grafts, the doctors had peeled away several additional layers of skin from the boy's buttocks and performed experiments involving the injections of T-lymphocytes.

Gone, too, were the strange people kept in the psychophrenic ward, as I called it then. I now know that Jimmy Dvorak, Frankie Haid, Billy Bierce, and other infamous Chicago killers of recent past were diagnozed as schizophrenics. But this was a word my parents did not know, and I had to make do with phonetics.

I only saw Celandine during therapy classes. Celly went to Wells public school, which was a lot closer to the therapy clinic.

I learned a lot about her. The fact that she was a child of thalidomide, that wonderful sedative that pregnant women were given until 1963, when it was banned. Her mother had been prescribed the brand name Kevadon and was herself eventually diagnozed with peripheral neuritis. Being young, I thought that was really keen. A drug that back-fired. In therapy, Celandine and I both practised the FeldenKrais Method. This was something invented by a former judo instructor to help improve posture and self-image. The latter was something I certainly needed. Celly was getting more beautiful by the day. I would long for the first, second, and fourth Wednesday of every month that summer. I found out that her mother was into holistic therapy, and that she gave Celly daily injections of aconite, which was really wolfsbane, no shit, and this presumably acted as an adjuvant of her "Vagus nerve," which was an ideal pain inhibitor. I often wondered later how much pain she had actually been in. Pretty, but still wearing frilly dresses instead of shorts and a blouse like most everybody else in Wicker Park, even the fattest of the girls.

And she liked me a whole lot.

My mother was glad that I had found a friendship in Celandine Tomei. Thinking back on it, I don't recall that they ever met during our days at Childermas. Celly and I would often walk hand in hand through Humboldt Park. She and her mother lived on Division and Hermitage, right next door to a holistic healing house that was usually tenanted by beat poets and abstract artists. Celly's father, before he died, worked as a steerer, someone who brought in potential poker players and gamers, at Mania's Lucky Stop Inn, a Polish bar on the other side of their building.

The first time I went over to Celly's house, I saw a framed quote, this being long before the cutesy arts-and-crafts-stitched logos. The bromide, in simple block letters, read:

HEALTH AND ILLNESS CAN BE
REPRESENTED BY A CONTINUUM.

Celly showed me her mother's bookshelves, Jan Smut's *Holism and Evolution*, Oliver Wendell Holmes's *Homeopathy and Its Kindred Delusions*, there were others. I remember seeing a book on EDTA. Not knowing what it meant, I thumbed through it. The letters stood for ethylene tetra-acetic acid. There were pictures in the book of dwarf-like skeletons and bodies in foetal positions. I read that EDTA chelated the calcium lost in body waste. I started to ask Mrs. Tomei what this meant, as she had walked into the room with cherry Kool-Aid, but she quickly took the book away, putting it up out of reach of Celly and me.

I stayed late that evening, because my mother was putting in over-time at the radium plant. I was supposed to be home before dark, but she wasn't able to make any calls, and I knew that crazy Anna Banana, the downstairs neighbour who was supposed to check on me, was at the horse track in Cicero.

We watched Walter Cronkite on the black-and-white blond-coloured Philco, talking very seriously about the latest Mercury space flight. And *that's* the *way it was*, July four*teenth*, 1967. We changed channels and watched *I Dream of Jeannie* and *Batman*. Catwoman shot the Dynamic Duo with sedated darts. Robin said "Holy D'Artagnan," and they both collapsed. It was Julie Newmar as Catwoman. The television picture wasn't snowy like our own, the Tomeis had ordered a Channel-Master from New York state (the only place that was marketing them), the first ones in the neighbourhood to have one, I think. You see them all over now; they look like double-sided rakes up next to the chimneys.

That night, after getting a ride home from Mrs. Tomei in their 1956 Olds Holiday, I had my first adult dream. It was of an older, fuller Cel-andine in the Catwoman outfit. My underwear was wet and it was hard to pee that morning. I felt guilty. I did not remember the dream itself until early that afternoon, then I kind of understood.

I went to see Celly that same day, the afternoon after my dream. Celly suggested that we play doctor. Her mother was out shopping at RB's, and I wondered if she would run into my father and spend extra time gossiping. We went into the back sitting room, the drapes flutter-ing every time the Paulina Street elevated thundered by like destiny.

Celly asked me if I was going to be afraid. I said of *what*, getting caught? She said no, and looked away.

I remember it all so clearly. The Westclox ticking a tattoo across the room, both of us bursting with fear and anticipation. We knew we'd never do anything more that day but look at each other naked. Celly's mother had left a package of Hit Parade cigarettes lying atop the bureau. I never had seen her smoke, and thought that the cigarettes were for her male visitors.

Celly was barefoot, still wearing the flowered dress. I moved forward to take the shoulder straps in my sweaty hands.

Something kicked me. It wasn't Celandine, unless she was able to lift up her leg double-jointed and plant one right in my thigh. She backed away quickly.

I was concerned that she had changed her mind. Another train went by and I started thinking about the time. I told her not to worry.

Celandine said that she would take the dress off herself.

"Close your eyes," she said. When I had them firmly shut, I heard her whisper, "You know I've never made fun of your head or eyes."

I opened my eyes. I thank the lesser gods that my deformity allowed for my eyes to not bug out any more than they already did.

I looked at Celly. She stood away from me, naked, her body hairless. But.

There was a part of a body growing out of her. Like in that book I had been looking at, the one Celly's mom had moved to a higher place on the bookshelf.

I realized that her rib cage was slightly bell-shaped. To accommodate the head that protruded from below the last of the left ribs. Its eyes were closed, peaceful-like, as if in sleep.

But that wasn't all.

Celly had a tiny leg growing out from her pelvic bone; that must have been what had kicked me. From the area around her flat stomach, I could see three webbed fingers.

A thumb with no thumbnail protruded from her navel.

I was only seven and a half, but you learn fast when you don't know what the next guy on the street is going to say or do to you. I told Celly that she looked beautiful, strong not vulnerable. Now I understood the reason for the Bohemian-style dresses. She began crying.

Still dressed, I went forward, carefully kissing her face. She responded in kind. After several minutes, I felt a tugging around my waist. I thought it might have been Celly's hands, working at my pants.

I looked down from the corner of my bigger eye.

The head below Celandine's rib cage was sucking on my shirt, pulling it into its mouth. Chewing on it.

I heard a noise and panicked, thinking the front door had opened. Celandine asked me if I was afraid. I said yes I was, that her mother might catch us.

Celly looked down and said that her mother didn't care that someone might see her this way. In what had to be her own mixed-up way, Mrs. Tomei was evidently proud that Celly was not afraid to show off her body.

When I backed away slightly, the head bobbed up. The eyes stared at me. The mouth did not relinquish my shirt.

* * *

Christ, I've looked up so many medical words in the time I came back to Chicago, to Celly. I tried looking up the phrase "maternal eclampsia" and couldn't locate it anywhere. Finally called the Harold Washington Library, a girl named Colleen told me that it meant that the mother would sometimes bleed to death during childbirth.

Celandine and I remained good friends throughout the next few years. We played doctor several more times when her mother wasn't around.

More often than not, we would just walk around Wicker Park, and I would sometimes, in the steel shadows of the elevated, lift up her dress, reach under and caress the twin's head. In the books about circus freak-shows, they were called "vestigial twins."

What Celandine's mother had was a foetal multiple cyst anomaly.

Nowadays, this is detectable by sonography. So Celly is certainly unique, especially that she lived. And the head was not stillborn.

Celly kept the leg, tiny like a chicken's, strapped around her leg with something along the lines of a Posey gait belt, the kind used to lift patients out of wheelchairs. The fingers were slowly being recalcified into her body, due to the added weight gain of her prepubescent years. Many times, I had read, a vestigial twin never formed because it had actually been recalcified into the stronger twin during the time in the womb.

Ray-Ban invented a pair of wraparound sunglasses about 1970, that fit my eyes perfectly, and Bankers Life Insurance picked up the bill. If I didn't have a full head of blond hair, I might have looked like one of the most intense punkers still visible in the old north side neighbourhoods. I think of all I know now, that I didn't know then. All the medical terms that didn't make a damn bit of difference to me. I loved Celandine Tomei.

You can find Celandine's anomaly, if you wish to call it something safe, under any book that lists Foetal Monozygous Multiple Pregnancy Dysplacentation Effects. In the Washington Library's reference book on birth defects, it says: SEE Also Michelin Baby Syndrome. Page 1433, no shit. Makes me think of John Merrick's disease and how it became known as "elephantitis" because his mother fell in front of an elephant during a parade in the early days of her pregnancy. I wonder if she ever ran into Tom Thumb's mother and swapped bad juju stories.

The head growing out of Celly was part of a foetal cyst that had skeletal dysplasia. Larger effusions of the cyst's organs were beneath Celly's subdermal region around her lower rib cage. Most thalidomide babies born this way had general effusions in the pleural and pericardial regions, that is, the lungs, heart, and spleen, and polyhydramnios may occur. I seem to recall a child at Childermas like this, the disease itself being excess water in the organs.

April, 1968.

Our happiness was short-lived. The spring after we had first seen each other nude, James Earl Ray assassinated Martin Luther King Jr. in Memphis. The neighbourhoods around us were burning to the ground. The biggest gang in the area was the Blackstone Rangers, and they vented their frustrations on the Puerto Ricans who were moving in to the west of us. There were daily rumbles with the Latin Kings.

The Friday that Ricky's Deli, on our corner, was firebombed, my parents broke their lease on the Crystal Street apartment. I had hoped that I would continue to see Celly at rehab classes when this whole thing blew over, but it wasn't to be. My father quit his job at RB's and we moved down to Shelbyville, Kentucky to live with relatives.

Celly and I exchanged letters, and she often wrote how bitter she was at how everyone, even the therapists, looked at her. I told her not to worry. My parents said we'd be moving back to Chicago soon, maybe a nicer neighbourhood around Albany Park.

"Soon" became 1970, and when we returned to the place I was born, I found that the Tomeis had moved. Out of state and somewhere west was all I could find out. I received several letters from Celandine, postmarked Iowa City and Thermopolis, Wyoming. She sounded increasingly depressed, saying how her mother was taking her to a climate that would help her feel more healthy. They might move to Albuquerque.

I watched MASH *and* All In The Family, *saw the Vietnam War end and Nixon resign. Around the time of the fall of Saigon, I received a letter from Celandine's mother in New Mexico. She told me that Celly had left home.*

In her room she found a ticket stub for Denver. She was going after her.

II. ZOMBIE TONGUE

The word freaks . . . sounds like a cry of pain
—Anthony Burgess

"You ain't gotten anything until you had yisself some zombie tongue." Several men on downtown Fremont Street repeated this like a litany the entire first night Norm and I were in Las Vegas.

We had taken a week off from our jobs, working at the Lion's Lair. Norm Brady was a bouncer, I was a disc jockey. Those wraparound Ray-Bans were quite the style now. It was June of 1987, and I had been living in the Denver area almost since I graduated from college six years before.

Viva Las Vegas, Elvis sang back when I was at Childermas with Celandine. *Visa* Las Vegas was more like it. Expensive as shit! Well, the shrimp cups were cheap. Looked like little sea monkeys, I recall David Letterman joking once.

We walked the seedier part of town, thinking our long thoughts and keeping them to ourselves. We were just damn glad to be out of Denver.

The cool neon of The Mint and the Golden Nugget that was so prominent on *Crime Story* were far behind us. Eighth Street was home to a bail bondsman and Ray's Beaver Bag. On Ninth, we saw The Orbit Inn, but couldn't enter because an armless fat man wearing a purple sweatshirt had passed out in the revolving door. No one inside seemed to care. We kept walking, amused at kids pitching pennies between the legs of butt-ugly whores. Looking back towards Glitter Gulch, all we saw was a tiny blob of pink and blue neon. That, and the memory of voices whispering conspiratorially about zombie tongues.

I had a BA in English Literature from the University of Illinois. Tried my hand at Behavioral Sciences, but I couldn't cut it. I guess it was because I still thought of Celandine. I was ten when she left Chicago for points west. I think it was the Holistic Center that told Mrs. Tomei that the drier air might do Celly good, by alleviating stress and "allowing a better view of oneself."

My actual thoughts were that the Tomeis wanted more privacy. The riots weren't just a racial thing. The blacks were hitting on the black handicapped, too. I could understand Josephine Tomei's concerns.

My family surprised me by moving back to the *south*west side of Chicago. Bridgeport, a few blocks from Mayor Daley's home on Emerald. A nice area then, the Stevenson interstate a new and wondrous thing, and most of the blocks filled with squalor had spanking new Tru-Link fences put up courtesy of da Mayor hisself. He did this several years before, because Chicago was going to be portrayed as a lovely town during the 1968 Democratic Convention, for all network television to see.

I had several mementoes of Celly; tactile things, not simply memories of her naked, and of her seeing me in the same way.

We had often exchanged books, and I still had one of her *Happy Hollisters* mysteries. They were on a ranch somewhere, is all I remember.

A menu from Ricky's Deli that we had played connect-the-dots with.

I had felt comfortable on Crystal Street, where we grew up. I realized this walking past the casinos and neon signs. Even in Las Vegas, as in Denver, no one thought of me as being different. Hell, I had both my arms, for chrissakes, and wasn't blocking a revolving door. That's how it was back in the Humboldt Park neighbourhood.

The older Poles liked us—not just *tolerated* us—because they weren't too far removed from the atrocities of Dachau. The kids our age, the normal ones, well, that was an entirely different tune altogether.

To them, we were freaks. There they go, the freaks. Some offered the opinion that my mother had fucked something in the gorilla house at Lincoln Park Zoo. And though Celandine's defects weren't easily apparent, she did have a slight stoop, like the older women who cleaned office buildings in the Loop after the rush hour ended.

The other thing that made Celandine a freak in the eyes of the other kids was that she hung around with me. This was before I got the black sunglasses and I looked like those creatures from Spider County on that *Outer Limits* episode. Celly kissed me in public. Those awkward, pre-adolescent kind where it's like kissing your sister. The saddest memento I had of Celly was a photograph my mother had taken, with white borders and the date printed on the right-hand side. When everyone from St. Fidelus was out on a class trip, my ma took the colour photo of Celly and me in front of the yellow brick entrance. To show off to relatives and coworkers who were never told that I was in actuality enrolled at Childermas. Ever. Always in a real world. James Trainor and Celandine Tomei, February 1967. Here in the real world.

In the real world, I graduated from college and left town. Found a job in a bookstore in Streator, then moved on to Navaoo, near the Mississippi. I was going west, too, you see. One night in the latter town, I came home from my job at the International House of Pancakes to find my place ransacked.

The memories of Celandine gone. Everything else didn't matter. I left the state that night. Carthage, Missouri. Colcord, Oklahoma. Whoever would have me. Not many places would. And the ones that did eventually found excuses. I was The fucking Fugitive, all through the early eighties. Just like in the tv show, I'd have some menial job, be there a few weeks, and then some self-righteous person or group would make up a rumour to get the funny looking bug-eye out of their safe little hamlet.

* * *

Until Denver. It was pure luck that I heard about the ADAPT program for handicapped people while I was passing through Sedalia, Colorado. I don't know why I shucked it for the dj gig; guess I liked the nights better. Denver's compact skyline, the Flatiron Mountains invisible until the grey of false dawn.

Best yet, I found a friend in Norm Brady. I was at the Wax Traxx on Twelfth Avenue in Capitol Hill, hunting down a copy of Robert Mitchum singing "Thunder Road" for one of the bar's theme nights. Norm had retrieved the last 45, seconds before I walked down the aisle. We struck up a conversation about Elvis and actors who should have never recorded albums, all the while walking down Colfax On The Hill. Norm lived in a studio apartment above the Metropolis Café on Logan; I was three blocks over on Galapago. Norm tended bar at a place on Wazee, over near the viaduct, in addition to bouncing at The Lion's Lair.

Living there was the best time of my life. Waking up to those beautiful and hypnotic blue mountains to the west, always covered with snow, even in July. Until we went to Vegas on a whim and I saw what the city and the real world had done to Celandine Tomei.

Our curiosity had gotten the better of us. We had gambled; breaking even, more or less. Neither one of us drank much. Alcohol has adverse effects on my health and I get massive headaches. So our decision was a sober one. A man dressed in lilac, a bargain basement Prince impersonator of the wrong race, told us where to find this . . . zombie tongue.

I was feeling natty; dressed in non-touristy black with an olive green jacket. Thin lapels, flowered tie, but mellowed out with a button of Elvis Presley playing the ukulele in *Blue Hawaii*. Norm was dressed in jeans and a Road Kill Press t-shirt he picked up back in Arvada, at The Little Bookshop of Horrors, topped off with a St. Louis Cardinals baseball cap.

The directions were not that difficult. Maryland Parkway connected with Rue H Street past Eleventh. In the middle of the three-way intersection, cross-hatched in shadows, there was a white building, railroad flat-styled. The logo was a woman in teal wearing a low-brimmed hat.

The name of the place, also in teal script, was BELLADONNA.

Celandine says she doesn't remember much about those days in Vegas. Hell, she doesn't remember much now, with the drugs she's still taking, trying to forget. A staff sergeant at Nellis Air Force Base tipped Celly to a way to make money, the kind of shuck you read in any of the Chicago classifieds. Celly knew that she'd never be working as a waitress in some greasy spoon off Flamingo Road.

The bar catered to those who really wanted a thrill, something different. Something obscene.

Amputees, burn victims. Parading on a stage. I wondered if the armless man propped in that doorway all those months ago ever visited Belladonna's.

Zombie Tongue.

Vegas is like the Miss America pageant. It uses you, and you use it right back.

The building vibrated with the passing of trucks on the parkway overhead. Overhead gels of red and blue, beaded doorways. Flashing squares of soft light on the floor, alternating in chequerboard patterns. Maybe a discotheque in a different time. The décor reminded me of the Go-Go bars in Calumet City, back in Illinois.

The woman on stage was a burn victim; in the light and nicotine haze you couldn't tell unless you were looking up at her. She was devoting most of her time to a gaggle of skeletons at the other end of the bar.

Where we were sitting, a dwarfish woman with hair growing out of a mole in her cheek passed by with an empty potato chip can. Money for the jukebox. The current song was some oldie but goodie from the seventies. "Fool For The City" by Foghat, maybe. Or "Toys In The Attic." Aerosmith always drew their biggest crowds at strip bars. The mole was the size of a .38's exit-wound. The woman blew away the long strands of hair from her mouth before trying to seduce us with a bloated, grey tongue.

It made me think about Celandine. And of myself. Time changes nothing but the contours of our bodies. (The burn victim on stage had no contours at all—we saw that when she moved our way; she was eternally young. A survivor of Vietnam, in fact. Her crotch smooth, like a Barbie doll.)

The hours passed and the drinks took their toll.

I had thought that the term "zombie tongue" was some street phrase for whores, like meth-moxie was anywhere else for drugs. But I couldn't leave. In the middle of a Windows of Whitechapel song—the burn victim grinding her smooth, gashless pelvis against the far wall—I tried loping over to the john. Green shag carpeting covered the walls and ceiling of the rooms down the hall. I was reminded of Elvis's Jungle Room at Graceland, the plushness acting as sound-proofing. I saw the sign marked

ME off to the right.

Near the opposite door, painted black, a tall guy with a shirt that read I LOVE YUMA, ARIZONA came out of the room, nodding his head in a "your turn" gesture. I noticed blood on his lip, purple in the thin track of lighting imbedded in the overhead carpeting. I was ready to go into the bathroom when my eye caught a glimpse of something beyond the still open black door.

A bookcase, and in the wedge of light, the unmistakable—to me, at least—yellow and red binding of a *Happy Hollisters* book. I thought, fuck, no. Squeezing every bit of emotion out of me, I pushed the door open. I saw Celandine.

She was naked and tied down spread-eagled on the bed. Her body was thinner than I might have expected. But I knew it was her, you see, because of the head. Celly's bush had grown up in a thin straight line, like a fuzzy black worm. Her nipples were small and pink. Sure enough, with age, the fingers that had protruded from her stomach had decalcified back into her. Where the small leg had been was a pale nub above the pelvic bone. Maybe it had been sanded smooth.

Celandine looked drugged or weary from crying. I could not look at her. But I found the courage to walk into the room. I looked around the sparse rectangle of living area. Hell, it was a mansion compared to the Cal City titty bars where you fucked the women on the stairwell landings, against the walls like it was Victorian England. If you fucked them in the ass, they spent the few moments reading the new graffiti.

Tubes of salve and Ben-Gay were crafted into strange stick-figures. Pill containers littered the vanity unit like perfume bottles. Tricyclic, anti-depressants like Elavil, stronger shit like Denzatropline. All labeled with a post office box in Groom Lake, Nevada. The doctor's name was unpronounceable. Blank postcards, her own mementoes. Deer feeding near Backbone State Park, Iowa. Thornton's Truckstop Diner (Con Mucho Gusto!) Beaumont, Texas. The Big Chief Hotel in Gila Bend, Arizona. The sun setting over Roswell, New Mexico.

Other, more "grown-up" books: Nelson Algren's *The Man With The Golden Arm*, and Frank Norris's *The Pit*. Theodore Dreiser's *Sister Carrie*, the collected Sherwood Anderson reader. All Chicago authors; Celly never forgot her roots. I saw a small cassette recorder on a table and flipped through the tapes. Came across Elvis's *Jailhouse Rock* soundtrack. Imagined him singing the title song, "You're So Young And Beautiful."

I heard a moan.

It was the head. Mouth open, like a dog begging for a biscuit. The tip of the tongue was bitten off. It *recognized* me. It was *showing* me.

JAILHOUSE ROCK

I ran out the door and into the john, vomit already nearing my teeth. Sweating, numb. And there he was in the doorless stall nearest the entrance, my new friend. The man who had been in Celandine's room before me.

The man with blood on his lip. He smiles then, said how the head felt no pain. He *knew* I knew what he was talking about. Said it was like raping a girl and then killing her after because she knows who you are.

Do the crime without doing the time.

When he smiled a bloody thin-lipped grin and compared it to having your cake and eating it too, hiking up his belt like a *real* man, I hit him. Caught him by surprise. I pummeled him until my knuckles were bloody. Left him face over the chipped porcelain bowl, hair hanging into the water like he had got a swirly.

I walked past the condom machines to the mirror. Took my Ray-Bans off and stared at my bulging face. Beat holy hell out of the mirror, out of my reflection.

But had the common sense to wash my hands and calm down.

Went back to the stage with my hands in my jacket pockets, told Norm I wanted to head back to the Plaza.

The girl dancing on stage as we walked out the door had two mastectomy scars.

That night, I dreamt horrible things, like a guy forced to sleep the night before he is to be strapped down into the electric chair.

I was back at Belladonna's, sitting front centre stage. Celly was dancing, glassy-eyed. Cradling the head as Patsy Cline belted out "I'm Back In Baby's Arms." The crowd going nuts.

Celly snake-dancing to "The Stroll," winnowing across the stage, the head dangling over the edge. Men stuffing dollar bills into its mouth. Celly standing and swinging her head back and forth, the cystic head below flopping like a colostomy bag. Celly oblivious to me, the head the only one recognizing me in the whole place, the whole city, the whole world.

Down on her hands and knees, shoving her ass in someone else's face. Inching down the stage, flashing red, blue, red, orange. Her nipples tiny points. Celandine's pussy seemingly enormous in the shadow of her body. The stage covered with wadded bills, spat out of the head's mouth.

The head with a mind of its own, making Celly move towards me.

So that the zombie tongue could lick the dried blood from my knuckles.

I woke up to find it was almost two in the afternoon. Norm was watching CNN. He told me that it was about time I got up, he'd been awake when I got back.

I asked him what the hell he was talking about.

He told me that halfway back to the Plaza, I got out of the cab and said I wanted to go back to Belladonna's. Then he told me to go do something about my breath.

We got back to Denver okay. Part of me wanted to go back to Vegas, to Celly. But I was embarrassed, shocked, even sickened at the depths I had lowered myself to. I took some spare Tegretol for my headaches. I tried for months to forget what I had seen at Belladonna's.

I watched the WGN superstation for Chicago news after the Cubs and Bulls games. Read about The Painkiller, killing wheelchair victims in the Loop back in Chicago in late '88, and of Richard Speck (still unrepentant) dying a day before his fiftieth birthday, bloated from distended bowel, although the cause of death was listed as emphysema, in December 1991. Everyone felt cheated that the drifter who had mutilated eight nurses in 1966—around the time Celly and I were getting to know each other better—got off so easily.

Norm Brady and I hung around The Lion's Lair in the evenings and I spent my days rereading old medical textbooks from the Denver Library on Seventeenth. I also read the *Rocky Mountain News*, my native city showing up increasingly as the civil war in the former nation of Yugoslavia continued unabated. My home town was indeed a melting pot, much of the coverage came from the Chicago wire services. Items about the Midwest in general, the Mississippi flooding from the Quad Cities to St. Louis, a crazed gunman killing patrons at a Kenosha, Wisconsin restaurant. A skinhead shooting a plastic surgeon who "dared" change someone's Aryan features; what would the neo-Nazi think of myself or Celly?

I dreamt about hot neon the colour of clotted blood, of deformed faces that looked as if they had been squeezed between unrelenting elevator doors. Sometimes I would realize that I had been awake and staring into a mirror.

Occasionally, I would come across copies of *The Chicago Tribune* at the library. Usually they only carried West Coast papers like the *Seattle Intelligencer* or the *Vallejo Vestry*.

One day six months ago, I read of a scandal involving a prominent Chicago network newswoman. Rumours circulated of a lesbian affair with a woman with an acardiac twin. This particular shit was slung because the woman was up for a national news desk spot. But, still. I flew back on United to see if the Tomeis were back in town.

Josephine and Celandine had been back in Chicago since the summer of 1991. Someone besides me had seen her in Vegas and knew an even better way to use her. A local writer exploited her for shock value in one of his novels, saying that she had become one of the highest paid call girls in the city, and that the head under the ribcage was dead and often mutilated.

The guy in Vegas was right. The head feels no pain.

But that doesn't mean you don't have to fix it.

She is asleep.

I stare out the window, the one facing east. Josephine Tomei died this past Christmas. It is just me and Celandine. I called Norm and told him I had family matters to take care of here.

I left things open.

She is asleep because she still is taking the drugs that she started on in Vegas. The only reason she hasn't lost all of her self-esteem. I swear I will get her straight. It is 5:30 and the sun is coming up.

I play the Elvis soundtrack to Jailhouse Rock. "I Wanna Be Free"; the title song. Finally, "Lover Doll."

I listen to the younger, pre-bloat King of Rock 'n Roll, singing about how he loves his lover doll madly.

I pull the sheets gently away from Celandine's drugged form. The head is still watching me. Dawn's light slashes a diagonal across Celly's black pubic hair. I pull off my shorts.

I reach forward, kissing Celly's closed mouth. It doesn't open. I lick her breast, the left one, then the right.

I reach into her cunt with my hand, one finger at a time. I can put three fingers in comfortably. She does not respond. My dick is still limp.

". . . let me be your lover boy . . ."

I take my fingers out of Celandine and stroke the head's hair. Its mouth opens. The eyes have a certain curiosity.

I swear I will get Celly off the drugs, get our lives together. Take her back to Denver with me.

I move towards the head, my dick growing to half-mast. There is early morning traffic outside. In the real world. Our real world.

Straddling Celly's sleeping body in a half-assed way, one foot on the ground, the other leg's knee near her armpit. Positioning myself over the head. Guiding my dick into its mouth.

It is not hard to believe that it begins sucking.

(For Denise Szostak)

The Spirit Wolves

Charlee Jacob

"The Spirit Wolves" was first published in *Into the Darkness* #4, 1995.

Charlee Jacob has published in the horror field for twenty years. Once a prolific writer, her disabilities and multitude of meds have forced her to stop writing. For a bibliography of her work, see her website at charleejacob.com

◆ ◆ ◆ ◆

FIVE YEARS AGO WHEN MILO was only thirteen he cut his mother's old bear rug into strips and then sewed these pieces to his flesh. It had taken the better part of one night of suppressing his cries of pain as he threaded the needle time and again with thick woolen thread and pushed it through in loop after loop to secure the fur to his body. It had become quite slippery with his blood but this only served to give it and him a magical sheen when he looked into the mirror afterward.

I have entered the pelt of an animal.

I have become the beast.

Then he ran away to join Fatima's Freak Tent outside the city limits. All the comely mutant ladies welcomed him, clucking and tittering with a singsong babble of delight. They touched him with their stumps and flippers, ran their bearded cheeks across his beardless ones, held fast his gasping face between their breasts that were either skeletal or mammoth mounds of perfumed fat. They cooed over Milo's ruined flesh and counterfeit hide, crawling around him on all fours, proclaiming,

"You are the king of the wolves!"

Then his mother came to drive him home before her with a stick, haranguing him every mile of the way.

If only she'd beaten him with her own hands, scratched at him until he bled. But she never touched him.

Had she ever touched him? Milo couldn't remember the feel of her hands ever. She pushed food at him, had even pushed the bottle toward him when he was a baby. Had left him, naked for days at a time, in his own excrement, before finally hosing him down.

But she must have touched him at some time. To teach him to walk, to take care of himself so that she wouldn't have to make contact. He didn't remember.

Had he wanted to be an animal? He'd seen the tantalizing women of Fatima's and he needed to be touched. He had always been too perfect. Milo wasn't only a handsome boy, he was a flawless beauty. It might have made him popular in his exquisiteness if it hadn't been such a dark beauty, so keenly edged that he seemed to have been carved from dark bone. And it would likely have helped his cause if he'd been willing to speak to people. But Milo mostly growled at folks, deep within his velvet throat like a beast. Most people around probably didn't know he could talk. And he never talked to his mother. What would he say if he did? Touch me! Hold me? Use your fists and teeth until I am raw with you.

His mother hissed, "Devilchild."

She'd left him on a dozen different doorsteps when he was an infant but the sheriff had always made her claim him. Why hadn't she left him at Fatima's then where he'd been so immediately accepted—even if he'd had to alter himself to do so? Was it because she'd become accustomed to brutalizing him from a distance? Had this granted her an outlet and an excuse for the ruin her own life had become?

Milo sat crosslegged before the mirror, butt naked on the cold floor, watching as his punctured skin slowly healed without scarring. No, he was too gorgeous for the holes to stay cut into his flesh. He wished the marks had remained, that he was pocked forever, for perfection marked him as being apart from all else. It made him furious, sitting there scratching himself, raking the elegant half-moons of his nails over his arms and face, desperate for touch, for sensation. Sometimes the need to be handled grew so frantic that mauling became a parody of contact. He dreamed of being torn apart by animals and that had to be a symbol of closeness burned in effigy. He healed, every time. The king of the wolves slunk ignominiously from Milo's sad life.

Fatima's special ladies turned away from him without recognizing him at all when his Uncle Rabe treated him to the carnival a few months later. They paraded their luscious deformities on the simple, ramshackle stage, shaking jelly mounds of flab or being wheeled on geek carts or doing perverse double-jointed calisthenics as they stared blankly into space. Smiles were frozen on their faces, refusing to acknowledge his presence at the foot of the stage, pleading up at them, craving a grope of their voluptuousness, wishing for any tidbit they might deign to grant this miserable, lonely boy.

Could it be that they had known who he was but realized that he wasn't one of them after all? He wanted to reassure them that he hadn't been laughing at them. It hadn't been a charade.

"I wasn't mocking you, Lizard Lady," he whispered as the pucker-fleshed damsel wriggled by. "I love you. I only want to stroke and be absorbed by your travesty."

She didn't look his way but did seem to slow down as she slithered past him in the procession.

"You say something, Milo?" Rabe asked in surprise. He'd never heard the kid speak before.

Milo growled a response, felt it itch in his throat.

Two years ago on Milo's sixteenth birthday he went to Caine's Tattoo Parlour and had himself covered with teeth. There were trenchant wolf sabers and yellow canine needles, bloody fangs, gleaming feral thorns, bared in snarling grimaces and in wide-open attack. His whole body became a dangerous mouth.

"Look like yer bein' et alive," his mother scoffed as she spat.

Grrrrrrrrrrroooowwwwwwwwwwllllllllllllll, he replied.

Was he being eaten or was it protective camouflage?

I enter the jaws of death.

I become the jaws of death.

Was to enter them the same as being?

Milo began to lift weights until his slender Adonis form put on coils of muscle, stretching the threatening shows of teeth into rictuses of animal agony, throes of creature passion. Biceps and triceps oiled and flexing, he bristled within his cage of fangs. He could feel the grazing by their rotted but powerful enamel against his skin. He would wake in the night straining against a dream of violence to find that some had broken the veneer of his flesh to leave Milo speckled in hot blood.

"This is interesting," he said to himself, smiling as he licked the blood off, reconsuming it. He turned his elbows back, his knees back as he'd seen Fatima's ladies do. He cleaned his genitals as well as he could, shaking flecks of spittle from his lips. It was a dusky flavor, copper and salt like the bodies of the freak women.

He imagined that the spirits of the beasts who owned the many teeth that had been inscribed in his skin crept up in the shadows of the night to claim their stolen jaws. Then they fled to hunt under a savage moon that didn't even need to be full like the stories said. A full moon was all right because it represented a haunch of meat, but a sliver of a crescent was just as well for it more nearly resembled a tooth. On slick ground they pursued the terror-stricken people and animals that Milo saw in his nightmares. And when they would catch their prey, oh, how they teased them, circling with wordless growls deep inside erotic throats. Reaching in to slash some meaty but otherwise non-mortal area, circling, biting, and bellowing thunder to the sky, laughing a jackal's laugh even as they showed a wolf's prowess. They then lunged to shake the soft, living bodies until riven meat steamed.

And Milo dreamed it, knew well what these spirit wolves were up to as they playfully snapped at squirts of arterial blood that took to the air like battalions of scarlet butterflies. As they rolled in the ribbons of ropy intestines like puppies with yarn balls. As they grew so aroused by the peppery carnal odor of carrion matted into one another's fur that they mounted each other indiscriminately. They licked each other's furry balls and assholes, domineered and submitted with howls of rage and rapture. Milo knew because he had worn the images of their fangs. The spirit wolves had taken their fangs back, and his spirit rode in their mouths as they committed their carnal crimes with the unbridled compassion of the predator. The graphic layers of carcasses spread open, the rutting, even ravishing the fresh corpses of the kill left Milo whining in his sleep, feverish from the ecstatic sensations of brute manipulation.

He'd wake up, feel the press of fangs on his flesh, the heat of blood across his skin that seemed to be more in evidence as each night passed. He was intoxicated by this rush of what had always been forbidden to him—contact. Even if it was brutal butchery. He had been there and tasted every scrap of gore, aching with its burn, savoring the pheromones of carnage and sex as they released like bubbles of boiling sugar. Had awakened close to his shroud of teeth, sticky and flushed.

Then one night upon opening his eyes he found a bloodied half of a breast on the sheets, the nipple bisected raggedly and the lymphatic glands trailing in uneven tendrils. Milo leapt up and raced to his mother's bedroom. He had to peek through the keyhole because she'd always kept the door locked against him. But he might have gotten in through her window, mightn't he? Had he murdered her at last, torn her callous body apart with his bare hands while he'd been dreaming of mercurial moonlight and the delirium to be found in galvanic homicide?

Her snore told him she was all right. He could see her flopping on the mattress and snorting, the sour stench of cheap whiskey gusting across the room. Milo shook his head in relief and confusion. Whose breast was it?

He searched the house and the yard. There were no other body parts. Was the blood on his skin not his own?

The next night the spirit wolves came to reclaim their teeth. He rode upon their tongues, clinging to the ballustrades of their honed incisors as they raced two counties over to kill three horses in a bluegreen pasture. The horses' eyes bulged as they reared, trying to defend themselves with their hooves. Wolves jumped onto their backs to sink lethal fangs into their necks and skulls. They screamed almost like people did. The phallus of one stallion had been as tough as an old boot, but the foal inside one of the mares was as tender as butter.

The dream faded and Milo struggled to wake up. He saw shadows leaving his room. He staggered out of bed and began to follow. Out in the yard their shapes humped, twisted, bent tortuously. And then they became men. He gasped. Were they not wolves in the spirit? Had they always possessed real flesh and bones?

Milo followed as they went beyond the edge of town, to Fatima's. Looking through a slit in the tent, Milo observed the freak ladies bathing the men, rubbing them down with fluffy towels, wrapping them in silk robes. They patted and caressed the men but never kissed them, never spread their legs for them. Their slavish devotions consisted only of touching, as they had been doing with Milo when he'd visited the tent years before.

Did the women know that these creatures had just been slaughtering livestock this night, human beings on other nights? Couldn't they smell the meat and blood on them?

He growled in the back of his throat, thinking. Yes, the women knew. And it didn't matter. They must have thought he was one of these when he'd run away to Fatima's when he was only thirteen, a bear rug stitched to his skin.

Or maybe they had only been humoring him, recognizing him as a would-be cub, a fledgling beast.

Milo inhaled sharply, frightened of what he was going to do next. He flexed his muscles to give him courage and then boldly walked into the tent. The women cried out in surprise and alarm to fall back to positions behind the furniture. The men jumped to their feet, eyes faintly red at the edges, black at the centers, like moons emerging from full eclipse.

"I know who you are. I wish to become one of you," he stated as if this was reasonable. Did he not wear their power on his skin in tattoo? Had he not ridden to their places of slaughter with them in the shadows of his nightmares?

The men glanced at each other, then turned back to him and grunted.

It made him angry that he'd broken his usual silence to speak to them. And they wouldn't speak back to him.

"Will you not help me?" he demanded.

One of the men stepped forward, wetting his lips from a cup of wine.

"We can't bite you," the man said with slurring, lispy words. "We have no teeth."

The men laughed, pink gums poking out in the half-light from the tent's lamps.

The freak women tittered behind the furniture, peering up shyly to stare at Milo.

"Please help me," Milo pleaded. "I want to live your life. I need to live it. It is the only touching I have ever known."

One of the men rubbed a stubbly chin. "There is one way," he replied tentatively. "Not just saliva carries the germ of the were. Semen does, too."

Milo started as if he'd been slapped. He imagined bending over a table so that each of these men could take their turns ramming their hardness into his rectum, until they were spent and he was contaminated. And by the nasty leers on their faces, he knew he would have to endure all of them, not just the one it might take to grant him their shifting powers.

But he wanted it so badly.

I enter the jaws of death.

I become the jaws of death.

After all, the wolves frolicking amid the pieces of their kills had fucked one another. It hadn't repulsed him then.

Even the most brutal touch was still a touch in a wasteland of isolation. And it had to hurt for he was sixteen and a virgin. And they were creatures addicted to very rough play.

Milo began to unfasten his trousers.

"No," said one of the men. "Not that way. The newest member of a pack must always submit."

They dropped their robes and stood, erect and ready in a gauntlet of anxious animals. Milo understood and sank to his knees before the first in line.

The freak women began to have sex with each other in an orgy of frustrated, voyeuristic passion. Skeletons rattled rocky pubes against the balloon faces of the fat women. Beards at both ends speckled with wet musk and occasional menstrual juices. Stumps thick as dildos vibrated with song. Lizard Lady's gills were opening and closing in a frenzy. The fetus of an aborted hermaphrodite in a jar was jiggled from its shelf as two entwined two-faced prodigies kept bumping into the table it sat on. It smashed to the floor and the enraptured women kept right on rolling over the top of it, the baby's elastic body pulping and the glass shards making them cry out in gurgling pleasure, embedding in their buttocks.

The men rocked above him. Their unusually long, black, curved fingernails raked his scalp and shoulders as he sucked them. He felt his blood coursing down his face into his eyes, flowing across his shoulders. He had his own erection, not from the act he was performing—but from the rust of his own blood, the scorch of it on his flesh. Its scent filled his nostrils as it crept down his face and he sucked it in great red drops, pulling it back into his head. He couldn't help but revel in it for this was touching. It was any kind of touching at all that made people and beasts aware that they were alive. He'd always wanted to be loved, and violence was a sort of love—a bond in contact between two participants intent upon release, upon getting dirty with the night. There was a grace in fury and a gift to be given with each outrage. Milo heard the man above him howl in inarticulate orgasm.

He tried to swallow the bitter semen but couldn't. It wouldn't go down. He tried to spit it out before sliding down to the next in line but it wouldn't be dislodged. He sucked until the next man came, then moved on to the next. He growled as he cupped his mouth around each shaft, snarling with the impulse to bite down at the most explosive of the meat. But he restrained himself.

Soon I'll be able to actually run with them . . .

But when he'd done them all—wiping at his chin, still unable to swallow or spit out their seed—Milo looked back to see that all the men were dead. Their faces were peaceful as if they were sleeping. They did not have the strained, sweaty faces of a mob that has been satiated with oral sodomy. The freak women were cradling the slightly shriveled bodies and smiling, cooing to them like the men had been husbands and sons who'd fallen in a worthy battle.

"You're the king of the wolves," the ladies told him through their happy tears.

Milo ran out of the tent, choking on the mouthful of semen.

He didn't go home. He collapsed in a field somewhere, exhausted, scratching at the tattooed skin, feeling the teeth press firmly against him, closing him in, hard as a kiss with open mouth and bared fangs.

The moon had risen by the time he woke up again. He stretched in the darkness and thought at first that his tattoos of teeth had gone black. But he rubbed it and it ruffled. It was hair sprouting all over him, tickling its way around his genitals and into the crack of his ass, filling the hollows of his armpits, flowing down his thighs. Itchy loving fingers crawled across his belly. His snout jutted forward and he thought he heard his nose bones cracking. His jaws became cavernous with wicked fangs.

He exulted and sniffed the air for signs of life somewhere, for the delicious odor of blood and the sound of a quickened heartbeat.

Inside him, the semen of the werewolves ceased to choke him. It coated his tongue, slimed his gums. He grinned like a maniac in the moonlight, that being what he was. Grinned as he ran off to hunt and to rip to pieces and feed, knowing that the spirit wolves were going with him, riding in his mouth. Wherever he roamed and whoever he slaughtered with his terrible love, they would dream in death of his exploits.

Godflesh

Brian Hodge

"Godflesh" first appeared in *The Hot Blood Series: Stranger By Night*, 1995, edited by Jeff Gelb and Michael Garrett.

Brian Hodge is the author of ten novels, over 100 short stories and novellas, and four full-length collections. Recent books include his second crime novel, *Mad Dogs*, and his latest collection, *Picking The Bones*, a 2011 release from Cemetery Dance Publications. He's also been busy lately converting his backlist titles into multiple e-book formats. By the time this sees print, he'd damn well better be done with his next novel, a sprawling thing that seemed to never want to end. He lives in Colorado, where he also indulges in music and sound design, photography, organic gardening, training in Krav Maga and Brazilian Jiu Jitsu, and mountain air.

Connect with Brian through his web site (www.brianhodge.net), on Facebook (www.facebook.com/brianhodgewriter), or follow his blog, Warrior Poet (www.warriorpoetblog.com).

The seeds of this story were planted by one of Feral House's classic books. Their second edition of Apocalypse Culture contains a fascinating article on various spiritual applications of gluttony and anorexia in history, plus select Gnostic groups' penchant for amputating whatever they could spare. It also referenced porn actress Long Jean Silver, whose missing foot inspired one of the story's tenderest moments. I've since had occasion to view one of her taped performances, an experience I can't particularly recommend, but if you insist, it's . . . memorable. Not long after the story's original publication, I was contacted by a representative of an amputee fetishist society in Chicago wanting to know one thing: "Do you have any MORE stories like this?"

◆ ◆ ◆ ◆

BEING AS SHE WAS A WOMAN who prided herself on walking her own
deliberate path, imagine, then, the irony: Her horizons were forever
broadened by the ecstatic man with no legs.

She was Ellen by day, and knew the aisles of the bookstore as well as
the creases in her palm, the smoky gray of her eyes, the finely-wrought
lines that inscribed the corners of her mouth and lent it warmth and
wisdom, as if etched by a loving sculptor. She walked the aisles with
her modest skirt brushing against her knees and could smell every page
along the gauntlets of spines. For the patient customer it was a trip well
rewarded. Every book should be so matched to a loving home.

There had been nothing different about that day right up to the
very moment they left the bookstore, she and Jude letting the evening
clerks take over. With that taut facelift, Jude could have been an older
sister, or so she thought. Thought she knew what made Ellen tick. A
common mistake, but then Jude's idea of a deep read was Danielle Steel
over Jackie Collins. Jude already had the endings worked out for most
anyone she could ever meet.

They left together for the parking lot down the street. The bookstore's neighborhood was like much of the city itself: old and charmingly
crumbled by day, not a place most would want to walk alone at night.
The peeling doorways, the odd bricks set just out of step with the others, the derelict and sagging smokestacks and chimneys . . . they hooked
strange shadows that worsened as day dwindled into evening, and the
shadows gave birth to night people.

They joined the flow, Jude's brisk footsteps clicking at her side. Urban
minnows, that's what they all were, and god forbid anyone should fall out of
step. Were it not for nights, Ellen knew she would one day tear out her hair,
an allergic reaction to this sunlight world and the pre-fab molds it demanded.

". . . and then do you know what that little doofus asked me?" Jude
was saying. "He asked, 'Do you have *The Old Man and the Sea* in Cliff's
Notes?' I told him the original was barely a hundred pages, so why didn't
he read that, and he just looked at me—"

They approached a break in the buildings, the mouth of an alley
that gaped back like a dirty, leprous throat. Yet inviting, all the same,
with mysteries lying just behind those crusty locked doors. Back rooms
often tweaked her curiosity.

"—just *looked* at me, like I'd suggested, 'Here, why don't you bite this brick in half.' So I said, 'Listen, I can summarize it for you in fifteen words or less: Man catches fish, man battles fish, man loses dead fish to hungry shar—'" Jude froze, except for her arm, as she began to point along the alley. "Oh. My. *God.*" Her arm recoiled back to her side. "Don't look, Ellen, just don't look."

It was the wrong thing to say, and too late anyway. Ellen wouldn't have missed anything that got Jude to interrupt herself.

The man looked to be in his early forties, and she'd never have mistaken him for one of the street people, one of those who cruised around in their wheelchairs with sad stories of cause and effect: car wreck and loss of livelihood; war wounds and loss of stability. From this distance—say, twenty feet along that wall?—his clothing looked neat and new, his hair well-barbered. He might have been any reasonably attractive man who'd made the best of his life after losing both legs at the hip.

Then again, he *was* masturbating. In his wheelchair. It did not look as if he were merely adjusting his crotch. He was wholly absorbed in the act—heart, soul, and both hands.

"He's—he's right out in the open!" Jude said, adding her disgust to that of the less self-absorbed passersby. "I . . . I don't think he's even aware anybody's watching!"

No. No, he wasn't, was he? His exultant abandon—Ellen found this the most fascinating aspect of the display. His choice of locale and timing may have been awry, but she saw on his face more passion and ecstasy than she'd noticed on the faces of last week's eight or ten lovers combined.

A Mona Lisa smile brushed her lips, unnoticed as Jude yanked at her arm.

"Come on, come *on,*" said Jude. "A nice proper thing like you, a sight like that can scar you for years. I had a neighbor? Liked to show himself to other neighbors? To this very day Sylvia Miller gets nauseated by the sight of knockwurst." Jude shuddered. "If only I had a bucket of water, I'd douse that pervert's fire. You shouldn't have to see things like that."

If you only knew, Ellen thought, and let Jude believe she was saving her from something she'd in fact watched maybe two thousand times before.

Ellen could be kind that way.

And the days took care of themselves.

By night, Elle. Just Elle. *"What's in a name?"* Shakespeare had asked, and she'd decided plenty. With the lopping off of a single letter she had created an entirely different life.

She even felt different when that was what others called her, what she called herself. "Ellen" was safe and respectable, a fine name to endorse on the backs of paychecks. But "Elle" rang with mystery and resonance, conjured a slick wet alchemy of surrender and seduction.

For years now that name had been eagerly welcomed by the sort of clubs that are frequented only by those who knew where to find them; whose new members arrived only by invitation and discreet word of mouth; where no one was ejected to the streets for improper conduct, because everyone there knew precisely what everyone else had come for.

Her beauty and willingness to experiment were prized. She was almost tall, not quite. Her raven hair, when unbound, contrasted with her pale luminous skin and ripe lips in delicious nocturnal severity. She had a twenty-three-inch waist but could corset it down to eighteen. Men and women alike loved to wrap their hands around it, or nuzzle over the smooth tight curves on their way to the drenched heat between her thighs.

Tonight's lovers were no exception, at times all six hands caressing her tiny middle, some lightly tender, others rough and groping with urgency. The club's name was the Inner Circle and variety was everybody's spice.

She'd spent the past couple hours as part of a foursome, one of her preferred configurations. Two men and two women—she found a perfect symmetry there, something intended by nature, along with the four winds and seasons, the cardinal points of a compass. The Inner Circle offered an orgiastic central room aglow with gauzy mood lighting, or more private quarters with plenty of cushions and sprawl, and they'd opted for the latter.

She filled her mouth with Daniel while Mitch filled her from behind; she cradled Jill, kissing her deeply, as the men traded off between the women's legs; she and Jill tongued one another's feverish clits while Daniel and Mitch were yet locked inside them; Jill straddled her mouth while holding her ankles wide . . . and in Elle's broad experience you usually needed more men, because their glands betrayed them and they wore out so much sooner. Still, they gave their all, and she drank it with her mouth, cunt, anus. She cried out loudly, in cycles, pulled the others into her singly, as pairs, all three. She made a dinner of semen, a dessert of the musky dew on Jill's swollen and petaled cleft.

And there was always so much silence when bodies fell still, unable to give or take any more. It always felt as if the world had just ended, and they all lay naked and wet in the ashes.

"You're ravenous," Daniel told her. Blond, well-toned, he lay in a sweaty half-curl near her side, reaching over with one finger to probe beneath the edge of the black corset. Jill and Mitch lay in their own raw exhausted tangle a few feet over. "I'd like to see you again."

"You might," she said. "I'm no stranger here."

"So I understand." Grinning, he elbowed closer, crawling like a soldier. "How long've you been coming here? Double entendre not intended."

"Look, you don't have to engage me in conversation, all right? I fucked you tonight, and I'll probably fuck you again."

He rolled onto his back, relaxed, unfazed. "I wish I was nineteen again," he sighed. "I could come five times a night when I was nineteen. But the sad thing was, I was alone for most of it." He peeked at her, hopeful. "Are you feeling pity for me yet?"

He was so obvious, and knew it, that Elle had to laugh in spite of herself. "You late bloomers, you're so maudlin when you start dwelling on what you've missed."

Daniel said he was valiantly fighting the pull of gravity, here on the downhill side of the sexual bell curve. Confessed he was thirty-five—coincidence, or karma? She was closing fast on thirty-five herself, but then weren't they all, for the first or second or tenth time.

She let him talk, and he was pleasant enough without seeming possessive. A few of the guys in these places, in spite of their laissez-faire posturing, they nailed you once and it was as though they'd staked a claim. So she let Daniel talk, but already her thoughts were drifting ahead. Tomorrow night, or the night after . . . future nights at other clubs, wondering where she'd be, what she'd be doing, who she'd be doing it with.

Maybe at the Purgatorium, with the rings through her hardened nipples and chained to a leather belt while some hooded dominatrix violated her with a strap-on.

Or maybe with the Jezebel Society, where gangbangs were a specialty, and where, on knees and elbows, she could be triply penetrated while massaging a cock in each hand.

Or elsewhere, with company even more exotic, but always sure to wring more from the experience than her partners. It was a kind of challenge, something bone-deep and primal.

And she wondered if, wherever she'd be, after she was sated and lay breathing heavily, she'd once more start dreaming of the next time before the sticky fluids of that night had even dried.

Could you even completely look forward to that next time when you could so easily forecast your pose by its end? Even in private clubs like the Inner Circle, the Purgatorium, the rest, sex could get as routine and predictable as some fat suburban couple's half-hearted hump scheduled for the second Tuesday of each month. It was only a matter of degree.

And she wondered if considering these things, in a room with three other nude people whose potent sexuality had just soaked the walls, meant that she was bored.

Figuring that, in the asking, she already had her answer.

A few days later Ellen came back from lunch, took one look behind the counter, and wondered if one of Jude's facial nips and tucks had begun to unravel. The woman's forehead appeared ready to burst veins.

"He's . . . upstairs," she said through clenched teeth.

Ellen frowned. "Who? Who is?"

"That . . . that *creature*." Jude seemed to need the counter to remain vertical. "From the alley."

"Ohhh," she said, and frowned again, more thoughtfully. "Was everything in place when he came in?"

Jude's eyes widened, horrified at the very notion she'd have glanced down to check. "You see, you see—it's types like his that make me think Affirmative Action is a terrible imposition on the rest of us. No telling what he's doing up there."

Ellen started for the stairs. "Maybe he needs help reaching a book. We don't have elevators for the shelves, did you ever think of that?"

"You're going up?" Jude clutched the counter, all bony white knuckles and maroon nails. "What if he has his willy out again?"

Over her shoulder, Ellen smiled with reassurance. "Then I'll suggest he find a more appropriate bookmark."

This befuddled poor Jude. Upstairs, Ellen began to check the aisles, the shelves older and taller and dustier up here, home to the store's used and vintage and rare books. She'd always accorded a greater respect to the browsers who spent their time here.

She found him in fiction, as sturdy and vital in his chair as if it were an outgrowth of him. He sat engrossed in a book, not so deeply that he didn't notice her approach. His face lit with a self-effacing smile, and she tried not to recall how it had looked the other day, self-pleasured and unashamed. And so powerfully attuned to his body. Not one in a thousand could get past his lack of discretion, and she supposed that finding this a simple matter made her the odd one as well.

"Can I help you?" she asked.

He pointed at the second shelf from the top. "Even chimps use tools to get what they can't reach, but . . . ." He spread his empty hands. "Eleventh from the left, if you wouldn't mind."

She stretched, pulled it down, looked over the cover before handing it to him. "De Sade, *Justine*. Not too much call for that."

His grin was apologetic, wholly engaging, set in a weathered ruddy face. A shock of hair tumbled over his forehead. "Loaned mine out and never got it back. Home feels incomplete without it."

Ellen smiled back. Or maybe it was Elle this time. Elle in daylight, rattling at her prison. "Myself, I'm partial to *120 Days of Sodom*."

He seemed merely delighted, not surprised. "I'm sure we each have our reasons." Vigorously, he patted *Justine*'s cover as if it were the shoulder of an old friend. "I appreciate his philosophy here. The utter lack of reward for living a virtuous life. And every one of these sick sons of bitches in here states his reasons for acting like a depraved monster with such eloquence it makes you want to cry." He shrugged. "But obviously you know that."

Her grin turned mildly wicked, and she checked to make sure they were alone. "You want to know what I found most eloquent? When Justine's captured by the bandit, and de Sade gets across the idea of a blowjob without using one concrete anatomical reference. I loved that."

And thus it went on, impromptu critiques and appreciation of the works of a man who'd scandalized a continent, whose debauches were legend, whose name itself had enriched the vocabulary of the erotic. Time got away from them, and once she started to laugh as she imagined what by now must have been going through Jude's mind downstairs. The poor woman frantic, calling paramedics, priests, a SWAT team. She should go quell Jude's fears.

"I'm enjoying this," he said at last. "I really am. You know the way you can just tell, sometimes, that you can talk to someone and let a half-hour go by and you won't even know it? I knew you'd be someone I could talk to."

"And how's that?" She had to know. He was either far more intuitive than Jude, and most of the day-herd who muddled through downstairs, or she'd let something of night inside shine free.

"You didn't look away on the street the other afternoon. You held your ground . . . and watched." His eye contact was bold, candid.

She stood there, tongue-tip wedged between her front teeth, clothed yet her garments may as well have been sheer. Caught. She was caught.

Knowing it had to come someday, but always taking for granted the person would at least have legs. *Caught.*

"It was the look on your face," she whispered. "I—I didn't even think you noticed me then."

As he laughed and rolled his eyes, she found his easy candor extraordinary. And while she'd known plenty exhibitionists, she got no sense that his pleasure had derived from being watched. It had been grounded in the physical, she was sure of it.

"I get carried away sometimes. I really shouldn't, but when it feels that good, and the mood strikes . . ." He shrugged, palms up. "You know, you may think it doesn't, but your face gives you away too. Like does know like, when it knows what to look for. I don't think I'm completely off-base here, am I?"

A blush threatened to warm her cheeks. Embarrassment? She'd not even thought it possible anymore. The challenge in her tone of voice was merely affectation: "What is it you think you see?"

He appraised. "In your eyes. It's always in the eyes. This look when your guard slips. Something unsatisfied, maybe a little angry. Okay. I know—it's like someone just stole the last sliver of chocolate torte right out from under your fork."

Ellen's laugh was soft, low, throaty, half-pleasure and half-challenge. Chocolate and sex. This man may have had no legs, but he most definitely had her number.

"Look," she said, "I have to be getting back to work. But I think I'm going to need your name . . . and some way of getting hold of you later."

His name was Adam, and the address he gave took her to a dim neighborhood where her footsteps were solitary echoes against walls of brick and stone, where the pale faces of residents peeped out from behind barred windows. Everything malingered beneath a stubborn dusting of industrial fallout, and the last of the year's greenery twined dead and brown around sagging wrought iron fences. Privacy would be valued here, and respected.

Adam played the proper host, skimming through his apartment and around corners as quickly as if he were on a basketball court. He mixed fine drinks, served hors d'oeuvres that hadn't come from a deli. He showed her his books, including the freshly reinstated *Justine*. He let her notice for herself his collection of fetish videos, and be the one to suggest slipping a disc into the player. There was a lot in the way of nipple clamps and whimpering, later the obligatory golden shower, and they were really just marking time here, weren't they? She might've yawned once. Adam shut it off before the end.

"It's been awhile since I've watched this," he said. "Been awhile since it even did anything for me."

"So why sit through this much if it's that passé to you now?"

He shrugged easily. "Humoring you?"

"Oh, that's a laugh," she said, and she was Elle again, had become Elle without one bit of effort. Adam recognized this. Like knows like, and from here it was a very short trip to the bedroom.

Unclothed, his body was a peculiar marvel. Incomplete, but hard and sculpted, like a magnificent Greek statue that vandals had smashed in two. His genitals seemed all the more for it, large and immodest. His lower trunk flexed with new rhythms she'd never felt without the normal counterbalance of legs. As he meshed with her, braced upon two powerful arms, she could run her hands along the tapering curve of his back, cup the clenching muscles of his ass. Could run her hands farther down and cup the smooth rounded stumps where his legs just *ended*. She couldn't think of him as an amputee. It felt as if Adam were complete, whole, and his hips met some other plane, where his legs existed in another dimension.

For hours they rolled, locking themselves into twisted new arrangements. Positions once denied her because of one set of legs or the other getting in the way were now accessible. And Adam was tireless, his commitment to ecstasy for a long time bordering on possession, then tipping far beyond. He had a whole body's worth of passion compressed into half the mass. Each time he came it was with a straining convulsion of ardor, racked with groans and shudders that might've been endearing were they not so intensely animal. For any less experienced a woman, Elle decided, his plunge into the heart of his own pleasure would've been frightening.

But for herself? It was maddening, feeling for the first time ever that she had been left behind, that there was no way she could draw more from the most ravaging of fucks than her partner. He had eclipsed her, and if at the bookstore he'd nearly prompted in her a flush of embarrassment, he had now done the unthinkable: He had inspired envy.

I want whatever it is you have inside, she thought, and lay as stunned as if a new galaxy had opened before her. Lay with him in the sweat-soaked afterglow, her cunt lips puffy and throbbing. It lasted long moments, even as Adam stirred, even as he traced a hand along her face.

Even as he said, "If you stay with me, you . . . you may not be seeing me this whole for much longer," and she found it a peculiar thing to say. But consider her life.

It certainly was no stranger than hearing someone confess his love.

Their relationship grew from that night, a happy co-existence of need and availability, willingness and daring. She didn't know how long it would last, but this was the way things were done on their level. Emotions and attachment rarely figured in. It was more the delight of connecting with someone who didn't judge, who understood that not everyone craved a permanent partner at his or her side through life. Who trusted the physical body's immediacy more than a bamboozled heart.

It saved time. It saved money. It saved pretense.

Adam happily listened to her recount various liaisons at her nocturnal haunts, his erection like a club curving away from the base of his body. He would close his eyes, smiling as she conjured for him images that would drive the average man to frenzied fits of jealousy and despair: Elle, flogging the back of a submissive man until he rimmed her with a quivering tongue; coaxing an orgasm from the sluggish genitals of an uncut transsexual; bending a girlfriend over her lap and paddling her bottom cherry red while a nervous old couple watched from chairs.

Adam listened, and Adam trembled. She had read, one memorable lunch break, that artist Salvador Dali could think himself to orgasm. She wondered if Adam wasn't far away from it himself.

"Your turn," she demanded once, in an uncharacteristic sense of quid pro quo. "You've hardly told me a thing about yourself. I want to know all the dirty stuff you did before you met me." Then, with a grin, "Besides pulling over for quickies with yourself in the alley."

He pretended to consider sharing. "I know some people. You're not the only one with a members-only pass."

He teased her with silence then. Adam's smile was annoyingly aloof; smug, even. He could be so superior when he wanted, all in fun, but he knew damn well how curious she was, that she wondered if he'd not had some esoteric training to channel sexual energy, let it feed upon itself like nuclear fusion. Something to do with Indian chakras, perhaps. Tantric sex magick. *Teach me too*, was the unspoken gist of her hunger. *Teach me or I'll strangle you.*

"So what does it take to meet these people," she asked, "or am I not good enough?" Guilt—that was a fair tactic. "You're ashamed of me, is that it? Not worth fucking in front of your friends?"

His weatherworn face creased with a heartfelt smile. "You may be ready after all." He ran a hand along her body, lingering here, there, anyplace where bones joined. "But then, Elle"—and it sounded anything but rhetorical the way he said it—"what have you got to lose?"

Adam took her to another unfamiliar neighborhood. This newest stop on the search for the bigger and better orgasm was a no-man's-land where residential met industrial and both had died of blight. The building of intent was a church whose congregation had long since moved away, broken up, lost faith . . . something. They'd left behind an orphaned edifice surrounded by trees stripped bare by smokestacks that had themselves died, all of them now in a stark eternal autumn. The church sat gothicly stolid, sooty and gray.

"Privately owned now," he said, and she wheeled him up a ramp at one side of the steps. It looked to be the only thing kept in good repair.

He unlocked the door, then stopped inside the nave, and before her eyes could adjust to the dimness, dangled a black strip of blindfold. "I'm afraid I have to insist."

Elle stiffened. His demand reeked of threat—how well did she really know him? Curious women died all the time, led to hellish ends by their hungers and strangers who betrayed misplaced trust. But back out now and she was a coward, a poseur. Adam knew that, of course, could easily exploit her sense of self.

She bent at the waist, let him fasten it around her head, and a cool cathedral night descended upon her. "If you cannibalize me," she said, "I'll haunt you 'til you die," then she bit firmly on his ear. He just laughed.

Elle rested her hand on one of the grips of his chair as he wheeled forward, let him lead her along as if blind. They passed through swinging wood doors. She shuffled her feet, seeking clues. Further still, and in this dark nucleus of intuition the room felt vast—the sanctuary, but a sanctuary redefined. It smelled of sex and sweat and ecstasies.

Her senses expanded, took in the others that surrounded them. Whispers on the periphery, a crawling sensation of being watched, appraised, admired. The menace of the unknown. Movement—were these others drawing closer?

Adam stopped, had her lower to the floor while he swung from his chair and joined her. His mouth pressed roughly to hers, and his hands rose to strip her clothes away. Moments later his hands were joined by others. Naked, blind, she was laid back on cushions that shielded her from a floor that felt old, nobody's priority.

"Beautiful," came someone's voice, "even if she *is* whole."

She submitted to the hands that stroked, caressed, and in their numbers lost track of Adam. He was subsumed into the mass around her. Her back arched, her mouth parted to suck a finger that slipped past her lips. Her nipples stiffened beneath circling palms. Their hands gave a hundred delights, promised a thousand more.

They opened her legs then, swung her ankles wide, and as one checked her wetness, then murmured approval, she heard the rustle of someone else moving into position. She was entered then, and gasped. It was huge, pushing deep, deeper still. What began as a groan became a wailing cry, treading that delicious threshold separating rapture from agony. She was filled near to being split, yet still wasn't aware of a male body hovering over her. There was no press of hips against hers.

Elle reached down with her hand, felt herself caught by Adam.

"One finger," he whispered in her ear, and she found him again. "One finger's all you get."

Trembling, slowly rolling her hips with the rhythm set up by the massive phallus, she extended one finger. His hand guided hers . . . and she touched, glided a few inches. Flesh. It was flesh, firm and hard.

"Satisfied?" he asked, and she was and she wasn't. Nobody could be that big . . . could he?

It wasn't for the mind to ponder—she let go of the thought, surrendered to the here and now, the reality of sensation. She drew a deep breath and braced herself, elbows on the floor. Took it. Took it all in. Thrust back with muscled hips and grunts through feral clenched teeth, feeling as if she were at war with this monstrous thing inside her. Riding it until it brought her low and sent her soaring, and her voice pealed from rafters gone dead with dust.

Drenched in sweat, she fell back into someone's arms, felt her lover withdraw, receding into a blackness that was total, her sole world. They waited until she got her breath, then a hand was on her chin, urging her lips to part. She obliged, eager to surmount exhaustion, prove herself worthy. Whoever these people were, she wanted to be one of them, take what they offered, give what she had. Her lips parted, and her tongue serpentined out to explore what her eyes were denied. She touched warmth.

It was at her mouth.

She smelled herself on the gigantic phallus, tasted herself a moment later. Opened wide, wider, could scarcely accommodate a few inches without her jaw cracking. *What WAS it?*, and she raised one hand, wrapped her fingers around it, felt firm flesh, muscle . . .

And it slowly withdrew, teasingly, before she could identify what seemed so familiar, so alien, so tantalizing. Around her, far and near, came soft murmurs of approval, appreciation, acceptance.

Adam's hands were at the back of her head, gently undoing the knot, and when the blindfold was drawn away she blinked into the light, forgot to breathe. Whatever she'd expected, it wasn't this.

She found herself in the center of the old sanctuary, beneath soaring ceilings and the watchful eyes of suffering figures in the stained glass windows, some pocked with vandals' holes. Pews and pulpit were gone, in their place a cushioned playground for these thirty-plus members who had welcomed her, even though she wasn't at all like them.

Elle looked straight into the eyes of the young woman sitting in the V of her outstretched legs. So this was her lover? There was a thin, wanton quality to her as she reclined on her haunches, meeting Elle's gaze with a hunger almost masculine. It was a role she played well. Elle followed the contours of her body, from the small breasts to the slim hips, to the tapering length of her left leg. There was no foot, just the smooth bony head formed by her ankle.

At the moment, quite wet.

And she had no right leg at all.

Elle whirled, met Adam's smile. His pride. And let herself be taken into his arms. At least he had them.

Not so, many of those around her. They were all missing bits and pieces, some more than others. Feet, lower legs, or the entire limb. A few, like Adam, had neither. Others had sacrificed arms along the way. A couple, she saw, were but heads and a single arm attached to naked trunks. They were smooth and they were sculpted, every one of them, and if they looked upon her with anything, it was with longing. Not to be like her again . . . but to make her one of them.

"You do it to yourselves, don't you?" she whispered to Adam. "These weren't accidents."

He grinned, got Freudian on her. "There are no accidents."

"I don't understand," but then, in looking around at them, an entire roomful of broken statuary, she couldn't say she didn't like it. Whatever their reasons, this was commitment, so far beyond the Inner Circle that she could never go back there.

"You will," Adam told her, then scooted off to new partners, as did the others. Recombinant pairs, trios, groups.

And she watched, a privileged witness.

They could do the most astonishing things.

Adam explained later, after the two of them had returned to his apartment. She was very quiet, cataloguing everything she'd experienced but finding that even in her vast erotic repertoire there was no place for this.

She drew herself together on the sofa, hands around a mug of coffee. Feeling loose inside, liquid, where muscles had stretched.

"How did it start?" she asked.

"How does anything start?" Adam said, then laughed softly to himself. "Transcendence. That's what anyone wants out of life, isn't it? Some way of getting past it. Or getting more out of it." He paused, changed gears. "Ever hear of the Gnostics?"

She seesawed her hand.

"They were several splinter groups from the early Church, a couple thousand years ago. Didn't last long, by comparison. The party line condemned them as heretics. Progressive in their day, in a lot of ways. But then they had this self-loathing kick they were on. Since the material world fell short of the spirit, it was bad, themselves included. So, automatically, anything that created them had to be bad too, so their lives were spent showing contempt for it all, until they could return to the spirit. Each branch had its ways. The ascetics denied themselves everything. The libertines, they pleasured themselves and fucked each other left and right. Overindulgence as the way to paradise . . . people after my own heart." Adam winked. "And yours too, *ma chérie?*"

Elle smiled weakly; felt rubbery inside and out. "I don't think my goals were that lofty."

"Oh mine neither, hell no," he said, laughing. "Anyway. Even among the Gnostics there was a lunatic fringe. Most all of them had the idea that the body was a prison that kept the spirit shackled, but this fringe, they did something about it. Had a habit of cutting parts of themselves away to reduce the size of the prison."

She began to piece it together then, amputation in an erotic context: The less body one has to dilute pleasure, the greater must be its concentration in the flesh that remains.

"And so the two of those approaches got combined, over time?"

"I don't know. Probably." Adam looked dumbfounded. "Who knows how anything really happens? It's not like we trace ourselves back for centuries, nothing like that. It's just something that someone stumbled onto awhile back, and found out . . . works."

Languidly, Elle slipped from the sofa, wandered to a window, stared into the night. A sickly glow of sodium lights cast pools amid the blackened hulks of brick and steel, withered hives of isolation. How she hated it out there, its cold hard rot.

"Everything revives," she said, "if you give it enough time."

Their procedures were strictly of a back room variety, the amputations performed by a surgeon no longer allowed by law to practice his craft. Who still liked to keep his hands active. It was an ideal arrangement, and the discarded parts were safely burned in an industrial incinerator.

Elle had him begin with her foot.

She found that phantom pains were scarcely a problem when you had done away with something voluntarily. She grew new skin, and beneath it, it seemed, new nerves. It was an awakening, and while the world slept beneath snow, she was healed enough to give this new sexual organ its first workout. Found she could come without a single touch between her legs.

At the bookstore sympathy flowed freely, especially from Jude, and they all remarked what a wonderful attitude Ellen had in spite of her accident. She was deliberately vague on particulars, felt touched by Jude's concern that it might now be more difficult for her to find a man, one who would overlook her handicap.

"If you have one tiny flaw," Jude said, "they can turn around and be such cold-hearted bastards," and then she smiled nervously and checked herself in a compact mirror. Ellen assumed it was time for another nip or tuck.

And Elle, with her mind already made up to proceed, wondered how she would ever be able to explain away the rest of her leg.

She was up and around again by spring, the itch of healing and new growth mostly behind her. Spending most of her free hours at the former church, crutching her way about as she explored both edifice and companions. They were an insular group, came to be with each other even when they left their clothes on. Of course—who else could they talk to? They'd cut themselves apart in more ways than one.

She often lay with Adam in the dying light of afternoon, both of them washed in colors the sun picked up as it streamed through stained glass. Overhead, the Virgin Mary held a little lamb; its fleece was dark with soot.

"You bastard," she said, "you didn't wait for me." But there was no anger in it, and it made Adam smile, made him laugh.

He touched her face with his sole remaining hand, an act she would relish for however long it might last. Not forever. Elle curled in closer, pressed her mouth over the smooth pink stub that jutted from his left shoulder, flushing in pleasure as he gasped.

"Has anybody ever gone all the way?" she wondered. "Cut off everything?"

Adam nodded. "There've been a few."

She groaned, murmuring wordlessly with fantasies of narrowing herself to a focused bundle of overloaded nerves, a single vast erogenous zone. "I wonder what it's like."

"I don't know. But I get the idea that . . . that it's like being a god." Adam stirred, flexed; seemed to ripple with each caress of hand and mouth, breeze and dust mote. "By that time, you know, it's up to everybody else to care for you. Take care of your needs. You're mostly a receptacle by then."

"What did the others say about it? And where are they now?"

"They quit talking," he said. "And pretty soon . . . they quit eating. But they still smiled."

They knew something, she thought. *Or felt something the rest of us aren't even close to yet . . .*

Yet.

She forced his hand down to her hip, the exposed stump hot, tingling. Raw and alive with promise. "I'll be better at it than you will. When I get that far. I'll feel more than you."

Said this with a tremor and a smile.

Could she cut herself down an inch at a time, feel gradations of pleasure with each successive chopping? If she lopped off a finger herself, would it be a new form of masturbation? Such paths to explore, down this avenue of the blade.

"We'll just have to see about that," he said, "won't we?"

And Elle wondered if she could convince him to hang onto that one last arm at least until she went in for her other leg, so that Adam might be the one to hold the scalpel for that first ceremonial incision.

That would be divine.

It would almost be something like love.

Every Last Drop

John Everson

"Every Last Drop" was first published in *Bloodsongs* magazine, Spring 1998, and reprinted in his collection *Cage of Bones & Other Deadly Obsessions*, Delirium Books, October 2000.

John Everson is the Bram Stoker Award-winning author of the novels *Covenant, Sacrifice, The 13th, Siren* and *The Pumpkin Man*, all released in paperback from Leisure Books. Limited collector's hardcover editions have also been released from Delirium, Necro and Bad Moon Books. He has had several short fiction collections issued by independent presses, including *Creeptych, Deadly Nightlusts, Needles & Sins, Vigilantes of Love* and *Cage of Bones & Other Deadly Obsessions*. Over the past 20 years, his short stories have appeared in more than 75 magazines and anthologies. His work been translated into Polish and French, and optioned for potential film production. For more on his fiction, art and music, visit www.johneverson.com.

I wrote a lot of erotic horror stories in the '90s for a variety of small press magazines, and "Every Last Drop" is one of my favorites. I think it really captured what can become an obsessive compulsion to follow the lure of the forbidden into the dark. I'd write about that theme again years later in my novel Siren.

♦ ♦ ♦

HIS BREATHING GREW RAGGED. In the shifting kaleidoscope of electric light, his grey eyes reflected obscene plays of color, did not shine out their own. The woman was tan, California style—no lines. Her lips were shiny pink, an erotic complement to the nipples of her bobbing brown breasts, currently matching—or more correctly, setting—the rhythm of his respiration. She flipped a strand of sand-blonde hair away from her face, ice-blue eyes flashing with lust, sweat collecting on her forehead, lips pursed and moaning . . .

The holovision abruptly went blank-blue, and Tony zipped up.

That was not your ordinary porno-blonde, he thought in admiration. Most of the blondes they used these days were like plastic dolls—the parts were all there, but the energy, the spirit—the spark that sometimes transfigured a 3-D bimbo into an orgasm-inducing fantasy—most just didn't have it. They looked bored. They looked . . . faceless. Tits and ass a dime a dozen—sex goddesses were hard to find.

On the cyberbooth door he paused a moment to read the obscene graffiti. He didn't know why, it was depraved and depressing and yet he always did. "Looking for black cock to suck? Call 546- . . ." "My wife screws you while I watch—ask for Leo (313) . . ." "Homos go to hell" . . . "The perfect blowjob: no names, no faces, no price, all privacy, unspeakable pleasure. Cum to Redroom Hotel #112 after 9 p.m."

He read the last one again and shook his head. Nobody gave the perfect blowjob for free. He couldn't *pay* Loni to give him one anymore at all. Tucking in his shirt he pushed open the door and walked quickly out of the back hall of the peep show. Men paced in the shadows, faces illuminated by the orange glow of silently smoking cigarettes, looking for the newcomer to proposition, waiting for the booth they wanted to free up. He grimaced in disgust and left the place, nodding at the wrinkled, bored cashier watching a "Dick Van Dyke Show" rerun.

Back when Loni had first gone out with him, she'd been eager to please, spreading everything for him just about anytime. She'd never been nuts about fellatio, but she serviced him dutifully. Their first couple years he'd nearly forgotten what the insides of these peep houses were like. Guys looking for anonymous sex with other guys, just for thrills or because they were too scared to admit they were gay and come out of the closet. Here it wasn't gay or straight, it was diversion. Businessmen on a lark, husbands on desperation runs. He wouldn't let these desperate men touch him, but he had no problem touching himself. If you couldn't get it at home, you had to go somewhere . . .

Tony gunned the car and screeched out into traffic. He hoped Loni was in a good mood tonight—the blonde with the ice-blue eyes and pure-copper bod had left him wanting more. The new cyberbooths at the adult video store he'd frequented for years were great—but even though the women surrounded you like real life, you still couldn't *feel* them. But thinking of that last scene made the crotch of his pants uncomfortable. He shifted in the seat and willed away an erection—which only served to increase its growth. Gripping his thighs together, he aimed the car onto the freeway and tried to relax. *That place was supposed to relieve the tension, not create more*, he grinned to himself.

Loni was not in a good mood.

"You're an hour late and I've got to make that train," she fumed, shimmying out of her skirt in their bedroom. At 34, she looked good, he observed, better than when they'd met. Her chest, while not that of the goddess, was ample, if over-nippled. Her middle was potting out a bit but her hips always nailed his eye to their hidden valley, something which, at this particular moment, did not work in his favor.

"I'm changing Tony, you've seen it before. Go get something to eat."

He reached out to massage her exposed behind. She slapped his hand away. "Go. There'll be plenty of time for that next week. Right now I'm late and you're pissing me off."

Her dark eyes pierced the mental fog that arousal always drew around him. Loni grew easily irritated with his physical obsessions. Sometimes it was flattering; now it was in her way.

"Alright, alright," he grumbled. "Did you leave me anything?"

"There's Chinese in the fridge, some spaghetti from last night. You'll have to warm it up yourself. If I miss this train, there's not another one until 11 and Angie will be sitting at the station waiting for me all night."

She finished pulling on jeans and drew a sweater over the bra strap Tony had been admiring from behind. She turned and caught him still staring.

"It's only seven days. Go rent *Vampy Vixens* or something. I've gotta go. She slipped on a pair of black flats and grabbed her suitcase from the bed.

"I'll call ya tomorrow. Now goodbye."

She pecked him on the lips and was out the door.

The ache in his crotch flared again as he realized *that* was all he was going to get for quite awhile. Shrugging in defeat, he shambled into the kitchen.

He decided on the Chinese, but after aimlessly poking through pea-pods and some mutant pygmy chicken, ended up re-Saran-ing most of it. He wasn't hungry, damnit, he was horny! He tried watching TV, but none of the canned laughs took his mind off the vision of pink lips wrapping around his erect member, a halo of beach-blown hair teasing his legs.

On a sudden impulse he pulled out the telephone directory and looked up the address of the Redroom Hotel. It turned out, as he'd expected, to be in a run-down section of the city, maybe a half hour's drive. He watched some more TV, knowing in some way that he was killing time. Waiting. Waiting . . .

. . . until the clock said 8:37. That would put him there around nine. Tony turned off the television and went to the garage.

Run-down is not the word for it, he thought as he pulled into the lot. The unlit sign (which was big enough that he still picked it out from a couple blocks away) didn't exactly promise the Hilton, and nobody seemed to be around. *Who knows how long that note had been markered onto the peep show door anyway,* he admonished himself. It was probably put there by someone in town for a night or two who was since long gone. He stopped in the hotel courtyard and shook his head. This was asinine. He could get mugged, get AIDS—maybe this was the site of ritual sacrifices. The newspaper'd just run an article about the rash of them downtown this year.

A clomping noise broke the pensive silence; made him whirl around, his heart kicking in double time. A sudden wind blew a drop of cold sweat from his forehead into his eye. There, on the brown brick wall at the end of the courtyard, a shadow grew, larger with each staccato slap. The clicking was footsteps, he realized, and they were coming his way. Go back—go forward—he didn't know which way to turn. And then, as the shadow reached gargantuan, grotesque proportions, its Dr. Frankenstein stepped into view—a short, Asian fellow carrying a briefcase and striding quickly towards the parking lot. He bent his head as he passed Tony, seeming intent on not making eye contact. Tony relaxed and abandoning his thoughts of turning back to the car, decided to check and see if anyone was in room 112. He was here after all, and had a whole night to kill.

Night cloaked the courtyard sidewalk in shifting mystery. Bushes and weeds poked tendrils across the path, slowing his progress, their cold, tenuous gropings of his legs and belly made him shiver. The encroaching undergrowth made him wonder if this hotel was still in operation, but then, when he glanced around, he realized there were lights on in some of the rooms. The sign was out, the sidewalk beacons were unlit, but a blue glow poked through the curtains of the occasional occupied room. Upon reaching 112, his fears were confirmed. No light at all. He knocked anyway, and the door creaked open an inch at his attack.

"Hello," he called through the black sliver of an opening. It was somehow darker in the room than it was outside. "Anybody home?" he drawled with mock levity.

There was no answer, only a heavy stillness that seemed to press against him like a smothering blanket. He wanted to turn and go home, but a stubborn duality drew him to stay. He wanted to *see* the room, *why* he didn't know. It was not like there was going to be some tangible remnant of sex-gone-by to see. Still, he pushed the squealing door open some more and stepped inside, his hand trailing along the wall for the light switch. He found it, flicked it, and nothing happened. Except the door slammed shut. Tony backed against the wall, eyes straining to make out something through the inky black air.

"Who's there," he said, trying to keep a desperate quaver from his voice.

"Shhsssssssssssssssssss," something answered. It could have been a rattlesnake or a cat as easily as a human.

Something touched him, grabbed him at the waist. Tony froze, not knowing whether compliance was safest or if he should strike—and possibly risk getting stabbed or shot by his unseen assailant. Actually, he supposed the hands on his body couldn't be accused of assault. He was the intruder here, after all.

The pressure on his left side abated and he felt a tickle at his crotch. His zipper protested in the dark, and then his belt loosened. Still he couldn't move. He was so scared he wanted to scream, to run, but he could do neither, only stand flat against the wall in the groping night as his underwear dropped to his feet and something cold and smooth brushed against his cock—which completely ignored the paralyzed fear of the rest of him and responded with an instant erection.

Which was first gripped and tugged by a cold hardness, *like the surgical probing of a doctor wearing rubber gloves for a prostate exam*, he thought. And then there was a wetness, an engulfing, and the two gripping appendages began working the rest of him, pinching his buttocks, sliding down his thighs, moving with icy grace across the hair of his chest. They were warming now, as was Tony, who had surrendered the fear, surrendered his questions. He pressed his hands to the wall as the caressing hands worked their erotic way across his skin, the unseen mouth working with unbelievable expertise up and down his hardened member. Teeth trailed lazily across just the right nerves, fingers pinched his nipples at just the right moment. As the tingling in his groin grew to a waterfall of breath-stealing sensation, Tony realized that this was, indeed, the perfect blowjob and closed his eyes as the moment exploded.

When he opened them again, the hands had receded. He was sitting on the room's short, sandpaper-rough carpet and could see now, sort of, in the darkness. There was no one else in the room.

"No names, no faces, no price," the peep show graffiti had said. "Unspeakable pleasure."

It delivered what it advertised, he thought, just as something small and hairy darted across his leg. Tony jumped up, ending his reverie with a shiver. Pulling up his pants, he left the room still buckling his belt. *Too weird,* he thought, hurrying back to his car. He was weak as he slid in behind the wheel. The experience had been so intense, so draining . . . *It was incredible,* he thought, *but too weird for me.*

"Tony? Tony?"

The vision of the blonde goddess from the peep show burying her head between his legs in a shadowy derelict hotel room vanished, replaced by the less welcome sight of his balding overweight boss, leaning over the desk and staring at him with a perplexed expression.

"Tony, you've been drooling into space for the past 15 minutes. Are you alright?"

Tony shook his head to clear away the stubborn ache of his daydream.

"Yeah, Bob. Sorry. I just . . . didn't get much sleep last night."

"Why don't you go lay down in the lounge for a few minutes?" Bob Mackenzie smiled. "I'd tell you to go on home, but I do need to have that Web report by the end of the week, you know."

"I know. You'll have it. I'm just having a little trouble concentrating today is all."

Bob chuckled, a dry, lifeless sound, and clapped Tony on the shoulder. "Well, wake up, man." He turned and lumbered back into his office. But Tony caught his watchful eye staring across the hall at him throughout the rest of the afternoon. And try as he might, the blonde kept nuzzling back into his consciousness. It was embarrassing. He couldn't leave his desk without first taking several minutes to meditate on bloody images of mutilated animals and abandoned babies to deflate the tent in his pants. First the incredible movie with the goddess and then the bizarre blowjob last night—the two were merging together in his thoughts, a union so powerful his sex was reacting as if he were a male dog surrounded by females in heat. When five o'clock rolled around, he moved like a zombie towards the door, praying nobody was looking at the zipper of his pants. It was bulging, and as he fumbled in his pocket for car keys he suppressed the almost unstoppable urge to grab and go for it, right there in the middle of the office.

Bob watched his trancelike gait from his desk and called across the office just before Tony reached the door.

"Get some sleep tonight, Ton."

"Uh-huh," he mumbled in reply. He knew what he was going to get tonight.

He threw the Chinese in the microwave when he got home, and this time managed to fork the mess down, though with little enjoyment. Loni called while he was rinsing off his dishes. He let her do most of the talking—she missed him, hoped he was fine. Did he eat the Chinese she left? She got in OK, her sister Angie was waiting on the platform with her husband Dan. They were going to the zoo tomorrow. Tony answered automatically when necessary, while his attention focused on watching the blonde goddess who had somehow materialized in his kitchen. She spread her legs apart on the dinner table, her shockingly pink lips opening and closing with mesmeric rhythm while her mouth whispered: "Come to me, Tony. Cum in me, Tony. Come to me, Tony. Cum in me, Tony."

"Tony."

"Huh?"

"Have you heard a word that I just said?"

"Yeah, hon, I just got, um, distracted. There's some kids running through the backyard."

"Well, go shag them out. I'll talk to ya tomorrow. I love you."

"Love you too, hon. Bye."

He cradled the phone in its receiver. The table was empty but for some delinquent grains of rice. But he could still hear her soft, crystalline voice—pleading like a ponytailed little girl, yet husky like a woman with a bad need for a man, any man.

Then it was nine o'clock and he was walking down the sidewalk towards room 112. He didn't really recall driving there, he realized, as he knocked on the door again. He didn't really remember what he'd done since hanging up the phone. But the door swung open with its raspy complaint and his cock was so hard he felt he might burst with anticipation.

The door closed behind him and this time there was no delay before the hands were taking down his pants. *It was strange, this silent sex,* he thought. There was no sound but his breathing, the beat of his heart, both increasing in tempo and timbre until he cried out in passion. "Yes. Yes. Suck me dry, baby. Take every last drop."

And with that command, somehow, she did. At the summit of orgasm he suddenly drew a breath of pain as her demand increased. He could feel her pulling him inside her, sucking him out through his penis. His head was spinning, a glittering fireworks display lit up before his eyes.

And then it was over, and he was collapsed on the floor, drained of the power to move. He had never experienced anything so powerful, so pleasurable.

"Who are you?" he whispered, as her hands pushed at his chest. He laid back on the floor as she directed and felt her hair trailing up his thighs to tease his belly. It was just like his daydream, he realized, and as he closed his eyes to imagine the glowing naked skin of the goddess, the woman between his legs began to work on him once more. This time when he reached his peak, he passed out.

It was after 3 a.m. when he crawled into bed, a painfully erect pole between his legs.

At 4 a.m. he was staring at the L.E.D. light on his clock radio, sweat streaming from his forehead, his hands uncontrollably glued to his cock.

This was insane. He'd seen a porno with a hot babe, and then gotten sucked off a couple times by some nut who freaked about being seen. Why couldn't he let it go? He'd never been this horny in his life. What would Loni think? She wouldn't care much about the movie or the little fantasies, and getting an anonymous bj wasn't exactly cheating—she ought to be happy someone took care of it for her, he thought. No, she wouldn't be too angry about that stuff. But if she saw him here sweating with lust over another woman—actually two, one of which he'd never in the strictest sense seen—that, she wouldn't relish. In an attempt to snap himself sober, he fastened onto an image he'd seen in a documentary. Soldiers dead on the battle field, arms and legs streaked with red, entrails leaking out from between clenched hands, heads lying 10 feet from the crater where the rest of the body was mangled . . .

The erection in his hands didn't even flag. And then his conscious mind lost control and the soldier with his guts hanging out suddenly stood up and pushed the bleeding mess back inside with one hand while unbuttoning his pants with his other. They fell to the ground and Tony saw the golden triangle of the blonde goddess below the ruptured belly. The soldier rubbed his face and her ice-blue eyes and pink lips were suddenly speaking to him.

"Come to me Tony, cum in me."

Tony rolled over and began to cry.

When 9 a.m. rolled around Tony was in his chair at the office, but Tony was not in. Black circles ringed his eyes and his right hand lay useless and twitching at his desk. His left hand was in his lap.

"Report coming along OK, Tony?" Bob asked from across the hall. He hadn't seen Tony move since he'd stumbled in a half hour before.

"Uh-huh," came the answer. But the man still didn't budge.

When afternoon arrived and Tony didn't seem any more aware, Bob sent him downstairs to the corporate doctor. There was a wet spot on the man's pants which left Bob praying silently that his key employee was not sicker even than he looked.

"Well Tony, your blood pressure is low today," Dr. Regsic chirped at him. "Let's get up on the scale." The meter flashed 156 lbs and she looked down at her chart.

"You've lost almost 20 pounds over the past couple months, Tony. Have you been on a diet?"

He shook his head no.

"Exercising?"

No.

She shook her head.

"Get up here on the table and unbutton your shirt."

He did as she asked.

"How did you get those?" she frowned and bent towards him for a closer look. He hadn't noticed this morning, but there were 10 red trawls down his chest, starting with a weak red glow at his shoulders and turning dark purple as they narrowed to converge in a single thick corridor at his bellybutton.

He was silent for a minute, and then offered: "My wife gets, um, excited."

"Drop your pants, Tony."

She didn't sound like she'd take an argument, so he stood and undid his belt. His pants slid down immediately, revealing first, that he'd somehow forgotten underwear this morning, and second that the purple bruise led downwards from his belly to the tangle of hair beneath.

The doctor gasped at the sight. Tony thought she was impressed with his size—he was, of course, still erect. But her eyes did not look lustful, rather, they were disgusted. He focused on the object of her stare and saw that it too was red and purple—and swollen to twice its normal size.

"Look, Tony. I don't want to tell you what to do in your bed, but if your wife is responsible for this—I'd consider divorce. I don't even want to know how this happened, but you'd better rule out sex for the next week or two. I'm going to give you an antibiotic just in case you've got that infected."

She walked over to the white cabinets across the room and pulled out a tube.

Instead of a dumpy fortyish woman in an overly long lab coat, Tony saw the bronze muscular buttocks of the goddess crossing the room, the dark lure of the crack between her legs led his hand to his lap. Her stride was lolling, casual. Her hips swayed suggestively, the ripples in her back and across her waist invited his tongue. She looked across her shoulder at him, flipping a mane of bleached hair over her shoulder. Her eyes touched his with electricity and she winked.

"Come to me, Tony."

She turned around to show him all.

"Cum in me, Tony."

"God, what is wrong with you?"

Dr. Regsic stood in front of him, her jaw hanging open.

"I'm not going to say anything about this Tony, but I am going to recommend a counselor."

She reached over and pulled a paper towel from a roll on the wall.

"Here. Clean yourself up and go home. I'll leave a prescription of antibiotic for that—you better hope it doesn't scar—and some ointment as well. Come back tomorrow, I want to see how you're doing."

She was there again at 9, just like before.

"Who *are* you?" he asked again, as his jeans bunched around his ankles. Still she would not answer, but her hands were hot tonight, full of rhythmic lust. He felt a sticky wetness on his leg. With the rest of himself, he felt only her power. Her fingers blazed trails of ice and fire across him, but it was her mouth that centered her magic. As she pulled him inside her, the pleasure radiated back into his body, a feedback of ecstasy. He knew now the purple trails across his chest were her conduits of pleasure, he could feel every pulling sensation electrify those paths with heat. It could have been the intoxication of the moment, but a dull cobalt illumination seemed to leak from the weave she worked upon him, growing brighter and dimmer with the waxing and waning of her pressure upon him. And as she reached up to carve another channel on his chest, he saw why she insisted on darkness. Her left hand was maimed. The thumb and pinky fingers were whole, their long red-capped nails raked his flesh as any woman's. But the middle three fingers lacked nails—in fact, they seemed to lack flesh as well. It looked as if she'd dipped her hand into a radiation soup. That would explain the hard coldness he had felt the past three nights as she first cupped and cajoled his loins. *With cold bony fingers* . . .

But her skill made up for any deformities. Again and again she brought him to orgasm, he groaned and begged her to suck him dry once more. And every time she did. Again the night ended with his losing consciousness in the throes of release. Again he awoke to find her gone, and spent the remaining hours tossing in his bed. And the next two nights were the same.

On Friday Bob put him on report and turned the Web project over to another department. Tony went back to Dr. Regsic.

She tried to keep the alarm from reaching her voice, while noting that his blood pressure had dipped dangerously low and he'd somehow lost another 10 pounds since Tuesday. But when he removed his clothes, her breath hissed with disgust. The purple bruising covering his torso looked like a gridmap. And it all led to a penis the size of a cucumber. Not an overly healthy looking one at that. She handed him the name of "a good doctor" at the hospital scribbled on her business card.

"Go there. Now," was all she said. It was three in the afternoon, but he went.

Not to the hospital, though, to the hotel.

As he pulled into the parking lot—for the first time in daylight—he saw how truly decrepit the place was. Weeds sprouted everywhere through cracks in the asphalt. A "For Sale" sign was tacked on below the big Redroom Hotel placard above the main office door—which was boarded shut. Apparently the Gentech Government Laboratories, whose fence butted up to the back of the hotel property, weren't bringing in enough business to support a hotel. Or maybe after the outcry a few years ago about GGL's genetic testing program, they had steered business away. The hotel windows that weren't covered in graffitied plywood were broken, ragged glass massaged gently by shredding curtains in the low breeze. Yes, this hotel had been closed for awhile, he supposed. *So how had there been lights on in some rooms the other nights? And how long had She been there?* This was probably a prostitution pit even when it was open for legitimate business, he guessed, wondering if his goddess had plied her strange trade here even then. *Were there others like her in the other rooms? Could the cold blue lights he had seen night after night have been the flares of others undergoing the same consuming pleasures as himself, not the glow of cathode ray tubes?* He found that he no longer cared, and strode unerringly towards 112. Closed or not, he knew of one room that had a vacancy.

The room was a lot creepier in the daylight than hidden in the moist shadows of night.

The paint, a dull, putrid green, was peeling away from the walls, especially in the corners where water damage had left brown stains on the cinderblock the paint was separating from. The carpet was once charcoal grey, but now was pockmarked with circles of brown and black stains. Portions of it were frayed and pulled up. Spiderwebs crisscrossed the corners, and something scuttled under the unsheeted bed when he stepped towards it. The mattress looked too dirty to sit on, let alone sleep on. Now he knew another reason she said to come after 9. It would be hard to get off knowing that you were likely taking rats, spiders, or any number of vermin along for the ride.

"Hello. Anybody home?" he called into the silence that seemed to hang around him like a breath taken and held.

Something rustled nearby.

"I know I'm early, but I couldn't wait."

She came out of the bathroom, her skeleton legs joining neat as knickers with golden skinned thighs and a blonde tuft of pubic hair. Her belly button was exquisite, a hollow darkness on a flat planed bed of sensual muscle that promised both pleasure and mystery. Her breasts were as tan and supple as her belly, full, alert and capped by the lightest shade of pink areolas. He saw now that both her hands were incomplete, but each by only two fingers—which was puzzling because he knew he'd seen three skeletal tips on one last night. But white-boned calves, feet, and fingers were not a turnoff to him now. And she could have hidden these odd deformities if she'd wanted to, he thought. Her face was the real problem. A lipless mouth showed the white teeth within glittering savagely against a gash of wet crimson. He could see her cheekbone jutting through pink flesh on one side, while the other half of her face seemed nearly complete, and as coppery brown as the rest of her fleshed body. Her eyes were piercing sapphires, but on the visible cheekbone side the eye was lidless, and the white line of her skull seemed to poke through above it. The lightly kinked, wind-blown blonde hair that turned him on so much ringed her face and draped across her shoulders. She held her arms out in offering.

"Is this what you want?" she asked. Her voice was gentle as a girl's, yet somehow throaty, wanton. But despite the velvet of her tone, without the cushion of lips, her words revealed themselves like daggers plied from carving meat.

"Yes," he said without hesitation. "But, *what* are you?"

She smiled with her eyes. Her ivory teeth ground cruelly.

"I'm your dream lover. Come to me, Tony. They designed me to be filled up by men. And it's really been too long."

He started towards her. She moved past him to the bed and laid down. He could see dots of scarlet and curdled cream on the bones that were her legs, and on her feet, tiny red lines that looked like unsheathed capillaries. She wiggled her toes and they clinked together invitingly. She spread her legs and he saw the heaven he'd thirsted for all week long. She *was* his dream lover. She was the girl from the porno vid. He could see it in the eyes now, in the perfect breasts, in the pinkness that glistened so invitingly. His crotch throbbed painfully while his head ached with fear and longing.

"Cum in me, Tony. Let me suck you down to make me whole."

His pants were so loose now they slid to the floor with no unbuckling. He realized briefly that however he'd written off his previous indiscretions with this woman, this was, unalterably, adultery. He knew somewhere in his head that Loni would be back Tuesday, and he should put himself back together by then. And he knew he wouldn't. Couldn't. And he didn't care.

He straddled her unfinished body and bypassed foreplay. She was visibly ready, and her hands now raked at his back as they had all week on his chest. He felt as though he were being diced and licked at the same time. Her tongue snaked out of her lipless mouth and teased and moistened his eyes, nose and neck. She bit him hard on the shoulder and then caressed his lips with her tongue. Her eyes sucked him into another world, her vagina was a utopian tunnel. He was making love like he never had before, bucking and pumping like a male hound on a bitch. Then she rolled atop him, the bones of her toes scratching at his calves, sounding like nails on hollow wood as they met the bones beneath his muscle. Yet he didn't howl; he could feel nothing but her forcefed ecstasy. And she drove him on, harder and harder, the trails in his flesh burned and froze in alternate coursings. He could see them glow with power released. And when at last he answered her plea and came, he knew with fatalistic certainty that it would never stop.

She laughed as he came and came and the skin on her cheek grew thick and tan and her lips went from baby pink flesh to full pouting sex teases.

. . . *And he came* and felt her legs pressed upon his own growing, the red and white seeds of flesh drawing the essence of him to her, nursing, nourishing their growth.

. . . *And he came* and as her shinbones ceased clicking together he heard his own begin to clatter. He felt light, empty, but trapped in some sick, twisted compulsion as his hips smacked against hers of their own accord.

. . . *And he came* and she laughed and pressed her arms upon his chest. Her fingers were perfect and whole and she said in that husky girl voice, "take me again, stud," and laughed when he did and she bent to kiss him and his tongue was caught in a vacuum; his cheeks sagged, receded. She lifted his arm in passion and he saw the white bones protruding from the unraveled skin of his fingers.

. . . *And* still *he came* and the night came and the morning too before she pushed his trembling bones away from her flesh.

She stood then, and stretched, a lithe cat of a woman. Running her fingers across supple, muscular skin, she drank in herself inch by inch in a shard of mirror across the room. Her body was whole, tan, California style—no lines. Her lips were shiny pink, an erotic complement to the nipples of her perfectly brown breasts. She flipped a strand of sand-blonde hair away from her face, ice-blue eyes flashing with abating lust, sweat drying on her forehead, lips pursed in humorous consideration. Gazing back at the bed, she saw the eyeballs in Tony's meatless cranium staring back at her, still with a longing, and, she felt, appreciation of her new form. She'd best finish the job.

She sighed and bent over him, tongue lasciviously ready. When she rose the skull was sightless, the bones no longer vibrated on the floor. A long transparent tube of skin trailed between his femurs. She pulled it off with a rip and swallowed it. "Every last drop," she murmured and licked her lips.

She pulled on his jeans, cinching the belt to its furthest hole. It left her thighs baggy and ill-defined, but it would do for now. She fastened one button of the short-sleeved blue cotton shirt, and tied the rest across her belly, leaving her midriff and much of her chest exposed. She pulled at the uncomfortable weight on her behind and came up with his wallet. Thumbing through $20s and $10s, her white canines flashed hungrily. Good. She didn't relish hanging around this dump any longer. As she went to flip the wallet closed, a snapshot of a woman caught her eye. She was raven-haired, dark-eyed, with high cheekbones and an intense look of vibrance in her mouth. The woman was *hot*. Just looking at the photo made her mouth dry, and even after its recent use, her groin ached with desire. *Probably his wife,* she speculated, checking his license to find an address. She *knew* where this house was, she realized, as Tony's cannibalized cells merged and shared their knowledge with her own. It had taken her too long to find a host after the Gentech engineer had abandoned her here to wither away. She laughed, thinking of his reward if she could track him down. Sex goddesses were hard to find—or make! And she intended to feed regularly to keep her full goddess form from now on. Maybe he could be one of her snacks.

Kicking the sated bones under the moldering bed, she wondered, in the meantime, if Tony's wife liked blondes. Opening the door to step with anticipation into daylight, she resolved to find out.

Blind in the House of the Headsman

Mehitobel Wilson

"Blind in the House of the Headsman" first appeared in *Brainbox 2: Son of Brainbox*, edited by Steve Eller, 2001.

Mehitobel Wilson has been publishing horror fiction since 1998. She is a Bram Stoker Award nominee, and many of her stories have been granted Honorable Mentions in the *Year's Best Fantasy and Horror* series. Recent stories appear in *Morbid Curiosity Cures the Blues, Zombies: Encounters with the Hungry Dead, Sins of the Sirens, Damned: An Anthology of the Lost,* and *Dead But Dreaming: New Excursions in the Lovecraftian Universe,* and selected stories have been collected in *Dangerous Red.* If you can't pronounce her name, call her "Bel."

◆ ◆ ◆

MAY WAS INSIDE THE WALL, and her eyes were open. Better on her back than on her knees; the shards of paneling would cut her throat, and her bruised knees couldn't take her own weight anymore, much less his.

Maybe, baby, Maybe, she heard, his name for her.

Maybe, baby. She blinked and stared at the clean studs, still fragrant, packed with nubby gray insulation that puffed lint into her eyes with each *Maybe* thrust. The back of the paneling was satiny and printed with blue letters, the closest ones clear, the rest shadowed. The few she could read ran through her head, AST, and she tongued her palate, chanting the letters silently.

Maybe. Maybe he had punched through her face instead, and her brain's best guess at peace was this space inside the wall. Maybe she was vibrating on the verge of death, the stabbing at her nape the last sparks of her spinal conduit. When death came, she would no longer remember him looming redfaced over her as she crabbed back onto the pillows, pressing her head against the wall, pulling his fist back and slamming it beside her face, catching one of her curls and tearing it from her skull as he punched through the paneling. *Maybe, baby*, maybe he hadn't gnawed her jawbone, steered her bloodied skull into the hole with a sustained bruise of a kiss, bitten her trachea and pressed her chin back with his hardboned face, shoved her head through, let the hole's edges score her forehead, her neck.

Maybe, baby, gusted the breath that powered his bloodstreaked cock, and she knew she was only in the wall.

May felt the cool glass of his ashtray settle on her sternum and knew this would take a long time. Her headless body lay before him. He would smoke an extra few cigarettes, she knew, and savor this. Her body was outside the wall. It was his.

AST AST AST ticked against the backs of her teeth, matching the rhythm. She felt the soft and dusty press, withdraw, press of insulation on her crown.

Her head was her own.

He owned the rest. In surgery, a wall of blue fabric had blocked her view of her own opened flesh. Sacs of saline were tucked beneath her pectoral muscles. He had used her vagina so thoroughly that it was as stretched as that of a mother thrice over. Dildos, fists, implements inspired by those he'd seen used in black-market Japanese films. He paid for her cunt to be tightened. Skin cultured in sheets from the cells of discarded foreskins, skin meant to reconstruct the features of burn victims, was trimmed into a new hymen and sewn to bridge her bruised soft walls. Nipped and tucked to be ripped and fucked. Again. All that lay on the far side of the sheet, and May, conscious, examined the warp and weft of the fabric, memorized the blue, called it cornflower, and felt none of the things they were doing to *his* body.

Two years later, he had undone all the work he'd bought between her legs, and had cultivated new tastes. Soon she would be on the table again, the saline sacs would be dragged from the muscles that had scarred around them, the natural tissue of her breasts would be scooped free and dropped into a Biohazard vat, and crescents of skin would be cut away, leaving her with the flat and aching chest of an adolescent. He'd tighten her again, of course, and he'd pay for electrolysis, leaving her mons bald as a child's.

For now, nothing beyond the wood was hers. May read the cornflower letters branded on the pressboard. She didn't feel it when he pulled his cock from her, didn't hear the foil tear or the latex snap, didn't hear the *tink* of his class ring against the bottle of Tabasco sauce, didn't feel the nuclear conflagration when his cock seared into her again. She ticked AST, still, against her teeth.

She let him have the body and the head knew nothing of it. May, behind the wall, thought of guillotines, of revolt and freedom. She tasted fiberglass on her smile.

Then she felt hands on her jaw, hands wet with blood and pepper sauce and viscid semen, and they fell to her throat and slipped firm behind her neck, fanned fingers open to cradle her skull and draw her forth from the wall. She made a small sound, disappointed, as she came forth into the world again.

Maybe, my beautiful little thing, she heard. She clenched her eyelids and felt sharp crusts of insulation clotted between them. The pillow was soft against the highest knobs of her spine when he lay her down. She knew she would bleed on the sham and that he would be angry later.

But for now, May was a good lay, a beautiful little thing. She felt him stroke her hair and tried not to wince as red pepper burned the cuts bristling with splinters across her forehead. She felt pressure from beneath her shoulders; he was pulling the bedspread up, cradling her. He wrapped the flannel around her and lifted her into his arms, held her head against his shoulder. Her eyes were closed, still. She swayed in his grip and he shifted her to one arm as he used the other to run the shower. She felt the air around her grow heavy with humidity.

He let her down and purred at her, helped her step blindly over the side of the porcelain tub and into the running shower. When the water hit her flesh she flinched before realizing that it was good, not the scalding rain into which he often cast her. He gently thumbed the insulation from her eyes. He was so very kind sometimes, like now, with the good water. He loved her so.

She opened her eyes and saw herself as he did.

May, outside the wall, saw nothing at all.

An Experiment in Human Nature

Monica J. O'Rourke

"An Experiment in Human Nature" first appeared in *The Rare Anthology*, edited by Brian Knight, 2001, Disc-Us Books.

Monica J. O'Rourke has published more than seventy-five short stories in magazines such as *Postscripts, Nasty Piece of Work, Fangoria, Flesh & Blood, Nemonymous*, and *Brutarian*, and anthologies such as *The Mammoth Book of the Kama Sutra, The Best of Horrorfind, Strangewood Tales*, and *Darkness Rising*. She is the author of *Poisoning Eros* I and II, written with Wrath James White, *Suffer the Flesh*, and the collection *Experiments in Human Nature*. She lives in upstate New York. Visit her at www.facebook.com/MonicaJORourke.

This story was inspired by Clive Barker's "Dread," though you would be hard-pressed to actually find any similarities. It also began my foray into writing hardcore (or splatterpunk) fiction and led to my collaboration with Wrath James White, Poisoning Eros parts I and II.

◆ ◆ ◆

ERNEST BRUSHED THE HAIR from his forehead with his fingertips and leaned against the wall, clumsily setting his glass upon the mantle.

Young men playing dress-up, sporting Ralph Lauren, knockoff rich man wannabees enjoying Ernest's parents' good food and good smokes and good single malt, crashing in the Tudor-esque McMansion that felt somehow misplaced among the Hampton elite. Animal heads suspended from the walls gazed at them with dead eyes. A billiards table sat unused in the corner.

"Okay," Ernest said. "I promised you something interesting, right? Now we see if you two have the jewels to go through with it."

Caleb uncrossed his spider legs and leaned forward. He set his cigar (the smoke was choking him anyway) in the oversized freestanding ashtray and rose to his full height. Stretching his arms overhead, his fingertips fell inches short of the eight-foot ceiling.

"This should be good," he said, cracking a smile.

Ernest smirked. "It wasn't easy, but I think it's worth it. Or will be, in the end. It's brilliant."

Ian, almost invisible in the corner of the room, said, "What'd you do?" His blue eyes were intense as he squinted at the two other boys. Curly auburn hair and a baby face, he was the youngest of the trio at nineteen, but only by two years.

Ernest closed the double doors. "Keep it down. Some of the staff may still be wandering around. They might hear us."

"Staff?" Caleb scoffed, knowing the huge staff was composed of a cook and a housekeeper. "So what's your big secret?"

Ernest cleared his throat and narrowed his eyes. "We swore that no matter what, we'd stick by each other, right?" He strummed his fingers on the edge of the table.

"Yeah, so? What's got you so freaked?" Caleb said, though he nodded. "What's your point?"

Ernest blinked, his long lashes almost dusting the tops of his high cheeks. "I'm not *freaked*," he snapped, and then composed himself. "A study in human nature. An experiment in perseverance."

"Blah, blah, blah . . ." Caleb snapped. "Get to the point."

Ernest ignored him. "You think you have the stomach for such an experiment? One that will be *messy*? One that, I guarantee, will end . . . badly?"

Caleb said, "Badly? What's that mean?"

"We'll be running some experiments. Okay? Just some tests. I got us a guinea pig."

"What kind of experiments?" Ian said, almost whispered.

Caleb cocked his head. "Guinea pig, huh? Why do I get the feeling it's not warm and furry."

Ernest smirked. "Oh, it's warm and furry all right . . ." He sat on the arm of the sofa. "Remember in Professor Klein's class when we studied about the strength of the human mind, and the ability of the body to persevere at any cost? What I remember most were the slides of the concentration camp survivors from the Holocaust, and the Japanese POWs. Remember?"

He paused briefly, looking from Caleb to Ian. "I've thought about that. A lot. Wondering . . . you know, what someone might do . . ."

"Might do if what?" Ian murmured. The air in the room felt heavy, as if coated in cotton. He pursed his lips, the color of his cheeks now matching his hair.

Ernest ignored him. "Thing is, there's no turning back now."

Caleb shook his head and said, "Get to the point. What did you do?"

Ernest stared at Caleb as if deciding how to proceed, whether or not to let Caleb in on the secret. "It's already begun. I need to know what to expect from you guys. Because let me tell you, if I go down, we all go down. One for all, and all that stupid Musketeers bullshit, okay?"

He sat back in the chair and rubbed his palm across his mouth. "Here's the thing. I think I can safely say I understand your character. I trust you guys. I think the three of us are of like minds."

There was no argument so far; the three were of like minds when it came to politics and religion. But Ian wasn't entirely sure he shared the same belief system as Ernest, or shared his ethics. He was willing to listen, however.

"I found a . . . a test subject. I'd like to see how much it will take to . . . to, um. For him to break."

"Break?" Ian asked. "What's that supposed to mean?"

Caleb snickered. "Are you saying what I think you're saying?"

Ernest shrugged and began to laugh.

"Oh, god," Ian said through fingers splayed across his mouth. He leaned forward in his chair, and his face brightened as he finally realized what Ernest was talking about. "You're talking about what? Breaking some guy's will? Right? Am I right? Holy shit, Ernest! Who'd you pick?"

"Nolan Pierson."

"Who?" Caleb asked, but Ian knew the guy. Nolan was in their psych class, and was in Latin and chemistry with Ian and Ernest. Nolan was rather forgettable, with butchered black hair and oversized Buddy Holly glasses. The scholarship kid. His father was a janitor in the Harper Building on the west side of the campus. Every school has at least one Nolan—the kid whose Sears suit was never quite up to par, whose Payless shoes always fell apart a few months into the semester. The kid who wanted to fit in but just couldn't afford to, his clothes and his efforts always being second rate.

Nolan was a throwaway human being.

And suddenly, the three seemed to realize almost simultaneously that they *were* of like minds. And like ethics.

"Him?" Caleb said. "I know who you mean. He won't last—the guy's a loser. He's on *scholarship,* for god's sake." He whispered the last part, as if naming a dreaded disease, as though naming his social status might inflict it on him.

"I think you're wrong," Ernest said. "And there begins our experiment. Who better than some poor schmuck who's had to struggle all his life to get what he wants? A guy who tries to fit in but never manages to. If he didn't have *some* strength of character, I think he'd've blown his brains out by now, n'est-ce pas? This guy has what we're looking for."

"You're awfully empathetic," Caleb remarked, his eyes at half mast. He snorted. "Like you really give a shit what this janitor's kid's been through."

Ernest opened his mouth but Ian cut him off. "What are you going to do to him?"

"Me? Not me—we. What are *we* going to do to him."

"Sure. Right. Then what?"

"Some tests." Ernest turned toward Caleb. "And to answer your question, dickhead—"

"I didn't ask any fucking question. All I said was you're full of shit. You talk about him being poor and struggling and all that but you don't care."

"Like you do?"

Caleb shrugged. "Never said I did. In fact, I don't. But you. You're full of shit."

Ernest smiled. "Oh yeah? I already have him in the house. Doesn't matter whether I feel sorry for him. All I wanna do is some experiments. Like I said, this has already begun. I invited him over and slipped some shit into his drink."

"Well, I guess it's started then," Caleb said. "I'm with you. I'm in."

"Just like that?" Ernest said.

"I trust you, man," Caleb said. "We're like brothers. And I think this sounds fucking exciting."

They stared at Ian. He chewed his bottom lip. "I'm in. You know I'm in."

Ernest slapped his hands together. "We have the house to ourselves. My folks gave everyone the night off since they're going into the city for the weekend. So there's no one left to, um, hear anything. Besides, Nolan's tucked away in a safe place. Soundproof."

"They gave everyone the night off, did they?" Caleb scoffed.

"Fuck you, assbag," Ernest said. "Not everyone has staff who wipes their dick for them." He led them across the room and reached behind the bookcase. "You see those old movies with the creepy old goth mansions that have these hidden passageways and shit?" He pushed a panel concealed behind a copy of *The 120 Days of Sodom* by the Marquis de Sade. A door disguised to look like part of the paneling creaked open. A light, musky air assaulted their nostrils.

"Oh gimme a fuckin' break," Caleb said.

"Shut up." Ernest ushered them inside and closed the door. They each held a flashlight, and Ernest led them down a hallway where the only sounds were their footfalls and the steady plinking of a leaky pipe.

They passed through several doors. At the last door, Ernest reached up and punched in a series of numbers on a keypad, locking it behind them. "Can never be too careful. We don't need company."

"Did you install that? It looks modern." Ian brushed cobweb remnants out of his eyes as they approached a small room. He smelled something burning.

Ernest told them, "I didn't install it, but I doubt my parents know about that secret panel upstairs, or even about this place. I just discovered it myself a few months ago. I wonder what kind of sick shit the previous owner got himself into down here."

Light overtook the blackness. In the center of the room was a large, thick butcher-block table. Tied naked and spread-eagle to the table was a young man with black hair. He was blindfolded, and his glasses had been placed on a tray beside his head. He was gagged, but that seemed unnecessary since he appeared to be unconscious. The slow rise and fall of his thin chest indicated he was still alive.

That burning smell . . .

Ian looked at the corner of the room. A large pot had been set up, and something inside was simmering on a platform above Sterno canisters. "What's that?" he asked.

"Metal," Ernest said. "A combination of metals, actually. Some old figurines, melted down. Lead and tin mostly. Silica. A bunch of stuff. Carefully mixed and tested."

"Tested? On what?" Caleb asked.

Ernest looked up. "Strays. Mostly."

"What, uh, what's the metal for?" Ian asked.

Ernest snapped opened a container of smelling salts and ran it beneath Nolan's nose. "You'll see."

Nolan's head jerked from side to side. He strained against his bindings. On a tray table beside the butcher block was an assortment of instruments. Ernest stood beside it and picked up a notebook and pen. He tried to hand them to Ian, who refused and backed up a step.

"You have to keep notes, Ian."

"Why me?"

"Because Caleb is stronger. I may need his help with . . . you know. Other stuff."

"No way. I don't want my handwriting in any journal."

"You idiot," Ernest said. "We're all in this. Someone has to keep notes, and I can't fucking do it. I'm going to be too goddamned *busy* to write, asshole. Besides"—he pointed at the camera mounted on a tripod in the corner—"I'm recording all of this. So fuck you and your handwriting. There's a permanent record."

Nolan screamed a series of desperate and incoherent sounds into his gag.

Ian snatched the notebook and pen out of Ernest's hand.

Caleb moved across the room and studied the tray of instruments. "Ernest, you are one seriously disturbed fuck."

Ernest handed him clamps. "Start with the nipples. Just don't cut them off."

"Me?" Caleb's face contorted. "Hey, isn't that kind of queer? I don't want to . . ."

Ernest sighed, rubbing his eyes with his index fingers. "Look—this is an experiment. It's medical, not sexual. If you get a hard-on while messing with his nipples, that's your hang-up. Otherwise, just goddamn do it. It's part of the experiment."

Caleb moved to the other side of the table. Frowning, he ran his palms over Nolan's breasts until the nipples stood erect. Using the clamps, he grabbed hold, Nolan writhing beneath him. "I still don't see what nipple clamps have to do with anything," Caleb muttered.

Ernest ignored him and turned to Ian. He said, "You ready? Before you write anything, I need you to help prep the subject. I want you to get a feel for this stuff."

Ian stepped forward, and Ernest handed him the next instrument.

"What the hell do I do with—"

"We're all pre-med," Ernest said. "Figure it out."

Ian knew what he was supposed to do with the tool, but—

"Can you handle it?" Caleb asked. "Need help?"

"You couldn't deal with a nipple clamp, but this you're okay with?" Ernest said.

"Fuck off."

Ian swallowed back a mouthful of spit. "I . . . yeah, but, I don't know how . . . I mean, I'm not sure."

"Just stick it up his ass," Ernest said.

"You got issues, man," Caleb said.

"I know where it goes," Ian said. "I just don't see what this has to do with your experiment."

"We start small, Ian. Clamps, a few tubes. Understand?" Ernest said. "Part of the experiment is a study in resilience, big and small. I have lots more planned."

"How will we know what he's feeling? Isn't that part of the experiment? Isn't that what you want me to write down?" Ian wasn't sure he wanted to know, or if he was stalling. He stared at the instrument in his hands, and it seemed to have become very heavy.

"How the hell do you think he's feeling?" Ernest smiled. "Never mind. We'll ask him in a minute."

"Oh." Ian lubricated the end of the tube and tried to push it into Nolan's anus. "I can't do this," he said. "It's, you know. He won't cooperate."

Ernest said to Caleb, "Make him cooperate."

Caleb nodded and took the length of metal tubing, which resembled a thin toilet paper roll, from Ian. He pressed it against Nolan, pushing and twisting until it found its way inside his writhing body, tearing the soft, delicate tissue at the opening of his anus. Blood tricked onto the table. Ernest tossed Caleb a roll of duct tape and instructed him to secure the tube as best as he could.

Nolan screamed into his gag and bucked his legs, but Caleb pushed the tubing in further. "It's secure," Caleb said. To Ian he said, "Just think of him as a cadaver. Easier that way."

"Good job," Ernest said. He leaned over Nolan's face. "I'm going to remove your gag now. I want to ask you a few questions."

Nolan's head bobbed like a float on a lake. Ernest removed the gag and Nolan screamed and begged for help. "Please!" he cried, lifting his head off the table. "It hurts! Take it out!"

Ernest stared at Nolan, a wry smile plastered on his face.

"You fucking psycho!" Nolan screamed.

Ernest stuffed the gag back in his mouth and clicked his tongue. "No use. He's just gonna be an asshole. How predictable. Anyway, the interesting part's coming up. I'll do it myself but may need some help."

He took a long thin metal tube—so thin it resembled a wire, but it was hollow, like the world's most narrow beaker—from the utensil tray.

Moving to the end of the table, he took hold of Nolan's penis, which failed to respond. "Grab it," he said to Caleb.

"No way! Nipples were bad enough. I'm not touching his dick."

"Look, dipshit, you're pre-med. You think you're never going to have to touch a dick? I didn't ask you to suck it, just hold it. I told you, there's nothing sexual about any of this."

"You like bringing pre-med up a lot," Caleb said. "Seems more like an excuse for you to play with this guy's dick." Looking away, he grabbed Nolan's penis. It lay unresponsive in his hand.

"I need you both to hold him as still as you can. Ian, pin down his chest."

Ernest grabbed Nolan's penis and tried to push the metal rod into the urethra. Nolan screamed into his gag, his head thrown back, the veins in his neck straining beneath the skin. His body was coated in a fine layer of sweat, and the smell in the room was a mingling of metal, blood, and musk.

"Shit," Ernest said, "hold him!" The rod kept slipping. Fitting it into the narrow urethra was more difficult than he had anticipated. "Get him hard," he snapped at Caleb.

"You fuckin' kidding me?" he yelled.

Finally, it slid inside his urethra. Ernest dropped Nolan's penis and stood back, panting. Turning to the camera, he said, "Goddamn. Okay. All tubes are in place."

Ian moved to the edge of the table. There was a small amount of blood on Nolan's crotch. It terrified Ian . . . yet somehow it was exhilarating.

"Ready to begin," Ernest said, grinning. He looked at Caleb and said, "Pick an orifice, any orifice."

Caleb ran his hands through his hair and shook his head. "You're seriously disturbed, man."

He tossed Caleb a pair of heavy-duty work gloves. "We'll start with the ass. That tube gets hot, so make sure you wear those. Hold the rod tight. Make sure it stays up his ass."

Caleb nodded.

"It cools pretty fast," Ernest said. "I considered putting him in water, but that would have been a real pain in the ass. Can you imagine if we'd had to start dragging bottles of water down here? That sink is useless." Ernest dipped the metal spoon into the simmering molten metal and stirred.

"We should be able to get enough into the tube if we work fast, before he starts flopping around too much. Otherwise it's just going to spill all over his legs." He filled the ladle and held it up, steam rising, the smell of the metal stronger now. "We don't want to get this on us. It's more than two hundred degrees, so be careful. And work fast. Got it?"

Caleb nodded, getting a better grip on the thick tube protruding from Nolan's ass. He affixed a large funnel to the end of the tubing. Ian stood off to the side, watching them with a transfixed expression of revulsion and horror.

"When I'm done, pull the tube out fast. Then cover up his asshole with the duct tape. Got it?" Ernest poured the contents of the ladle into the tube. Seconds later the liquid reached its intended destination and Nolan went berserk, flailing against the ropes, his agonized screams muffled against his gag. Moments later, he was still.

"He dead already?" Caleb blurted, pulling the metal rod out of Nolan's ass, covering it with bandages and tape to keep the liquid from leaking out.

Using the stethoscope from the instrument tray, Ernest listened for a heartbeat. He shook his head. "No, not dead. Strong heartbeat."

Ian dropped against the wall and buried his face in his hands. "Oh my god," he croaked. "Oh my god."

"Get a grip," Ernest said. "We're not through." He removed the gag from Nolan's mouth, and a trace of spit and vomit trailed away with the cloth.

"Now what?" Ian asked, choking back tears, trying not to cry.

Ernest picked up the smelling salts. "We continue with the experiment. Should we remove the blindfold now?" He didn't wait for an answer.

"But . . ." Ian scratched his head and stepped forward. "But then he could identify us."

The other two exchanged glances before turning back to Ian.

"What did you think was going to happen here?" Ernest asked. "He's got a metal block up his ass. Did you think he was going to just walk away?"

Ian swallowed and shrugged.

"I told you earlier that this wasn't going to end well."

"Yeah, Ernest, but—"

"And you promised! You said you wanted to be part of this, that you would always be one of us. You swore along with Caleb and me, fucking told us we were your brothers!"

"I didn't know you meant murder!"

Ernest looked at the floor before speaking, using a patronizing voice not unlike his father's. "I told you this would be difficult. I told you this would end badly. I told you we would be sharing secrets for life. What about all of that didn't you understand, you fucking idiot? What the fuck did you think I was referring to?"

"Come on, Ian," Caleb said. "You've got to see Nolan for what he is. A non-person, just an asshole getting a free ride. He's a leech, a guinea pig. He's a goddamned lab rat."

Ian looked from Ernest to Caleb and knew they planned to finish. Could he see Nolan as just a giant lab rat? He tried to justify what they were doing to the slab of meat on the butcher block table, hidden away somewhere in a room that reeked of damp, dead wine, a room lit by a naked bulb dangling by a single thin wire. The expressions on the faces of his fellow scientists were feral, somehow evil. They were enjoying this too much and would never need to justify their actions. Ian tried to reason that this was all for posterity, tried to forget that this was how Nolan would spend the last minutes of his pathetic life.

"Okay," Ian whispered. "I'm with you." He didn't know whether or not he really meant it. For now, he did mean it. For now, he would stand with them.

Ernest handed him the notebook and pen. "Good. Let's get going then. First entry was, say, 6:00 pm. Let's see . . ." He played with the webbing between his thumb and index finger. "Level One. Subject gagged and blindfolded. Nipple clamps and insertion of rods and tubes. Slight bleeding. Subject . . . uncomfortable.

"Level Two. Jot down, like 6:45. Level Two, melted metal enema injected. Subject in extreme pain and passes out. I guess this is where we begin Level Three."

Glancing at his watch, he said, "Blindfold and gag removed. Subject will be revived and questioned for response. Start Level Three at 7:00 pm."

Ian wondered what sort of doctor Ernest would become and then remembered his particular fondness for forensic medicine.

Ernest continued his dictation. "About to revive subject." Then he grinned. "Level Three. Wake the fucker up."

Caleb waved the salts beneath Nolan's nose. There was no reaction. He waved them for another few seconds, and then lifted the vial to his own face and sniffed. He jerked back his head and snorted. "Nothing wrong with these!"

"Oh, god," Ian moaned, peering into Nolan's face. "What's wrong with him?"

Ernest rolled his eyes. "Are you serious?" To Caleb he said, "Keep working those salts. See if you can revive him."

Caleb waved the salts and slapped Nolan's cheeks.

He continued the dictation. "Level Three. Subject unresponsive. Efforts to revive subject have been unsuccessful. Unsure at this point what—"

Nolan rocked his head away from the salts. His eyes rolled around in their sockets, trying to focus, unable. The whites of his eyes were tinged with pink, distorted Easter eggs.

Ernest leaned over, his mouth by Nolan's ear. "Can you hear me?"

Nolan moaned.

"Nolan? Come on, man, wake up. We need to know how you feel. For posterity." Ernest looked up at Ian. "Jot this down: subject unwilling or unable to respond. In great deal of pain."

Nolan's eyes focused. He blinked and tried to press himself into the table. Opening his mouth, all that escaped was a belching groan.

"Next level before he passes out again," Ernest said, moving to the simmering pot.

"Burns . . ." Nolan groaned. "Help me . . ."

Ernest said, "This is going to be tricky. Ian, your turn. Grab his dick. Put on the gloves first."

Ian got into place and did what Ernest instructed.

"Hold it up, as straight as you can. Hold it steady." He turned back to the pot.

"Wha . . ." Breathing came as gasping hitches, making speech impossible for Nolan. Tears streamed, dampening the hair along his temples. His eyes were glistening gems, brilliant and dying at the same time, a beautiful comet blazing to oblivion.

Ernest held up an oversized syringe. "Hold him steady. I'm going to inject this." The rod in the urethra was narrow, much thinner than the needle on the syringe. "Okay, hang on. He'll thrash around, so hold him. Steady now."

He stuck the syringe into the tip of the rod. Moments later, the liquid metal traveled the length and filled the inside of Nolan's penis.

His shrieks reverberated off the cellar walls. He strained against the ropes, as if in the throes of a seizure. A sudden snap followed Nolan's trailing screams before he passed out.

Ernest tossed the stethoscope to Caleb and traced his fingertips over the damaged flesh and bone of Nolan's broken leg. "Jesus Christ, that was a hell of a reaction. He broke his own goddamned shinbone."

Ernest examined the rest of the body. The flesh on the other ankle was torn and bloody, but the rope had held. He secured the broken leg to the table with another length of rope before checking on Nolan's wrists.

Ian pulled the rod from Nolan's body. The liquid metal inside his penis had already begun to harden.

"Hold it up," Ernest said. "If you put it down the liquid will drip out."

Caleb held up the stethoscope. "He's still alive."

Ernest smiled and wiped his brow with his sleeve. "Level Three was a success, I would say."

"Look at this," Ian said, pointing to the underside of the penis. "The skin's burning away over here. But nothing's leaking out. I think it's already solid."

"I can't believe he's still alive," Caleb said, shaking his head. "If it was me, I'd sure want to be dead."

Ernest glanced at his watch. "Write this: Level Three achieved at 7:20 pm. Subject in agony, yet continues to live. Asked for help. Barely able to speak, yet screamed his head off a minute later. Level Three consisted of pouring liquid metal into his urethra, creating a permanent solid block in his urinary passage."

He cleared his throat. "Now at . . . 7:35 pm, we will attempt Level Four. Will see if administering liquid to victim while asleep revives him at all."

Ian raised his eyebrows. His hands trembled as he wrote the notes, jotting every word, wishing this ordeal was over. He leaned against a wall, exhausted.

Caleb handed him a small bottle of water. "You okay?"

Ian nodded, chugging the water down his parched throat.

"Hey, look at this," Ernest said. Nolan's penis—ramrod straight and granite solid—jutted up and rested against his stomach. "Come on, break's over. Let's do Level Four."

He held up two small cylindrical tubes. "Ian, write down whatever I say. Try to capture whatever he says or does. If he wakes up."

"You have to hold his head back tight, Caleb. If he went nuts before . . . I don't have a clue what he might be capable of. These are going up his nose now. If he shakes his head, that shit's going everywhere. Hold him as tight as you can."

"Up his nose?" Ian said. "Won't that kill him? That'll, like, fry his brains."

Caleb shook his head. "Why didn't you get something to hold him still, like Flunitrazepam or something, man?"

"Date-rape drug?"

"Yeah. Like you don't have access to that shit."

"Why would I want to use anything that would paralyze him? I want to see his reactions, asshole. I want to see the little fucker squirm."

"You're sure taking this little 'experiment' personally, don't you think?" Ian said.

Ernest thought for a moment and chose to ignore this line of questioning. "I'm not sure whether this'll fry his brains, but in other tests I've run, it didn't kill the subjects right away. They kind of went nuts, but they didn't die right away."

"You still talking about small animals, man?" Caleb asked.

Ernest ignored him and instead tilted Nolan's head back and inserted small metal tubes into each nostril. Nolan's breathing became whistling gasps, and his mouth popped open to breathe.

"He's waking up," Caleb yelled, bending low and holding on tight to Nolan's head.

Dipping two metal turkey basters into the pot, Ernest filled them with the liquid and rushed back.

Before Ernest even touched him, Nolan responded, crying out and bucking on the table.

Ernest yelled at the camera to be heard above Nolan's steady stream of guttural and hysterical cries. "Level Four! Pour liquid into nasal passages!"

Nolan fought, spit and sweat and blood flying everywhere, horrible grunts and animal growls erupting from his destroyed body. Placing the tips of the basters into the tubes, Ernest injected the boiling liquid into Nolan's nasal passages.

Inhuman screams poured out of him, seeming to come from some other level of existence. He strained against the ropes securing his body, fighting and stretching so spastically and furiously that sinewy cords snapped up and down the length of his body.

Blood gushed from deep ruts in his skin. Then he passed out.

Ernest collapsed. "Oh my god," he panted. "Level Four complete. Did you get all that, Ian?"

Ian's heart pounded and his head thudded. "I feel sick."

"We're almost done. Hang in there."

"Can't," Ian said. "Gonna be sick."

Ernest said, "We can't stop now and leave him hanging. We have to put him out of his misery. Take a deep breath. Get a fucking grip, man."

The three stood around Nolan. His once not-quite-handsome face was now a gnarled and hideous ruin, a distorted parody of his former self. Metal patches stuck to his skin and hair. His cheeks were open sores, oozing pustules of flesh and exposed bone where metal had leaked through. The lining of his nostrils were two solid metal caves. Blood trickled out of the corners of his eyes and mouth.

Ian gently squeezed the nose and felt the soft metal shift beneath his fingers, felt the spongy mass of tissue give beneath his touch. His stomach flipped, and he wished he'd ignored that strange compulsion to touch Nolan.

"Level Five," Ernest said. "We end this. See what sort of resolve or strength this freak has left."

Caleb listened to Nolan's chest with the stethoscope. "His heart's strong, I guess," he said, licking his lips, stepping away from the body. "It's still beating, anyway."

"I thought he'd be dead by now," Ernest said, staring off at nothing. "Let's do this. Final level."

He grabbed a length of tubing from the tray. "This is flexible, like a garden hose, but it's metal. Coiling of some sort. I snagged it from the garage, when the mechanic wasn't looking. Open his mouth."

"His mouth?" Caleb asked.

"His fucking mouth!" Ernest shrieked.

Caleb tipped Nolan's head back and pried open his mouth. Ernest fed the tube down his throat.

"Write this down: eight pm. About to attempt Level Five. Tubing has been fed into subject. The tube acts as a sort of trachea. Get ready, guys. This is it."

Ian nodded and licked his lips. His heart pounded so fiercely his temples ached.

"Hold him tight, Caleb!" Ernest placed a funnel at the end of the tubing in Nolan's throat. He turned back to the pot and filled a quart-sized metal measuring cup, and he then dumped the molten metal down the tube and into Nolan's throat. He pulled the tube out as the throat and mouth filled with the liquid, the neck and throat bulging.

"Level Five!" Ernest cried, a look of triumph filling his eyes and spreading into an enormous grin. "Subject appears to be suffocating. His eyes are—"

Nolan's movements were lightning-fast and unexpected; in the throes of his mindless, adrenaline-powered paroxysm, he broke through the last of the thick cords and bolted upright, his head whipping. Blood poured from deep gashes across his body where moments before he'd been restrained. His arms and legs pinwheeled and struck out in every direction at once, searching for help, his brain now mush, his actions primal, mouth gasping for air.

Metal, blood, and vomit flew everywhere, coating the walls and the young men. Nolan's pupils disappeared, and he searched and pawed blindly, trying to scream through the terrible obstruction in his throat, trying to pull it out, gasping and retching, stuffing his fingers into his mouth and reaching down his throat, his body trying to vomit out the foreign objects.

Nolan was free from his restraints but his actions were primal and desperate. His bulging eyes had focused enough so that they trained on a terrified Ernest, who was now trying in a blind panic to remember where he had left the exit.

Nolan grabbed Ernest from behind, searching for help, a desperate young man tortured beyond recognition, searching for someone to save him from his living hell. So it was his fortunate luck, and Ernest's piss-poor luck, that he was able to exact his revenge without even knowing it.

For in his final moments, Nolan—weighed down by the metal filling every major cavity in his body—gurgled and sputtered his final gasping breaths, falling forward, impaling Ernest's tailbone, piercing major organs with what was possibly the world's hardest and sharpest dildo.

This contorted mess of twisted body parts fell forward into the table, crashing to the floor. The metal-filled pot overturned, spilling its boiling contents on Ernest's head. He howled, arms flailing, the liquid hardening into a layer on his head and shoulders, the skin beneath bubbling and dissolving off his bones.

He died melting like a crayon in the sun, his colon impaled by his very own test subject, who was dead as well.

Some time later, Ian pulled himself up off the floor. In a daze he extinguished the light and pulled the door closed, shutting the carnage in behind him. His mind was numb, his body trembling.

He remembered earlier walking through a series of doors and now just walked down the passageways shell-shocked, trying to recall the way they had come just a couple of hours before. It felt like he had been down there for days. He realized it would be years before the bodies would be found, if ever.

When he reached the third door, Caleb was sitting on the floor. Ian shined the flashlight beam in his glazed eyes.

"I forgot about you, man," Ian said, sitting on the floor beside him. "When did you sneak out here?"

"Right after Nolan fell on Ernest. I got the fuck out of there. I thought you fainted or something."

"They're both dead. What are we going to do?"

Caleb exhaled and ran his hands through his hair. "Do? We're royally fucked, Ian. Unless you know the combination. Look." He shined the flashlight in the air and the beam fell on the lock, a keypad with the series of numbers 0–9.

Ian stared at it, remembering only that the combination was seven digits long.

"Oh, shit," he squeaked, quickly getting up and entering random patterns of numbers into the keypad. "We can figure this out. I mean, how many combinations can there be?"

Caleb raised his eyebrows. "Are you serious?"

Ian pounded away at the keypad. He wailed on the solid oak door as well but only succeeded in smashing his knuckles and cutting the fleshy pads on his hands.

"What are we gonna do?" he cried, kicking Caleb, who stared into the darkness.

Ian searched the basement for an exit, a window, a crawlspace. All he found was hallway after hallway of solid rock.

Two weeks later the food supply was rotten beyond even their desperation. Every last drop of dead blood—their only source of liquid besides the small reserve of bottled water and their own urine—had been consumed.

Starving now, Ian, whose fingernails were bloody pulps from his efforts to tunnel through solid rock, his throat raw from screaming for help hour after hour, wondered how long he would be able to survive on Caleb's dead body.

Caleb was wondering the same thing . . . only he wondered if Ian would last longer if consumed while still alive. Wondered if the body parts would heal, providing Caleb with an endless food supply. Wondered what warm blood tasted like.

Staring at one another from opposite ends of the torture chamber, Ian and Caleb began another experiment in human nature.

The Burgers of Calais

Graham Masterton

"The Burgers of Calais" was first published in *Dark Terrors 6, The Gollancz Book of Horror*, edited by Stephen Jones and David Sutton, 2002.

Graham Masterton was a young newspaper reporter when he wrote his first novel *Rules of Duel* with the encouragement of his friend William Burroughs, author of *The Naked Lunch*. He went on to become editor of *Penthouse* and *Penthouse Forum* magazines before penning his first horror novel *The Manitou* which was filmed with Tony Curtis playing the lead role. Since then he has published over a hundred horror novels, thrillers, historical sagas, short stories and best-selling sex instruction manuals. He lived in Cork, Ireland, for several years, and has written a new crime novel about a female Irish detective, Katie Maguire. He now lives in England. His wife and agent Wiescka established his name as the leading horror novelist in Poland, but passed away in April, 2011. He dedicates this story to her memory. Website: www.grahammasterton.co.uk.

"The Burgers of Calais" is both a pun and a metaphor on the suffering of the people of Calais who were almost starved to death in a siege by the English in 1347, and had to eat rats to survive. They were saved only by the self-sacrifice of six eminent burghers who agreed to surrender themselves and hand over the keys of the city. But it was mostly inspired by Eric Schlosser's book Fast Food Nation which describes how foul the ingredients of most American fast food actually is. Not rats, but pretty close.

♦ ♦ ♦ ♦

I NEVER CARED FOR NORTHERN PARTS and I never much cared for eastern parts neither, because I hate the cold and I don't have any time for those bluff, ruddy-faced people who live there, with their rugged plaid coats and their Timberland boots and their way of whacking you on the back when you least expect it, like whacking you on the back is supposed to be some kind of friendly gesture or something.

I don't like what goes on there, neither. Everybody behaves so cheerful and folksy but believe me that folksiness hides some real grisly secrets that would turn your blood to iced gazpacho.

You can guess, then, that I was distinctly unamused when I was driving back home early last October from Presque Isle, Maine, and my beloved '71 Mercury Marquis dropped her entire engine on the highway like a cow giving birth.

The only reason I had driven all the way to Presque Isle, Maine, was to lay to rest my old Army buddy Dean Brunswick III (may God forgive him for what he did in Colonel Wrightman's cigar-box). I couldn't wait to get back south, but now I found myself stuck a half-mile away from Calais, Maine, population 4,003 and one of the most northernmost, easternmost, back-whackingest towns you could ever have waking nightmares about.

Calais is locally pronounced "CAL-us" and believe me a callous is exactly what it is—a hard, corny little spot on the right elbow of America. Especially when you have an engineless uninsured automobile and a maxed-out Visa card and only $226 in your billfold and no friends or relations back home who can afford to send you more than a cheery hello.

I left my beloved Mercury tilted up on the leafy embankment by the side of US Route 1 South and walked into town. I never cared a whole lot for walking, mainly because my weight has kind of edged up a little since I left the Army in '86, due to a pathological lack of restraint when it comes to filé gumbo and Cajun spiced chicken with lots of crunchy bits and mustard-barbecued spare ribs and Key lime pies. My landlady Rita Personage says that when she first saw me she thought that Orson Welles had risen from the dead, and I must say I do have quite a line in flappy white double-breasted sport coats, not to mention a few wide-brimmed white hats, though not all in prime condition since I lost my job with the Louisiana Restaurant Association which was a heinous political fix involving some of the shadier elements in the East Baton Rouge catering community and also possibly the fact that I was on the less balletic side of 289 pounds.

It was a piercing bright day. The sky was blue like ink and the trees were all turning gold and red and crispy brown. Calais is one of those neat New England towns with white clapboard houses and churches with spires and cheery people waving to each other as they drive up and down the streets at 2 1/2 mph.

By the time I reached North and Main I was sweating like a cheese and severely in need of a beer. There was a *whip, whip, whoop* behind me and it was a police patrol car. I stopped and the officer put down his window. He had mirror sunglasses and a sandy moustache that looked as if he kept his nailbrush on his upper lip. And freckles. You know the type.

"Wasn't speeding, was I, officer?"

He took off his sunglasses. He didn't smile. He didn't even blink. He said, "You look like a man with a problem, sir."

"I know. I've been on Redu-Quick for over six months now and I haven't lost a pound."

That really cracked him up, not. "You in need of some assistance?" he asked me.

"Well, my car suffered a minor mechanical fault a ways back there and I was going into town to see if I could get anybody to fix it."

"That your clapped-out saddle-bronze Marquis out on Route One?"

"That's the one. Nothing that a few minutes in the crusher couldn't solve."

"Want to show me some ID?"

"Sure." I handed him my driver's license and my identity card from the restaurant association. He peered at them, and for some reason actually *sniffed* them.

"John Henry Dauphin, Choctaw Drive, East Baton Rouge. You're a long way from home, Mr. Dauphin."

"I've just buried one of my old Army buddies up in Presque Isle."

"And you *drove* all the way up here?"

"Sure, it's only two thousand three hundred and seven miles. It's a pretty fascinating drive, if you don't have any drying paint that needs watching."

"Louisiana Restaurant Association . . . that's who you work for?"

"That's right," I lied. Well, he didn't have to know that I was out of a job. "I'm a restaurant hygiene consultant. Hey—bet you never guessed that I was in the food business."

"Okay . . . the best thing you can do is call into Lyle's Autos down at the other end of Main Street, get your vehicle towed off the highway as soon as possible. If you require a place to stay I can recommend the Calais Motor Inn."

"Thank you. I may stay for a while. Looks like a nice town. Very . . . well-swept."

"It is," he said, as if he were warning me to make sure that it stayed that way. He handed back my ID and drove off at the mandatory snail's pace.

Lyle's Autos was actually run by a stocky man called Nils Guttormsen. He had a gray crewcut and a permanently surprised face like a chipmunk going through the sound barrier backward. He charged me a mere $65 for towing my car into his workshop, which was only slightly more than a quarter of everything I had in the world, and he estimated that he could put the engine back into it for less than $785, which was about $784 more than it was actually worth.

"How long will it take, Nils?"

"Well, John, you need it urgent?"

"Not really, Nils . . . I thought I might stick around town for a while. So—you know—why don't you take your own sweet time?"

"Okay, John. I have to get transmission parts from Bangor. I could have it ready, say Tuesday?"

"Good deal, Nils. Take longer if you want. Make it the Tuesday after next. Or even the Tuesday after that."

"You'll be wanting a car while I'm working on yours, John."

"Will I, Nils? No, I don't think so. I could use some exercise, believe me."

"It's entirely up to you, John. But I've got a couple of nifty Toyotas to rent if you change your mind. They look small but there's plenty of room in them. Big enough to carry a sofa."

"Thanks for the compliment, Nils."

I hefted my battered old suitcase to the Calais Motor Inn, changing hands every few yards all the way down Main Street. Fortunately the desk accepted my Visa impression without even the hint of hysterical laughter. The Calais Motor Inn was a plain, comfortable motel, with plaid carpets and a shiny bar with tinkly music where I did justice to three bottles of chilled Molson's and a ham-and-Swiss-cheese triple-decker sandwich on rye with coleslaw and straw fried potatoes, and two helpings of cookie crunch ice-cream to keep my energy levels up.

The waitress was a pretty snubby-nose woman with cropped blonde hair and a kind of a Swedish look about her.

"Had enough?" she asked me.

"Enough of what? Cookie crunch ice cream or Calais in general?"

"My name's Velma," she said.

"John," I replied, and bobbed up from my leatherette seat to shake her hand.

"Just passing through, John?" she asked me.

"I don't know, Velma . . . I was thinking of sticking around for a while. Where would somebody like me find themselves a job? And don't say the circus."

"Is that what you do, John?" she asked me.

"What do you mean, Velma?"

"Make jokes about yourself before anybody gets them in?"

"Of course not. Didn't you know that all fat guys have to be funny by federal statute? No, I'm a realist. I know what my relationship is with food and I've learned to live with it."

"You're a good-looking guy, John, you know that?"

"You can't fool me, Velma. All fat people look the same. If fat people could run faster, they'd all be bank robbers, because nobody can tell them apart."

"Well, John, if you want a job you can try the want ads in the local paper, *The Quoddy Whirlpool.*"

"The what?"

"The bay here is called the Passamaquoddy, and out by Eastport we've got the Old Sow Whirlpool, which is the biggest whirlpool in the Western hemisphere."

"I see. Thanks for the warning."

"You should take a drive around the Quoddy Loop . . . it's beautiful. Fishing quays, lighthouses, lakes. Some good restaurants, too."

"My car's in the shop right now, Velma. Nothing too serious. Engine fell out."

"You're welcome to borrow mine, John. It's only a Volkswagen but I don't hardly ever use it."

I looked up at her and narrowed my eyes. Down in Baton Rouge the folks slide around on a snail's trail of courtesy and Southern charm, but I can't imagine any one of them offering a total stranger the use of their car, especially a total stranger who was liable to ruin the suspension just by sitting in the driver's seat.

"That's very gracious of you, Velma."

I bought *The Quoddy Whirlpool.* If you were going into hospital for a heart bypass they could give you that paper instead of a general anesthetic. Under "Help Wanted" somebody was advertising for a "talented" screen-door repair person and somebody else needed an experienced leaf-blower mechanic and somebody else was looking for a twice-weekly dog-walker for their Presa Canario. Since I happened to know that Presa Canarios stand two feet tall and weigh almost as much as I do, and that two of them notoriously ripped an innocent woman in San Francisco into bloody shreds I was not wholly motivated to apply for the last of those positions.

In the end I went to the Maine Job Service on Beech Street. A bald guy in a green zip-up hand-knitted cardigan sat behind a desk with photographs of his toothy wife on it (presumably the perpetrator of the green zip-up hand-knitted cardigan) while I had to hold my hand up all the time to stop the sun from shining in my eyes.

"So . . . what is your field of expertise, Mr. Dauphin?"

"Oh, please, call me John. I'm a restaurant hygienist. I have an FSIS qualification from Baton Rouge University and nine years' experience working for the Louisiana Restaurant Association."

"What brings you up to Calais, Maine, John?"

"I just felt it was time for a radical change of location." I squinted at the nameplate on his desk. "Martin."

"I'm afraid I don't have anything available on quite your level of expertise, John. But I do have one or two catering opportunities."

"What exactly kind of catering opportunities, Martin?"

"Vittles need a cleaner . . . that's an excellent restaurant, Vittles, one of the premier eateries in town. It's situated in the Calais Motor Inn."

"Ah." As a guest of the Calais Motor Inn, I couldn't exactly see myself eating dinner in the restaurant and then carrying my own dishes into the kitchen and washing them up.

"Then Tony's has an opportunity for a breakfast chef."

"Tony's?"

"Tony's Gourmet Burgers on North Street."

"I see. What do they pay?"

"They pay more than Burger King or McDonald's. They have outlets all over Maine and New Brunswick, but they're more of a family business. More of a *quality* restaurant, if you know what I mean. I always take my own family to eat there."

"And is that all you have?"

"I have plenty of opportunities in fishing and associated trades. Do you have any expertise with drift nets?"

"Drift nets? Are you kidding? I spent my whole childhood trawling for pilchards off the coast of Greenland."

Martin looked across his desk at me, sitting there with my hand raised like I needed to go to the bathroom. When he spoke his voice was very biscuity and dry. "Why don't you call round at Tony's, John? See if you like the look of it. I'll give Mr. Le Renges a call, tell him you're on your way."

"Thanks, Martin."

Tony's Gourmet Burgers was one block away from Burger King and two blocks away from McDonald's, on a straight tree-lined street where the 4x4s rolled past at 2 1/2 mph and everybody waved to each other and whacked each other on the back whenever they could get near enough and you felt like a hidden orchestra was going to strike up the theme to *Providence*.

All the same Tony's was quite a handsome-looking restaurant with a brick front and brass carriage-lamps outside with flickering artificial flames. A chalkboard proudly proclaimed that this was "the home of wholesome, hearty food, lovingly prepared in our own kitchens by people who really care." Inside it was fitted out with dark wood paneling and tables with green checkered cloths and gilt-framed engravings of whitetail deer, black bear and moose. It was crowded with cheery-looking families, and you certainly couldn't fault it for ambiance. Smart, but homely, with none of that wipe-clean feeling you get at McDonald's.

At the rear of the restaurant was a copper bar with an open grill, where a spotty young guy in a green apron and a tall green chef's hat was sizzling hamburgers and steaks.

A redheaded girl in a short green pleated skirt sashayed up to me and gave me a 500-watt smile, complete with teeth-braces. "You prefer a booth or a table, sir?"

"Actually, neither. I have an appointment to see Mr. Le Renges."

"He's right in back . . . why don't you follow me? What name shall I say?"

"John."

Mr. Le Renges was sitting in a blood-red leather chair with a repro-duction antique table beside him, on which there was a fax-machine, a silver carriage-clock, and a glass of seltzer. He was a bony man of 45 or so with dyed-black collar-length hair which he had combed with something approaching genius to conceal his dead-white scalp. His nose was sharp and multi-faceted, and his eyes glittered under his overgrown eyebrows like blowflies. He wore a very white open-neck shirt with long 1970s collar-points and a tailored black three-piece suit. I had the feeling that he thought he bore more than a passing resemblance to Al Pacino.

On the paneled wall behind him hung an array of certificates from

THE BURGERS OF CALAIS 195

the Calais Regional Chamber of Commerce and the Maine Restaurant Guide and even one from Les Chevaliers de la Haute Cuisine Canadienne.

"Come in, John," said Mr. Le Renges, in a distinctly French-Canadian accent. "Sit down, please . . . the couch, perhaps? That chair's a little—"

"A little *little?*"

"I was thinking only of your comfort, John. You see my policy is always to make the people who work for me feel happy and comfortable. I don't have a desk, I never have. A desk is a statement which says that I am more important than you. I am *not* more important. Everybody who works here is of equal importance, and of equal value."

"You've been reading the McDonald's Bible. Always make your staff feel valued. Then you won't have to pay them so much."

I could tell that Mr. Le Renges didn't quite know if he liked that remark. It was the way he twitched his head, like Data in *Star Trek*. But I could also tell that he was the kind of guy who was anxious that nobody should leave him without fully comprehending what a wonderful human being he was.

He sipped some seltzer and eyed me over the rim of the glass. "You are perhaps a little *mature* to be seeking work as a burger chef."

"Mature? I'm positively overripe. But I've been working in the upper echelons of the restaurant trade for so long, I thought it was time that I went back to basics. Got my hands dirty, so to speak."

"At Tony's Gourmet Burgers, John, our hygiene is second to none."

"Of course. When I say getting my hands dirty—that's like a metaphor. Food hygiene, that's my specialty. I know everything there is to know about proper cooking times and defrosting and never picking your nose while you're making a Caesar salad."

"What's your cooking experience, John?"

"I was a cook in the Army. Three times winner of the Fort Polk prize for culinary excellence. It made me very good at home economics. I can make a pound-and-a-half of ground beef stretch between two platoons of infantry and a heavy armored assault force."

"You're a funny guy, John," said Mr. Le Renges, without the slightest indication that he was amused.

"I'm fat, Tony. Funny goes with the territory."

"I don't want you to make me laugh, John. I want you to cook burgers. And it's 'Mr. Le Renges' to you."

He took me through to the kitchen, which was tiled in dark brown ceramic with stainless-steel counters. Two gawky young kids were using microwave ovens to thaw out frozen hamburger patties and frozen bacon and frozen fried chicken and frozen French fries. "This is Chip and this is Denzil."

"How's it going, Chip? Denzil?"

Chip and Denzil stared at me numbly and mumbled "'kay I guess."

"And this is Letitia." A frowning dark-haired girl was painstakingly tearing up iceberg lettuce as if it were as difficult as lacemaking.

"Letitia's one of our *challenged* crew members," said Mr. Le Renges, resting one of his hairy tarantula hands on her shoulder. "The state of Maine gives us special tax relief to employ the challenged, but even if they didn't I'd still want to have her here. That's the kind of guy I am, John. I've been called to do more than feed people. I've been called to enrich their lives."

Letitia looked up at me with unfocused aquamarine eyes. She was pretty but she had the expression of a smalltown beauty queen who has just been hit on the head by half a brick. Some instinct told me that Tony Le Renges wasn't only using her as an iceberg lettuce tearer.

"We take pride in the supreme quality of our food," he said. Without any apparent sense of irony he opened a huge freezer at the back of the kitchen and showed me the frozen steaks and the frost-covered envelopes of pre-cooked chili, ready for boiling in the bag. He showed me the freeze-dried vegetables and the frozen corn bread and the dehydrated lobster chowder (just add hot water). And this was in Maine, where you can practically find fresh lobsters waltzing down the street.

None of this made me weak with shock. Even the best restaurants use a considerable proportion of pre-cooked and pre-packaged food, and fast food outlets like McDonald's and Burger King use nothing else. Even their scrambled eggs come dried and pre-scrambled in a packet.

What impressed me was how Mr. Le Renges could sell this ordinary, industrialized stuff as "wholesome, hearty food, lovingly cooked in our own kitchens by people who really care" when most of it was grudgingly thrown together in giant factories by minimum-wage shift-workers who didn't give a rat's ass.

Mr. Le Renges must have had an inkling about the way my mind was working.

"You know what our secret is?" he asked me.

"If I'm going to come and cook here, Mr. Le Renges, I think it might be a good idea if you told me."

"We have the best-tasting burgers anywhere, that's our secret.

McDonald's and Burger King don't even come *close*. Once you've tasted one of our burgers, you won't want anything else. Here—Kevin—pass me a burger so that John here try it."

"That's okay," I told him. "I'll take your word for it. I had a sandwich already."

"No, John, if you're going to work here, I insist."

"Listen, Mr. Le Renges, I'm a professional food hygienist. I know what goes into burgers and that's why I never eat them. Never."

"What are you suggesting?"

"I'm not suggesting anything. It's just that I know for a fact that a proportion of undesirable material makes its way into ground beef and I don't particularly want to eat it."

"Undesirable material? What do you mean?"

"Well, *waste products,* if you want me to be blunt about it. Cattle are slaughtered and disemboweled so fast that it makes it inevitable that a certain amount of excrement contaminates the meat."

"Listen, John, how do you think I compete with McDonald's and Burger King? I make my customers feel as if they're a cut above people who eat at the big fast-food chains. I make them feel as if they're discerning diners."

"But you're serving up pretty much the same type of food."

"Of course we are. That's what our customers are used to, that's what they like. But we make it just a little more expensive, and we serve it up like it's something really special. We give them a proper restaurant experience, that's why they come here for birthdays and special occasions."

"But that must whack up your overheads."

"What we lose on overheads we gain by sourcing our own foodstuffs."

"You mean you can buy this stuff cheaper than McDonald's? How do you do that? You don't have a millionth of their buying power."

"We use farmers' and stockbreeders' co-operatives. Little guys, that the big fast-food chains don't want to do business with. That's why our burgers taste better, and that's why they don't contain anything that you wouldn't want to eat."

Kevin came over from the grill with a well-charred burger patty on a plate. His spots were glowing angrily from the heat. Mr. Le Renges handed me a fork and said, "There . . . try it."

I cut a small piece off and peered at it suspiciously. "No shit?" I asked him.

"Nothing but one thousand percent protein, I promise you."

I dry-swallowed, and then I put the morsel in my mouth. I chewed it slowly, trying not to think about the manure-splattered ramps of the slaughterhouses that I had visited around Baton Rouge. Mr. Le Renges watched me with those glittering blowfly eyes of his and that didn't make it any more appetizing, either.

But, surprisingly, the burger actually tasted pretty good. It was tender, with just the right amount of crunchiness on the outside, and it was well-seasoned with onion and salt and pepper and the tiniest touch of chili, and there was another flavor, too, that really lifted it.

"Cumin?" I asked Mr. Le Renges.

"Aha. That would be telling. But you like it, don't you?"

I cut off another piece. "Okay, I have to confess that I do."

Mr. Le Renges whacked me on the back so that I almost choked. "You see, John? Now you know what I was talking about when I told you that I was called to enrich people's lives. I keep small farmers in business, and at the same time I give the people of Calais a very important community venue with the best food that I can economically serve up. Well, not only Calais. I have Tony's Gourmet Burgers in Old Town and Millinocket and Waterville and I've just opened a new flagship restaurant in St. Stephen, over the river in Canada."

"Well, congratulations," I coughed. "When do you want me to start?"

I dreamed that I was sitting by the window of Rocco's restaurant on Drusilla Lane in Baton Rouge, eating a spicy catfish poboy with a cheese fry basket and a side of brown gravy. I had just ordered my bread pudding when the phone rang and the receptionist told me in a clogged-up voice that it was 5:15 in the morning.

"Why are you telling me this?" I asked her.

"You asked for an alarm call, sir. Five fifteen, and it's five-fifteen."

I heaved myself up in bed. Outside my window it was still totally dark. It was then that I remembered that I was now the *chef de petit dejeuner* at Tony's, and I was supposed to be over on North Street at 6 a.m. sharp to open up the premises and start getting the bacon griddled and the eggs shirred and the coffee percolating.

I stared at myself in the mirror. "Why did you do this to yourself?" I asked me.

"Because you're a nitpicking perfectionist who couldn't turn a blind eye to three mouse droppings at the Cajun Queen Restaurant, that's why. And they probably weren't even mouse droppings at all. Just capers."

"Capers schmapers."

It was so cold outside that the deserted sidewalks shone like hammered glass. I walked to North Street where Chip had just opened up the restaurant.

"Morning, Chip."

"Yeah." He showed me how to switch off the alarm and switch on the lights. Then we went through to the kitchen and he showed me how to heat up the griddle and take out the frozen bacon and the frozen burgers and mix up the "fresh squeezed" orange juice (just add water).

We had only been there ten minutes when a young mousy-haired girl with a pale face and dark circles under her eyes came through the door. "Hi," she said. "I'm Anita. You must be John."

"Hi, Anita," I said, wiping my fingers on my green apron and shaking hands. "How about a cup of coffee before the hordes descend on us?"

"Okay, then," she blinked. From the expression on her face I think she must have thought I said "whores."

But they were hordes all right, and once they started coming through that door they didn't stop. By a quarter after seven every booth and every table was crowded with businessmen and postal workers and truckers and even the sandy-haired cop who had first flagged me down as I walked into town. I couldn't believe that these people got up so early. Not only that, they were all so *cheerful*, too, like they couldn't wait to start another day's drudgery. It was all, "Good morning, Sam! And how are you on this cold and frosty morning!" "Good morning, Mrs. Trent! See *you* wrapped up warm and toasty!" "Hi, Rick! Great day for the race—the human race!" I mean, please.

They not only looked hearty and talked hearty, they ate hearty, too. For two hours solid I was sizzling bacon and flipping burgers and frying eggs and browning corned-beef hash. Anita was dashing from table to table with juice and coffee and double orders of toast, and it wasn't until 8:00 that a sassy black girl called Oona came in to help her.

Gradually, however, the restaurant began to empty out, with more back-whacking and more cheery goodbyes, until we were left with nobody but two FedEx drivers and an old woman who looked as if she was going to take the next six months to chew her way through two slices of Canadian bacon.

It was then that one of the FedEx drivers put his hand over his mouth and spat into it. He frowned down at what he had found in his burger and showed it to his friend. Then he got up from the table and came over to the grill, his hand cupped over his mouth.

"Broken my darn tooth," he said.

"How d'you do that?" I asked him.

"Bit into my burger and there was *this* in it."

He held up a small black object between his finger and thumb.

I took it from him and turned it this way and that. There was no doubt about it, it was a bullet, slightly flattened by impact.

"I'm real sorry," I said. "Look, this is my first day here. All I can do is report it to the management and you can have your breakfast on us."

"I'm going to have to see a darn dentist," he complained. "I can't abide the darn dentist. And what if I'd swallowed it? I could of got lead poisoning."

"I'm sorry. I'll show it to the owner just as soon as he gets here."

"This'll cost plenty, I bet you. Do you want to take a look?" Before I could stop him he stretched open his mouth and showed me a chipped front incisor and a mouthful of mushed-up hamburger.

Mr. Le Renges came in at 11:00 a.m. Outside it was starting to get windy and his hair had flapped over to one side like a crow's wing. Before I could collar him he dived straight into his office and closed the door, presumably to spend some time rearranging his wayward locks. He came out five minutes later, briskly chafing his hands together like a man eager to get down to business.

"Well, John, how did it go?"

"Pretty good, Mr. Le Renges. Place was packed out."

"Always is. People know a good deal when they see one."

"Only one problem. A guy found this in his burger."

I handed him the bullet. He inspected it closely, and then he shook his head.

"That didn't come from one of our burgers, John."

"I saw him spit it out myself. He broke one of his front teeth."

"Oldest trick in the book. Guy needs dental work, he comes into a restaurant and pretends he broke his tooth on something he ate. Gets the restaurant to stump up for his dentist's bill."

"Well, it didn't look that way to me."

"That's because you're not as well-versed in the wiles of dishonest customers as I am. You didn't apologize, I hope?"

"I didn't charge him for his breakfast."

"You shouldn't have done that, John. That's practically an admission of liability. Well, let's hope the bastard doesn't try to take it any further."

"Aren't you going to inform the health and safety people?"

"Of course not."

"What about your suppliers?"

"You know as well as I do that all ground beef is magnetically screened for metal particles."

"Sure. But this is a bullet and it's made of lead and lead isn't magnetic."

"They don't *shoot* cows, John."

"Of course not. But anything could have happened. Maybe some kid took a potshot at it when it was standing in a field, and the bullet was lodged in its muscle."

"John, every one of our burgers is very carefully sourced from people who are really *evangelical* when it comes to quality meat. There is no way that this bullet came from one of our burgers, and I hope you're prepared to back me up and say that there was absolutely no sign of any bullet in that customer's patty when you grilled it."

"I didn't actually *see* it, no. But—"

Mr. Le Renges dropped the bullet into his wastebasket. "Attaboy, John. You'll be back here bright and early tomorrow morning, then?"

"Early, yes. Bright? Well, maybe."

All right, you can call me a hairsplitting go-by-the-book bureaucrat, but the way I see it any job has to be done properly or else it's not worth getting out of bed in the morning to do it, especially if you have to get out of bed at 5:15. I walked back to the Calais Motor Inn looking for a bite of lunch, and I ordered a fried chicken salad with iceberg lettuce, tomato, bacon bits, cheddar and mozzarella and home-made croutons, with onion strings and fried pickles on the side. But as comforting as all of this was, I couldn't stop thinking about that bullet and wondering where it had come from. I could understand why Mr. Le Renges didn't want to report it to the health and safety inspectors, but why didn't he want to have a hard word with his own supplier?

Velma came up with another beer. "You're looking serious today, John. I thought you had to be happy by law."

"Got something on my mind, Velma, that's all."

She sat down beside me. "How did the job go?"

"It's an existence. I grill, therefore I am. But something happened today . . . I don't know. It's made me feel kind of uncomfortable."

"What do you mean, John?"

"It's like having my shorts twisted only it's inside my head. I keep trying to tug it this way and that way and it still feels not quite right."

"Go on."

I told her about the bullet and the way in which Mr. Le Renges had insisted that he wasn't going to report it.

"Well, that happens. You do get customers who bring in a dead fly and hide it in their salad so they won't have to pay."

"I know. But, I don't know."

After a double portion of chocolate ice-cream with vanilla-flavored wafers I walked back to Tony's where the lunchtime session was just finishing. "Mr. Le Renges still here?" I asked Oona.

"He went over to St. Stephen. He won't be back until six, thank God."

"You don't like him much, do you?"

"He gives me the heeby-jeebies, if you must know."

I went through to Mr. Le Renges' office. Fortunately, he had left it unlocked. I looked in the wastebasket and the bullet was still there. I picked it out and dropped it into my pocket.

On my way back to the Calais Motor Inn a big blue pick-up truck tooted at me. It was Nils Guttormsen from Lyle's Autos, still looking surprised.

"They brought over your transmission parts from Bangor this morning, John. I should have her up and running in a couple of days."

"That's great news, Nils. No need to break your ass." Especially since I don't have any money to pay you yet.

I showed the bullet to Velma.

"That's truly weird, isn't it?" she said.

"You're right, Velma. It's weird, but it's not unusual for hamburger meat to be contaminated. In fact, it's more usual than unusual, which is why I never eat hamburgers."

"I don't know if I want to hear this, John."

"You should, Velma. See—they used to have federal inspectors in every slaughterhouse, but the Reagan administration wanted to save money, so they allowed the meatpacking industry to take care of its own hygiene procedures. Streamlined Inspection System for Cattle, that's what they call it—SIS-C."

"I never heard of that, John."

"Well, Velma, as an ordinary citizen you probably wouldn't have.

But the upshot was that when they had no USDA inspectors breathing down their necks, most of the slaughterhouses doubled their line speed, and that meant there was much more risk of contamination. I mean if you can imagine a dead cow hanging up by its heels and a guy cutting its stomach open, and then heaving out its intestines by hand, which they still do, that's a very skilled job, and if a gutter makes one mistake *floop*! everything goes everywhere, blood, guts, dirt, manure, and that happens to one in five cattle. Twenty percent."

"Oh, my God."

"Oh, it's worse than that, Velma. These days, with SIS-C, meat-packers can get away with processing far more diseased cattle. I've seen cows coming into the slaughterhouse with abscesses and tapeworms and measles. The beef scraps they ship out for hamburgers are all mixed up with manure, hair, insects, metal filings, urine and vomit."

"You're making me feel nauseous, John. I had a hamburger for supper last night."

"Make it your last, Velma. It's not just the contamination, it's the quality of the beef they use. Most of the cattle they slaughter for hamburgers are old dairy cattle, because they're cheap and their meat isn't too fatty. But they're full of antibiotics and they're often infected with *E. coli* and salmonella. You take just one hamburger, that's not the meat from a single animal, that's mixed-up meat from dozens or even hundreds of different cows, and it only takes one diseased cow to contaminate thirty-two thousand pounds of ground beef."

"That's like a horror story, John."

"You're too right, Velma."

"But this bullet, John. Where would this bullet come from?"

"That's what I want to know, Velma. I can't take it to the health people because then I'd lose my job and if I lose my job I can't pay for my automobile to be repaired and Nils Guttormsen is going to impound it and I'll never get back to Baton Rouge unless I fucking walk and it's two thousand three hundred and seven miles."

"That far, hunh?"

"That far."

"Why don't you show it to Eddie Bertilson?"

"What?"

"The bullet. Why don't you show it to Eddie Bertilson. Bertilson's Sporting Guns and Ammo, over on Orchard Street? He'll tell you where it came from."

"You think so?"

"I know so. He knows everything about guns and ammo. He used to be married to my cousin Patricia."

"You're a star, Velma. I'll go do that. When I come back, maybe you and I could have some dinner together and then I'll make wild energetic love to you."

"No."

"No?"

"I like you, John, but no."

"Oh."

Eddie Bertilson was one of those extreme pains-in-the-ass-like people who note down the tailfin numbers of military aircraft in Turkey and get themselves arrested for espionage. But I have to admit that he knew everything possible about guns and ammo and when he took a look at that bullet he knew directly what it was.

He was small and bald with dark-tinted glasses and hair growing out of his ears, and a Grateful Dead T-shirt with greasy finger-wipes on it. He screwed this jeweler's eyeglass into his socket and turned the bullet this way and that.

"Where'd you find this?" he wanted to know.

"Do I have to tell you?"

"No, you don't, because I can tell *you* where you found it. You found it amongst the memorabilia of a Viet Nam vet."

"Did I?" The gun store was small and poky and smelled of oil. There were all kinds of hunting rifles arranged in cabinets behind the counter, not to mention pictures of anything that a visitor to Calais may want to kill: woodcock, ruffed grouse, black duck, mallard, blue-wing and green-wing teal.

"This is a 7.92 Gewehr Patrone 98 slug which was the standard ammunition of the Maschinengewehr 34 machine-gun designed by Louis Stange for the German Army in 1934. After the Second World War it was used by the Czechs, the French, the Israelis and the Biafrans, and a few turned up in Viet Nam, stolen from the French."

"It's a machine-gun bullet?"

"That's right," said Eddie, dropping it back in the palm of my hand with great satisfaction at his own expertise.

"So you wouldn't use this to kill, say, a cow?"

"No. Unlikely."

* * *

The next morning Chip and I opened the restaurant as usual and by 8 a.m. we were packed to the windows. Just before 9 a black panel van drew up outside and two guys in white caps and overalls climbed out. They came down the side alley to the kitchen door and knocked.

"Delivery from St. Croix Meats," said one of them. He was a stocky guy with a walrus moustache and a deep diagonal scar across his mouth, as if he had been told to shut up by somebody with a machete.

"Sure," said Chip, and opened up the freezer for him. He and his pal brought in a dozen cardboard boxes labeled Hamburger Patties.

"Always get your hamburgers from the same company?" I asked Chip.

"St. Croix, sure. Mr. Le Renges is the owner."

"Ah." No wonder Mr. Le Renges hadn't wanted to talk to his supplier about the bullet: his supplier was him. I bent my head sideways so that I could read the address. US Route 1, Robbinstown.

It was a brilliantly sunny afternoon and the woods around Calais were all golden and crimson and rusty-colored. Velma drove us down US 1 with Frank and Nancy Sinatra singing *Something Stupid* on the radio.

"I don't know why you're doing this, John. I mean, who cares if somebody found a bullet in their hamburger?"

"*I* care, Velma. Do you think I'm going to be able to live out the rest of my life without finding out how an American cow got hit by a Viet Cong machine-gun?"

It took us almost an hour to find St. Croix Meats because the building was way in back of an industrial park—a big gray rectangular place with six or seven black panel vans parked outside it and no signs outside. The only reason I knew that we had come to the right place was because I saw Mr. Le Renges walking across the yard outside with the biggest ugliest dog that I had ever seen in my life. I'm not a dog expert but I suddenly realized who had been advertising in *The Quoddy Whirlpool* for somebody to walk their Presa Canario.

"What are you going to do now?" Velma asked me. There was a security guard on the gate and there was no way that a 289-pound man in a flappy white raincoat was going to be able to tippy-toe his way in without being noticed.

Just then, however, I saw the guy with the scar who had delivered our hamburgers that morning. He climbed into one of the black vans, started it up, and maneuvered it out of the yard.

"Follow that van," I asked Velma.

"What for, John?"

"I want to see where it goes, that's all."

"This is not much of a date, John."

"I'll make it up to you, I promise."

"Dinner and wild energetic love?"

"We could skip the dinner if you're not hungry."

We followed the van for nearly two-and-a-half hours, until it began to grow dark. I was baffled by the route it took. First of all it stopped at a small medical center in Pembroke. Then it went to a veterinarian just outside of Mathias. It circled back toward Calais, visiting two small dairy farms, before calling last of all at the rear entrance of Calais Memorial Hospital, back in town.

It wasn't always possible for us to see what was happening, but at one of the dairy farms we saw the van drivers carrying cattle carcasses out of the outbuildings, and at the Memorial Hospital we saw them pushing out large wheeled containers, rather like laundry-hampers.

Velma said, "I have to get back to work now. My shift starts at six."

"I don't understand this, Velma," I said. "They were carrying dead cattle out of those farms, but USDA regulations state that cattle have to be processed no more than two hours after they've been slaughtered. After that time, bacteria multiply so much that they're almost impossible to get rid of."

"So Mr. Le Renges is using rotten beef for his hamburgers?"

"Looks like it. But what else? I can understand rotten beef. Dozens of slaughterhouses use rotten beef. But why did the van call at the hospital? And the veterinarian?"

Velma stopped the car outside the motel and stared at me. "Oh, you're not serious."

"I have to take a look inside that meatpacking plant, Velma."

"You're sure you haven't bitten off more than you can chew?"

"Very apt phrase, Velma."

My energy levels were beginning to decline again so I treated myself to a fried shrimp sandwich and a couple of Molson's with a small triangular diet-sized piece of pecan pie to follow. Then I walked around to the hospital and went to the rear entrance where the van from St. Croix Meats had parked. A hospital porter with greasy hair and squinty eyes and glasses was standing out back taking a smoke.

"How's it going, feller?" I asked him.

"Okay. Anything I can do for you?"

"Maybe, I've been looking for a friend of mine. Old drinking buddy from way back."

"Oh, yeah?"

"Somebody told me he's been working around here, driving a van. Said they'd seen him here at the hospital."

The greasy-haired porter blew smoke out of his nostrils. "We get vans in and out of here all day."

"This guy's got a scar, right across his mouth. You couldn't miss him."

"Oh you mean the guy from BioGlean?"

"BioGlean?"

"Sure. They collect, like, surgical waste, and get rid of it."

"What's that, 'surgical waste'?"

"Well, you know. Somebody has their leg amputated, somebody has their arm cut off. Aborted fetuses, stuff like that. You'd be amazed how much stuff a busy hospital has to get rid of."

"I thought they incinerated it."

"They used to, but BioGlean kind of specializes, and I guess it's cheaper than running an incinerator night and day. They even go round auto shops and take bits of bodies out of car wrecks. You don't realize, do you, that the cops won't do it, and that the mechanics don't want to do it, so I guess somebody has to."

He paused, and then he said, "What's your name? Next time your buddy calls by, I'll tell him that you were looking for him."

"Ralph Waldo Emerson. I'm staying at the Chandler House on Chandler."

"Okay . . . Ralph Waldo Emerson. Funny, that. Name kind of rings a bell."

I borrowed Velma's car and drove back out to Robbinstown. I parked in the shadow of a large computer warehouse. St. Croix Meats was surrounded by a high fence topped with razor-wire and the front yard was brightly floodlit. A uniformed security guard sat in a small booth by the gate, reading *The Quoddy Whirlpool*. With any luck, it would send him to sleep, and I would be able to walk right past him.

I waited for over an hour, but there didn't seem to be any way for me to sneak inside. All the lights were on, and now and then I saw workers in hard hats and long rubber aprons walking in and out of the building. Maybe this was the time for me to give up trying to play detective and call the police.

The outside temperature was sinking deeper and deeper and I was beginning to feel cold and cramped in Velma's little Volkswagen. After a while I had to climb out and stretch my legs. I walked as near to the main gate as I could without being seen, and stood next to a skinny maple tree. I felt like an elephant trying to hide behind a lamppost. The security guard was still awake. Maybe he was reading an exciting article about the sudden drop in cod prices.

I had almost decided to call it a night when I heard a car approaching along the road behind me. I managed to hide most of me behind the tree, and Mr. Le Renges drove past, and up to the front gate. At first I thought somebody was sitting in his Lexus with him, but then I realized it was that huge ugly Presa Canario. It looked like a cross between a Great Dane and a hound from hell, and it was bigger than he was. It turned its head and I saw its eyes reflected scarlet. It was like being stared at by Satan, believe me.

The security guard came out to open the gate, and for a moment he and Mr. Le Renges chatted to each other, their breath smoking in the frosty evening air. I thought of crouching down and trying to make my way into the slaughterhouse behind Mr. Le Renges' car, but there was no chance that I could do it without being spotted.

"Everything okay, Vernon?"

"Silent like the grave, Mr. Le Renges."

"That's what I like to hear, Vernon. How's that daughter of yours, Louise? Got over her autism yet?"

"Not exactly, Mr. Le Renges. Doctors say it's going to take some time."

Mr. Le Renges was still talking when one of his big black vans came burbling up the road and stopped behind his Lexus. Its driver waited patiently. After all, Mr. Le Renges was the boss. I hesitated for a moment and then I sidestepped out from behind my skinny little tree and circled around the back of the van. There was a wide aluminum step below the rear doors, and two door-handles that I could cling on to.

"You are out of your cotton-picking mind," I told me. But, still, I climbed up onto the step, as easy as I could. You don't jump onto the back of a van when you're as heavy as me, not unless you want the driver to bounce up and hit his head on the roof.

Mr. Le Renges seemed to go on talking forever, but at last he gave the security guard a wave and drove forward into the yard, and the van followed him. I pressed myself close to the rear doors, in the hope that I wouldn't be quite so obtrusive, but the security guard went back into his booth and shook open his paper and didn't even glance my way.

A man in a bloodied white coat and a hardhat came out of the slaughterhouse building and opened the car door for Mr. Le Renges. They spoke for a moment and then Mr. Le Renges went inside the building himself. The man in the bloodied white coat opened the car's passenger door and let his enormous dog jump out. The dog salaciously sniffed at the blood before the man took hold of its leash. He went walking off with it—or, rather, the dog went walking off with him, its claws scrabbling on the blacktop.

I pushed my way in through the side door that I had seen all the cutters and gutters walking in and out of. Inside there was a long corridor with a wet tiled floor, and then an open door which led to a changing-room and a toilet. Rows of white hard-hats were hanging on hooks, as well as rubber aprons and rubber boots. There was an overwhelming smell of stale blood and disinfectant.

Two booted feet were visible underneath the door of the toilet stall, and clouds of cigarette smoke were rising up above it.

"Only two more hours, thank Christ," said a disembodied voice.

"See the playoff?" I responded, as I took off my raincoat and hung it up.

"Yeah, what a goddamn fiasco. They ought to can that Kershinsky."

I put on a heavy rubber apron and just about managed to tie it up at the back. Then I sat down and tugged on a pair of boots.

"You going to watch the New Brunswick game?" asked the disembodied voice.

"I don't know. I've got a hot date that day."

There was a pause, and more smoke rose up, and then the voice said, "Who *is* that? Is that you, Stemmens?"

I left the changing-room without answering. I squeaked back along the corridor in my rubber boots and went through to the main slaughterhouse building.

You don't even want to imagine what it was like in there. A high, echoing, brightly-lit building with a production line clanking and rattling, mincers grinding and roaring, and thirty or forty cutters in aprons and hard hats boning and chopping and trimming. The noise and the stench of blood were overwhelming, and for a moment I just stood there with my hand pressed over my mouth and nose, with that fried shrimp sandwich churning in my stomach as if the shrimp were still alive.

The black vans were backed up to one end of the production line, and men were heaving out the meat that they had been gleaning during the day. They were dumping it straight onto the killing floor where normally the live cattle would be stunned and killed—heaps and heaps of it, a tangle of sagging cattle and human arms and legs, along with glistening strings of intestines and globs of fat and things that looked like run-over dogs and knackered donkeys, except it was all so mixed-up and disgusting that I couldn't be sure what it all was. It was flesh, that was all that mattered. The cutters were boning it and cutting it into scraps, and the scraps were being dumped into giant stainless-steel machines and ground by giant augers into a pale-pink pulp. The pulp was seasoned with salt and pepper and dried onions and spices. Then it was mechanically pressed into patties, and covered with cling-film, and run through a metal-detector, and frozen. All ready to be served up sizzling-hot for somebody's breakfast.

"Jesus," I said, out loud.

"You talking to me?" said a voice right next to me. "You talking to *me*?"

I turned around. It was Mr. Le Renges. He had a look on his face like he'd just walked into a washroom door without opening it.

"What the fuck are *you* doing here?" he demanded.

"I have to cook this stuff, Mr. Le Renges. I have to serve it to people. I thought I ought to find out what was in it."

He didn't say anything at first. He looked to the left and he looked to the right, and it was like he was doing everything he could to control his temper. Eventually he sniffed sharply up his right nostril and said, "It's all the same. Don't you get that?"

"Excuse me? What's all the same?"

"Meat, wherever it comes from. Human legs are the same as cow's legs, or pig's legs, or goat's legs. For Christ's sake, it's all protein."

I pointed to a tiny arm protruding from the mess on the production-line. "That's a baby. That's a human baby. That's just *protein*?"

Mr. Le Renges rubbed his forehead as if he couldn't understand what I was talking about. "You ate one of your burgers. You know how good they taste."

"Look at this stuff!" I shouted at him, and now three or four cutters turned around and began to give me less-than-friendly stares. "This is shit! This is total and utter shit! You can't feed people on dead cattle and dead babies and amputated legs!"

"Oh, yes?" he challenged me. "And why the hell not? Do you really think this is any worse than the crap they serve up at all of the franchise restaurants? They serve up diseased dairy cows, full of worms and flukes and all kinds of shit. At least a human leg won't have *e-coli* infection. At least an aborted baby won't be full of steroids."

"You don't think there's any moral dimension here?" I shouted back. "Look at this! For Christ's sake! We're talking cannibalism here!"

Mr. Le Renges drew back his hair with his hand, and inadvertently exposed his bald patch. "The major fast-food companies source their meat at the cheapest possible outlets. How do you think I compete? I don't *buy* my meat. The sources I use, they pay me to take the meat away. Hospitals, farms, auto repair shops, abortion clinics. They've all got excess protein they don't know what to do with. So BioGlean comes around and relieves them of everything they don't know how to get rid of, and Tony's Gourmet Burgers recycles it."

"You're sick, Mr. Le Renges."

"Not sick, John. Not at all. Just practical. You ate human flesh in that piece of hamburger I offered you, and did you suffer any ill effects? No. Of course not. In fact I see Tony's Gourmet Burgers as the pioneers of really decent food."

While we were talking, the production-line had stopped, and a small crowd of cutters and gutters had gathered around us, all carrying cleavers and boning-knives.

"You won't get any of these men to say a word against me," said Mr. Le Renges. "They get paid twice as much as any other slaughterhousemen in Maine; or in any other state, believe me. They don't kill anybody, ever. They simply cut up meat, whatever it is, and they do a damn fine job."

I walked across to one of the huge stainless steel vats in which the meat was minced into glistening pink gloop. The men began to circle closer, and I was beginning to get seriously concerned that I might end up as pink gloop, too.

"You realize I'm going to have to report this to the police and the USDA," I warned Mr. Le Renges, even though my voice was about two octaves above normal.

"I don't think so," said Mr. Le Renges.

"So what are you going to do? You're going to have me gutted and minced up like the rest of this stuff?"

Mr. Le Renges smiled and shook his head; and it was at that moment that the slaughterman who had been taking his dog for a walk came onto the killing floor, with the hellbeast still straining at its leash.

"If any of my men were to touch you, John, that would be homicide, wouldn't it? But if Cerberus slipped its collar and went for you—what could I do? He's a very powerful dog, after all. And if I had twenty or thirty eye-witnesses to swear that you provoked him . . ."

The Presa Canario was pulling so hard at its leash that it was practically choking, and its claws were sliding on the bloody metal floor. You never saw such a hideous brindled collection of teeth and muscle in your whole life, and its eyes reflected the light as if it had been caught in a flash photograph.

"Kevin, unclip his collar," said Mr. Le Renges.

"This is not a good idea," I cautioned him. "If anything happens to me, I have friends here who know where I am and what I've been doing."

"Kevin," Mr. Le Renges repeated, unimpressed.

The slaughterman leaned forward and unclipped the Presa Canario's collar. It bounded forward, snarling, and I took a step back until my rear end was pressed against the stainless steel vat. There was no place else to go.

"Now, *kill*!" shouted Mr. Le Renges, and stiffly pointed his arm at me.

The dog lowered its head almost to the floor and bunched up its shoulder-muscles. Strings of saliva swung from its jowls, and its cock suddenly appeared, red and pointed, as if the idea of tearing my throat out was actually turning it on.

I lifted my left arm to protect myself. I mean, I could live without a left arm, but not without a throat. It was then that I had a sudden flashback. I remembered when I was a kid, when I was thin and runty and terrified of dogs. My father had given me a packet of dog treats to take to school, so that if I was threatened by a dog I could offer it something to appease it. "Always remember that, kid. Dogs prefer food to children, every time. Food is easier to eat."

I reached into the vat behind me and scooped out a huge handful of pink gloop. It felt disgusting . . . soft and fatty, and it dripped. I held it toward the Presa Canario and said, "Here, Cerberus! You want something to eat? Try some of this!"

The dog stared up at me with those red reflective eyes as if I were mad. Its black lips rolled back and it bared its teeth and snarled like a massed chorus of death-rattles.

I took a step closer, still holding out the heap of gloop, praying that the dog wouldn't take a bite at it and take off my fingers as well. But the Presa Canario lifted its head and sniffed at the meat with deep suspicion.

"*Kill*, Cerberus, you stupid mutt!" shouted Mr. Le Renges.

I took another step toward it, and then another. "Here, boy. Supper."

The dog turned its head away. I pushed the gloop closer and closer but it wouldn't take it, didn't even want to sniff it.

I turned to Mr. Le Renges. "There you are . . . even a dog won't eat your burgers."

Mr. Le Renges snatched the dog's leash from the slaughterman. He went up to the animal and whipped it across the snout, once, twice, three times. "You pathetic disobedient piece of shit!"

Mistake. The dog didn't want to go near me and my handful of gloop, but it was still an attack dog. It let out a bark that was almost a roar and sprang at Mr. Le Renges in utter fury. It knocked him back onto the floor and sank its teeth into his forehead. He screamed, and tried to beat it off. But it jerked its head furiously from side to side, and with each jerk it pulled more and more skin away.

Right in front of us, with a noise like somebody trying to rip up a pillowcase, the dog tore his face off, exposing his bloodied, wildly-popping eyes, the soggy black cavity of his nostrils, his grinning lipless teeth.

He was still screaming and gargling when three of the slaughter-men pulled the dog away. Strong as they were, even they couldn't hold it, and it twisted away from them and trotted off to the other side of the killing floor, with Mr. Le Renges' face dangling from its jaws like a slippery latex mask.

I turned to the slaughtermen. They were too shocked to speak. One of them dropped his knife, and then the others did, too, until they rang like bells.

I stayed in Calais long enough for Nils to finish fixing my car and to make a statement to the sandy-haired police officer. The weather was beginning to grow colder and I wanted to get back to the warmth of Louisiana, not to mention the rare beef muffelettas with gravy and onion strings.

Velma lent me the money to pay for my auto repairs and the Calais Motor Inn waived all charges because they said I was so public spirited. I was even on the front page of *The Quoddy Whirlpool*. There was a picture of the mayor whacking me on the back, under the banner headline HAMBURGER HERO.

Velma came out to say goodbye on the morning I left. It was crisp and cold and the leaves were rattling across the parking-lot.

"Maybe I should come with you," she said.

I shook my head. "You got vision, Velma. You can see the thin man inside me and that's the man you like. But I'm never going to be thin, ever. The poboys call and my stomach always listens."

The last I saw of her, she was shading her eyes against the sun, and I have to admit that I was sorry to leave her behind. I've never been back to Calais since and I doubt if I ever will. I don't even know if Tony's Gourmet Burgers is still there. If it is, though, and you're tempted to stop in and order one, remember there's always a risk that any burger you buy from Tony Le Renges *is* people.

Ecstasy

Nancy Kilpatrick

"Ecstasy" was first published in *Master/Slave*, edited by Thomas Roche and published by Venus Books in 2004.

Award-winning author Nancy Kilpatrick writes and edits in the horror, dark fantasy, mystery and erotica genres. She has published 18 novels, including the popular 4-book *Power of the Blood* vampire series. A unique reprinting (in slipcase) of her seven novel erotic horror series *The Darker Passions* (writing as Amarantha Knight) is available from MHB Press.

Some of her roughly 200 published short stories have worked their way into 5 short story collections. You can read a few of her recent pieces in *Blood Lite, Blood Lite 2—Overbite* (both Pocket Books), *Hellbound Hearts* (Pocket Books), *The Bleeding Edge* (Dark Discoveries), *The Living Dead* and *By Blood We Live* (both Night Shade Books), *Don Juan and Men* (MLR Press), *Vampires: Dracula and the Undead Legions* (Moonstone Books), *The Bitten Word* (Newcon Press), *Campus Chills* (Stark Publishing), *Darkness on the Edge* (PS Publishing), *Vampires: The Recent Undead* (Prime Books), *Best New Vampire Tales #1* and *Best New Zombie Tales #3* (both from Books of the Dead Press). Upcoming stories will appear in *The Moonstone Book of Zombies* and *The Mammoth Book of Ghost Stories by Women*.

She has also written one non-fiction book *The Goth Bible: A Compendium for the Darkly Inclined* (St. Martin's Press), and has edited ten anthologies, the latest (from Edge SF&F Publishing) being a horror/dark fantasy anthology *Tesseracts Thirteen* (co-edited with David Morrell, 2009), *Evolve: Vampire Stories of the New Undead* (www.vampires-evolve.com , 2010), *Evolve Two: Vampire Stories of the Future Undead* (August 2011). A new anthology is in the works.

For Brainstorm Comics, she scripted three of her short stories in *VampErotica* #5, 6, and 13 and these comics and stories combine with interviews to create the graphic novel *Nancy Kilpatrick's Vampyre Theater*, out in 2011. You can find out the latest about Nancy on her webpage www.nancykilpatrick.com and follow her on facebook.

Ecstasy came out of my perception of how far some people will go to be loved.

◆ ◆ ◆ ◆

THE WORLD, IT SEEMS, IS BOUND FOR HELL. You grip the hand basket tighter, holding onto your life.

This is the first time you have come for him, and that unnerves you. With luck you will find him. With more luck, you won't. Either way, intuition implies you are not in a good position, despite what you now believe.

Everywhere you turn, white light assaults your eyes as if it were the white-light tunnel of death instead of moonlight glinting knife blade sharp off snow. Harsh air forces you to pull inward, shrinking back to yourself, shriveling, becoming smaller to hide from the cold. Nowhere you have been was the environment this inhospitable to human survival, although you realize other places on the planet are worse. Still, you haven't been there and, in the midst of this trauma your cells suffer in anticipation of freezing to death, speculation seems pointless.

You have searched this city for hours with this lanky sexy prostitute by your side. Together you visited places where Kevin has been seen. Inquiries here, there, his identity verified by photo, all painting a fresh trail, or so your companion assures you. "Listen, Fran," Didi said at the last transvestite bookstore, your name on his crimson lips sounding far too intimate, "we'll find him. There are only so many places a broken boy can hide." That was many hours ago. Between then and now: dozens of taxi rides taken, club entrance fees paid, drinks bought in bars, seedy hotel clerks questioned, meals eaten and coffees drunk in greasy-spoons and diners frequented by she-males as Kevin likes to identify himself. You are not naive; this world is not the one you glide through ordinarily, yet it is not entirely alien. So many personas, each in its own way demanding love and acceptance. How you envy their seduction techniques; how they terrify you.

The last club was in the middle of a ghetto and as you left it, once again, you congratulated yourself that you only paid this pretty hustler a fraction of the promised money—he will make efforts to keep you unharmed to get the rest. "Listen, sweetie, taxis won't answer calls to this neighborhood we're going," Didi assured you. "We'll hike it. Just you and me, romping through the snow!" Said with a Madonna toss-of-the-head and a devilish sparkle to almond-eyes. That he plays with you, laughs at your expense does not bother you. Since long before Kevin's treatments began, before his breasts swelled and his voice rose an octave and his body hair thinned, all of it leading to "the change" as he calls it, you have been to hell and back many times. Nothing bothers you anymore. Except for one thing. The nightmare.

This northern city's mean winter streets leave you hopeless. Life does not exist here in the dead of a cold night. No one sane walks around at 3 a.m. The last vehicle to pass inspired a fantasy of jumping in front of the bumper and pleading with the driver, "Take me home! I just want to go home!" But there is no home, not anymore. Mother is gone. Father was too often there. Kevin is all you have. You do not even care that your baby brother is becoming your baby sister. You just want to find him before, as the nightmare leaves you feeling, things have gone too far.

Hands and feet half frozen, you finally reach a wide street, but you are so far from downtown that here it is deserted, of people, vehicles, shops. Life has ended, or so it seems. What must it be like in daylight? You shudder to think about the corruption that will be exposed when the ice melts. Now, a ridge of danger lingers, danger and desolation, two emotions that, combined, combust and leave a raw scar from a wound that runs deep to the marrow. A wound you have suffered. A scar you still possess. You know it is the same with Kevin.

Your companion points ahead gleefully. "See! I told you!" he cries, as if you did not believe he would find this place, and in truth you had doubts. The building resembles a burnt out factory: windows not boarded up are blacked out; bricks smoked and charred; aluminum siding covered by graffiti in various languages. It amuses you to think that tagging might bridge linguistic solitudes.

There appears to be no door, no sign. "It's here somewhere," Didi insists, voice reeking with false confidence which relaxes into real confidence the moment a cab pulls up and two persons of indistinguishable gender emerge. They know right where the door is, a crack in the aluminum wall, a spike for a handle. "This is the place, Fran," Didi says, as if you are dim, unable to see the world for what it is.

This door would go unconsidered if you had not seen for yourself that it could be opened. Apparently no secret code is needed to enter. You open it now. Heat rushes out at you, and sound, loud, a cacophony of panting tongues and beating hearts and angry fists pounding flesh. Once you step inside, the sound swallows you.

You fight hard to hold onto yourself, caught in an audio intensity that forces you beyond your normal rhythm and into a power-drill mode of being. Remember why you're here, you remind yourself. Kevin is more lost than you are. He needs you more than ever. The bad dream told you this, and more.

A man, or a large woman skimpily dressed glares at you as if you are an insect to be crushed, definitely not worthy of admittance. You know the look is real, but the true function is other. The function involves money. Didi whispers "Fifty. Each," in your ear. Reluctantly you pull large bills from your nearly depleted wallet and slap them into the hot hand this monolith shoves inches from your chest. A smile erupts on the heavily made-up face, one more sinister than sweet. The cash is theatrically slipped down between the breasts encased in black latex, down further past the exposed stomach, down into the leather pants, up under the crotch. All the while dark eyes mock you, patiently awaiting a reaction, but you show none. Life holds few surprises. A flicker of disappointment accompanies the thumb pointing behind.

Didi removes his fur, and his dress, leaving his body clad only in a white lace bra, g-string panties and garter belt of the same fabric, the last holding up white hose. He hands everything else over the counter with a *No Drugs!* sign attached to the wall that almost brings a cynical smile to your lips. A muscular tattooed arm reaches out of the darkness towards you, waiting. Didi turns. You shake your head. You have no intention of leaving your coat, let alone undressing. Fabric is the only protection you might have here, and fifty dollars should pay for your eccentricity. "Whatever," Didi says, obviously disappointed by not seeing you near naked. "Still gotta tip, sweetie," he/she smiles, and you hand over five dollars and do not receive change.

A dark plastic barrier is held open, like a vulva, or the entrance to a womb. You follow Didi in, the Amazon making sure you brush against him or her, but your coat protects you from contact.

Sound slams into you, rasping, raping your body through every orifice, beating your pulse into submission, racing towards the target, your heart. You gulp in oxygen to ensure you are still alive. The air is clotted with smoke that chokes you, and you cough uncontrollably. Your eyes tear then blur and you realize you cannot distinguish anything here, objects, people; although the room is lit with red and blue lights, the colors do not make things discernible.

You have come this far, and you know Didi has no more ides. To retreat is unthinkable. You must find Kevin. For once in your life, you need to act on his behalf, and on your own.

You step further into the room. Suddenly the floor shifts down a level, half as deep as a step, and you fall forward. Your knee buckles and you struggle for balance. You have always been sharp on your feet, thank God! and manage to right yourself, feeling not so much foolish as vulnerable—what you cannot see *can* hurt you, Mother! But she never would hear you, or Kevin, and now cannot.

The throbbing techno drives you to the edge of insanity. It makes you angry. At life, for inflicting all this craziness from birth onward. At your parents for solidifying the madness. At Kevin for being weak, for leaving you to struggle alone. You are furious at yourself and your misguided hands-off philosophy that gave your brother *carte blanche*, immersing him in unconditional love, extending extreme unction for his soul to pass into other worlds. You destroyed the power of conditions that led to self-responsibility. The degree to which you rein yourself in is the same extreme of permission he enjoys.

Your senses cringe in terror. You argue with your optic nerve, willing it to clear your vision. When it does, shapes become apparent. Bodies dot the walls like giant cockroaches. One nearby drags on a cigarette, the yellow glow of fire casting hellish illumination onto harshly-angled features. Not a friendly face, but the eyes look too distant for this to be an enemy.

You inch forward, now feeling with your feet for dips in the floor level that seem to be everywhere. The mallet-sound changes, like a hammer passed from one hand to the other of an ambidextrous person. The beat is the same. It punches through your nervous system, producing more fury that you battle, and throbbing at your genitals. Most of these patrons must be high on ecstasy. This music would stimulate them in a different way, or so you have read about E.

Finally you stumble upon the bar, close by the dance floor. A girl— or a good imitation—leans over, her Nazi cap low over kohl-lined eyes, minimal breasts bare, tiny pierced nipples erect and staring at you. She does not ask you what you want. You have an impression of deep disinterest. Didi shouts his order and gestures for you to do the same. You lean in and her face shows distaste as she eyes the coat you clutch to your body, her look implying you are not brave enough to be here. Above the pounding, you scream "Jack, straight up!" Without a nod, she turns her back on you, and fades into the darkness. You glance to the right to watch the dozen or so dancers.

Young. Slim. Naked. Sweat dripping down sinewy bodies that have never known fat. These Danse Macabre figures writhe and jump to the beating noise, eyes rolled up so the whites glow in flashing black light strobe, tongues lolling, corpse-like puppets yanked on strings. One penis, erect, suddenly shoots into the air like a fountain. Two dancers fall to their knees to lap up the discharge.

The light allows you to see patrons next to you at the bar, others across the dance floor, stripped of clothing, waiting, watching, fondling themselves and one another. All are skeletal, ribs jutting, hip-bones prominent, many bald, skulls so large compared to the child-like bodies, enormous fetuses. They resemble drawings of aliens, photos you have viewed of victims in interment camps. Watching them makes you hot, and you feel like a pedophile. Or a necrophile. You wonder when it became sexy to look as if you're starving to death.

The harsh tapping on your shoulder goes almost unfelt—the rhythm is the same as the music, the same as the fingers around you groping, the same as your heartbeat forced to synchronize to all of this. But you do notice, eventually, and turn to find your drink. Behind it, one hand still on the glass, the other fondling a ringed nipple, the capped bartender releases your shot to hold out an open palm in much the same way as the door person, the coat check. You have the impression of beggars, starving, willing to take anything from anyone, but of course they will not take less than they demand. The image is titillating in its obscenity. You offer bills that are snatched away even before reaching the palm.

You want to ask Didi questions, about this place, about the preponderance of the thin, the beautiful who may live fast and die young for all you know, but the music prohibits verbalization. You only know this place is called *Ecstasy*, a 24-7 club that is more than a club, that is a lifestyle Didi assured you, frequented by transvestites, transsexuals, gay men, lesbians, bisexuals, straight couples and singles, fetishists, hardcore SM players, everyone with the need to be ecstatic, in Didi's words.

Kevin, you know, loved to get high. Most of his life he gravitated towards anything that would obliterate his pain. You watched your brother transit sexual preferences, chemical intoxicants, liquid libations, extreme physical ritualistic practices, various cults, and endless trendy diets to reduce the bulk he is prone to, all designed to take him out of the mud of this physical realm he loathes and lift him to spirit. You stood by helplessly for the thirty years you have known Kevin, unable to even aid yourself, let alone him. Each of his ventures was the answer, the salve to soothe the wound of living in a terribly imperfect world. Each would bring him the love and acceptance he longs for. Each was abandoned, or incorporated into Kevin's perpetual morphing. You understand him, only too well. He acts out the inner turmoil you silently endure daily, turmoil that has driven you to three quiet suicide attempts, that causes you to sleep more hours each day than you are awake, that leaves you alienated and too depressed to make contact, or even to exhibit symptoms of your despair. Only the bulimia you battle in secret is evidence of your pain, and that goes unnoticed in a twisted world that values minimalism in everything to the point of praising your rejection of nourishment.

Kevin has tried it all, and you have watched like a voyeur, living vicariously through his efforts. Someone getting the thrills without the risks. You encouraged him, perhaps to placate the demon within you that demands extremes. When Kevin told you about his plans for the operation, and how if he were female instead of male, if he had been you instead of himself, life would be different, fulfilling, accepting, that night you had the first of what would become a recurring nightmare.

Stuck at the bottom of a dark empty well, you look through a soulless mirror that liquefies. This noir river begins to flow into you, your nose, mouth, ears, anus, vagina, even your pores. Little animals with barbed bodies scratch this tender penetrated flesh, stimulating you almost beyond endurance. You are poised in mid-air, air black as night, body throbbing with desires that will not allow release. And only when the black fire of passion forces a scream of exquisite agony from your lips do you wake in your lonely bed, covered with sweat and tears, thighs slick with juices. And no amount of stimulation releases your volatile frustration.

Eventually, when you had dreamed this enough, and cried miserable tears until your ducts emptied, it dawned on you what had been happening all along. And now, like the religion that both of you turned away from when it failed you, you have come with no answers to save Kevin from himself. But in the process of trying, perhaps you will be rescued as well.

Didi nudges you and you follow, away from the safety of the bar, around the outer corners of the room. You pass between people, and hands reach out to touch you, finding fabric instead of flesh. You smile, happy to have thwarted their expectations. But then one hand discovers your secret and worms beneath the fabric, inside your blouse, down under your bra, the body pressed hard against your own, following, in step, bony fingers tweaking your nipple in time to the pounding beat, forcing your head back, your mouth open, the black river flowing once again—

"This is it, what we came for," Didi says. The hand is gone, leaving your nipple burning, your body freezing.

Didi opens a door and enters. You step into a cathedral of ice, with lighted grottos on each side of you. As you walk down the aisle, you pass these "rooms." On the left a man is suspended by his wrists and ankles. Four naked attendants shave his head, strip the hairs from his torso with wax, pluck out his eyebrows, and the hairs around his anus . . . To the right, a bald woman's bare body is cut with a scalpel, little cuts, deep enough to bleed, not enough for permanent injury, her flesh a canvas of tiny crosses, out of her mouth deep erotic pleas for forgiveness . . . A genderless being is having finger- and toenails clipped very very short, eyelashes singed, dead skin cut from the feet . . . You bend to peer inside a small door to find three pale and slender bodies prone on blond-wood shelves, sweat pouring off them as an attendant splashes water onto steaming rocks . . . Another grotto, a woman with her finger down her throat, vomiting, peeing, shitting, bleeding from her vagina, all at the same time . . .

You have seen each of these worlds in one way or another, and they do not shock you. All your life you have known that to rid the body of everything leads to purification, to spirit. Every major religion reinforces this value. The culture in which you reside prays for the destruction of the flesh.

At the end of this corridor of pain and humiliation is a white door with a white Gothic arch above folding inward. Didi opens the door and you realize that somewhere along the way she has discarded the rest of her clothes. You move up the three steps to this altar of rejuvenation.

The inner sanctum glows with twinkling lights, bright as stars. All here is colorless, odorless, pure and uncorrupted: walls, floor, hospital gurney, sheets atop it. A frail woman lies still as death, attended by skinny hairless beings dressed only in white latex gloves and milky rubber shoes.

Didi puts a finger to lips, and you stare into her liquid eyes, realizing that they remind you of the black liquid fire. Her body is lean, angular, the dead refusing to die. Your vagina spasms.

This side show is interesting, but you remind yourself of the purpose of this quest. The pounding techno is a fraction dimmer here, enough to allow thought. Kevin is not here. You turn to leave.

"Fran?"

The voice catches you in a net of fragility. You glance back at the gurney, and the languid corpse-like form lifts its skull. Unnaturally bright eyes—familiar—peer into yours from deep in their sockets, as if beckoning.

"Kevin?"

"I'm Fran now," he tells you, and your body jolts with this confirmation. "I need you for the reinventing."

It *is* Kevin, or what is left of him. Instantly you move beside the gurney as if it is a coffin. He has no hair, no eyebrows, lashes, no finger- or toenails. His body is covered with pale stitches, like a rag doll repaired too many times.

"What's . . . happening to you?" you ask.

"Ecstasy," he says, his voice more feminine than masculine, the tone otherworldly.

"Drugs—"

"No. True ecstasy."

You stare at his body, breasts plumped like white plums, his penis gone, replaced by . . . by . . . nothing! This is disturbing, but what leaves you unable to speak is his once thick-fleshed frame, now lighter than air, an exoskeleton.

"I'm thinner than you are," he whispers with a smile so grotesque you shudder.

You can only shake your head, confused, horrified, resigned in your failure.

Suddenly, as if they are meant to distract, you notice the apparatus—clear tubes removing blood, suctioning fat from the body, washing out the intestine's contents. You watch as one of the attendants pulls skin together over Kevin's stomach where fat cells have been suctioned out, cuts the flab, stretches the skin taut, sutures . . .

"My stomach is stapled now, so I don't need to eat," Kevin whispers, eyes gleaming.

"What? . . . why? . . ." But you can no longer form sentences.

"To be you," he says, the words so simple. The message clear as a crystal bell. This is your nightmare, your legacy. What you have created in your own distorted image. What you cannot show the world but what Kevin displays on your behalf. You gave him permission to reflect your darkness. Now that you see yourself with clarity, you cannot bear the sight.

He stares at the ceiling as if seeing God, as if he is ascending, and your eyes fill with tears.

Didi gently pulls the coat from your ravaged body, your clothes, then fingers find you through all your barren openings, filling them with black fire.

At long last, the heavy basket slips from your grip. Finally, you descend.

Pop Star in the Ugly Bar

Bentley Little

"Pop Star in the Ugly Bar" was first published in *Outsiders: 22 All-New Stories From the Edge,* edited by Nancy Kilpatrick and Nancy Holder, ROC, 2005.

I originally wrote this story in 1992 for an anthology titled Shock Rock, edited by the Hot Blood team of Jeff Gelb and Michael Garrett. They like the story and accepted it, but a month or so later, I received word that Pocket Books' lawyers were not so thrilled. I was never sure whether they thought the story was obscene and thus open to prosecution, or whether they were afraid that Madonna, who had just come out with her Sex book, might be in the mood to sue. Either way, they banned the story. Three years on, after several rejections in the interim, Poppy Z. Brite accepted it for her anthology Razor Kiss. Unfortunately, she soon got word from the lawyers that they could not allow her publisher to include my story, and I received notice that once again the piece was banned.

Finally, a full decade later, "Pop Star in the Ugly Bar" appeared in the anthology Outsiders, thanks to editors Nancy Holder and Nancy Kilpatrick, and the brave people at ROC. No one sued, the world didn't end, and now it can be reprinted here for your reading pleasure.

◆ ◆ ◆ ◆

SHE WALKS IN, THE POP STAR. Arrives with her retinue, wearing a black leather outfit that shows part of one tit and is supposed to be revealing but just doesn't cut it here in the bar. I can tell she's slumming, looking for action. The second she walks through the door she's acting as if she owns the place, and she tries to appear nonplussed when she finally figures out no one's paying attention to her. She's wearing a wig, pretending she wants to travel incognito, but now that no one notices her, she stands in her most recognizable pose, desperately willing people to recognize who she is.

Nobody does.

I do, but I don't say anything, just watch. I've seen her videos, read about her in *Playboy* and *Rolling Stone* and *TV Guide*, read how she's outrageous and into kinky sex, how she likes to pick up young black hitchhikers and have her way with them, and I see her now, this pampered bitch, and I have to laugh. Wild and outrageous? I'll show you wild. I'll show you outrageous.

Welcome to the Ugly Bar.

She said in an interview that she likes to be spanked, something pretentious about there being a fine line between pleasure and pain and that for her the two sometimes overlapped. Old news. Shocking maybe for grandpa in Kansas but babytalk here in the bar. I look at her smoothly unblemished carefully moisturized skin and I know it's never experienced true funpain. I think of Desdemona, the time I carefully flayed her left buttock and rubbed vinegar and lemon juice on it while Deke pissed in her mouth, and I can't see the pop star going for that.

Well, I can, but I can't see her liking it.

Control freak. That's what we have here, folks. Walks on the wild side carefully modulated, well-planned. Little fantasy trips with safe, padded boundaries, escape routes if things get too real, if the monster gets too hairy.

Pleasure and pain

Are almost the same

To me

Isn't that a line from one of her songs? One of her videos? I look at her, at her Hollywood costume. Almost the same? I suddenly want to make her prove it. No matter that it's an act, that she's just entertaining people, trying to titillate them. The fact that she's here in the Ugly Bar means that it's no longer just an act, that she's starting to believe her own press, that she really thinks she's daring and provocative and out there.

I glance around the bar, catch the nods, catch the looks, and I know they all want to be in on it.

I walk up to her, ask if I can buy her a drink. Her eyes take in my mask, my codpiece, and I see, for a second, fear. She's afraid. Not of me, specifically, but of losing control. She might say in her interviews that she likes big men, hung men, that she's looking for a man who has enough between his legs to really satisfy her, but I can tell that now that she's seen one, she's scared. She doesn't like it at all.

I push aside her bodyguards, and two of the Others come out of the shadows and drag them quietly off, taking them away. She says with all of the confidence she can muster, all of the confidence her money and power have bought, that, yes, she'd like a drink. The bartender pours it, holds it between his legs, stirs it with his cock, lets a couple drops of bloody jizz fall visibly into it and hands it to me.

I grin, give it to her. "Here, bottoms up."

She grimaces, puts it down an arm's-length on the bar, pulls back. "God."

The other patrons laugh derisively, and I think she realizes for the first time that she's just an amateur here.

She looks around for her bodyguards, notices that they are gone, and I see the fear on her face again, but she pretends she's not afraid, and she walks away from me, to the other end of the bar. She walks now with the grace and confidence of a dancer, the athlete she has to be in order to perform her stage show, but when I am through with her she will not walk that way. She will be hobbled and crippled, cleaned out with the razorcock perhaps, or violated to hemorrhage by the first three feet of Mr. Pole, and she will never be able to dance again. Each step she takes will be filled with pain and will remind her of her former pretenses and her forced knowledge of reality.

What if I cut her off at the kneecaps, cauterize the wounds with lighter fluid and fire, use the leftover blood to lubricate her bottom two holes?

Could she handle living on stumps?

She looks at me from the safety of the other side of the bar, faces me. "How big are you?" she asks, feigning boldness.

"Cock or arm?" I say.

She blinks.

"Two feet cock, four arm. More reach with the arm, too. I can maneuver around in there, feel out the womb, stroke those babygrowing sides with my fingers. Ain't nothing like it, babe."

She looks sick, looks like she wants to say something, looks like she wants to bolt, but her bodyguards are gone, she's a long way from the door, and she's been left here and hanging and knows she'd better make the best of it.

A crowd is gathering. The Mother and Zeke and Mr. Pole and the Roothog. Ginjer and Liz. There's an animal smell in the air. Lust. Sexual lust. The lust of victors for more victims.

The bar is never satisfied is it?

I drink her drink with the drops of bloody jizz, walk over.

The Roothog approaches. "A question," he says. "Do you have to be in love to have sex?" It's clear he still doesn't know who she is.

She stares in open horror at his whiplike pizzle, and she nods slightly, tentatively. Her voice is a little girl's voice, frightened. "Yes," she lies.

"Love is spending time together," he says to her. "Sex is just sex." He grins, cackles, and pulls on his pizzle, and I realize that he does know who she is. He's just thrown a quote from her book at her.

And she's scared.

Sometimes the Ugly Bar surprises me.

She starts for the door. The Mother blocks her way.

I nod casually toward the Roothog's pizzle. "He's good with that," I say.

"Let me out of here!" She tries to maneuver around The Mother, who moves to the side, blocks her again.

"You want another drink?" I'm trying not to laugh.

"I want out of here!"

"Then why did you come in?"

She looks at me, doesn't answer. I'm the only one she's really spoken to, and she thinks that's established some sort of relationship between us, she thinks I'll feel sorry for her and take pity on her because I've looked into her eyes, but she doesn't know shit about the way things really work.

I stroke my codpiece. "I'll take you," I say. "I'll even hurt you if you want."

"Let me out of here!"

"No."

The flatness of my refusal throws her. Did she have lipstick on when she came into the bar? It's gone now. Her lips are thin and dry. There's a tic starting in her left eye.

"You don't know who you're fucking with," she says. "There'll be a lot of people looking for me. A lot of people. You don't know who I am—"

"I know who you are," I say.

She stops, stares at me, and what little color she has left drains from her face, leaving it a beautiful porcelain white.

"Come on," I say.

I take her hand. It's soft, thin, I can feel the bones. I start to pull her toward the door to the Back Room.

"I—I'm having my period," she lies.

I grin at her. "The more blood the better."

"Oh God . . . Oh God . . . Oh God . . ." She's crying. Scared and frightened. Runny mascara tears. Clear snot. She doesn't look much like a pop star now.

"Please . . ." she begs, sobbing.

And I lead her into the Back Room.

The waterbed is filled with sperm and blood, piss and placenta, but I don't take her to the bed, I take her to the table and strap her into the stirrups. She is pliant and pliable at this point and I can do anything I want with her. She looks around, takes in the bones and the babies, the devices and the animals. Dazed, she tentatively touches the sticky wall next to the table with a finger, slowly puts the finger to her tongue as I strap her in, then she's gagging, spitting so she won't puke, and Liz comes and licks the spit off her face, off her mouth.

She struggles, squirms, and Liz slaps her face. Five times. Quickly.

The games have begun.

The pop star looks at me, mouth open, nose bleeding, eyes teary.

"Make a fist," I order.

She does, and holds it up, and Ginjer jumps on top of it, sliding slowly down, already slippery wet. The pop star reacts instinctively, cries out in disgust, tries to shake Ginjer off, but Ginjer's cunt is like a steel trap and she'd clamped on tight and not letting go and she starts spinning, round and round on the pop star's arm, squealing wildly with each successive climax.

"Get if off!" the pop star screams. "Get it off!"

But Ginjer's still spinning, and the juice dripping down the pop star's arm is starting to mix with blood.

I'm not sure if it's Ginjer's blood or the pop star's.

The Roothog steps up, pizzle in hand, starts whipping her with it.

She's screaming. More fear now than pain, although that will change.

Ginjer's already ground off the fist, and blood is streaming down the pop star's arm. Her chest is bruised purple by the pizzle.

They all want in on it, all the patrons of the bar. I'm not greedy, I'm willing to share, but her mouth is mine. I've earned it. I stake my claim, pointing, and there are no objections. Zeke holds down her forehead, while I bust out her teeth. She stops screaming, fainting I think, but that makes no difference to what I want to do. There are shards of teeth left, and I clean them out with a piece of bone. Her mouth is filling with blood, just the way I like it, and she comes to, gagging, and I open my codpiece and take out my cock, and start feeding it to her.

Her bladder lets go, but Liz is there to bathe in the spray.

It's gone too far, I realize. She's not going to make it. I wanted to leave her changed, marked, not dead, but there's no turning back now, and if that's the way it's gotta be, that's the way it's gotta be. Fame or no Fame. There are no exceptions.

Everyone's the same in the Back Room of the bar.

We take our time, and she's alive for much more of it than I would have thought, but eventually we finish her off, and by the time it's all over and done with there's not even much of her body left.

What remains is thrown in the slush pile.

We celebrate with drinks.

They come in later, official representatives of the Law outside, looking for the pop star, but no, officers, we haven't seen anyone matching that description. Lemme look at the picture. Nope. Haven't seen her. Any of you seen someone like that in here?

There is a slit-eyed older lieutenant in on the hunt, a Harvey Hardass, a faded jaded seen-it-all, and I catch the eyes of the other regular patrons, see the nods and the smiles, and I look again at the cop who thinks he's seen everything.

His friends are already moving away, out the door.

I nod to the Others, letting them know that they're to snag him if he tries to leave.

I look at him, catch his eye.

Confused, maybe a little frightened, he looks around the darkened room, then back at me.

I grin.

Welcome to the Ugly Bar.

The Sooner They Learn

Wrath James White

"The Sooner They Learn" was first published in his collection *The Book Of A Thousand Sins*, 2005, from Two Backed Books.

◆ ◆ ◆ ◆

PAIN IS THE NERVOUS SYSTEM'S primary indicator that we are doing something that might compromise the integrity of our bodies. It prevents us from destroying ourselves. To not know pain is to not understand what it takes to survive and succeed. Darrell was an educator, a teacher of pain. He had a warehouse of agonies concentrated within him that he needed to share, to diffuse amongst all those who had yet to know it, those who needed to learn.

The boys walked past Darrell, followed by the pungent aroma of tobacco. They were perhaps only eight or nine years old. Way too young to be smoking. The larger of the two boys held out a pack of Newports to his shorter friend as he coughed and choked on the coffin nail dangling from his own lip. He was obviously not used to smoking. Perhaps he could still be saved? Darrell began to follow the two boys, listening to their conversation, looking for the perfect opportunity to issue his sermon.

"Hey Sam, take a hit off this," the larger boy said, shoving the pack of Newports into his friend's hand.

"Naw, Joey. You know I don't smoke. Besides, my mom would kill me if I came home with my breath smelling like an ashtray."

Sam tried to hand the smokes back to Joey, who snatched them from his hand.

"Damn Sam! You's a little bitch! I thought you was down? I was going to pick up some weed later. I suppose you wouldn't smoke that neither?"

"Hell no! My mom would beat the hell out of me if she smelled that shit on me!"

"I can't believe what a little punk you are. You scared of your mom? The bitch is like in her fifties! What the fuck is she going to do? I'd smack the hell out of my mom if she tried to talk some shit to me. I do whatever the hell I want!"

Joey took another long draw on his cigarette, smoking it down to the filter. He dug into his pack of Newports and pulled out another, looking around to make sure the other kids in the playground were watching so they could see how cool he was.

Darrell sat across the playground on a park bench, watching Joey. A tear rolled down his cheek. The anger built within him into a tempest, spilling from his emotion filled eyes into the air around him.

"Another child that we have failed," he whispered, wiping away the tear with the tattered sleeve of his mangy plaid fur coat.

That kid knows nothing about pain, Darrell thought. *He knows no consequences for his actions. It's all fun and games to him. I have to teach him.*

Darrell knew all about life, all about pain. He knew that it built character, made you strong, taught you discipline. He knew that it was something every child needed to know about.

Darrell freely acknowledged that he had failed his own children. He had let the world take them and it had broken them like kites in a hurricane. He watched them spin out of control into the maelstrom of drugs and crime until their shattered fragments had fallen headlong into the abyss, one in the grave and the other in prison. It was his fault. He'd been too permissive, too liberal. He'd allowed them to make up their own minds, make their own mistakes, hadn't set down enough rules, hadn't taught them about consequences and repercussions. Linda and Jake had grown up thinking the world revolved around them, that they were invincible. Now they were lost and it was Darrell's fault. He had failed them. But, there were many other children in the world and he would not fail them. He would teach them all.

Darrell rose from the bench and stalked out of the park after Joey.

"The sooner they learn," he mumbled as he closed the gap between them.

Joey's eyes burned from the thick miasma of tobacco smoke that choked the room. He coughed repeatedly and started to retch. The unmistakable click of the revolver's hammer cocking back immediately silenced his coughing fit. Quickly, he put the cigar back to his lips and sucked down more smoke.

He looked over at the huge disheveled old man that sat beside him, holding the revolver. Joey's frightened bloodshot eyes pleaded with him, but the old man's were ruthlessly silent. Joey coughed again. Darrell leaned over and placed the cocked and loaded .38 caliber Colt revolver directly to Joey's head. The boy winced as he felt the chilling bite of the metal pressed against his temple, still he continued to dry heave. He had already regurgitated all the contents of his stomach. His throat was raw with the acid burn of stomach bile and the caustic fumes raking at his esophagus as he was forced to inhale more of the pungent smoke. The boy's body began to hitch with sobs as tears raced down his cheeks.

Joey wanted to beg Darrell to let him stop, but held himself back. He had begged the old man just minutes before, only to be snatched out of his seat by the jaw and dragged within inches of the man's enraged countenance, which had twisted into a horrible scowl. The old man stared into Joey's eyes looking as if he was about to bite his face off, then he spun the cylinder on the revolver and dry-fired the gun against the boy's temple. The hammer fell on an empty chamber with a dull hollow click. Joey's anus clenched up and his testicles rose into his stomach. A violent trembling shook his entire body and he nearly fainted. He had seen the old man put three bullets into the revolver. He knew that the chances of him surviving another round of Russian roulette were not good.

The old man took the cigar from the boy's lips and pressed it into his own palm where it sizzled as it scalded his flesh. "You stop smoking again and this is going in your eye," he said in a voice that was hoarse and raspy, as if he had just smoked 6 boxes of cigars himself.

Joey put the cigar back to his lips and sucked down more smoke. He had never felt so sick or scared before. He was woozy and his stomach rolled as he sucked on the huge cigar. It no longer felt cool. It no longer made him feel like a man. Six empty cigar cartons lay on the floor amongst the butts and ashes of nearly a hundred cigars and six more cartons sat waiting for him. Joey felt like he was going to die. If the cigar smoke didn't kill him, then he knew Darrell probably would.

Darrell was a child's nightmare. He was the real boogieman. Draped about his neck was a necklace of severed Barbie doll heads, pacifiers and the miscellaneous limbs of broken action figures. The moth-eaten fur coat that Joey had originally thought was plaid was, in fact, fashioned from the hides of fur toys, Teddy bears, stuffed rabbits and big purple dinosaurs. Most of them still had their little glass eyes intact and they stared out of that bizarre collage of artificial pelts, as if beseeching you to rescue them. Some of the fur looked real, however, and were in the perfect shape of small dogs and cats. Some of these still appeared to have their skulls intact, though minus the eyes. It looked like some last minute attempt at a homemade Halloween costume or the place where childhood dreams found their death.

He was a huge man, well over two hundred pounds with a hard athletic build. He had a head full of gray hair that was wild and unwashed. His skin looked like some type of hard wrinkled leather. From the weathered landscape of his face, cold gray eyes stared without emotion, except when they flashed brilliantly with rage. Joey had passed him numerous times in the playground as he sat on the swings. They jokingly called him the Boogieman and made up stories about him kidnapping and punishing bad kids. Joey had noticed the haunted look in some of the other kid's eyes when he made Boogieman jokes, but he had always laughed it off, thinking they were just little punks scared of a fairytale. Now, he knew that he wouldn't be making jokes like that again. Now, he knew the stories were real.

Joey finally fainted, just short of finishing his last box. Darrell stepped back, dropping the pistol from the boy's head to allow the limp body to fall to the concrete floor. He left the door open as he left. When Joey awoke, he'd realize that he'd been only yards away from his own house in his dad's tool shed. He'd crawl into the house and try to sleep off the whole experience. He wouldn't tell his dad what happened though. They never tell. They knew they deserved it.

There were no more good parents. The kind who knew when a child needed a trip to the woodshed and a belt or a switch pulled from an old tree lain across his backside 'til the welts ran with blood. The kind who knew how to pinch you until your flesh turned purple for giggling in church during service, while daring you to make another sound.

Nowadays, the child ruled the parent. They threw tantrums when they didn't get what they wanted and parents gave in just to keep them quiet. Didn't they know how easily quieted the child was who knew that a scream would immediately bring a slap across the face? Didn't they know that one day these kids would have to learn that the world did not bend to their wills and may even roll right over them, leaving their broken bodies behind? There were no more good parents to teach these lessons. That's why they needed Darrell.

It was already getting dark when he left Joey's back yard. The shadows had locked arms to form battalions of night that laid siege to the entire town. Darrell locked arms with the shadows too. They were his friends, his allies. He moved among them easily. Few people even noticed him as he traveled among his tenebrous troops. He was just another penumbra in an army of darkness.

The couple making love in the Cadillac Escalade parked by the curb didn't notice him either. Darrell would have likewise paid them no attention if it hadn't been for the fact that he saw the school books in the backseat of the car as he passed.

"Children," Darrell hissed in disgust. "Children fornicating in public."

The disheveled old man drew back a fist wrapped tight in rags and punched it through the back window, just as the boy's scrawny naked ass rose into the air preparing to impale the eager virgin beneath him with his throbbing young cock. He grabbed the boy by the hair and dragged him out through the passenger side window, in a hail of tempered glass.

When the boy hit the ground and rolled over, his face snarled up into a grimace of rage and confusion, Darrell could see that the kid was barely fourteen years old, not even old enough to be driving, let alone fucking, in his father's car. The boy wasn't even wearing a condom.

"You think you're ready to be a father?" Darrell growled as he snatched the boy up by one arm. The boy swung at him with his free hand, missed, then bent down to pull up his pants and underwear to hide his diminishing erection.

Darrell reached down and grabbed the boy by his genitals, balls and all. The boy let out a helpless squeal.

"I asked you a question, boy."

"Leave him alone!" The girl had shrugged her clothes back on and was yelling at Darrell through the shattered window.

Darrell let go of the boy's arm and slapped the girl back into the car. "I'll deal with you later," he said turning his attention back to the boy. He tugged on the boy's penis, stretching it out until it felt like it would tear right out from between his legs.

"Aaaaaaargh! Fuck man, that shit hurts! Let me go motherfucker! What are you her father or something? We were just having a little fun. Jesus, don't hurt me! Arrgh! Heeeelp!!! Fuck! Let me go!"

Darrell leaned in close until his foul breath, reeking of rotten candy, steamed in the boy's face. "I should rip it the fuck off and keep it on ice until you're old enough to know what to do with it!" He reached into the car and dragged the girl out of the car by her hair. He seized her by the throat and held her against the car. "I'm not your father. I care a hell of a lot more than that. So, I'm only going to say this one time. If I ever catch you two going at it again, then I'll make sure you never have to worry about ruining your lives by catching AIDS or herpes or hepatitis or getting pregnant. I'll rip your cock right off and I'll fill your pussy full of super glue and sew it the fuck closed! You are too young! Do you understand me?"

They both nodded with eyes filled with tears. He let them go and they ran off down the street. When they were a block away the boy turned around and yelled, "You crazy motherfucker! I'm calling the cops!"

Maybe he would. Maybe he wouldn't. Darrell really didn't care either way. He knew one thing for certain though. That relationship was over. As the boy ran off down the street, Darrell aimed at the center of his back and squeezed off a shot. The boy's back erupted and bloomed bright red. He pitched forward onto his face, hitting the asphalt with a wet smack. His prone body convulsed for a second and then lay still. He wasn't dead, but Darrell knew that the bullet had likely shattered his spine. He wouldn't be getting any young girls pregnant now and definitely wouldn't be catching AIDS. The horny little bastard wouldn't be able to feel anything below the waist for the rest of his life. The girl screamed and ran even faster, disappearing around the corner. Darrell chuckled to himself and continued down the street sticking tight to the shadows, just in case the police were already out looking for him.

Darrell walked another four blocks to the big shopping mall on Market Street. He entered the Sears department store and wandered around in a trance. He was thinking about his own children again when he heard the child screaming over in the toy section. Linda and Jake used to scream like that when they wanted something. He'd always given in after they'd embarrassed him, enduring the looks of pity and disgust on the faces of other parents as they watched him struggle with his undisciplined brats. He remembered the look on their faces that asked, "Why doesn't he give those two little monsters a good spanking?" Back then, he'd felt that corporal punishment was cruel. Now, after seeing how they'd turned out—staying out all hours of the night, drinking, using drugs, getting into fights, having sex at ages thirteen and fourteen, stealing, dropping out of school, one eventually going to prison and the other becoming a crack whore who overdosed on heroin after being used and discarded by half the perverts in town—he realized that not disciplining them more harshly had been the true cruelty. They had never listened to a damn thing he said to dissuade them from their self-destructive behavior and now they were lost forever.

The sound of that child screeching for his harried mother to buy him a new PlayStation video game brought back all those memories. Darrell stormed over to them fuming mad and dangerously close to exploding.

The screaming, crying, cussing, undisciplined little cur threw a convulsive tantrum while still clinging to its mother's leg. Darrell was amazed as the little beast balled up its fingers into a fist and punched his mother in the abdomen. The redheaded little terror was barely five years old and already in control of his parent.

"I want it! I want it! I want it!"

"Stop it!" The woman yelled back in a voice that quivered with emotion. She was near the breaking point, teetering on the edge of a nervous breakdown. Her hellacious offspring screeched at her in a shrill whine that raised the hair on Darrell's neck. The redheaded demon threw itself on the floor and began to kick like an overturned cockroach. This was another one who still believed that the universe should bend to its will and that any frustration to its desires could be easily dispelled with a few well-placed and infinitely irritating screams. Every moment that he went undisciplined was another day in jail, or on drugs, or selling his ass on the streets. He had to be taught.

The entire store seemed to be staring at the little shrieking harpy and its mother with disapproving eyes, awaiting the moment when the obviously overwhelmed woman would actually begin to act like a parent and silence her son's fit of egocentric rage with some corrective discipline in the form of a slap. It would never happen, not until the child was too old for it to do any good. The moment dragged on and on, the mother withering beneath the child's aural assault, slowly being conquered, just on the verge of admitting defeat and giving in to her son's whim.

In a last ditch effort to regain a control that had obviously been abdicated long ago, the mother gave voice to her parental inadequacies with a cry of defeat that masqueraded as a threat, but only symbolized failure and imminent resignation to all those who heard it, including the delinquent it was meant to correct. "Wait 'til your father gets home! Do you want me to call Daddy?"

This was followed immediately by words that told all that witnessed the irksome spectacle that there was no respite in sight. "Do you want a time out?!"

Darrell's stomach rolled. What the hell had happened to parents? He had tried that tactic himself. The fool who invented it should be roasted alive on a spit, in Darrell's opinion. It was just another admission of the parent's loss of control.

The boy answered his mother predictably and appropriately. "Fuck you!" The words flew out of his mouth along with a spray of spittle.

The child began to punch at its mother again. Darrell could take no more. The woman was staring up at the ceiling, as if praying to god to rescue her from her own child, when Darrell charged down the isle, looking like a troll from under a bridge in some long forgotten fairytale. The ankle-biting little rug-rat was still yelling and screaming. Darrell pushed the mother aside and slapped the child to the floor with a back-handed swing that collided with his mouth with the sound of a gunshot. The kid's head bounced off the tile with a loud smack that effectively cut off his shrill ranting. A trickle of blood ran down from the crack that bisected his lip. With eyes glazed in shock and dizzy from the blow, he looked up at Darrell. The child trembled as he met Darrell's feral gaze, feeling like a rabbit cornered by a voracious wolf.

The little redheaded monster screamed for his mother. Darrell drew back and backhanded him again, this time with a closed fist. The force of the blow knocked the boy over backwards. He landed face down on the tile floor. When he looked up, his left eye was nearly swollen shut with a tremendous black and purple bruise that went from cheek to temple. It looked as if he'd just gone twelve rounds in a boxing match.

Darrell leaned over and pointed a long gnarled finger into the boy's face. His eyes seethed with rage and madness burning like an electrical fire. "You yell one more time and I will beat the life out of you. Do you hear me?"

The child nodded, his jaw still hanging open in shock. He looked over Darrell's shoulder, searching for his mother.

She finally overcame her own shock enough to protest. "What the hell are you doing to my baby!"

She charged the gray-haired old man who'd just battered her son, swinging a fist and hooking her fingernails into claws, reaching out for Darrell's face, determined to make him pay for hurting her child.

Darrell turned and casually caught the woman by her throat, pinching her windpipe closed just enough to guarantee her silence.

"Shhhhh!" he said, then turned back to the child, still holding his mother in an iron grip. He had to concentrate to keep his rage in check so that he didn't crush her esophagus.

Why do they even bother having children if they don't know how to control them? he wondered.

"I want you to apologize to your mother for disobeying her and embarrassing her like that in public. SAY IT!!!"

"I—I'm sorry mommy!" the child cried and tears began to flow from his eyes steadily.

"And if you ever disobey your mother again, I'll be back for you. Do you understand?"

"Yes."

Darrell released the kid's mother and she rushed to scoop up her son. They held each other and cried as Darrell turned and walked toward the exit. On his way, he passed a cherubic, blonde-haired, three-year-old baby girl sitting in a stroller with a pacifier in her mouth. She was being pushed along by an overweight woman, roughly Darrell's age, who was obviously her grandmother. The child's real mother was probably little more than a teenager. As Darrell passed, he reached down and overturned the stroller, dumping the child out onto the floor and leaving the toddler screaming as if it had been fatally assaulted. Darrell bent over and retrieved the baby's pacifier, adding it to his necklace. He carried the stroller away with him as both parent and child screamed at his back.

"The sooner they learn the better," he muttered, twisting the stroller into a mass of warped metal and plastic. The little girl had been nearly four years old, at least three years too old to be riding in a stroller and sucking on a pacifier.

"The sooner they learn," he repeated.

He walked out of the mall and tossed that tortured relic of some years ago baby shower into the dumpster, wondering almost casually if he was perhaps taking his crusade too far. He reassured himself that all the kids he had disciplined were bad kids who would have only gotten worse if not for his intervention, that he was doing it for their own good. But, he wondered if he was also getting a little pleasure out of it, if perhaps he was not seeking to save the children but to punish them, to hurt them. He wondered if he was seeking revenge. Maybe, it was the parents he should have been punishing and not the children? Parents like him, who had failed their children, allowing them to become the brats that they were. Maybe, it wasn't enough to teach the kids? Maybe, he needed to include the parents in his education?

"Let me get another hit off that, mom."

Darrell's head whipped around so fast he nearly broke his own neck.

There stood the answer to his musings in the form of a mother and daughter dressed identically in skintight halter-tops, sans brassieres, and mini-skirts so short that you could tell they were not wearing panties beneath them and that they had recently shaved. They were both smoking cigarettes and passing a bottle of Crown Royal back and forth. The girl couldn't have been more than twelve years old. It was obvious that she and her mother were prostitutes, just like Darrell's baby girl Linda, who'd died in an alley with a needle in her arm and the semen of the more than a dozen different men she'd fucked that night still leaking out of her. Darrell wanted to scream. He wanted to yell at the top of his lungs. A parent was supposed to want better for their child than what they had. They were supposed to guide them, steer them away from making the same mistakes they made. What this mother was doing was abominable. She had to be punished.

How could she let her child do that?!!!

He wanted to rip her apart. He would show that little girl what became of women who sold themselves on street corners. He reached into his coat and closed his hands around the hunting knife in his left pocket and the Colt revolver in the other.

"The sooner they learn," he muttered as he stalked after them.

"Let's go back to the motel, relax, and smoke these last couple of rocks before we hit the stroll again tonight. Okay baby?"

"Cool! I need a little pick me up. I feel like shit tonight."

"Get it together honey! There's a convention in town tonight. There'll be twice as many tricks on the strip tonight and that means mo' money."

Acid roiled in Darrell's stomach as he fought to hold in his rage and revulsion. As much as he wanted to attack them right then and there, he needed to be alone with them.

He followed closely, matching their footsteps as he slipped from shadow to shadow. He ducked behind some bushes just yards from where the mother stopped to squat by the curb and relieve herself. He could smell the acrid ammonia of her urine wafting from the gutter. His stomach lurched and this time he did regurgitate. Luckily, they had already moved off down the road and did not see him drop to his knees and throw up his lunch in the same gutter where the whore had just urinated. His body trembled with fury as he rose and continued his pursuit.

Darrell kept thinking of his little girl. Her anus and vagina had been bruised and torn, her nipples bitten, there were welts and cuts on her back and buttocks, livid blue and purple contusions around her throat from manual strangulation. He couldn't believe that she hadn't been murdered. Darrell had gotten sick then too, when the coroner told him that many of the bruises were old and healing at different rates. They'd been acquired at different times and most likely at the hands of different men. Trophies of her profession. This is what that little girl had in store, the path her mother was leading her toward. A life where a needle full of heroin and a cardiac arrest would be the greatest kindness she could hope for. Darrell gritted his teeth and flicked open the blade of his hunting knife.

The little girl kept looking back over her shoulder, peering into the darkness as if she could sense him there. Most likely, it was just her normal paranoia, heightened by cocaine use. Finally, they turned the corner and the mother began fishing into her purse for her keys. Darrell moved in closer as they approached the door to one of the rundown rooms.

The two whores staggered up to the motel, reeling from alcohol and a cocktail of illegal drugs. They never saw the powerful looking old man in the multi-colored fur coat as he came rushing at them from behind a nearby parked car. He forced them into the room, slamming the door behind him.

Darrell had bound them both in duck tape. He'd left the mother's ankles unbound to allow him access. He didn't gag her either. He wanted her daughter to hear her scream.

"Stop hurting my mommy!" screamed the twelve-year-old girl. Mascara ran down her face like black tears and lipstick smeared across her lips and cheeks like bright red welts. Darrell punched his entire arm into her mother's dilated vagina up to the elbow.

"Pleeeease! Stop hurting my mommy!"

A wet, sticky, ripping sound accompanied each thrust as he drove his arm in deeper, tearing her reproductive system apart. The bottle of Crown Royal he'd shoved into her rectum shattered. Her vagina continued to tear until cunt and asshole became one gaping orifice, dripping blood in a tremendous pool that saturated the piss-stained motel carpeting. The woman had stopped screaming and now only whimpered helplessly. Her eyes were vacant, fixed and dilated. Her mind had snapped. Tears still streamed down her cheeks, turning brown as they ran in rivulets through the feces that covered her face from when Darrell had defecated upon her.

"Is this what you want? Is this how you want to end up? You still want to be just like your mommy?" Darrell growled, staring directly into the young girl's face as she continued to scream.

"You'd better get your ass back in school and make something of yourself or I'll personally make sure that you suffer worse than this."

Darrell withdrew his arm from the mother's vandalized twat with a hideous "Shlorp!" It was covered in blood, excrement, and tissue. Darrell scowled as he looked about for a place to clean it. He went into the bathroom to wash up, leaving the two whores bleeding and crying on the bedroom floor. When he returned, he had his knife open.

"Watch this, little girl. Watch what men like me do to whores."

He grabbed the girl's mother by the hair and flipped her over onto her back. He knelt down on top of her and began to saw off her breasts. She began screaming again. Twisting her nipple and stretching her breast taut, he sawed down to the white of her ribcage and tore her entire mammary gland free of her chest. He worked her over with the knife for the better part of an hour. Her terrible anguished screams grew deafening in the tiny apartment. She began to convulse in agony as Darrell cut a long incision around her face and began peeling it off of her skull. When he finally left the room, he took the woman's breasts, face and vagina with him, leaving her hollowed out remains writhing and shrieking in an ever-widening pool of blood. He never touched the little girl. There had been no need.

"If you don't get your life in order, go back to school and stay off these streets, you will see me again."

She got the message.

By the time the old man left the apartment, it was well past midnight. The streets were bustling with activity and he was exhausted and feeling decidedly anti-social. He just wanted to go home. Today had been more exciting than most and he was drained. There were so many children to save and he was just one man. He had miles to walk to his home on the other end of town. He scrambled along quickly, imagining snuggling beneath his covers with a good book and a cup of warm tea. He tried to stick to the shadows as much as possible as he made his way toward home. He knew that the cops would be looking for him and he was not exactly inconspicuous.

He barely noticed when the car full of kids pulled up alongside him. Until they jumped out and attacked him.

"That's him!" a tiny hoarse voice cried out from the car. It was Joey, the smoker.

One of the larger boys lunged out of the car and swung a baseball bat at Darrell's head. It connected with a loud crack that sent the old man sprawling onto the floor.

"That was my fucking brother you almost killed, you fucking freak!"

It happened so fast that he didn't have time to go for his gun. The kids held him down and searched his pockets, removing both his knife and his revolver before they began kicking and punching him.

Boots, sneakers, a baseball bat and what may have been a pipe crashed down on his head and face, cracked his ribs, crushed his hands and shattered his kneecaps. They were beating him to death. Darrell was barely conscious when he felt the splash of liquid being poured all over him, followed by the pungent odor of gasoline. Then, he was burning. He could even hear the children's laughter over his own screams.

They never learned.

Joey and his big brother Mike snuck back into the house through the basement window and tip-toed all the way upstairs to their bedrooms on the second floor, careful not to wake their parents. They still smelled like smoke and gasoline. They both lay in their beds and tried to shut out the image of that old bum's face sizzling and running off his skull like frying lard as the flames consumed him. Joey had just managed to quiet the screams in his head when he heard the window slide open and that same burnt pork smell that had lingered in the air after their impromptu cremation came wafting into the room, roaring up his nostrils.

He opened his eyes just as Darrell's charred skeletal face moved towards him, blocking the moonlight. Joey was sure that the old man had been dead when they left him smoldering on the sidewalk. When he examined the man's face—eyes missing, teeth gleaming through where his lips had burned away, bits of burnt tissue clinging to an otherwise bare skull, other bits flaking away and fluttering to the floor as ash—he saw nothing to contradict his original assessment. Darrell was indeed a corpse. He tried to scream, but the old man pinched his windpipe closed before he could utter a peep.

Darrell sparked the flame on the Bic lighter clutched in his blackened fingers and held it up to Joey's face.

"You have to learn not to play with fire, Joey."

Joey tried to scream again as the crazy old dead guy aimed the flame up his right nostril. Joey's flesh began to sizzle. He writhed on the bed in nerve-searing anguish, but Darrell held him firm.

The boy had learned at least one of the lessons. He knew now that there were things in the world that could hurt him, that he was not invincible and that he could not get away with anything he wanted. The other lessons would take longer and be much more painful. But, Darrell had time. The boy had to learn.

Darrell would not let him grow up to be a criminal like his son Jake, on death row for murdering a drug dealer. He would teach the boy better. The old man moved the lighter to Joey's eyelid and smiled as his eyeball sizzled and popped.

Addict

J. F. Gonzalez

"Addict" originally appeared in *Insidious Reflections* #5, January 2006.

J. F. Gonzalez is the author of over a dozen novels of horror and dark suspense including *Back From the Dead, Survivor, Primitive, The Beloved*, and the upcoming novel *They*. He is also the co-author of the popular *Clickers* series of novels (co-written with Mark Williams and Brian Keene respectively). He writes in a variety of media including print, screen, and the corporate world. A native of Los Angeles, California, he relocated temporarily to Pennsylvania, where he now resides and is trying to escape from. Learn more about him at www. jfgonzalez.com.

♦ ♦ ♦ ♦

IT WAS A PLACE HE STOPPED BY occasionally on his way home from work and, like most underground porn flea markets, it moved around periodically. This time it was in a modern three-bedroom tract home in Alhambra. Dennis Hillman stopped by shortly before 2 p.m. after having left work early for the day.

He tried to stifle a yawn as he flipped through home-made magazines containing photos of various sexual acts. Normal garden variety in-and-out didn't do much for him anymore. It hadn't in a few years. The deeper he got into it, the more hardcore his pornography had to be. It was his unique tastes in pornography that led him to seek out places such as Carl Grossman's group a year or two back. You couldn't find bestiality or scat stuff in neighborhood porn shops. Or women being fucked by guys with dicks the size of those little souvenir baseball bats you could pick up at Dodger Stadium.

There were half a dozen other porn junkies browsing through Carl's wares this afternoon. Dennis ignored them as he silently sifted through the materials. None of it excited him anymore. He felt a slight sense of disgust with himself as he leafed through a rape magazine. Violence didn't even turn him on anymore.

Carl Grossman lumbered over. "Got something I think you might enjoy." Carl was a huge fat man; he looked like a crowd of fat people squeezed into a tight suit. His trousers were wearing thin, the tails of his white shirt was coming out from his pants. Even though Carl didn't work a normal job, he still tried to dress as if he had a regular nine-to-fiver. His tie was stained with grease and ketchup.

"What is it?" Dennis said, already bored.

"Come this way," Carl beckoned. He turned and Dennis followed him down a dim hallway to the rear of the house.

"Just got this in the day before yesterday," Carl said, weaving his way through boxes piled on the floor. He opened a box and rummaged around inside it before he found what he was looking for. Dennis let his eyes stray around the room as Carl looked for the thing he wanted to show him; this was where Carl kept stuff for the hardcore freaks. His eyes rested briefly on a still from a bestiality film depicting a young woman with thin limbs and heroin sculpted cheekbones on her hands and knees being fucked by a large monkey. "Here it is," Carl said, handing Dennis the item.

Dennis picked it up. It was a magazine, the cover showing a woman with blonde hair lying on a bed. Her throat was slit, a great cascade of blood spilling down her chest and on the mattress. Her eyes were open and glazed over.

Dennis handed the magazine back. "It's snuff, and every snuff film I've ever seen is fake. Don't try to pawn this shit on me."

"It ain't snuff," Carl said, handing the magazine back to Dennis. "Take a better look at it."

Dennis sighed and began flipping through the magazine, growing more disgusted with himself. What he should be doing was working at the office; he had to finish that CPM spreadsheet for a meeting next week. But the pull of desire was strong and he needed an outlet. *Admit it*, Dennis thought, his hands trembling slightly as he flipped through the pages of the magazine. *You're a hardcore porn junkie. You're addicted to this shit and you know it.*

The photos in the next few pages showed the same woman from different angles. The next few pages showed a young man, about twenty years old, climbing onto the bed with the woman and embracing her. The next few pages had photographs of the young man sticking his cock between the woman's lips and shoving it into her mouth. That particular set of photos ended with the man vaginally penetrating her.

"What is this, some kind of special effects thing?" Dennis asked, his curiosity only slightly aroused.

Carl shook his head, a sick grin on his face. "Keep looking."

The next few pages showed different subjects. One was of what appeared to be an old man, his belly puffy and distended, the flesh of his torso the color of dark storm clouds. A woman who looked like a junkie was sucking his flaccid penis. It wasn't until he got to the old woman—what Dennis *thought* was an old woman—that he stopped and stared at the picture, his stomach curling in his belly.

He flipped back through the magazine, looking at the photos again. His eyes were wide. "You mean . . . this shit is *real?*"

Carl grinned. "As real as they get, Dennis."

The photo that had stopped Dennis in his tracks was that of an old woman. She must have been Caucasian because her hair was straight and long. Her skin was black and blue and green in places, some of it wet-looking. There were spots of white in various parts of the body. As Dennis flipped through it the photos got perversely worse. There were close-ups of her decayed face, the eyelids sunken in. There were close-ups of her rotting breasts, the flesh falling off her arm bones. It wasn't until the man entered the picture that Dennis held his breath. Even though he found it hard to go through the rest of the magazine, he did so anyway. His eyes were riveted on the scenes of the faceless man's cock buried in the rotting woman's pussy, the close ups of the man's penis with brown, maggot-ridden, rotted flesh caked to it amidst creamy semen.

Dennis closed the magazine. He couldn't breathe, he was that excited. "Where did you get this?"

Carl shrugged. "Just got it in a few days ago. A local outfit. You want it?"

"How much?"

"Fifteen hundred."

Normally Dennis would have paid for it, but he hadn't come prepared to pay that much money for something. "I'll have to get back to you on that," he said, handing the magazine back to Carl. "I'll call you."

Carl smiled and put the magazine back where he'd found it. "You do that."

Dennis exited the house with a sense of shaking excitement that chased him on the drive home. He couldn't get his mind off that image of the corpse of the old woman being fucked by the faceless stranger.

* * *

"Dennis, are you okay?"

"Hmmm?" Dennis snapped awake, banishing the daydream that had been floating through his mind. He was replaying the images of the necrophilia photo in his dreams again, wondering what it felt like to fuck a rotting corpse. Trying to imagine what the sensation must feel like on your dick.

"You've been awfully quiet tonight. Everything okay at work?"

"Yeah, everything's fine."

Dennis was sitting up in bed watching the evening news. His wife, Carrie, was sitting next to him doing her nails. Their son, Justin, was in his room doing God knew what on the internet and their daughter, Elizabeth, was in her room talking on the phone with her friends. Dennis had hardly paid attention to his children when he got home this afternoon. All he'd been able to think of were the images from that magazine.

Carrie lolled on the bed, her hair up in curlers. Dennis tried not to look at her; she'd grown increasingly flabby in the past five years. Her ass was a mile wide, the cellulite on her thighs quivered like Jell-O. Dennis tried to get his wife to accompany him to the gym, but she showed no interest. "I've got an early morning and late afternoon meeting tomorrow," he said, flipping through the channels, "so I won't be home till late. That okay with you?"

"Fine with me," Carrie said, finishing her nails. "What's on Channel Two?"

And that's the way things went every night. It was the way things had been for fifteen years. The minute they began to have kids, their sex life took a nosedive. And to compensate, Dennis sought to relieve his outlet through other means. Pornography.

And the more he got into it, the more he needed to satiate his needs. Where before he couldn't stomach an anal sex scene, within a few short years he began to crave it . . . where before he flinched at the barest suggestion of S&M, within a few years he was exploring every aspect of that subculture. Where before he'd gagged at the site of a woman sucking a Great Dane's cock, or some redneck fucking a sheep, now bestiality films held a strange fascination for him. And while he had heard of snuff films over the years, the closest he'd ever come to seeing one was an extreme hardcore loop Carl Grossman sold him. The clip showed a woman being viscously whipped, then burned with a hot piece of metal as she dangled from the ceiling in an abandoned warehouse. The first time Dennis saw the clip it disturbed him. Later viewings turned him on. He currently kept the tape in a safe in his study and only brought it out when he knew he was going to get at least four hours to himself at home, which was rare.

Now the only thing that could get him off was the hardest of the hardcore. Currently he possessed two additional films other than the torture film, which were the only things that could bring him to orgasm, all three he kept in the safe. One was a film showing a woman being fucked by an Orangutan; it was followed by a guy screwing a female German Shepard. The other tape was a rape film showing the very real rapes of a twelve-year-old girl, a forty-year-old toothless crack addict who looked like he was seventy, and an eighteen-year-old man who already looked like he was in his mid-forties courtesy of hard-living. Carrie would never dream that both tapes resided in a locked safe in Dennis' study.

Before they settled down to sleep Carrie said, "Oh, I forgot to tell you. Bob Lansing called this afternoon."

"Really?" Dennis felt his stomach clench. "What did he want?"

"To talk to you," Carrie turned over. "He sounded surprised, like he thought you would be home."

"Bob gets confused sometimes," Dennis said, the lie springing to him easy. "He must have forgotten I had that meeting at our West LA office and thought I'd gone home early."

Carrie didn't say anything. Dennis waited for a response, and when none came he rolled over on his right side, facing the wall. He waited until he heard the calm breathing of his wife sleeping beside him, and then he closed his eyes and tried to get some sleep himself. But it was a long time in coming.

He had a meeting on his calendar the next morning but he skipped it, stopping by Carl Grossman's instead. He'd gone to the bank on the way and had the fifteen hundred dollars for the necrophilia magazine; he simply couldn't get it out of his mind. He'd woken up in a good mood so why not splurge? Carl shook his head as Dennis asked for the magazine. "Sorry. Shoulda bought it yesterday. I sold it last night right after you left."

Dennis felt his hopes deflate. "Oh. That's too bad." He didn't know the magazine would sell so quickly.

"But you're in luck," Carl said, moving to a corner of the living room that he referred to as his "office"; it was crammed with a small desk and filing cabinet. He rummaged around on the desk for a business card and copied a name, address, and phone number on it. "You might want to talk to the guy that bought it. He's a big collector. You and he have similar interests. Maybe he can help you find another one." He handed the card to Dennis, who slipped it into his pocket.

"Thanks," Dennis said.

Dennis took a look at the card in his car. The name on the card—Harvey Panozzo—was unfamiliar to him. At first he wasn't going to place the call; after all, he had to get to work and start giving his employers the impression he gave a shit about his job. But he finally succumbed to his desires and punched Harvey's number in his cell phone.

The phone was picked up on the other end. "Panozzo here."

Dennis quickly introduced himself and told Harvey how he came by his number. "Carl suggested I call you since we have similar interests."

"Are you busy later today?"

"Not at all."

"Why don't you stop by? We'll chat then. You have the address?"

"Yes." Harvey was in Monrovia, just down the freeway from Pasa-dena where Dennis lived. He jotted down the directions and hung up, his nerves on edge at the thought that he was going to see more of the type of material he was becoming enamoured with.

The next few hours were spent at work. He made phone calls to various business contacts, did some work on the CPM spreadsheet. Bob Lansing poked his head in his cube and asked where he was yesterday. Dennis told him he'd been stuck in traffic, which was why he was late to the CPM meeting in West LA. Bob nodded, then asked him how the meeting this morning was. Dennis made something up and Bob left, seemingly satisfied with his answer.

He spent the remainder of his day cruising the internet, always making sure to keep a spreadsheet open, and to be on alert in case anybody came by. There'd been a few close calls when Dennis had fumbled with the icon at the bottom of his screen for the spreadsheet, thus blocking out whatever porn website he was on. Thank God for quick fingers.

He visited ten porn sites that afternoon including his favorite: the rape page. He also did some searches on Google for necrophilia pages. He couldn't find any.

He left the office at his normal time and arrived at Harvey's house ten minutes early. Harvey Panozzo lived in a nice neighborhood with tree-lined streets and ranch homes. He met Dennis at the front door dressed in tan slacks and a white shirt; he looked like he'd just come home from work. He appeared to be around Dennis's age—early forties—and had thinning black hair and a dark mustache. He also looked like he spent a lot of time out in the sun.

"Nice to meet you," Harvey said, holding out his hand.

"Thanks for meeting with me," Dennis said, shaking his hand. "I really appreciate it."

Harvey invited him inside the house and Dennis followed the man, his nerves twitching. One time he'd met an extreme hardcore fetish enthusiast in the hopes of scoring some bloodsport videos and was tackled from behind by another character who was lying in wait. Looking back on it now, Dennis realized that they were going to rape him, probably torture him to fulfill their own desires, but Dennis was lucky. Working out at the gym every day gave him an advantage a lot of guys his age lacked, and he was able to fight off his attackers ruthlessly. He was careful in meeting like-minded freaks, and now as he followed Harvey Panozzo down the hall toward a rear bedroom, his senses were on heightened alert.

"Carl is a trusted friend and ally," Harvey said, motioning for Dennis to have a seat. "I knew you were okay when you mentioned Carl sent you. I don't trust people that are referred to me by people other than Carl."

"Neither do I," Dennis said.

"You said you were going to buy the necro publication Carl had?" Harvey asked.

Dennis nodded. "Yes. He said you bought it last night, that you're a fellow . . ."

"Enthusiast?" Harvey smiled. "I suppose I am." He paused for a moment. "I take it you are interested in similar material?"

Dennis nodded. "Very much so."

"I think I may be able to help you."

Dennis felt a burst of excitement. "That would be great."

"Tell me something," Harvey said, leaning forward, elbows resting on his knees. "What do you do for a living?"

Dennis hesitated a moment, then plunged on ahead. "I'm a financial analyst."

Harvey nodded. "I see. The reason I'm asking is that the group has pretty specific membership requirements. They like for fellow members to be professionally employed."

"Well . . ."

Harvey smiled. "Don't worry. I take it that with your job title you have at least a Bachelor's Degree and that you make at least fifty k a year. Correct?"

Dennis nodded. Actually he made quite a bit more than that but he wasn't going to tell Harvey.

Harvey rose to his feet. "Come with me. I think I have just what you're looking for."

Dennis followed him to the next room, which appeared to be an office. Harvey opened a file cabinet with a key and rifled through it. He extracted a glossy paged magazine wrapped in plastic and handed it to Dennis, who took it in trembling hands. "Is this the kind of material you're looking for?"

Dennis looked at it. The dead girl with the severed throat glared at him, her eyes lifeless. Dennis nodded. "Yes."

"If you'd like, I can give you some time alone with it. Perhaps thirty minutes?"

"That would be great." Dennis tried to keep his excitement at bay.

"After that, all I have to ask of you are three things," Harvey said. "The first: make sure you stay employed. We have our reasons for insisting on this policy, the main reason being that when you begin to acquire a taste for the type of material we're into, it can get rather expensive. We'd rather have you indulge with money you are making honestly. We have no desire to have the police come poking around should you resort to a life of crime in order for you to pay for your habit. Agreed?"

Dennis nodded. "Yes."

"Good. Number two, your being employed is actually a benefit. It automatically separates you from a lot of the other hardcore freaks out there. We have no desire to associate with drug addicts, ex-porn stars, the homeless, or other degenerates. What we do is in the privacy of our own homes. We don't hurt anybody. We are simply working professionals with similar interests. Agreed?"

Dennis nodded. "And the third?"

"That when you are finally admitted to our group you bring us some materials. An offering, if you will." Harvey smiled. "It doesn't matter what it is . . . a loop of some junkie getting fucked by a Doberman . . . a torture flick . . . some chicken hawk stuff for the pedophiles in our group. But you'll score big points if you can procure some necro flicks or some snuff. And not the fake crap, either. We're seasoned veterans and we can spot fake a mile away."

Dennis nodded. "Yeah, I think I can do that." *What the hell are you thinking? Where the hell are you going to find more of this kind of stuff?*

Harvey clapped him on the shoulder. "I'm sure you will. Now why don't I leave you alone for awhile?"

And he did just that. Harvey left Dennis alone in the office, pointing out a box of Kleenex and a bottle of lotion on the desk. He closed the door behind him, leaving Dennis alone.

Dennis sighed, opened the magazine to the spread of the decayed old woman, and felt his dick grow hard at the sight of the anonymous penis penetrating the rotting flesh of her stomach, and then he began to jack off.

When Bob Lansing called Dennis into his office the following day he was exiting another meeting regarding the CPM project. Dennis thought Bob wanted to pick his brain some more about the project, but as he closed the door to Bob's office he saw his superior's features were grave. "Sit down, Dennis," Bob said.

Dennis sat down, his stomach growing leaden. He'd been feeling uneasy since exiting Harvey Panozzo's house yesterday. He'd driven home wondering if anybody saw him leave the house. Ever since bringing himself to orgasm yesterday courtesy of the necrophilia publication, he felt like he was under scrutiny now, as if everybody around him suddenly knew he was different from them. It was a feeling that had chased him throughout the day.

"What's up?" Dennis asked Bob as he settled into his seat.

Bob pushed a set of papers across the desk at Dennis wordlessly. He refused to meet Dennis' eyes. Dennis picked up the paper and scanned the document. At first he thought it was computer code, but then he recognized it as website URLs. His eyes widened in surprise as he recognized the URLs as websites he visited at work. "I don't understand," he said, trying to sound casual but doing a terrible job of it.

"Those are the websites you've been visiting during your work day," Bob Lansing said, jabbing a finger at the document. He looked at Dennis unsympathetically. "I got an IT tech to download some software on your PC yesterday when you were out and run a check. Human Resources gave me a call the day before that to inform me an anonymous call was placed to their Sexual Harassment hotline informing them you were viewing sexually explicit material at work, so we had to investigate. And *this* is what we came up with."

The news was hitting Dennis like a sledgehammer. Despite the fact the evidence was staring him right in the face, he still tried to talk his way out of it. "There must be some kind of mistake," he stammered. "I don't—"

Bob Lansing leaned forward. "Can the bullshit, Dennis! Between you and me, it would be one thing if you were visiting the Playboy Website and looking at a little T & A. Human Resources would still want me to fire you, but I'd fight for you because I like you, and I like your work. But the crap you've been looking at on *our* computers, on our *time*?" He emphasized this by jabbing his finger down on the paper, his tone of voice becoming hoarse with anger. "Frankly I don't have much respect for guys like you that get off on watching women being degraded like that." His left hand dipped down to his desk drawer and emerged with a document and a green envelope. He slid them across the desk to Dennis. "Consider yourself fired. You're getting off easy; if the material you'd been viewing in your cubical involved children, so help me God I would have waited until after work and then I would have kicked the living shit out of you and damn the consequences."

Dennis was shocked; he didn't know how to respond. Bob Lansing glared back at him with anger and disgust. "Now get the fuck out of my office. You *disgust* me."

Dennis rose to his feet slowly, feeling the burning of Bob's gaze on his back as he exited his office. A tall African-American man from building security was already at his cube, waiting to escort him out of the building. The security guard stood at sentry duty as Dennis gathered the few personal items he had in his cubical and then he left the department, not even aware of the furtive whispers of his co-workers as the gossip mill started.

Dennis was at home when Harvey Panozzo called. He picked it up in the extension in his study upstairs. "Hello?"

"Dennis! Harvey here. Are you ready?"

"I'm afraid I won't be able to join just yet," Dennis said, lowering his voice. He was still reeling from the events at work today and was pouring through his business rolodex, coming up with a list of contacts. He had enough money to float on for a while, but he would have to get another position fairly soon. "Some things have come up and—"

"Oh, but you don't have to worry about joining, Dennis." Harvey's voice was soothing. "Consider yourself a charter member."

"Well . . . *thanks*, but—"

"The reason I'm calling, actually, is to see if you've held up your end of the bargain."

Dennis' mind drew a blank.

"Don't you remember? You were supposed to contribute something to the circle? A film? Photos perhaps?"

Dennis couldn't believe what he was hearing. "I just met you yesterday. You expect me to come up with something in twenty-four hours?"

"Why not? Surely you have something in your own collection that would suffice."

Dennis felt his nerves tremble. "Well, yeah . . . I guess I do."

"Great! How about you swing by on your way home from the office tomorrow and drop it off?"

Dennis told him that was fine and hung up. He spent the next thirty minutes staring out the window. He was so involved in his thoughts that he barely noticed when Carrie arrived home with the kids.

Dennis left early the next morning dressed in his normal work attire just like any other day. He didn't go to the office, however. Instead, he headed straight for the nearest coffee shop.

He bought a copy of the *Los Angeles Times* and sat in a corner booth, sipping coffee and circling the job listings. He also had a good breakfast: pancakes, scrambled eggs, sausage, hash browns, orange juice. He left the coffee shop at ten-thirty, taking the paper with him, and leaving the waitress a satisfying tip.

His house was silent and empty when he got home. Just as he thought it would be.

He headed straight to his study where the safe was. He got the safe opened and took out the rape video. *This should satisfy them*, he thought as he closed the safe. *They probably want something really hardcore and this is the hardest I have.*

He spent the rest of the day at the library making phone calls from his cellular phone, making connections, trying to set up some meetings. He was able to get a few interviews set up, and by the time he set out for Harvey Panozzo's place that afternoon he was already starting to feel better.

When he pulled up to Harvey Panozzo's home he saw the garage door was open. The silver Mercedes he'd seen in the driveway yesterday was absent. A group of kids were messing around on skateboards on the driveway. Dennis walked up the driveway, briefcase in hand. One of the kids, a twelve-year-old boy with curly black hair, looked up as Dennis approached. "If you're looking for my dad, he isn't home yet."

"Oh." Dennis frowned. "When will your dad be home?"

The boy shrugged. "Probably after six. He said he had a meeting."

"Okay. Thanks." Dennis walked back to the car, his feeling of apprehension growing again.

It turned to dread when he pulled into his neighborhood and saw the police car parked in front of his house.

The officers were at his front door talking to Carrie when Dennis approached his home. Carrie saw him and he could tell by the look on her face that she was worried and confused. "They're here to see you, Dennis."

Dennis tried to act casual. "What can I do for you, officers?"

The officers stepped off the porch and approached Dennis. They were around his age, both of them slim, nice-looking men, a blonde guy and an African-American cop. "We got a call that you're dealing in illegal pornography," the African-American cop said.

Dennis almost exploded. He looked at his wife briefly and motioned for the cops to huddle close to him so he wouldn't have to talk so loud. "Look, I don't know who called you about that, but it's *bullshit*, okay? If this has to do with work, and I'm sure it does, some asshole planted some shit on my computer and got me fired for it!"

The African-American cop cleared his throat. "Um, excuse me, sir, but we realize the allegations against you probably *are* trumped up, but still . . ."

Dennis looked at the officers with numbing horror. "You mean . . ."

"Do you mind if we look around a little bit?"

Dennis was just about to say no when an alarm went off in his head. To say no now would only spell trouble down the road. They'd get a search warrant and he might not be able to get the tapes out of his safe. If he let them poke around they might not even *see* the safe, much less ask to see what was inside. Ditto on his briefcase. He sighed. "Go ahead."

As the two officers poked around his living room, he herded Carrie into the kitchen. Carrie's eyes were wide and scared-looking. "Dennis, what's going on?"

He told her. Not about his recent Internet activities, nor his deviant pornography addiction, but about his being fired from his job. He told her Bob Lansing had been out to get him for a long time now, and that he was fairly sure Bob had gotten that information planted on his computer. Carrie swallowed the story, hook, line, and sinker. "And now he's trying to get you *arrested*? Why, that's *outrageous*!"

"I know," Dennis said, his voice low and trembling. It just occurred to him that whoever had complained about him at work was now anonymously calling the police. Whoever it was, they wanted to get him bad. "And that's why we're going to fight this thing tooth and nail."

The police didn't search for very long. After poking around the living room, the den, and his study and bedroom for a few minutes, they emerged looking sheepish. "Sorry to have troubled you, Mr. and Mrs. Hillman."

"No problem," Dennis said, seeing them out the door.

By the time he stowed his briefcase away and began to undress, Carrie was getting steamed about the whole incident. "I can't believe somebody would stoop so low just to have you fired. That's outrageous! I bet it was that Bob Lansing; he's been envious of you ever since you got that position. I wouldn't put it past him to come up with something like this. In fact—"

Dennis grinned as he changed into casual clothes. As long as he had Carrie believing him, he was home free.

The following day he left the house dressed in usual business attire. With Carrie knowing he was now unemployed, it would be easier to keep odd hours. Giving her the illusion he was job hunting was his chief source of cover. She left at her usual time this morning, carting the kids to school on her way to her job as an executive secretary, while Dennis dressed and made phone calls to prospective employers. When they were gone, he went to his study and extracted the rape tape and placed it in his briefcase. Then he left the house.

Harvey Ponozzo had left a message on his cell phone last night and instructed him on where they were to meet today to make the drop-off for the tape. Dennis returned the call late last night, telling Harvey he would be there, and now as he made the drive to Colorado Boulevard, looking for Phan Liquor store, he hoped to have all this swept under the rug as soon as possible. Get Harvey the tape, then he could resume his life. He was positive he could get a new job soon and when he did, he wasn't going to look at a porn magazine or website ever again. In fact, he was going to expand his job search and consider positions out of state. The further away he could get away from Los Angeles, the better.

He made the drop-off quickly. Harvey was waiting for him in his silver Mercedes and Dennis handed him a brown paper bag containing the tape. "I'll call you later this afternoon," Harvey said, starting his car. He pulled out of the parking slot and Dennis went back to his car, feeling as if a heavy burden had been suddenly lifted from him.

The rest of the day would have gone smoothly except for one thing. Harvey Panozzo never called him.

Dennis began to worry about it that evening as he feigned normalcy in the den. Carrie was watching the evening news. The kids were . . . well, who knew where the kids were this time of the evening. Dennis made a half-hearted attempt at getting his resume updated and actually visited a pornography addicts support group on the Internet. He'd been thinking about his actions all afternoon, and how they'd affected his job and his life. He was finally coming to terms that he had a problem and he had to face it, deal with it, correct it. He still didn't want Carrie or the kids to know about it, and he hoped that keeping it away from them while secretly trying to conquer his problem would do the trick. He still had to stay away from the stuff. He hoped Harvey Panozzo didn't call him back.

"How'd the job search go today?" Carrie asked from her spot on the sofa.

"Good," Dennis lied, rustling the paper. "I updated my resume, made a few phone calls. I'm hoping to get at least one interview by next week."

"Think you'll have something by then?" Carrie looked concerned. "Our house taxes are going to be due pretty soon. With Wendy's college tuition coming up in Fall, it's going to be kinda tough."

"We'll be fine," Dennis said. *Shit*, he thought. He'd completely forgotten about the goddamn taxes. Without a job to cover him, Wendy's college tuition was in jeopardy. The money he had in the bank was already earmarked for it. The house taxes would eat all that up.

"Are you sure?" Carrie was looking at him with concern.

Dennis smiled. "We'll be fine, honey. I promise."

He told himself that over and over all night until he was convinced things would be fine. And they would be. He was sure of it.

Harvey called him the following morning.

"How'd you like to make some money?" Harvey asked.

Dennis was sitting at his desk in front of his computer. He had just updated his resume and printed ten copies on nice bond paper. The *Los Angeles Times* Employment section was spread out in front of him and he'd circled five job descriptions that appeared to match his skills and educational background. "Doing what?" he asked. He was immediately suspicious.

"Don't worry, it's legit."

"I think I can find a new job on my own," Dennis said. "Thanks for the offer of help, though."

"I want to help," Harvey continued. "Like I told you a few days ago, we prefer our members be professionally employed. That includes being able to network with us, allow us to help each other."

"I don't think I'm interested," Dennis said. "In fact, I've changed my mind about the group. I no longer want to be a member."

"You have three more tapes in your house," Harvey said. "The police didn't find them yesterday, but they will if they make another visit. While possession of bestiality films are only punishable by a small fine, possession of a necrophilia film will probably carry a murder charge."

"What are you talking about?" Dennis felt his stomach drop. *My God, did Harvey call the police and have them search my house? Did he get me fired from my job? If so, how?*

"The film," Harvey continued. "The one showing that guy screwing corpses. They're murder victims, Dennis. Unsolved murders, I might add. The man in the videos is a hardcore junkie like you who's a necrophile. Surely you don't want your wife—your *children*—to know that you're a—"

"I don't *have* any such film in my safe," Dennis stammered.

"You do now, and it's not in your safe. It *is* in your study, though. When you were gone yesterday, one of our operatives broke into your home and planted it."

Dennis felt all the spit dry up in his mouth.

"Go ahead and call the police and tell them about us if you want to," Harvey purred. "They won't be able to prove the group exists. The tape will have *your* fingerprints on it. We can arrange it so that the evidence of murder points to *you*. And with your . . . unique tastes in pornography, you could be in jail for a long time, Mr. Hillman."

"What do you want?" Dennis felt his entire body go slack with shock. He felt totally helpless.

"All we want is your cooperation," Harvey continued. "Your membership in the group. You're one of *us* now. We're here to help you. Stray from us, we have to risk exposure. We can't afford that. Surely you understand our concerns for security, don't you Mr. Hillman?"

"Y . . . yes," Dennis stammered.

"I'm calling you from my cell phone. I'm parked right outside your house. I expect to see you walk out your front door in fifteen seconds. If I don't see you, I call the police and alert them to the location of the tape."

"Wh . . . why . . ."

"When you exit your home, you will walk to my car and enter the front passenger side," Harvey continued. "I will take you to the job I've mentioned. Do you understand?"

Dennis didn't know what to say. His eyes darted around his study, trying to find something out of place, some clue that would tell him where the tape was planted.

"Dennis?"

"Yes?"

"Do we have an understanding?"

"Yes."

"Good. Fifteen seconds, Mr. Hillman. From the time I hang up. I'm hanging up now. I expect to see you shortly." The line went dead.

Dennis was up and out the study in a flash. He grabbed his wallet and keys and left the house, locking it behind him, and headed down the front walkway and saw Harvey's silver Mercedes parked at the curb across the street. He walked around the front of the vehicle, feeling the dread build inside, entered the car and sat down in the front passenger seat. Harvey started the vehicle and pulled away from the curb. "Good," Harvey said as he drove out of the neighborhood. "I'm glad you came out."

"Why are you doing this?" Dennis asked.

"I want to help you," Harvey said as he piloted the Mercedes out of the neighborhood. He headed toward the 210 Freeway. "Relax. You'll be well taken care of."

Dennis found it hard to relax. He kept thinking, *what did I get myself into?* as Harvey took the 210 into the foothills of the San Gabriel mountains. Harvey's demeanor was casual and laid back. He was dressed in casual business attire—tan slacks and a white polo shirt. The interior of the Mercedes was spotless. For the first time, Dennis wondered what Harvey did for a living.

"What do you do for a living?" Dennis asked, trying to sound casual.

"I'm in the insurance industry," Harvey said. He kept the car at the speed limit. "I'm just a corporate drone like yourself. That's all."

"What's this job you told me about?"

"You'll see."

Forty minutes later Harvey pulled the car up to a ranch-style house nestled in a small valley deep within the San Gabriel mountains. He turned off the engine and got out of the car. "Come, follow me," he said.

Dennis followed, still wondering what this was about. He'd managed to get Harvey to admit that the work in question was for a fellow member who needed a database built of various hardcore pornography media. "We're building a lending library," Harvey had said. "It's still in the early stages, but neither of us have the time to build something sophisticated. That's why you're here."

"And you'll pay me?" Dennis asked. Despite how things were shaping up, he still felt a trifle nervous as he followed Harvey to the front walkway.

"Of course," Harvey said. He unlocked the door. "Perhaps we can get you to make some money at this as well. How would you like that?"

"I don't know," Dennis said.

"If you had an opportunity to make twenty-five grand screwing a dead chick, you wouldn't do it?"

"I just like to watch," Dennis said. "I don't want to actually *do* these things."

"Ah! You're merely the customer, right?"

Dennis shrugged. "I guess."

"Wonderful!" Harvey grinned. "Come this way, Mr. Hillman."

Harvey led Dennis through a large foyer to the rear of the house. Dennis could hear the sound of a television and he saw the flickering light of the screen spilling in the shadowed room. Whatever was playing it was either a horror movie of some kind or—

Dennis stopped at the threshold of the room as the image on the large screen TV rolled on. What appeared to be the elderly woman from the necrophilia film was being brutally beaten by two masked men. Her cries of pain were real, genuine. Dennis could tell that the minute he laid eyes on the film. He turned to look at Harvey and as he did so, his eyes rested on two figures lying on the floor like large, bloated lumps. Dennis took a step forward and recoiled, his stomach roiling as he saw that the figures were two adult dead males. They were naked, their bodies livid and white. Dennis noticed one had a small hole in the center of his forehead. His eyes were half-open, the lids like droopy shutters. Dennis took an involuntary step backward. "Hey, look, I don't think this is—"

"You don't think this is what, Mr. Hillman?" Harvey stood at the threshold to the large den, smiling. The old woman on the large screen TV screamed in pain as something horrible happened to her.

Dennis turned to Harvey, his heart racing. "Those guys . . ." He couldn't finish what he was going to say.

"Are dead. Yes, I know that Mr. Hillman. I thought that's what you liked."

"I'm not gay," Dennis said quickly. He wanted to get the hell out of here, but something kept him rooted to the spot.

"Of course not," Harvey said. "Andy Wilkes, one of the dead men you see there, was very much into young men, though. Take a look at the other one. Surely you'll recognize him."

A spike of fear dripped down Dennis's spine as he took another look at the bodies. One of the bodies was that of a fat middle-aged man with thinning gray hair. He looked familiar . . . vaguely familiar. He looked like the type of guy who'd be . . .

Dennis put a hand to his mouth to hold back the scream. *"Oh my God! That's Carl Grossman!"* His knees threatened to buckle and Dennis leaned against the wall.

"Yes, that's Mr. Grossman. He was the supplier. Nice that we have all three of you here, don't you think? Customer, supplier, and the manufacturer."

Dennis looked at Harvey. He was shaking so badly. "Wh-wha-what are you talking about?"

Over the agonizing screams of the old woman on the screen, Harvey continued. "Almost twenty years ago my mother and son were kidnapped. My son was only eight years old. They were never found. I looked everywhere; the police, the FBI, they looked everywhere. I used every available resource I could. I became so obsessed with their disappearance that my wife left me. There was no sign my mother took my son and changed their identities. There *were* signs that they were taken against their will, though. A witness reported that on the last day they were seen, two men were observed talking to my mother and son at Alondra Park in Gardena. My mother was a very accommodating, very helpful woman. This same witness saw my mother and son walking with the two men out to the parking lot. Perhaps they told her they needed some kind of help. We'll probably never know. Needless to say, they disappeared from that park. My mother's car was found still parked there without a trace of them. Later, much later, about thirteen years ago while chasing down a lead, I came across this tape." He motioned toward the TV screen. One of the masked men was cutting the old woman's throat while another one forced a small boy, who appeared to be eight or nine years old, his face red and wet from crying, to watch.

"Don't ask me where I got it," Harvey continued. He reached into his slacks pocket and pulled out a gun. He pointed it at Dennis as he continued. "To make a long story short, I did more research and found out my son later died. He'd been held as a sex slave for a group of perverts and eventually ran away. He was so scarred, so traumatized, that he became insane. He was tracked down by this ring of pedophiles and perverts and again abused horribly for profit." Harvey picked up Dennis's rape tape from the top of the large screen TV. "*Your* tape, Mr. Hillman. You have the only copy. My son's suffering was made for *your* pleasure. You *paid* to watch my son suffer!"

"No!" Dennis said. "I swear, I didn't!"

Harvey's face was twisted with rage and grief. "I've waited a long time for this . . . to get back at the people responsible for this . . . this *filth*! It took me years to track down Carl Grossman, but I did. I got him, and I got the bastard who killed my son, and now I've got the sonofabitch who paid for it." He pointed the gun at Dennis.

"Please . . ." Dennis stammered. "Y-Y-you don't want to . . . to . . . d-d-*do this*!"

"Sure I do," Harvey said, his grief suddenly as gone as fast as it came, his face erupting into a sick smile and then he pulled the trigger.

The .38 caliber slug tore into Dennis's head, ejecting brain and bone into the wall behind him. The force of the shot propelled Dennis back and he slumped against the wall, eyes opened and glazed. Harvey watched as Dennis's dead body rolled over and beat a convulsive tattoo on the carpeted floor before finally stopping.

Harvey knelt down and felt for Dennis's pulse. Except for the dwindling sound of the dying woman's screams coming from the snuff film on the TV, the house was silent.

Harvey grinned. He felt good. Wonderful. He never thought it would have felt so great, so fulfilling, so powerful! He stood up and replaced the revolver in his front pants pocket. He turned the VCR off with the remote control and rewound the tape and began making preparations for the owner of the house to arrive. According to his research, they were due back home in about three hours. Harvey had already set up all the video cameras at strategic places in the house, and he would turn all of them on with one flick of the remote when it was showtime. Then, he would wait for them to walk in and welcome them home, all four of them: mother, father, two adorable kids. Then they'd have some fun. He was looking forward to it now that he'd gotten warmed up. And getting warmed up was important. He'd gone through this stage with Carl, Alan, and Dennis to make sure he had the stomach for it. It was one thing to watch this shit everyday for the past twenty years; it was quite another to actually cross the line and do it.

Marveling at how well his fabricated story about his mother and son had gone over with Dennis Hillman, Harvey Panozzo made sure all the weapons were ready. Then he sat down in the darkened living room and waited.

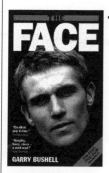

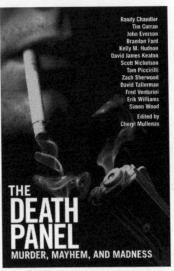

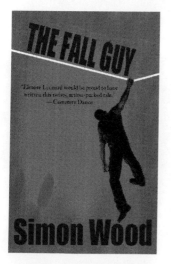

Comet Press is an independent publisher of
horror and dark crime.

Get the latest updates on our website at
www.cometpress.us

Visit the blog at
www.cometpress.us/blog

and follow us on twitter and facebook:

twitter.com/cometpress
facebook.com/cometpress

Made in the USA
Lexington, KY
21 October 2013